The Hou

A Novel

For Dan: Rachel / With love and a prayer for you.

R.T. Lawrence

RIVERSONG
BOOKS

An Imprint of Sulis International
Los Angeles | London

Cover design by Sulis International Press.
Sky and clouds photo by Sam Schooler.
Drawing of Rose-Marie by Audrey Lawrence

Library of Congress Control Number: 2019936741
ISBN (paperback): 978-1-946849-38-0
ISBN (eBook): 978-1-946849-39-7

Riversong Books
An Imprint of Sulis International
Los Angeles | London

www.sulisinternational.com

Contents

Dedicated to Jerry and Dianne Myhan

Acknowledgments

Many people have contributed to the hard work of editing and reviewing the multiple drafts leading to the final book you have before you. If you find yourself enjoying the story, I want you to be aware of some people to whom you and I are both indebted:

Laura Lawrence, my wife, editor, and source of perseverance throughout the sometimes tedious writing process.

Jerry Myhan, a nurse practitioner, who has introduced generations of medical professionals to work in the developing world, and the one who introduced me to Haiti.

Michael Justus, whose wisdom as a physician, voracious reader, and encourager provided the inspiration for turning this work into more than a private story.

Luckson Previl, the Haitian boy, now a man, who ensured the Creole in this story was authentic.

DeeAnn Martin, nurse and friend, who worked at L'Hopital Sacre Coeur in Milot after the earthquake and helped ensure the scenes in this story are faithful to what volunteers experienced.

Allan Underwood, friend and minister, who generously read the raw draft and provided helpful insights.

Abigail and James Rucker, missionaries in Haiti, who read the manuscript and offered a balancing perspective.

Ada Lawrence, the teenager who once said that every time she goes to Haiti, her family gets a little bigger; she reviewed the manuscript and made sure the story is right for all ages.

Introduction

Just before sunset on January 12, 2010, a powerful earthquake hit Port-au-Prince, Haiti. Within a few terrifying minutes, over one-hundred thousand men, women, and children were killed. Thousands more were critically injured, and millions were displaced to rapidly erected tent cities or hospitals across the country. Swiftly came the international response. Health care professionals from every corner of the world dropped their work and descended on Haiti. Among them were surgeons, nurses, and other health care professionals. Some arrived unprepared for the chaos of working in austere conditions, but this did not stop them from being Good Samaritans who unselfishly gave all they had. The work was rewarding.

Then something happened. As the dust cleared, many volunteers found their world was also shaken by the recognition that the victims were not just nameless people. They were daughters and sons, fathers and mothers, farmers, teachers, laborers, seamstresses, cooks, machinists, pastors, soldiers, taxi drivers, grocers, and students. They were a mix of the sort you find in any neighborhood. Most who responded to the disaster say that at least one person, usually a patient, broke their hearts. Many remember the moment it happened. The name of at least one patient is forever seared into the person's memory. Many can tell you the moment that he or she looked down and first recognized that it was no longer a patient for whom he or she was caring, it was a neighbor. This is a story of what happened to one of those volunteers.

"Let my heart be broken with the things that break the heart of God."

— *Bob Pierce, founder Samaritan's Purse*

1

The Doctor

On January 2010, a powerful earthquake struck southern Haiti, leveling the capital city.

Six days later, a trauma surgeon sat at his desk in a Seattle clinic. He opened an email containing images from the earthquake. Each picture revealed destruction on a scale unimaginable in peacetime. Some images were repulsive and others captivating. One grisly photograph drew the surgeon's attention. He leaned forward. His gut tightened. The gruesome image brought to mind a thousand horrific words, all captured in one frozen moment of suffering.

The surgeon was Philip Scott. He had been a trauma surgeon for over a decade and was accustomed to the sight of wounded bodies, but this image was different. He rarely saw trauma like that caught in the photograph: suffering in its raw form. Paramedics and emergency room physicians provided him with a buffer to the carnage. They reported accidents to Philip in cold medical jargon, but Philip seldom saw the actual scene. He met victims in a surgical setting long after screams had subsided into whimpering fears. By the time suffering reached Philip, it was draped in the sterile blue of an operating room.

The photograph before him was unlike anything he had seen. Taken far from a hospital, it captured the unsterile emotion of a father holding his mangled daughter amidst the ruins of a disaster. The young girl with ebony skin dangled limply in the man's arms. Grey dust obscured her delicate features. Her leg was bent in half at mid-thigh, and a bone protruded through the skin of her upper arm. She was dead, or at best unconscious. Her lifeless head hung across the man's arm in a way that made her eyes bulge in a fixed, dilated stare at the camera as large drops of blood fell from her mouth. The tears of her gaunt-faced father were smeared across his dust-covered cheeks. The picture had been taken mid-scream; the man's mouth was open toward the sky with his neck muscles tightened in a state of pure agony. Slightly out of focus behind him was a city street of flattened concrete buildings, structures crumbled in disorganized layers upon which men could be seen pulling at debris in the beams of light that fell through billowing grey dust.

Below the photo was a message from the dean of the University of Washington. He made a short plea for humanitarian aid and requested volunteers willing to travel on behalf of the school to provide disaster relief.

A physician sitting at another desk saw Philip wince, "Looks like you got the memo. Disturbing, isn't it? Are you thinking about going?"

Philip slipped a sarcastic cough, "To Haiti? Not a chance."

The sound of a woman clearing her throat interrupted them. Philip heard her and rotated in his chair to see Aryanna Vito, his resident, standing in the doorway.

Aryanna wore the white coat of a surgeon-in-training. She addressed Philip formally, speaking in a smooth alto, cautious in her tone but confident in her posture, "Good morning, Doctor Scott. Mr. Palmer's asking for a refill. He's complaining of severe pain."

Aryanna was an erudite, olive-skinned daughter of an Italian businessman and an American fashion designer. She was gifted with the attractive features of a model and the steady hands of a surgeon which, when added to her love of sports and keen intellect, made her a sought-after resident in the world of sports medicine. She had one particular weakness: a sort of phobia of interpersonal conflict which caused her to avoid confrontation, especially with her superiors. On the playing field, she rose to any challenger matching strength for strength, but off the field, in the midst of an argument, she felt herself a coward, more likely to bend to pressure than to resist confrontation. She stood in the office doorway looking at her feet as if ashamed to report unwanted information.

Philip wrinkled his forehead so that his eyebrows cast a shadow over his lower face, "So, what did you tell him?"

Aryanna rocked on her heels with her hands planted in the pockets of her white coat, a chart under her arm. She had been warned about giving out pain medications.

She lifted her eyes but not her head. Her sunken orbits accentuated the dark circles under her emerald, sleep-deprived eyes, "I explained the policy. No more refills. But the lady with him was pleading. She's so sweet, and I think she just cares about him."

Philip leaned back and squeezed his chin between his fingers, "Tell me, Doctor, does your patient meet criteria for surgery?"

"No sir, I don't think so. He's got a compression fracture, but no nerve involvement. I think it's just an exacerbation of his pain. His wife said it's gotten worse. I believe he is really hurting. He can't stand without assistance."

"Then send him back to talking doctors. You are a surgeon. Your hands are trained to incise and repair, not pass pills. Cut him loose."

"But don't you think given his injury, he may—warrant an extension?"

Philip glared at the young doctor. Her inability to handle a manipulative drug addict irritated him. He grabbed the chart and walked toward the exam room.

Philip stopped before entering. He flipped through the chart to remind himself of the patient's medical problem.

He saw the name: Thomas Palmer, an elderly man who a year earlier, having fallen from a ladder, had been rushed to the hospital for spine surgery. Philip had stabilized his spine, but Mr. Palmer's pain became severe. For several months he had come for refills of medication.

Without knocking, Philip walked into the room. The musty smell of aftershave and old clothing filled the air. A startled elderly couple sat beside the exam table.

Thomas sat up in his wheelchair. He remained poised but without remaining still, subtly rocking and squirming in discomfort. He had grey hair combed to one side, well-trimmed in a military style. He wore dark-tinted glasses behind which his eyes drooped at the edges, pulling forward his heavy ears. His suit coat gathered in a wrinkled wad on his withered shoulders.

A thin elderly woman sat next to him. She had bronze skin and white braided hair held in place by a wide band printed in floral hues that matched her lavender polyester dress. She coddled Thomas' hand. As Philip entered, the woman glanced up. Her thin eyes studied Philip from behind her high round cheeks, but she did not speak.

Thomas saw his surgeon, and he reached up to shake hands. His voice was like grinding rocks, "Good day, Doctor."

Philip took Thomas' hand. It was callused with oil-stained cuticles and veins woven under age spots and benign skin cancers that marked the seventh decade of the man's life. But the grip felt to Philip as pincers, firm, and brief. Then Thomas slumped back into the wheelchair.

The old woman next to Thomas began speaking rapidly with a soft voice, "Thank you for coming, Doctor. Thomas is still suffering. He was getting better until just last week when he was trying to help me and twisted his back."

"I see. And can Mr. Palmer still move his legs?"

"Well, yes, but it hurts him so very much."

"Is he incontinent of urine or stool?"

"I don't know what that means."

"Is he peeing on himself?"

"No, doctor. He goes fine. Why do you ask this?"

"I'm trying to ascertain whether the nerves in his back have been injured. Can the man speak for himself?"

Thomas raised his head and removed his glasses. His pupils had become tiny specks encircled by ghost-grey irises, the eyes of an elderly man robbed of his soul. He folded the glasses in his lap and spoke in slow, hesitant breaths, "Sorry to bother you, doctor. I know you're a busy man. I'm still suffering. I can't sleep. The pain is terrible, especially at night. Please, just one more month."

Philip pointed his finger and raised his voice to a volume more suited to the outdoors over a distance, "Mr. Palmer, stop the show. Your injury was over twelve months ago. I fixed your problem. I've given you a second chance. You're on your own now. Get up and start depending on yourself or find a candy man of a family doctor. But don't come back to this clinic until you're ready to have something cut. I am a surgeon, not your savior."

Philip threw the chart at Aryanna and turned to walk back to the office with his head aloft, satisfied with himself for successfully modeling how a busy surgeon should engage a difficult patient.

Aryanna followed him back to his office with her jaws clenched as if seething in silent anger.

Philip turned to face her. He saw her glare. Without speaking, he invited her question with a quick raising his eyebrows.

Aryanna bit her lower lip and cut her eyes upward, "Isn't there anything we can do to help this man? I mean, it's like my grandparents are sitting in there, and I can't help them. I'm sure he's gotten too dependent on the drugs; I get that.

But it seems like we have something to offer, maybe physical therapy, or rehab, or something."

Philip rolled his chair up to Aryanna and took her hands, turning her palms upward and studying the creases he said, "These hands are beautiful. They are gifted. With them, you will perform miracles. The lame will walk because of you. Broken bodies will be mended by your skill. But you must learn when to pull back. Learn how to keep a distance. We fix the problem, but we must learn to step away and allow patients to determine their own destiny."

Aryanna pulled her hands away. She grabbed another chart and walked out.

As she departed, Philip turned to his colleague, "She may disagree with me today, but in a few years, she'll come to see I'm right. Some lessons are hard when you are young and idealistic."

Philip's pager beeped. The number was from the orthopedic clinic on the university campus. The office manager who answered passed along a message, "Chairman Henske has asked to meet with you. Are you available in an hour?"

"I can be. Is something wrong?"

She answered in a script-like monotone, "I just make the calls, sir. May I put you down for the appointment?"

2

The Assignment

Michael Henske was the chairman of the orthopedics department. A meeting with the chairman meant promotion or demotion, or possibly reassignment. The chairman never called for social chats.

Philip believed he deserved a promotion. No professor in the department could match his experience or his drive. Patients, and not a few medical students complained about Philip's bedside manner, but colleagues never questioned the quality of his work or his ability to manage complex injuries. Philip published his work in respectable journals, and his peers nominated him for Top Doctor in Seattle Magazine. He brought national attention both to the university and to the residency program as a featured conference speaker. Beyond a doubt, Philip Scott believed he deserved professional recognition. And more than the honors, he craved the financial rewards that came with that recognition.

Most of his work took place at the Harborview Medical Center, a 1930s-era hospital that stands on a hill overlooking Seattle, Washington.

Other clinics in the orthopedics department were spread out across north Seattle. The chairman's office was on the northwest edge of the University of Washington campus, normally a quick drive for Philip, if not for the afternoon traffic.

Philip raised the hood of his raincoat and walked out of Harborview. He made his way to the staff parking garage. Thoughts of a promotion added energy to his pace. His polished cherry red sports car with gleaming chrome wheels was strategically parked in the garage to maximize visibility and minimize damage. He revved the engine and pulled out of the gate in an accelerated turn causing wheels to screech over the wet pavement.

For him, the car was a badge of honor; driving a fast car communicated to the world that he was going places. And even more, it was a physical statement of freedom, an impulse purchase after his divorce.

Philip knew the interstate route would be congested, so he took back streets, traveling north behind Capitol Hill and then descending to the Montlake Bridge. This took him onto the southern side of the University of Washington campus. Husky Stadium rose like a colossal ship to his right and the sprawling medical center extended down the waterfront to his left. Rainier Vista, a long thin field of grass rose up the slope before him toward Drumheller Fountain. He could see students walking down the lawn in front of the fountain, many with umbrellas raised against the dripping grey sky.

He turned left onto Northeast Pacific Street, passing the University Medical Center and the School of Medicine. Memories of better days passed through his mind. At least one half of his life had been spent in the buildings along that one street. College. Medical school. Residency. Associate professorship. He got married on the dock along the waterfront behind the medical school. His two children were born at the medical center. He called them his little Huskies, children of the University of Washington. He studied biology as an undergraduate; then he was accepted into the medical school and later secured a spot as an orthopedic resident. Philip knew the halls of those buildings better than his own house; the drive was for him like driving down the streets of his hometown.

Philip arrived at the chairman's office with a few minutes to spare. The office manager saw him and smiled. She pointed to a chair in the lobby, "Good afternoon, Doctor; the chairman will be with you shortly. May I get you something to drink?"

Philip leaned over the counter, "Nothing now, thank you. But maybe after work I could interest you in a drink?"

The young woman raised an eyebrow. She pushed her hair over her left ear, conspicuously flashing a ring, "Too late, doctor. This one's taken."

Philip raised his palms in surrender, "Ok, I see that. Can't blame a man for trying."

Within a few minutes, Doctor Henske opened the door and greeted Philip with a handshake and quick grin, "Phil, please come in. I apologize for the short notice; I needed to speak with you as soon as possible."

The chairman led Philip down a long hall. As they turned into the chairman's office, Philip asked, "More complaints?"

"Well, now that you mention it, yes; I have received a few grievances. Two medical students claim you're demeaning them on rounds, and a patient's mother filed a complaint with the department because you forced her son to walk too soon after his surgery."

Philip's face reddened, "They're all complaining about the same incident. The kid busted his tibia. That woman's as ignorant as our students! The boy's never going to heal unless he starts putting weight on that leg. You know that. Give me those complaints; I'll answer them myself."

"There's no need Phil. I'll respond to the letters. I called you here for another reason. Make yourself comfortable."

Philip took a seat in one of the plush leather chairs.

Doctor Henske sat on the corner of his desk crossing his arms, "Did you receive the dean's email?"

Philip answered with a note of sarcasm, "The one about Haiti?"

"Yes."

"Yeah, I got it; a real tragedy *for them,* I thought."

Henske peered over his glasses, "This is no joke, Phil. They're reporting deaths in the tens of thousands. They say it's like a bomb was dropped on Port-au-Prince. Streets are impassible. The city reeks of decaying bodies. They're burying the dead in mass graves. The real tragedy is that hundreds of thousands have survived, though barely; there are thousands of victims."

Philip shrugged and shook his head. "I don't mean to sound cold, but it's probably for the best don't you think? That country's been an overcrowded drain on the resources of our hemisphere for decades."

"That does sound cold."

"I'm sorry; I mean no disrespect. But if you put a million people in a city of made of cinder blocks right on a major fault line—this story just has no way of ending well."

Doctor Henske's lips pursed to slow a deep breath as he studied Philip like a businessman preparing to negotiate. Then he slid a sheet of paper across his desk, "You know, Phil, sometimes tragedy opens the door to an opportunity."

Philip raised his eyebrows and leaned forward, "What are you selling?"

Doctor Henske handed Philip the sheet of paper. It was a typed memo, printed on university letterhead. Doctor Henske looked out the window as Philip scanned the document. In it, the dean gave instructions for putting together a group of health care professionals to respond to the earthquake.

Philip looked up from the memo, "So, the Dean wants us to put together a humanitarian team?"

"That's right, a team of surgeons."

Philip raised an eyebrow, "I'm not interested in charity work. It's not my thing."

"Think of it as an opportunity, Phil. The University of Miami already has a team on the ground. Their residents are getting an incredible experience. The administration sees it as a win-win. Send a team from UW. The residents get a once-in-a-lifetime experience. The program gets good press."

Philip laughed, "So why not send fuzzy-headed interns. They're always looking for a chance to scrub in."

"Come on, Phil. Haiti's been dealt a blow on a massive scale. They need trauma surgeons. King's men like you who know how to put Humpty back together."

Philip asked, "So, what's he thinking? Send a few residents down for a week or so?"

"Four weeks, actually. He wants us to put together a team of faculty members and three or four residents."

"So, why are you twisting my arm? I have no interest in third-world work. Get someone else."

Doctor Henske smiled, "I've asked Anderson Hu from the Ballard clinic. He jumped at the chance. He's been before. He tells me it was a great experience."

Philip shook his head and tapped on the leather of the chair, "Ok, who else?"

"There's no one else. The two of you are best prepared for the assignment."

Philip's face pulsed red; he heard only coercive half-truths, "Come on, Michael. This isn't about skill. Tell me the truth. This is about availability isn't it?"

Doctor Henske dropped his shoulders. He looked at Philip and sighed, "You're single, Phil. The rest of us have family or kids at home. Your kids live with Amanda, and you've got—well, you've got time most of us don't have."

Philip clenched his jaw. That phrase felt to him like a manipulative undercutting punch. He did not appreciate judgmental insinuations. He gave his life to the practice of medicine. He had traded in a marriage. He barely knew his kids. He did not have—time to spare; any time he had, he gave to the University long ago. Torn between the reflexive desire to storm out of the office and his better judgment, he swallowed his pride and remained silent, glaring at his boss until the anger receded; then he shoved the letter back.

But Doctor Henske was not provoked. He took the letter, folding it calmly as he continued his offer, "Phil, my apologies. I don't mean to suggest you are idle. You are one of the hardest working men I know. What I hoped you would see is the opportunity."

He looked out the window as winter rain trailed down the pane.

Philip's eyes were fixed on his boss, "I'm listening."

"I'm an old man. In three years, I'm up for retirement, and the administration's asked me to recommend a successor. I'd like that person to be you. No one's better positioned to take this department forward. But if my recommendation's to be taken seriously, I need your help."

"Help with what?"

"This position requires a certain level of—diplomacy. You have a reputation for action, not tact. I believe a humanitarian trip would look good to the administration. It will show them you've got a heart." Doctor Henske turned to look at Philip, "You do have a heart?"

Philip responded with a quiet sneer.

Doctor Henske smiled, walked across the room and placed a hand on Philip's shoulder, "I'm not trying to twist your arm, Phil. Give it some thought. It's January. They say the Caribbean's nice this time of year."

3

Seeking Permission

Philip drove up Interstate 5 to Edmonds, Washington. He crept to a stop in front of an old house with brightly painted wood siding and a large porch framed by trimmed shrubs. Light reflected off a stained glass image on the front door shaped to depict a dove in flight. A sign beside the door read, WELLNESS PSYCHOLOGICAL SERVICES of WASHINGTON.

Philip noticed moist prints on the dark leather steering wheel. He sat in the car for several minutes preparing mentally for a confrontation. He knew he had to speak with his ex-wife in person. A decision to leave the country, even for a short trip, would require her consent. But the issue could not be discussed by phone. Whether it could even be discussed face-to-face was yet to be determined. A few minutes passed; then, once his confidence matched his resolve, he shut off the engine and crept up the walk, looking back over his shoulder frequently as if afraid to be seen walking into the clinic.

Behind a low wall in the waiting room, a college-age woman wearing a white coat sat at a desk. She saw Philip enter, his eyes scanning the room as he stepped through the entrance. She spoke warmly, "Good morning; how may I help you?"

Philip felt paranoid. He had been conditioned to keep up his guard since conversations with his ex-wife tended to become caustic. He glanced around the room; at least one camera was pointed at him. Behind the lady at the desk was a closed door with a nameplate that read Amanda Ward, Ph.D. Philip cleared his throat and spoke just above a whisper, "My name is Philip Scott. Dr. Ward is expecting me."

Amanda Ward was a woman whom Philip both loved and hated. She was a graceful woman, short in stature but ever poised, with unblemished skin, red lips and gentle features. Her physical beauty compounded by a disarming way of dealing with people served her well professionally. She was a clinical psychologist. Most people called her, Doctor Ward. But she and Philip had an understanding. She called him Philip. And despite a decade of turbulent waters having passed under the bridges of their relationship, she allowed him to call her Mandy.

Amanda greeted Philip with a professional air, adding a gentle kiss on the cheek, "Good morning, Philip. What brings you to Edmonds?"

"May we speak in private?"

"Of course. Come into my office."

She led Philip to her office and motioned for him to sit on the couch. She took a chair and faced him with her ankles crossed and her hands comfortably at rest in her lap, "So, what is on your mind?"

Philip leaned forward trying to find his composure on the low seat of the couch, "I've got a favor to ask. The department's asked me to go on an extended assignment. The University's sending a group to Haiti, you know, for humanitarian relief."

"How do you feel about this assignment?"

"Come on, Mandy. I'm not here as a client. Don't turn this into a counseling session."

"Ok, so tell me about the assignment. Why are you interested in going?"

Philip answered, "Well, truthfully, I'm not interested. It's not my thing. But, then again, I agreed to go, so I guess I am interested, just not for reasons you'd think."

Amanda raised an eyebrow, "Did you join some cult?"

"What?"

"You sound like someone brainwashed you. Are you going for a religious photo op with starving kids?"

"No, of course not; I have no interest in religion."

"So, what's the problem?"

"The time away, that's my problem. They asked me to lead an orthopedic team. I've agreed to go. It could be good for my career, but it means being away for a few weeks."

"Have you made arrangements for the children?"

"Well, that's why I came to see you. Would you consider keeping them for a few weekends?"

"Are you insane? Do you think my weekends are free? I can't just rearrange the calendar on a whim."

Philip raised his hands in an open-palm gesture, "It's only for a few weeks."

"The time is irrelevant. They're barely teenagers, Philip. They need their father every day. They only get time with you on weekends as it is. I can't bear the thought of your walking out on them again."

"Don't go there, Mandy. I'm not the one who walked out."

"No, you just never came home."

Philip put his face in his hands. Every conversation with Amanda eventually deteriorated into a demoralizing rehash of bad memories.

They had met while Philip was in medical school and Amanda was in her doctorate program. Their class schedules were intense, but so was their infatuation with each other. Amanda's confidence was irresistible. She would listen to Philip's descriptions of learning medicine and make him feel like he was preparing to do the greatest work in the world. As he looked back, he concluded she was just practicing on him. He was a project; her first client. As time passed, however, Philip became a form of security for

Amanda, mostly financial. She would introduce him as her man who was going to become a rich doctor.

A son was conceived, unplanned, in Philip's fourth year of medical school. They married in the first trimester. The ceremony was elegant yet simple, held on the docks of a bay behind the medical school. Amanda was opposed to a church wedding. Instead, their parents and few college friends showed up to witness the vows. A professor from the philosophy department served as the officiant. The ceremony was beautiful, but the reception was a disaster. Philip planned a surprise getaway. He rented a sailboat for a post-wedding party in the waters around Seattle. The boat was decorated in flowers from bow to stern with a flag waving from the mast bearing the message, "Just Married!" He thought the whole thing would be romantic: a sailboat pulling up to the dock to whisk away the beautiful bride and her lover into the sunset. But Philip was a young doctor; he should have known better than to plan a boat ride for a pregnant woman in her first trimester. Amanda spent the evening bent over the rail vomiting into Lake Union.

A few months later, their son entered the world, born at the University of Washington Medical Center. They named him Max after Amanda's favorite uncle. But Philip had few memories of his son's birth. He was there when it happened; however, those were the days of staying up for thirty-six hours at a stretch and having learned to sleep standing up, he dozed through most of the labor and delivery. All he recalled was the joy of having a son and dancing with Max in his arms after the delivery. A daughter, Alexa, was conceived a year later. Philip did not remember much from her birth either. But he did remember ceasing to be the center of attention in the home. Amanda's attention had turned fully to her little Huskies.

So, Philip turned back to work for accolades. The school gave him awards, and his colleagues provided recognition no longer found in his home. He swiftly moved up the career ladder, grasping rungs reached only by the few willing to put in long hours in the operating room. He was driven by the intellectual rewards of scrubbing in on interesting cases. His superiors repeatedly recommended Philip for promotion; this put him on a fast track toward professorship.

The contrast between the way Amanda ridiculed Philip at home and the ways he was honored at work became stark. Surgery became his passion, his mistress. She provided him with fame and glory, and her allure became all the stronger when he was trapped at home. Philip's desire for being in the operating room amplified Amanda's feelings of resentment toward him. He was an inattentive husband and absent father. She retaliated with scorn. Her requests for more of his time became a nightly drip of complaints which eventually became outspoken dishonor as she openly ridiculed him in front of Max and Alexa. This was strategic. She knew where he was vulnerable. In their home, she suppressed any evidence of his success. She even kept Philip's diplomas and certificates boxed in the basement. Like a sick psychology experiment, she withheld what he needed most.

Philip exploited her weaknesses, too. While in school and residency, they were in debt, not wealthy. Philip ran up credit card charges for what Amanda called mere toys. He bought a sailboat and a big screen TV. Then Philip ridiculed Amanda for not managing the money. He told her he had to work longer and take on moonlighting opportunities just to stay afloat. In reality, he was just looking for ways to avoid coming home; but the thought of poverty terrified Amanda, and Philip played on her fear. He knew that a threat to her security was a stab at her heart.

It eventually backfired. She sought and found security in another man's home. One day Philip came in after two full days at the hospital. The house was empty, except for a lone box of framed awards, certificates, and diplomas sitting in the middle of the living room.

The subsequent divorce proceedings were tense. Philip had neither the interest nor time to mount a solid defense. Amanda, by contrast, had made friends in the legal world. In the end, Philip was allowed to see his children on the weekends, though he ended up being responsible for the entirety of their expenses, at least until they turned eighteen. Such was the court-ordered child support. Amanda took care of their schooling and general upbringing, Philip paid for their existence. But he loved his children. In them, he saw beautiful fruit growing from the compost of a failed marriage.

Amanda married a man named Stanley Duberstein, a wealthy Australian with a broad face, thin build, and wavy golden hair who worked as a freelance writer, though in reality, he did not need to work. He published his work as a hobby; not for income. He lived off the interest from a third-generation family trust with which he offered Amanda a comfortable lifestyle. For professional reasons, Amanda kept her maiden name, Ward.

Philip never liked Stanley, mostly out of spite. In truth, he was a good catch for Amanda. He treated her fine and was a good role model for the children. Philip thought he and Stanley might have become friends had they met at the pub or at the gym. But Philip never counted Stanley as a friend. In his mind, the new husband was an opponent, an adversary who walked onto the playground of Philip's life and stole his team. Worse, they all walked off with him and never looked back. It irritated Philip to see the new husband, as a mere writer, working half as hard with half the education living with Amanda and the kids in a picturesque waterfront house. Philip believed it was the life that should have been his.

Philip looked up, "Mandy, please don't make this difficult for me."

Amanda crossed her arms, "Difficult for you? I'm sorry. From where I'm sitting, it appears that you want to make things difficult for me."

"That's not true."

"So, you drove up here to ask me to put *my* life on hold so you can fly off to the tropics to help whom? Me? Certainly not your children."

Philip raised his voice, "This is not about us. Have some compassion. I've been asked to go help people suffering a tragedy. I'm just asking you to watch the kids for a few weekends until I get back."

Amanda's eyes narrowed, "Is that girl going with you? What's her name? Rita?"

"Her name is Raina. And no, she is not going. She and I have come to—an understanding. She's no longer in the picture."

Amanda grinned. She had the upper hand and knew how to twist the situation to her advantage. "I'm sorry for your loss, Philip. I hope she knows what she's given up. But I must say, you were right to end that relationship. Max and Alexa told me she speaks ill of you behind your back. She is a snake."

"She's gone. Her character is no longer my concern."

"No, but I see how her absence explains your sudden need for someone to watch the children."

"So, do you have a problem with them staying with you a few weekends?"

"Yes, I do have a problem with that. Max and Alexa need you, now more than ever. They're barely teenagers. You're their father. You've been helping 'other people' your whole life. How about showing your own children a little compassion?"

Philip nodded as if to feign agreement, "Well, then, I could just take the kids with me. You know, introduce them to a new culture and the joys of international travel."

As soon as the words left his lips, Philip knew his dig was not received well.

Amanda's jaws tensed. Any residual self-control disappeared from her face. Her posture straightened. Her eyes flashed red. Philip had seen that look before, many times. He braced for an emotional explosion. She pointed a finger at his face, "I will destroy you before I ever let you threaten to take away my kids. How dare you? How dare you attempt to blackmail me with our children?"

Philip threw up his hands, "Ease up, Mandy. I'm not serious. I have no intention of taking them with me. I'm just asking for a little help. I'll give you money to cover the extra time, and I'll make it up to you when I return."

Amanda's eyes cut to her desk. She reached over and picked up a legal notepad. Her tone became curt, "Here. I want it in writing. Every detail—signed."

Philip pushed the pad away, "What's your problem? I'll make it up to you when I get back. I'm not asking for an addendum to our agreement. This is temporary. Just a few weeks. I'm asking for a little bend in the plan, that's all."

Amanda held out the pad again, "You're a man of words, not action. I want exact dates and firm amounts."

Philip took the notepad in a sluggish swipe, "Ok, how about two hundred dollars per weekend?"

"Five-hundred."

"Five-hundred? Are you out of your mind?"

Amanda crossed her arms and leaned back, "Five-hundred, per child. Paid in advance for every weekend you plan to be away."

"Mandy, that's extortion. Our kids don't cost us that much to care for."

Amanda placed a hand on an appointment book that was sitting on the edge of her desk. Her eyes cut upward, "You're asking me to cancel weekend appointments for what, a month? I'm asking you to cover my lost revenue. So, unless you think you have the time to hire a lawyer to convince a judge to appoint a mutually agreeable sitter, I'd say you're getting a good deal."

Philip scratched out a few lines on the note pad and pulled out a checkbook. His nostrils flared, and his temples pulsed. With the pen pressed hard enough to indent every remaining check in the book, Philip wrote out the amount.

There were no further pleasantries. Philip was much too upset to speak. He stormed out of the clinic and slammed the front door with sufficient energy to shatter the stained-glass transom window. "Perfect!" he screamed, "Just send me a bill for that too!"

As he drove away, Philip converted emotion into forward motion and applied enough force to the gas pedal to leave a streak of burnt rubber on the street in front of the clinic. It was all very therapeutic.

4

Preparing for the Tropics

Philip had only two weeks to prepare for a trip to the Caribbean. Doctor Anderson Hu, an orthopedic oncologist who had been to Haiti several times, agreed to arrange the travel. Three orthopedic residents and one medical student also volunteered.

There was no time to meld as a team prior to departure; each person had surgeries and clinics or classes to squeeze in before leaving the country. So, Doctor Hu sent emails with guidance on how to prepare. Pack light. Purchase a mosquito net. Make sure passports are current. Read up on tropical diseases. Bring a headlamp and plenty of batteries. Get the recommended shots. And take malaria pills.

Tropical medicine was not something Philip had thought about in a long time. He recalled the names of a few tropical diseases from medical school with tongue-twisting names such as elephantiasis; schistosomiasis; and cholera; however, when it came to treating any of these, he felt woefully unprepared.

Philip remembered someone who could help, a friend in the infectious disease department named Heidi Kapoor. One afternoon, between cases, he picked up a phone in the doctor's lounge and dialed her number.

The woman answered with the rising pitch of a person with a generally cheerful disposition, "Phil, what can I do to help?"

"Hello Heidi, this is a personal call, not a consult. I have a favor to ask."

"Sure, anything you need."

"The department has assigned me to a relief team. We are being sent to Haiti, and we leave in less than two weeks. I wonder if you'd have time to get me up to speed? You know, tell me which shots I need and what bizarre things to be prepared for."

Heidi Kapoor was a global health infectious disease specialist. She had a string of letters after her name, but it was her ambition and kindness, not the depth of her education that made her trustworthy. Doctor Kapoor had traveled the globe studying the world's most frightening diseases: Ebola; multi-drug resistant tuberculosis; smallpox; and anthrax. She was on a mission to save the world, a woman in search of a cure for the greatest causes of suffering. If there were something to worry about in the Caribbean, Doctor Kapoor would make sure Philip was sufficiently armed.

She laughed, "You are better prepared than you think, Phil. But there *are* a few things you should know and, I'll tell you what: stop by my clinic. Our nurse will draw some blood and give you any necessary vaccines. Then let's talk over lunch. Are you available Friday?"

That afternoon Philip went to the travel clinic. A jovial nurse with biceps that stretched the seams of his white scrubs welcomed Philip with a firm handshake and a wide open-mouth smile. He spoke in a Caribbean accent, "You must be Doctor Scott. Sit down, sir; be comfortable."

He placed a tourniquet and started drawing blood, "Kapoor tells me you are traveling to the Caribbean. Ha. Ha. That's where I'm from, you know. What takes you there this time of year? Vacation? Conference? A little winter sunshine?"

"No, just work."

"Work, you say? In the Caribbean?"

"I'm being sent with a group to Haiti. You know, because of the earthquake."

The nurse's eyes widened, "Ooh, Haiti? You are a brave soul. Bless you for going. It is a terrible tragedy. So much suffering. My parents still live in Jamaica, and they are terrified. They say everyone is scared."

"Did your parents feel the quake?"

"No, sir; it was too far away. But you know Jamaica's on the same fault as Haiti. Our day's a coming."

"So, what do you know about Haiti?"

"Ah, I never go there. But I knew people from there. Lots of them came over on boats when I was a child. Haiti is a rough place. No food to eat. Terrible diseases. They say it's crowded from one end of the country to the other. And they worship spirits."

"I'm not worried about the ghosts; I'm worried about the parasites."

"Ha, then you've never heard of zombies?"

He made reference to the undead with the ease and seriousness of a man talking about the weather, but Philip could not imagine an educated person being serious about zombies. He assumed the nurse was kidding and raised his eyebrows to let him know he caught the joke.

But the nurse lowered his voice. "I can see you do not believe me. But, trust me, Doctor, there are bodies of people in Haiti who have no soul. You will see them. They were dead. They were buried even. And then they were raised by sorcerers. Most of them sold into slavery." He flicked at an upheld syringe, "Now bare your arm for me, sir."

Philip pushed up his sleeve. Then he pressed the nurse for more relevant information, "Ok, so I need to watch out for zombies. Any other advice?"

"Ha, ha. The zombies will not even know you're there. They're harmless. You must watch out for the men who make zombies. Don't cross anyone. If you offend someone, make it right. You never know who might grow angry and pay a sorcerer to do you harm."

Philip's foot bounced impatiently, "So, can you tell me anything about the real world of parasites or bacteria?"

"Ha, ha. No, I just work here. I draw the blood and give shots. And sometimes I tell tales. Kapoor will give you the real story." Then he handed Philip a bottle of pills, "I am supposed to give you these; take two of these each week until after you return. They're for malaria. The zombies are harmless, but the mosquitos will kill you dead. Like my grandfather used to tell us, *the little axe cuts down the big tree*. Ha, ha."

Two days later Philip met Heidi Kapoor in her clinic. He arrived holding two boxed meals from the hospital cafeteria for which Heidi made room amid stacks of journals and folders that lay cluttered about her desk. The scent of fresh coffee billowed from a carafe giving the room an aromatic air of productivity.

Heidi cleared documents off the chairs, "Please, grab something to eat, and sit down. Let's review your labs and talk about your trip."

Philip looked around the office at the stacks of paper and journals, "Looks like you're doing a little reading, doctor."

Doctor Kapoor placed a hand over her chest, "Forgive the mess; I'm preparing for a lecture. But now, my time is yours. I am so excited to hear about your trip. I have been running full steam all morning to make sure we would have time to visit without interruption."

Philip laughed. Doctor Kapoor provoked a strange desire in him, not a physical or romantic attraction, but a jealousy of the vibrant energy she possessed in boundless quantities. Like most people, Philip enjoyed being around her. She was a magnet, attracting and realigning steel minds to her own singular purposes. Philip raised a cup,

"Heidi, you've been running full steam since the day we started med school."

She sat down next to him, studying his face as if it were a piece of art, "So, tell me about your trip. Where are you going?"

"Well, we're flying into Northern Haiti and working at some hospital outside Cap-Haitien. The main hospital in the south was destroyed. Survivors who can tolerate the trip are being moved to the north for surgeries and treatment. I don't really know what to expect. And I have to be honest, I don't really want to go. It's just an assignment, one of those things you agree to do when your arm is professionally twisted. I'm going with a colleague and a handful of residents."

"Are you afraid?"

"I'm afraid of wasting my time. We'll go and do a few surgeries and set some bones, maybe perform a few amputations. But I've seen the pictures. It's chaos. That place needs to be bulldozed and rebuilt, not just patched up. All I can offer is a speck of sand in the tons of concrete that will be needed to rebuild that place. Even if I had your energetic superpowers, the most I could do is put a few injured people back on the street."

"I think you will be surprised, Phil."

"By what?"

"I predict that in one week, you and your students will see more pathology than you have seen in your entire career. You will treat malaria, leprosy, tuberculosis, typhoid, dengue, AIDS, and quite likely cholera. Treating individuals with these diseases will be like putting ice on a twisted ankle. It's a great opportunity for them, and for you. You are going to learn so much."

Philip grabbed his forehead, "Ok, so I have not even thought about some of those diseases in years. This is where it gets scary. I don't have time to learn all this."

Doctor Kapoor grinned, "Well, maybe a little refresher would set your mind at ease."

She walked to her shelf and removed a green hardcover book. Then she took a rectangular piece of paper from her desk upon which she scribbled a note, folded it and placed it in the book, "Take this with you; it's my favorite reference on tropical disease. Keep it handy. Most of the pathology you see will be familiar, but when you come across something unfamiliar, I think you'll find help in here."

"Thank you. I'll not let it out of my sight. So how did my blood work turn out?"

"It's excellent. You're medically boring. Your vaccination titers are good, so no need for more shots, other than the typhoid vaccine you received. Your blood type is O-negative, which is great; you're a universal donor; however, I have to tell you, after a trip to Haiti you cannot donate for a year. I hope you already gave at the office."

"What's the risk with donating blood?"

"If you are bit by a mosquito with malaria, the parasite can remain dormant in your liver for many months. When you return from that part of the world, the risk of transmitting the malaria in a transfusion is just too high."

"Why do I not find this reassuring?"

Doctor Kapoor smiled, "I would not worry about malaria. Any risk is far outweighed by the benefit of this experience for you. It will change you, Phil. You will have to work very hard to remain the same man you are today. It happens to all of us. No one is immune. There is no vaccine against the change. We call it 'the good infection.'"

5

The Coolest Dad

That afternoon, Philip drove to Edmonds to pick up his children in a routine Friday evening exchange. Max and Alexa waited on the front steps of the Duberstein house with bags packed. When Philip drove up, they sprinted to the car and fought over the front seat.

Philip walked up to the porch extending his hand to greet Stanley. Then he gave Amanda a hug that amounted to little more than a rigid pleasantry. As he leaned forward, he asked her, "Did you tell them about my trip?"

Amanda replied under her breath, "Not in any detail. I just told them you had to go for work."

Philip nodded and wished Amanda and Stanley a good weekend. Once buckled into the car, he revved the engine, lowered the top on the convertible and accelerated down the street, hair flying backward in the wind. Philip grinned at the sight of Amanda in the rearview mirror, standing with her arms crossed as they dashed away.

Their destination was a pizza parlor tucked in a strip mall on the edge of the University District in Seattle. The restaurant was famous for deep-dish pizza, and it functioned as a popular hangout for university students. For Philip, it was a venue for getting reacquainted with his kids after being apart for five days. The owner had a table waiting for them, a personalized nook for realigning the comminuted fragments of their week.

The teenagers sipped on soda as they waited for the pizza. Philip asked predictable questions, "How's school? What events are coming up? Anything you want to do over the weekend?"

Max and Alexa were uninterested. Both of them played on their phones and gave short, hollow answers. Somewhere along the way, Philip had lost the ability to communicate with his children. It was a strange handicap. During the day, he carried on scholarly conversations with some of the smartest people on the planet. But when it came to having simple conversations with his teenagers about everyday life, he was a foreigner speaking a dead language, or worse, he was a deaf-mute, unseen by his own children. It was not that he did not care; he wanted to know what was going on in their lives. Who knows what pressures they faced? Were they experimenting with alcohol or maybe drugs? Max at age fifteen had unkempt hair and a baggy way of dressing. His grades had fallen. Did he have a sloppy attitude toward life in general? Alexa at age thirteen remained academically strong, but she was withdrawn socially. Philip did not know any of her friends. He knew they both spent hours alone, and he wondered if they thought about serious issues. What careers interested them? Did they struggle with depression? Did their mom talk to them about sexual identity, or were they sexually active? Could they stand up for themselves at school? Philip wanted to enter their universe and speak with them as a father, but he did not have the vocabulary.

Philip grinned, pulling out his cell phone he typed a text to Alexa, "How R U?"

She did not look up. Her thumbs continued pounding out words in rhythmic taps on her phone.

A message appeared on Philip's phone, "ha ha dad."

Philip slapped both palms on the table with just enough force to capture the attention of Max and Alexa without making a scene, "Alright, electronics go in your pockets. Put'm away. It's time to talk. I've got an announcement."

Alexa sneered, "Can it wait? I'm in the middle of something. Let me finish."

Max rolled his eyes, "What's the lecture on tonight?"

Philip was not deterred by their juvenile contempt or self-centered insistence on virtual seclusion. On most weekends he tolerated their generational quirks, but not that night. He had important news. He drew their attention with a silent gaze followed by a growled ultimatum, "Either the devices go in your pockets now, or they go in my pocket for the weekend. It's your choice."

Alexa sighed, "What's with you?"

"What's with me? You're my daughter. I'm your dad. We're eating dinner together. I think it's quite normal for a family to talk every now and then. You have a problem with that?"

Alexa smirked, "I'm cool. Just surprised. Why the sudden happy family routine?"

Philip answered in a firm whisper, "Listen to me. We were not a perfect family. I get that. But we *are* family. And like it or not, I'm your dad. There was a time when that meant something to you. Someday it will mean something to you again. But for now, we'll just have to put up with each other. I know you think I'm out of touch, just some parent you have to tolerate on the weekends. And for the last twenty minutes, I've tolerated your sitting right beside me while you're talking to the rest of the world. Tonight that changes. Let's practice the art of talking to the people who are actually with us for a change."

Alexa put her phone in her lap and grabbed two spare straws. With them she tapped out a rhythm on her glass, her attention drawn momentarily back to her dad.

Max hid his phone out of sight, "So, Dad. What's up?"

"I've been asked to go on an assignment. I may not see you for a few weeks."

Alexa broke into a drum roll on her glass. She looked at Max and nodded, "Yeah, Mom told us."

Philip leaned back and crossed his arms, "What did Mom say about it?"

Max looked back toward the kitchen, "Well, she's not happy, I can tell you that. When's the pizza coming?"

"It's not microwave pizza, Max. It will get here in a few minutes. Did Mom tell you where I'm going?"

"She mentioned the Caribbean."

Alexa looked at Max and giggled, "She said the Bermuda Triangle was a good place for you."

Max laughed.

Philip felt the hair rise on his neck, "Keep your mother out of this. I'm sorry I asked."

A waitress approached and lowered a pizza onto the middle of the table. The smell of the fresh baked pizza drew their full attention.

Max and Alexa grabbed at pieces that were still so hot that the cheese stretched from their plates to the pan. They each devoured a slice and reached for another.

Philip poked at a slice with a fork, allowing the flavors to meld as it cooled. He struggled to shove the conversation forward, "They're sending me to Haiti."

Max started to speak. His voice was muffled by hot pizza, "That sounds interesting."

"Yeah, they had a big earthquake, and they're sending me to help. Lots of people were injured."

Alexa grabbed another slice. She had one hand under the table and was looking down while chewing. Max knew what she was doing and called her on it, "Seriously, Alexa. While you're eating? Dad said to put it away."

Alexa slipped her phone back into her pocket and gave her dad a contrite look, "Sorry."

Philip tried to engage them further by reciting things he had picked up in his reading, "So, do you know anything about Haiti?"

"Nope."

"Do you know where it is?"

Max looked at his dad and spoke in a sarcastic tone, "Can I use my phone to check?"

"Nice try, but no."

Alexa spoke out of the corner of her mouth while sipping from her straw, "It's in the Caribbean."

Philip tried to kindle the spark of enthusiasm in her voice, "Did you know that Haiti is where Columbus first landed in the Caribbean?"

"Nope."

"Did you know they won a revolution against Napoleon?"

"Nope."

Every attempt at engaging either of them was met with painfully short answers that communicated distant disinterest in the subject, or worse, a disinterest in being with their father.

Philip leaned forward, "You want to hear something really cool?"

Alexa rolled her eyes. Max shrugged, "Sure, Dad, whatever."

Philip looked both ways as if to clear the area of prying ears, and then he whispered, "My friend says in Haiti, they've got zombies—real ones."

That was all it took. For the rest of dinner and for several hours thereafter, Max and Alexa probed for more stories and asked innumerable questions. That night Philip became the coolest dad in America.

6
The Truth is Hard to Hear

Philip refused to hire a housekeeper. He kept his home clean in the hygienic sense, but organizationally his living space was a cluttered mess. He considered his place functional, not fancy. Magazines lay stacked on stairs, dishes were spread upon the kitchen counter, and pieces of orthopedic hardware, relics from work, were placed along a wall in the living room. For him, the smell of home was a mix of aging carpet and disinfectant spray, the kind of fragrance that hits a person walking into a freshly cleaned locker room.

A few days prior to departure, Philip transformed his living room into a staging ground for his reluctant voyage to the developing world. Anderson Hu advised Philip to pack light which, though a reasonable recommendation for a journey to any tourist destination, seemed woefully inadequate for a trip to a disaster zone. Philip knew nothing about life in Haiti, but he was fairly certain there would be no convenient way to replenish depleted or forgotten items. He used a step-wise approach to packing. Start broad. Spread everything out as if preparing for an expedition. Then pare down the jumbled collection of supplies and clothing to the absolute minimum. Philip stood over the muddle strewn about the floor pondering which items were essential and which could stay behind.

Then his doorbell rang.

A man in his twenties stood on the porch dressed comfortably in ripped jeans and faded tee shirt. The amber light reflecting off his wavy blond hair gave him a look more in line with a loafing juvenile than a young professional. In reality, Sam Verity was a mix of both. He was a resident, ambitious in work and carefree in persona. He lived for busy nights in the emergency department; the rush of adrenaline at meeting unknown trauma turned him on. For him, a trip to the scene of a disaster resonated with his longing for adventure. He greeted Philip, flicked his thick hair to the side and held out a carton of bottles, "E'vning, Doc. Want a beer?"

Philip answered, "More than you know. Come in. Have a seat if you can find a place to chill, but keep your drinks off my leather."

Sam slumped back in a chair and picked up a remote control. He studied the buttons and flipped through stations, "You've got a sweet screen. This new?"

"Brand new. See if a game's on."

Sam pointed the remote, "When I get money, I'm putting one of these in my pad."

Philip shouted from the kitchen, "So, what have you been up to? Haven't seen you at the hospital."

Sam laughed, "Don't even ask. I've been on the oncology service. Can't say much for the pace over there. Hu told me about the trip, though, and I signed right up." Sam looked around the room, "Man, it looks like you're prepared for about anything. You know, if you can't get it done with all this, you ought not to be doing it."

Philip called back, "Funny, Sam. It's not all going. I'm trying to figure out what I really need."

Sam asked, "Are the others coming over?"

Philip returned and sat back on the couch, throwing his arms back over the cushions, "As far as I know. Hu set up the meeting. He wants to go over details before our flight out."

"You think he'll be here?"

"Hu's in charge; why would he not be here?"

"Well, 'cause he wasn't in clinic. His nurse said she'd heard he had some emergency."

"Maybe he had a case come up at the hospital. I think he'd have called if something serious occurred. He'll be here soon."

Sam tapped the arm of the chair, "So, when did you sign up?"

Philip shook his head, "Can't say I really did. Henske says jump, and we smile and say, 'how high?' Know what I mean? How did you get pulled into it?"

Sam threw a relaxed leg over the arm of the chair and took a drink, "Sounded cool. I read about some residents working down in Port-au-Prince after the quake. They've been doing intense work, and I thought it'd be a good experience."

The doorbell rang.

Two other residents stood at the door. The first was Connor Wayman, an academic type with round glasses and a tall, thin physique. He was dressed in khakis and a well-pressed button shirt. The second resident was Aryanna Vito. She stood next to Connor holding his arm with delicate fingers. She looked over Philip's shoulder and bit her lip, "Um, Doctor Scott, you know we're leaving in two days?"

"I'm acutely aware of our imminent departure. Don't mind the mess. I work better under deadlines."

Connor and Aryanna stepped over the boxes and moved clothing off the couch. They sat down together. Aryanna rested her bare arm on Connor's shoulder as she rubbed the hair behind his ear.

Connor looked at Philip, "Well, we solved your rash mystery."

"The post-operative hip? Was it dermatitis or something?"

"Not even close. We took biopsies; the pathology came back as vasculitis. Turns out the gentleman is experiencing a metal hypersensitivity."

Sam wiped beer from his lips, "Hey, it's an English-only zone here. You sayin' the guy's allergic to something?"

Connor nodded, "Yep, his implant. It turns out the new hip is the culprit. The guy has a rare allergy to metal alloy. He never had a rash or reaction like this before. The rash started right after his hip replacement. It all makes sense, now."

Philip shook his head, "Tough luck. I guess it's back to the operating table for him, huh?"

Connor shrugged, "He's on the schedule for tomorrow morning to remove the hardware. Could have been worse, I suppose. Without the skin reaction, we may not have caught the problem before it got worse. The rash may have saved his ability to walk."

Sam raised his bottle, "Well, alright then. I propose a toast. To my esteemed colleague, Connor Wayman, better known as Doctor Cranium, the medical genius who makes rash decisions."

Aryanna laughed.

Philip saw Aryanna smiling at Connor. The way she looked at him stirred something in Philip. Jealousy. Not covetousness; he had no desire to insert himself into their relationship. It was her love that caught his eye. The way she touched him and the way her perfectly shaped eyes locked onto Connor resurrected a feeling he once knew when he was a student and Amanda looked at him that way.

In a few minutes, the doorbell rang again. This time a young lady in light blue scrubs, short in stature, with black hair, a round face and a square frame, stood at the door bouncing on her toes.

She looked up at Philip and smiled with her whole face, speaking in high pitched elongated syllables with a rising quality that made each statement sound like a question, "Hello, my name is Paulita Sanders. Is this the Scott residence?"

"Yes, it is. I'm Phil Scott. You must be our medical student."

"Oh, Doctor Scott. It is so good to meet you. Call me Pauley. Doctor Hu told me so much about you. He told me we were meeting at your house tonight. I hope that's correct. Am I in the right place?"

"Well, Pauley, I can't say any of us are in the right place. But this is where we're meeting, yes."

Aryanna called out Pauley's name and leapt from the couch, reaching out to her in a welcoming embrace, "I'm so happy you're here. I didn't know they were going to let you go."

Pauley bounced again, "Well, I signed a ton of papers to say I was going at my own risk and all, but I needed an elective credit, and my advisor worked out this plan to count the mission as a rotation in international medicine. Doctor Hu agreed to be my preceptor. So, it worked out perfectly."

Philip looked at both of them and stated the obvious, "So, you two know each other."

Aryanna nodded, "Pauley did a rotation with us last fall. She's on her way to being a fine surgeon."

Philip gave an approving nod, "Ambitious. I like that. Sorry about the slim selection of food. I didn't have time to pull much together. Drinks are in the refrigerator if you want something."

Hospitality was not a skill Philip possessed, nor was he inclined to acquire such a virtue, but he cleared space on the coffee table and set out an assortment of sandwiches. His home had been selected for the pre-trip meeting, not because he was a good host, but because his townhouse apartment was in a geographically convenient neighborhood near the campus.

Aryanna took a small sandwich, "It's hard to imagine that we're going to a place where people don't have even this much to eat."

Pauley's smile turned into a downward somber frown, "Doctor Scott, is it safe to eat the food there?"

"I wish I could answer that. I assume meals are provided. But I'm taking snacks just in case."

Sam laughed, "I'm not eating anything that's not wrapped with a label written in English. You won't find me on the toilet with the Hershey squirts."

Aryanna scowled, "Really, Sam. That's gross."

Connor leaned forward, "Here's the rule when you travel: boil it; peel it; cook it or forget it."

Aryanna turned to Philip, "Have you done this type of work, Doctor Scott?"

Her question caught Philip off guard. He had been practicing medicine his entire adult life. Aryanna had been in his program for several years; she was well aware of his 'type of work.' Either her question sprung from a deeper curiosity about something larger than Philip's understanding of what he did every day, or she was tactfully pointing out his lack of experience.

Aryanna interpreted Philip's expression as confusion about her meaning. She looked at Connor and then back at Philip, "I just mean, I was surprised to see you'd volunteered to go with us."

Philip's face reddened, "Really, and why is that?"

"Well, you've just never struck me as the—humanitarian type. I mean you're great and all. I've just never pictured you working in a place like Haiti."

"Maybe I did not volunteer. I can tell you when I travel I don't pick destinations inundated with disease, filth, and political turmoil. And if by humanitarian you mean those people who toss change to the panhandlers of the world and expect an award, then you're right, I'm not a humanitarian."

Sam reacted with a short laugh, "So, you're in it for the rush, right?"

Philip scowled as he answered using slow, measured words, "Let's just say my presence on this trip results from a clause in my contract that says I'm subject to performing 'other duties as assigned.'"

The eyes of each person shifted to the floor. Philip's harsh reply elicited an awkward silence. He knew his reaction caused the change in mood, but he was not apologetic. He wished he had the idealism or sense of adventure of his students. But, he did not. As he saw it, the wages of altruism are heartbreak, and worse, poverty, and the danger in thrill-seeking is the inevitable bad outcome, usually set off by some high-profile patient who dies on the table, thereby angering an unfriendly legislator or catching the skeptical eye of a reporter; though the operating room is full of people, the whole affair reflects most poorly and almost exclusively on the surgeon, and the negative publicity all but erases any promotional opportunities. Philip had learned these lessons early; as professionals, his apprentices needed to learn that in this world everyone looks to doctors for a handout, and then discards them as scapegoats. Countries are no different. And Philip thought that doctors must learn to resist the sacrificial tendency to give away skills for free or put themselves at increased legal risk without proper compensation.

Though he would later be ashamed to admit it, at the time he misinterpreted their silence as thoughtful reflection as if the truth was just hard to hear. Philip chose to let his point sink in and avoided the pressure to break the moment with what he considered further meaningless chatter.

The silence was finally broken, not by a comment, but by the ringing of the doorbell.

Anderson Hu stood on the doorstep. A baseball cap shaded his eyes but could not darken the bright smile that permanently rounded his cheeks. Though short in stature, he usually stood tall as if always at attention, but this night he leaned forward on a pair of crutches. He held one knee flexed, lifting his foot off the ground while resting his weight fully on the other. The raised foot was splinted. A woman stood beside him holding a covered dish.

Doctor Hu shook his head, "Phil, so sorry to drop in late, but I've got tough news. I tore my Achilles. I'm scheduled for surgery next week. Believe me, I regret doing this to you, but I won't be able to make the trip."

Philip felt his heart pound. The group depended on Anderson's experience. He set the itinerary. He arranged the travel. Without Anderson, there could be no trip. Philip suppressed the welcome thought that this injury, though personally inconvenient to Anderson, may mean the trip would be cancelled, a conclusion which Philip would welcome, "That's terrible, Anderson. What happened?"

"Playing ball last night after work. I went up for a rebound and 'wham' it hit me like an electric fence across my heel. It's not a fun feeling, I tell you."

Philip leaned forward, "What does that mean for our trip?"

Anderson turned to the woman beside him, "This is my wife, Monica. She's my driver. And she's a first-rate baker. Here, we brought dessert. May we come in?"

"Yes. I'm sorry. Of course. Of course."

Anderson hobbled on his crutches into the living room. He saw the mess and laughed, "You guys need some packing advice? Looks like you're ready to tackle Rainier."

"Just trying to sort out the indispensable." Philip waved Sam out of the chair. "Let the doctor have a seat. We've been waiting on you, Anderson. What can I get you to drink?"

Anderson reached out and handed Philip a shoulder bag and hopped to the recliner. He leaned back in the chair and elevated his splinted foot, "Just water, thanks. You've got a nice place, Phil."

Sam leaned forward and tapped Anderson's splint, "So how long until you're able to travel?"

"I think you know the answer to that. It's my Achilles; a total rupture. I'm out for weeks. We'll see how things heal up."

Aryanna looked concerned, "Does this mean we have to call off the trip?"

"Well, I thought it might come to that. I called Henske to let him know about my injury and see who else could fill in. It's too late to get a replacement. But our flight into Haiti has been chartered, and the bulk of our medical supplies are already in Florida ready for transport. Henske says Doctor Scott can lead the team. And I think he's right. Phil will do a great job."

His words fell on Philip like a hot spotlight. Every head in the room turned to look. But Philip's eyes remained fixed on Doctor Hu. Then he asked in a firm voice, "Anderson, may I talk to you in private?"

Anderson grabbed his crutches and shuffled behind Philip to the back of the kitchen. There, Philip lit into him, "Listen to me. You can't just drop this kind of thing on me without warning. I don't know the first thing about tropical medicine, and I was coerced into going on this trip in the first place. We have no idea what we're walking into down there. I can't commit to being responsible for our residents, and I certainly can't be responsible for that medical student on a trip like this; the risk is too great."

"They volunteered, Phil. They are aware of the risks. If you back out now, they will be sorely disappointed. And, besides, you won't be alone. Other programs are already on the ground. You're not the only ones going in. I've done this kind of trip many times. You'll do just fine."

"But this was not the plan. It's not what I signed up for."

"Here's your first lesson, Phil: be flexible. In Haiti, if your plans won't bend, they'll break. Just roll with the challenges and do your best not to get too rigid. Accept each day's circumstances and do what you can. In fact, when you land, just put your watch away. The roosters will be your alarm, and the sun will be your clock. Don't worry."

He pointed to the shoulder bag Philip was still holding, "Open it up, Phil. Everything you need is right there. The itinerary, contacts, evacuation insurance. I included a step-by-step guide for getting through customs in Haiti. There's cash for the group and a department credit card. My cell number's on the contact list. Call me anytime. I know it's a lot to dump on you. But Henske insisted. He says you're the type of leader who works well under pressure."

"Leadership requires preparation. I'm not prepared. How can I be expected to lead people into a situation I know nothing about? They're barely adults. None of us has been to this place. We don't know anyone there. I have a real problem with this."

"Well, if it's any consolation, I've arranged to have you picked up at the airport in Cap-Haitien by a man I know well. His name is Victor Santile; he was our driver when I went to Haiti. He is absolutely trustworthy, and he will get you from the airport to the hospital compound. From there, the hospital supervisor will provide you with an orientation and schedule."

Philip pulled out one of the folders and thumbed through the pages, but he was not reading. He was thinking, contemplating a way out, a clean exit that would allow him to save face. But no matter how hard he tried, he was unable to summon a convincing argument. Everything that came to mind sounded like a spoiled child pouting about having to do chores.

Philip closed the folder and placed it on the counter, "I just don't know. If I had a month to plan, maybe, but this is too sudden. It's all too unexpected."

Anderson smiled, "You're a trauma surgeon, Phil. Being ready for the unexpected is the core of your specialty. But I hear what you're saying. And you're right; it's a lot to drop on you without warning. Why don't you take the evening to think it over? If you don't feel prepared to lead the group, perhaps the department can just postpone the trip."

Whether it was his intent, Anderson's comment struck Philip at his weak, most vulnerable, selfish core. Philip was more than prepared to lead. It was not a question of ability. It was a question of desire. He understood that altruistic trips were popular among some people. But he failed to see how the trip would add anything of value to his life. Had Anderson spoken with Henske? Was this comment a subtle reference to his ability to lead the department? If so, this was nothing short of cruel hazing.

Philip shook his head and pushed Anderson out of the way as he walked back into the living room.

The moment Philip entered the room the volume of excited jabbering dropped into silence. All eyes turned to look at him. Philip stood still for a minute. He looked at each person, studying their faces. Connor gave him a stiff confident grin. Sam winked and lifted his bottle. Aryanna crossed her arms and raised an eyebrow.

It would be a long time before Philip recognized that on that night when Connor Wayman, Sam Verity, Aryanna Vito, and Paulita Sanders sat in his home, amidst the mess of his life, that his eyes were about to be opened to a larger understanding of the world. At the time, he was not yet ready to see it. He was blind to the real reason he had been selected for the trip, and he was deaf to any calling outside his own will. Indeed, the truth can be hard to hear.

It was Pauley who finally spoke. She looked at each of them and then looked at Philip, "So, Doctor Scott, are we going to Haiti?"

7

First-Class Ticket to the Third World

On the southern ramp of an international airport in Fort Pierce, Florida, just outside a missionary aviation hanger, sat a brightly polished vintage aircraft, a DC-3, with blue and white stripes, its nose angled upward as it rested on its tailwheel in a proud pose. Like an old man surrounded by grandchildren, it sat motionless among the bustle of modern business jets.

This particular DC-3 was built in 1944, constructed in the closing years of World War II after the likeness of its larger cousins the B-17 and B-29. The DC-3 was tough, heavy yet nimble, able to land on short dirt strips while carrying a heavy load. After World War II, this particular DC-3 continued to fly. Its oil-guzzling, radial engines and large propellers had flown sailors, marines, and supplies for the U.S. Navy until 1965 when a civilian company purchased the plane for commercial use. Then twenty years later a mission aviation company in Florida purchased it and put it to use flying missionaries and supplies to remote locations around the Caribbean. Twice a week, the old warbird flew to Haiti. It was a well-maintained aircraft with roomy seats and a clean interior.

Philip walked out of the small hanger into the cool morning air. When he saw the airplane, he stopped; mesmerized by the beauty of a flying vestige of his grandfather's era, he studied the plane from head to tail as if counting every rivet. The polished aluminum wings reflected orange rays of dawn which, against the backdrop of departing night, gave the plane a majestic glow. It looked like a museum artifact on display. Philip remained as still as a statue before the old relic. Then he said, "This is unbelievable."

Aryanna came up from behind him and touched his shoulder, "You alright, doc?"

Philip stood still, "It's beautiful."

"It's just a plane," answered Aryanna.

"I see that," said Philip, "But you understand we're looking at a piece of history."

Sam laughed, "A piece of work is what it is."

Philip answered, "Don't be stupid. People pay thousands of dollars for a flight in one of these old birds. I think we're in for a once in a lifetime ride."

Philip followed the stream of passengers entering the back door of the old plane. Once each person was seated, a tall, grey-haired, confident fellow with a bushy mustache entered the cabin. He was older in years but, like the plane, well-maintained. He smiled in a way that caused the corners of his mustache to spread out like wings. Then he introduced himself, "Good morning folks, I'm your captain. I'll be taking you to Cap-Haitien this morning."

After a few cheerful comments regarding the route of flight and operation of seatbelts, he became most serious and explained it was the custom to begin the flight with a prayer. Then he started praying. With a lowered brow and breathy voice, he prayed aloud, not with fervor, but with the same mix of joy and solemnity with which he had just briefed the passengers.

Philip had never prayed in his life. When he saw the captain bow his head, and other passengers follow suit, he felt suddenly out of place. Like most educated people, he accepted the fact that a prayer worded by clergy may be appropriate for like-minded individuals in private gatherings. But this was not a wedding or funeral or religious ceremony. They were on an airplane that had not even taken off. Perhaps a prayer during severe turbulence or an inflight emergency would be forgivable. But compulsory prayer before starting the engines seemed excessive, even offensive.

Furthermore, the otherwise dignified captain was committing what Philip considered intellectual suicide. Public displays of religious practice are a sign of ignorance. Philip assumed the captain was well trained to fly the aircraft, but he could not see any connection between the professional proficiency of a pilot and private religious beliefs that, frankly, were irrelevant. It was not ancient religious manuscripts that taught men to fly, and sophisticated people did not gain the respect of others by publicly displaying private religious acts. As a child, Philip once asked his father why people close their eyes to pray. Never long with explanations, his father told him, "People who pray close their eyes to reality." That summed up Philip's religious training. He understood that spiritual beliefs held deep meaning for some people, and he respected the right of people to practice whatever religion they chose; but religious beliefs, regardless of their depth, should be kept private. That was what Philip believed.

Philip sat in quiet respect until the captain was finished; then he turned to Sam and whispered, "I can't express how disturbing this is to me."

Sam chuckled, "You mean because the plane is as old as my grandfather or because the pilot seems to think we need to make peace with our maker before the flight? Ten bucks says they take up a collection to start the engines."

Laughing, Philip shook his head, "What did I get us into, Sam?"

Two hours later they were flying over the Bahamas. The combination of jet lag, the hum of radial engines, and the reduced oxygen at altitude had a sedating effect. The travelers were fast asleep, except for one. Philip remained wide awake. Sam dozed next to him. Aryanna was in front of them resting her head on Connor's shoulder. Pauley sat across the aisle curled up next to a well-dressed Haitian; both were slumbering. Philip, however, could not sleep.

The roar of the engines and slow climb over the Atlantic Ocean took Philip back to a childhood memory. As a child, lying awake late at night he would gaze at the model airplanes hanging from his bedroom ceiling and imagine piloting one of them in a wartime adventure. In a way, the flight in a DC-3 was a dream come true. During such an experience, he dared not sleep.

Philip asked the flight attendant if it would be possible for him to see the view from the cockpit. She agreed to ask and walked to the front of the aircraft. She returned smiling, "Go up whenever you like. The pilots say they'd enjoy the company."

Philip's heart skipped a beat. He stepped over Sam and made his way up the aisle, rising onto his toes with each step, suppressing the instinct to bounce into the air in the anticipation of seeing the view from up front. He bent over into the cockpit and placed a hand on the captain's shoulder. Yelling over the engine noise, he said, "The stewardess said I could watch you guys for a minute?"

The captain motioned to the co-pilot, who removed his headset and handed it to Philip. Then the co-pilot climbed out of his seat and motioned back toward it as he shouted, "Here, take my seat for a while. I'm getting a cup of coffee."

Philip took the headset. His eyes grew wide, and he looked at the co-pilot, "You're not serious."

"I'm perfectly serious," replied the co-pilot, "Who knows? Captain may recruit you."

Philip placed the headset over his ears. Instantly, the noise of the aircraft faded into a distant static, and he heard the captain speaking in a measured baritone, "Have a seat, brother. Make yourself comfortable."

Philip slid into the co-pilot's seat, taking great care not to bump the countless levers, switches, and dials. The yoke in front of him gently rocked back and forth as if moved by an unseen spirit.

A thousand questions poured through Philip's mind, but for the moment he sat in frozen wonder, afraid that a wrong move would send the plane into an unrecoverable dive.

The captain noticed Philip's trepidation. He demonstrated how to secure the shoulder harness and reassured Philip that nothing delicate fell within his reach. After a brief orientation to the instruments and controls, the captain asked, "Have you flown in one of these before?"

Philip smiled, "No. I've waited my whole life for this."

The captain smiled, his moustache scraping at the microphone as it flared outward, "Well, I can tell you after thirty years of doing this, it never gets old. Are you a pilot?"

Philip answered, "No, I'm a surgeon. But I went through a phase when I was a kid. I wanted to be a fighter pilot. I read books on planes and built models. On my ninth birthday, my dad and I built this model of a B-17."

The captain nodded, "Ah, the Flying Fortress."

Philip answered, "Precisely. I played with that thing for years, flying imaginary missions over our yard. I can't tell you how many times I dreamed of what it would be like to actually sit in that cockpit with shrapnel exploding around me on some bombing run. Now here I am."

The captain agreed, "You know, this plane is not much different than the bombers."

"You've flown them?"

"No, but I go sit in one every now and then; at air shows and what not. My dad died on one when I was just an infant. He was a gunner. They crashed on take-off some-where in the Pacific. So, though I never knew the man, any chance I get to sit in one of the restorations makes me feel like I'm spending a little time with him."

Philip responded politely, "I'm sorry for your loss."

"No matter now. He was a good man. Served his coun-try. Loved the Lord and loved my mother. In some ways, I'd like to think I'm just following in his footsteps."

Over the next hour, Philip asked questions in anxious bursts like a nine-year-old with limited time. Unable to contain his excitement he probed the captain's knowledge of the history aviation, the pilots of old, and the maneu-vers that set apart great pilots.

The captain acted the role of a tour-guide, navigating the conversation with the same ease with which he guided the plane over the Caribbean.

At one point, the conversation entered a natural pause. As the plane droned over uninhabited islands, Philip leaned forward to watch turquoise waters pass below. In the distance, a successive line of flat, verdant isles stretched to the horizon, each one surrounded by a patch of white and green that contrasted with the deep blues of the distant ocean. The scene transported Philip back to another period of his childhood when pirates and fantasies of surviving alone on uncharted islands filled his imagina-tion. He thought about what life would be like on one of those islands. What would it cost to own a piece of Car-ibbean real estate? He imagined swinging on the porch of a private bungalow shaded by palm trees, fishing in the shallow waters, traveling between islands by catamaran, sipping tropical drinks. For Philip, that would be success. That would be paradise.

After about an hour, the co-pilot returned to reclaim his spot and Philip thanked both pilots for the experience. He returned to his seat and stared out the window at the verdant islands. Eventually, his daydream gave way to a deep sleep.

A while later, he awoke to abrupt turbulent heaving as the plane descended through cumulous clouds that billowed along the border of the islands. Philip rubbed the sleepy haze from his eyes and looked around the cabin.

Several people were pointing out the windows as they approached a very different-appearing island. Unlike the flat isles of the Bahamas, this island was monstrous, with faded slopes of brown and green rising directly out of the sea. Each ridge was situated in front of successively taller mountains. Smoke rose from valleys in between these mountains and along coastal villages where tin and thatched-roofed huts dotted the shoreline. Philip looked down and saw wooden boats with triangular sails cutting across waves parallel to the shore.

Pauley saw Philip stretching his neck to see out her window. She yelled from across the cabin, "Is this Haiti?"

Philip shrugged, "I can only assume."

The captain flew inland for several miles, circling back over a large bowl of flat fertile land rimmed by tropical peaks. Dirt roads divided the green fields below like a plaid quilt. Toward the northern shore, Philip saw Cap-Haitien, a cement city bordered by the sea and protected on the west flank by a lone deforested mountain. From the air, the city looked old and worn, like an enormous piece of rusted tin, bent and broken, lying by the sea. It did not appear to Philip like a city of a million people. There were no skyscrapers or lofty offices that characterize cities of its size. Low plastered buildings were connected to each other, each rising to varying heights in an extended arrangement of concrete blocks which gave the city the appearance of a pixilated topographic map with perhaps an indistinct border between urban and rural landscapes. Tired huts clung to the hills around the edge of the city precariously exposed to the elements. As the plane descended, Philip could see cattle and goats grazing along the runway and a boy running behind one of the cows with a stick driving the gaunt animal away from the airport.

The captain landed and taxied to the terminal. Then, when the propellers stopped spinning, he walked down the aisle and opened the door at the rear of the plane. Hot salty air filled the cabin. The captain looked back with a smile, "Welcome to Haiti, folks; please watch your step."

Philip stepped from the plane into the bright equatorial sunlight. For a moment he could not see. The world flashed white in the glare of rays reflecting off the white tarmac. He squinted and raised his hand to shield his eyes.

Philip followed the line of people walking toward the terminal, a one-story concrete structure, which looked to Philip like a dilapidated strip mall.

Along the edge of the ramp, hundreds of people massed along a chain-link fence watching passengers disembark. One man in the crowd stood out. He was large, a head taller than most with skin the color of coffee and a shaved head that reflected sunbeams in a way that made his scalp glow. He had the look of an imposing bodyguard or bouncer wearing sunglasses and a maroon knit shirt that fit tightly, accentuating his large chest. Philip felt like the man was looking straight at him. More ominous was the way the man turned and walked along the fence all the while watching Philip as he approached the terminal.

Other planes had arrived at the same time, and Philip blended himself into the crowd of arriving passengers. His eyes adjusted to the shade of the packed terminal. He saw two lines of people, each moving toward different windows. Philip was unsure of which way to go. He felt his heart race. Signs were written in a different language. The immigration process was unclear. Philip felt a rising frustration with people pushing on him in a line of cramped human dominoes. The combined effects of jet lag, heat, noise, and apparent pandemonium left his head pulsating in a growing headache. He reached into his pocket and pulled out a bottle of ibuprofen.

At the front of the line, a stoic man in a blue uniform stamped Philip's passport and pointed to another crowded area. Philip moved into the larger room where a fan blew the smell of humid body odor over people waiting for baggage. If there was a system to follow, its rules were lost on Philip.

Luggage came through an opening in the wall, and a line of Haitian men pushed the bags down a raised ramp of rollers. Connor and Sam identified and stacked containers of medical supplies as Aryanna and Pauley grabbed luggage.

A line of men opened and inspected the luggage. Then a man in a tan uniform approached Philip. In broken English he asked, "Excuse me, Monsieur, are you the leader?"

Philip looked around, "I came with these people if that's what you mean."

"You must come with me."

Philip followed the man into a back room where a middle-aged woman with high cheekbones and penetrating black eyes sat behind a small desk. She wore a dark sports coat and a white blouse upon which hung a faded and peeled identification tag. The office, a confining space, had walls painted in a faint dirty yellow. A fan mounted in the upper back corner sagged downward; unplugged, its blades only rocked in the brief wafts of dust-laden air filtering through the screened window. A lone picture of the president of Haiti hung on the wall behind the woman.

The woman did not smile, but greeted Philip in a heavily accented monotone, "Welcome to Haiti. Is this your first time here?"

Philip looked around. The uniformed man blocked the door like a guard, and the woman sat before him with the confidence of an interrogator. Philip stumbled over an answer, "Uh, yes. This is my first trip."

"Did you pass a good journey?"

"Yes. It went fine."

"How many are in your group?"

"Uh, six—No, I'm sorry, one could not make it; there are five of us."

The woman spoke in Creole to the man in uniform. He responded with indecipherable words and gestures.

The woman looked back at Philip, "You are a doctor?"

"Yes, ma'am, a surgeon."

"You have medications with you?"

"Some medication, yes—mostly surgical supplies."

The woman pulled out a receipt pad and scribbled out an invoice with a list that Philip could not read but for the dollar figure next to each item. Then she typed out a series of calculations on an old calculator and turned the display to show Philip the sum; three hundred dollars.

Philip's heart became lead. He did not know what to do. Was this legitimate? Was he being robbed? He looked at the woman, puzzled, "What's the meaning of this? Is it an entry fee? We're not tourists; we're here to help."

The woman responded in an apathetic monotone, "It is the tax for bringing medical supplies into my country."

Philip suspected extortion. He was too exhausted to think, much less argue, but he could not let this go. His face tensed and he pointed at the woman, "I think you're ripping me off. I wasn't told about any tax. These supplies are to help your people. You can't just charge arbitrary taxes. We're not here to sell this stuff. You'll just have to excuse me. I'm leaving!"

The woman motioned to the official who held out his arm to hold Philip in the room. Then she typed again on the calculator and displayed a new number; this time it read two hundred dollars. But she added, "Sir, if you do not pay the tax I must confiscate your supplies. You will not be allowed to enter Haiti with your possessions."

Philip's face pulsed crimson; he removed two hundred dollars from a money pouch and slapped the bills on the desk as he said under his breath, "You're worse than my ex-wife."

Either the woman did not hear the insult, or she did not care. Regardless, she did not respond. And Philip walked out into the baggage claim area with a handwritten receipt bearing a stamp of the Haitian government.

Suddenly, skinny men in red shirts grabbed Philip's supplies. They moved the containers and bags out the door. Sam yelled at Philip over the crowd, "Hey Doc, where are they going with our stuff?"

Philip noticed the large man with a shaved head and dark glasses standing by the door. It was the same man who had been eyeing him outside. He appeared to be using the men in the red shirts to carry the luggage away. Philip walked up preparing himself for a confrontation.

As Philip approached, the man took off his glasses revealing the meek eyes of a person who had few worries. His physical build, however, was imposing enough to end an argument before it began. With flat emotion and a sharp accent, the man said, "You are a friend of Doctor Hu?"

"Yes. I am Phil Scott."

The man looked at the containers and luggage being carried passed, "Perhaps you plan to stay awhile, I think." Then he turned to follow the last container.

Philip grabbed the man's shoulder, "Excuse me, I'm supposed to find a man named Victor Santile."

The man turned back and looked at Philip, his jaw muscles bulging. He looked right at Philip with a piercing gaze. Then, once the tension fully ripened, he broke into a wide, round smile, "It is no problem, my friend. You may relax. Victor Santile has found you."

"So, you know him."

"Oui. I know him well. I am him."

8

The Drive to the Hospital

Philip followed Victor out of the terminal. He took in the hot, sticky air and felt beads of sweat run down his back. He again squinted against the tropical light and raised a hand to shield his eyes.

Victor walked toward a white truck parked in an isolated patch of shade near the airport terminal. The truck was a diesel-type flat-bed over which a blue canopy was stretched to shade passengers. Benches were welded around the perimeter of the bed. It was clean except for streaks of rust forming along the back rail where the passing of supplies had abraded the otherwise pristine veneer. A line of Haitian men stood behind the truck, passing luggage and containers up to another man waiting in the bed. The man in the truck received each item and tossed the supplies into a tight stack just behind the cab.

Once the luggage was loaded, a Haitian boy wearing faded pants and tattered tennis shoes held a ladder against the back of the truck. As each person climbed aboard, the boy patted his chest and spoke in stuttering English, "I-I-I am your friend."

Philip climbed in last, taking a seat on the back edge of the bench. The boy tossed the ladder at Philip's feet and then walked to the front to join Victor in the cab. When Victor fired up the engine a puff of hot, oily smoke drifted under the canopy, eliciting a flurry of waving hands until the grinding of gears caused the truck to rev and surge forward. Impulsively everyone in the back grabbed for something secure to prevent falling as the smoke drifted away behind them.

Victor departed the airport and merged into the traffic along the crowded main street leading east out of Cap-Haitien. Dust rose around the traffic like a dry mist, stirred up by feet and passing trucks in the heat of the day. In halting motion with sudden stops, blaring horns, and a hasty grinding of gears, Victor edged forward through the undulating stream of people and vehicles.

All around him, Philip heard the roar of engines and grinding of tools competing with music blaring from roadside shops, all at a volume so loud that any conversation required the force of a shout. He rubbed his forehead while studying the unfamiliar world around him.

Rows of connected businesses, over which living spaces were built, bordered each side of the dusty, pothole-ridden street. The quality of masonry varied. There was little sense of unity or consistency among the buildings. Some appeared solid, beautiful even, with French-styled balconies and turrets, while others were small, tilted buildings that bulged at mid-wall. There were no lighted signs or posters. The dust-covered façades of most buildings were painted with large letters or pictures indicating the sort of business. Philip could not read the Creole words, but he deduced the meanings. He saw a barber shop, a pharmacy, a mechanic, a restaurant, and more than a few lottery stands.

Sam yelled out comments reflecting early stages of culture shock, "How can this many people be crammed into one place?"

Connor pointed to the cinder block buildings overshadowing them. He thought about Seattle, with its towering offices and multistory apartments. To him the connection was clear, "I think people just build up. You know, like back home. People just adapt by living on top of each other."

Aryanna thought of pictures she had seen of Port-au-Prince after the earthquake. She shook her head, "No wonder so many people died. Can you imagine being in one of these during an earthquake? It must have been horrifying. Even if you got out alive, you'd be crushed under the next building."

Pauley shouted toward Philip, "Did people die here in Cap-Haitien?"

Philip called back over the noise, "Unlikely. The earthquake was a hundred miles south. I don't think it caused much damage here. It leveled the capital. The death toll there is in the hundreds of thousands."

Pauley raised an eyebrow, "So, why didn't we go to Port-au-Prince?"

Philip yelled again over the revving engine and flapping canopy, "Doctor Hu had connections up here. The Port-au-Prince hospital was severely damaged, so cases are being flown to other places. We're supposed to work in a private hospital in a town called Milot."

Victor laid on the horn and swerved to miss a motorbike carrying three grown men. Sam raised his arms, "Aren't there any driving laws? If people rode like that back home, somebody'd be going to jail."

They passed a heap of garbage full of warm, decaying matter. Smoldering ribbons of smoke rose from isolated spots around the mound, and a goat with a triangular wooden collar stood atop, chewing rotting food. The smell of decomposing material wafted through the truck. Philip reflexively held his breath. Connor wrinkled his nose and became pale, "I think I'm going to be sick."

He turned outward leaning over the side of the truck, but women bearing fruit on their heads were passing right beside him, so he turned back to the center and leaned over his feet.

Aryanna saw Conner heave. She grabbed the ball cap off her head and handed it to Connor who emptied his stomach of its contents into the cap. Then, Aryanna tossed the soiled cap into the next trash heap.

A short while later the truck came to a full stop. A loaded wooden cart with two wheels being pulled by a wiry shirtless man blocked the traffic. The gaunt man, his skin glistening under the heavy midday sun had the poles of the cart under his arms, struggling forward like a human ox. But the cart would not move. One wheel of the cart was stuck in a pothole. As horns blared and people yelled at him from the crowd, the man fought to get the cart to budge while traffic crept around him.

As they passed, Pauley looked just as a black cloud of exhaust from the truck blew over the man. She turned to Philip, her eyebrows converging as her bottom lip quivered, "Doctor Scott, can't we stop to help?"

Philip pointed to the streets, "He's got plenty of his own people to help."

Pauley's shoulders fell. Her eyes became moist as she watched the man struggle until her view of him was obscured by the traffic and crowd. Aryanna saw Pauley's expression and patted her on the shoulder, "You've got a good heart, girl."

The concrete and asphalt landscape of the city eventually gave way to rural roads bordered by sugar cane fields and plantain trees. Lush mountains shaded by towering clouds became the backdrop to an expanse of farmland. In the direction of travel one mountain had an unnaturally squared-off peak. A fortress or castle had been built on top of a mountain in clear view of the entire plain. The boy leaned out the passenger window of the cab, and pointing toward the mountain he yelled, "You s-s-see Citadel?"

Over the next half hour, they passed by collections of pastel huts and single-story concrete houses with rusting tin roofs, many shaded by old growth mango trees. Cactus hedges marked the borders between packed dirt yards. Small children with swollen bellies ran from the huts to the road.

Aryanna saw the children, many wearing only shirts with no pants, waving as the truck passed. She waved back shouting, "They're so adorable."

Adorable was not the word that came to Philip's mind. These children were living in pure austerity. Many were standing outside of mud-walled homes. Emaciated chickens ran free, and dogs with visible ribs and hip bones lay in the yards. Women in tattered attire sat on low wooden chairs leaning over cooking pots. Others sat along muddy creeks washing clothes. How did people survive such poverty?

In the distance, Philip heard the approaching roar of an aircraft. Then a grey helicopter passed low over the field beside them. The markings on the side read—NAVY.

Soon, the flow of vehicles met a rising tide of people. Here the road became congested by a mass of traffic moving slowly in both directions. The people walking along the roadside were no longer just Haitian. Many appeared to be from other countries, some wearing medical attire.

Sam pointed to a sign at a crossroad, "Look, this is Milot."

At one point, a modified SUV with the markings of an ambulance approached and crept around the truck, its bullhorns blaring as it pushed ahead.

The Navy helicopter had landed in an open field near the road. As they passed the field, Philip saw four men in white smocks carry a body from the helicopter on a stretcher. They loaded the patient into the back of the ambulance. From where Philip was sitting the patient appeared young. A victim of the earthquake, perhaps.

Victor passed the ambulance and after a few hundred yards pulled up beside an iron gate which stood in front of a two-story white building with green trim. A statue of a robed figure with upheld hands looked down from a second story alcove. Under this statue was the name of the building, Hôpital Sacré Coeur.

The little boy who had helped the team onto the truck appeared from the cab and again held a ladder for each person to disembark. As they descended he patted his chest, "You remember me? I-I-I am Luckson."

The smell of exhaust saturated the air, and Philip's shirt stuck to his back. Philip patted the young man on the shoulder, "Ok, Luckson. Where do we go?"

Luckson held up his hand to indicate the team should not move; then Victor called out, "You wait here. I will find the person you are to meet."

Philip surveyed the area. His head pounded from the unfiltered noise of revving diesel engines, air horns, and shouting crowds. The two-lane street in front of the hospital was packed with people and vehicles moving in an uncoordinated, creeping vacillation of traffic.

A woman with a headscarf sat nearby under the awning of a small market stand built of rough cut planks. She watched Philip grab his forehead and in a show of compassion held up two oranges.

Philip just shook his head and looked away.

The ambulance soon arrived and rocked cautiously through the gate, passing through a crowd of people before turning toward the back of the compound. Moments later a tap-tap, a small covered pickup truck that served as a Haitian taxi, stopped in front of the hospital, its brilliantly painted covered bed was weighed down with at least twenty people. Several women wearing faded medical scrubs stepped from the back and pushed by the group from Seattle.

Philip and his team remained at the gate peering through the bars at the crowd of people. Philip scanned the entry area which held hundreds of individuals, some standing, others sitting. Many wore pressed dresses as if prepared for a special occasion. But they were somber; the occasion was clearly medical. Children with sunken eyes and distant stares lay across the laps of women who dabbed the young foreheads. Some of these women looked back at Philip. He noticed their countenance was resigned like people at a wake.

Aryanna took out her camera. She took pictures of the hospital entrance and the crowd of waiting patients.

Sam pointed at the crowd, "I guess the waiting room is already full, huh Doc?"

More than the people, Philip's attention was focused on the actual building. It was tiny. He had traveled five thousand miles to provide trauma support in one of the greatest natural disasters of all time. No one told him that he would be working in an oversized closet. Philip was accustomed to working in a level one trauma center. If a city in the Pacific Northwest suffered an earthquake of such magnitude that the casualties reached into the hundreds of thousands, every major hospital in the northwest would have to open rooms to accommodate the injured. But Philip and his team were standing in front of a structure no larger than a county clinic. Philip grabbed his hair with both hands, "Tell me this is a bad dream."

Aryanna looked at him, "Doctor Scott? What's wrong?"

"What's wrong? You can't run a trauma unit out of a shoe box. Look at this place. There's no room for patients, much less surgeons. I don't know what I was expecting. But when I was told we would be working in one of the country's main hospitals, I anticipated we'd be working in a facility that took up a little more real-estate. Please tell me this is not the main facility."

Sam punched Philip's shoulder, "Come on, Doc. It'll be like the emergency room on a Friday night. We'll just treat'm and street'm."

At that moment, Victor and Luckson approached a fair-skinned woman kneeling in front of a crippled child in the crowd. Her back was to the gate. When Victor reached her, she stood, greeted him, and turned to look toward the group from Seattle.

When Philip saw her face, his heart skipped. She was a lady of such beauty that in that multitude of faces, her face alone was the one he would remember. The smooth contour of her cheeks and her vibrant eyes bore the resemblance of a European actress. She wore a white dress which covered her poised shoulders and hung with elegant modesty over her trim hips and well-molded legs.

The woman saw the group of Americans standing at the hospital gate. They were dressed like Caribbean tourists wearing sunglasses, bright shirts, cargo shorts, and ripped jeans, each one standing back from the crowd avoiding contact with those around them. One was taking photographs.

The woman heaved a sigh. *They keep coming,* she thought, *egotistical adventure seekers bent on expense-paid philanthropic vacations.* The woman was exhausted; she did not have the energy or patience to drag another group through the unpredictable, cruel realities of disaster management. She needed experienced reinforcements; this group looked like an imposition, dressed like rich kids standing around a cheap resort. She quipped under her breath, *We need people willing to get dirty and save lives; they look like they've come to play golf.* Still, the hospital was overwhelmed. They needed the help. So, the woman stood tall, looked up at the sky and breathed a soft phrase, "Grant me strength to equal this task."

The woman forced a smile. She approached Philip with the confidence of someone in charge and spoke in a French accent, "Welcome to Milot. You are the team from Seattle, no? We've been expecting you. My name is Lynn Sable. The staff here calls me Nurse Lynn. I am assigned to give you an orientation. Would you like to see where you have come to work?"

9

The Operating Room

The hospital consisted of several concrete buildings roughly laid out in a rectangle around a central courtyard. Lynn showed the team into a recovery room. About ten patients were arranged tightly in a room with little space to walk. The patients lay still on rusty beds. They had amputated limbs wrapped in blood-tinged bandages. Caregivers sat on the bedside or on the floor.

Connor started writing in his notebook, "So, how many beds do you have?"

Lynn motioned toward the remainder of the compound, "We are a seventy-three-bed hospital, but if you count the school classrooms across the street and the temporary tent wards, as of this morning's count we have four hundred and thirteen patients. We are getting up to twenty airlifts a day, and the surgical teams are doing around thirty procedures every day. You will be busy."

Sam gasped, "Whoa. Four hundred patients crammed into one place. That's unbelievable."

Connor cut his eyes upward, "I think Harborview back home has four hundred beds."

Sam laughed, "That's radical. It's like taking our entire hospital and squeezing every patient in the emergency department."

Aryanna looked at Lynn, "How do you keep track of all the patients?"

Lynn sighed; her shifting eyes reflected a weary desire to give a better answer. "It has been difficult. It's getting better, but I can't say we've addressed every challenge. We can only do our best. Patients arrive with no records. The common language is Creole, but very few of our volunteers know it. Patients get misplaced. Your stamina will be tested. Family members sometimes help, but so many come to us without family. The people of Milot have been excellent, opening their homes, and helping around the compound. We find that people do well if they have at least one caregiver. But in so many cases, we're working blind. We feel our way through each day trying to identify and treat those most in need."

Lynn led them off the compound to see the pre-operative staging area. As they walked across the street, Luckson grabbed Philip's hand and pointed to one of the pens in his pocket, "You g-g-give me one Bic?"

Philip handed Luckson a pen which the boy put in the pocket of his ragged shirt. Then he pointed to Philip's wrist, "You give me w-w-watch?"

Philip slapped his hand away, "Don't push your luck, kid. I'm not a walking welfare station."

Luckson left Philip and ran up to Aryanna. He held her hand for a moment and then pointed to her wrist.

Philip saw Aryanna remove her watch and place it on Luckson's wrist. Philip shook his head. If Aryanna had a fault, it was her inability to say no. She was an excellent surgeon, but her heart was larger than her judgment.

Luckson beamed with pride and began walking with his head held high, his hand grasping Aryanna's hand.

The building across the street was a school that had been converted to an extension of the hospital where student desks and benches had been aligned to form improvised beds. Entire classrooms had been converted into trauma wards. Philip peered into one of the rooms. A Haitian nurse held an intravenous bag of fluid over an injured man in the corner. The man was lying perfectly still with his eyes closed. When the nurse touched his arm, his face suddenly grimaced, and he moaned as his whole body extended into a rigid arch with his back off the bed.

Philip asked, "What's wrong with him?"

Lynn shook her head, "He's contracted tetanus. We are giving him antibiotics and a sedative, but the slightest noise or stimulation sends him into a painful spasm. We think he's already broken vertebrae from the severity of the contractions."

Philip wanted to turn away. In his career, he had ordered tetanus shots on thousands of patients, but he had never once seen an active case of a botulinum tetani, the bacterium that causes tetanus. Seeing the effects first-hand made him grimace. *Calling that "lockjaw" is an understatement or at best misleading*, he thought, watching in stunned silence. Neurotoxin had taken control of every nerve in the man's body causing his neck, torso, and legs, not just his jaw, to lock up in a bone-breaking spasm.

Philip's legs became weak. He could not believe what he was seeing. No one should have to suffer such a fate. *Tetanus is absolutely preventable*, he thought, *it's a simple vaccine; prevention costs pennies*. Philip turned to Lynn and said, "Where I come from, this man would be placed in the ICU on a ventilator heavily sedated with muscle relaxers until the symptoms pass."

Lynn spoke without emotion, "Not in Haiti. Perhaps this provides each of you with a blunt introduction to the realities of health care in our world."

Philip leaned on a door post and stared at the man in pain. He clenched his own teeth as a way of containing an emotional reaction. Despite all his medical training, when it came to tropical medicine, Philip was in an unfamiliar classroom, uneasy, powerless to prevent the paroxysms of a fellow man's preventable disease.

Suddenly, a Haitian nurse wearing a pressed white dress entered the room. She handed a sheet of paper to Lynn and spoke in rapid Creole, clearly distressed.

Lynn gave the nurse her full attention, then she turned to Philip, "I apologize, but I must end your tour and beg your assistance. Would your team be willing to take on a case? The helicopter has brought us a new patient. She is being taken to one of our overflow operating rooms. The other surgeons are occupied in the main theater. If you are ready to get to work, I will scrub in with you."

Perhaps it was her accent, but Philip thought her request floated off her tongue as smoothly as if she was asking him to join her for dinner. Philip was exhausted. He was covered in sweat. He craved water and sleep. But he could not say no. He winked at Lynn and answered, "Well, I guess we came to work. Where do we scrub in?"

Lynn walked out saying, "Follow me."

She led them back across the street to the main campus of the hospital. They passed two operating rooms where teams of people worked in blood-tinged surgical attire.

Lynn turned into a small clinic room separate from the larger operating rooms. In the center of this room stood an old exam table, the type found in a doctor's office. An oxygen tank was positioned at the head of the bed and a few surgical supplies sat on shelves along the wall. An instrument tray stood beside the table next to a procedure lamp articulating over the table from atop a flexible stand.

As they entered the room, a gecko ran out from under the exam table and wiggled up the wall. Luckson saw the gecko and leapt to catch it. Then he walked back to Aryanna and placed the wriggling animal into her cupped hands, a traded gift in return for his new watch.

With everyone pressed into the room, the group had little space to maneuver. Philip sensed the impending pang of claustrophobia, an equal and opposite feeling to the awe of standing in the expanse of space within which he usually worked. Philip remembered seeing a cruel prank as a child where a person was wrapped to a pole with plastic. That is how he felt standing in that miniature operating room, unable to move. He sighed, "Please tell me this is only a pre-op room?"

Lynn shook her head, "The hospital only has two operating rooms. Those are being used. We had to convert a few of our clinic rooms to handle the additional volume. This is one of the added rooms."

Philip took a deep breath and pushed his way to the exam table. He leaned on the table with both hands to test its stability. The table rocked under his weight, "Forgive me. I will not have my team operate in such obscure and unsterile settings."

Lynn stood erect, "Then your patient will die."

Philip asked, "What exactly do you expect us to do here?"

Lynn looked down at her clipboard, "The patient has a festering crush injury to her left leg and is showing signs of sepsis. She was airlifted here for evaluation. The triage team suggests an amputation."

Philip lost his temper, "Amputation? Here? You cannot be serious. Where's anesthesia? Where's your ventilator? Where's your monitor? This is beyond unbelievable. Are you actually considering performing a major surgery in this closet?"

Lynn was unmoved. With professional solemnity she allowed Philip to finish, and then she answered, "It will be our third case in this room today."

Philip's neck muscles tightened, "May I speak with you outside?"

"Of course; come this way." Lynn led Philip to the shade under a palm tree in the courtyard.

Philip grumbled, "Pardon me for being blunt. I'm sure you are a fine nurse. But we are surgeons. We expect a basic level of surgical support. Your facilities are clearly deficient. Can you help me understand how you expect us to perform a major procedure under these conditions?"

Lynn looked at Philip, studying his arrogant posture as if in anticipation of a confrontation. She was not the type to tolerate the condescension of a pompous professional regarding her vocation or the hospital within which she worked. She stood tall and answered with conviction, "I understand it is a unique environment. Even our experienced visitors tell me it takes a case or two to get used to the simple setting." Sarcasm crept into her tone, "If you need help, I can guide you through the procedure."

"I do not need your guidance," Philip said sharply, "I can perform an amputation in my sleep. But I do need proper instruments and the ability to practice standard precautions. You're just asking for a bad outcome."

Lynn leaned forward and spoke softly, "Doctor Scott. This girl may die no matter what you do. The outcome is already dire. Surely, if you do nothing, the result will most certainly be her death. She will die from lack of a beneficent doctor. But you came to this place to give her a chance. She needs you. The room in which she meets you is incidental, irrelevant really. She needs you to do what you can with what you have. Have courage. Your skill may save her life, and in turn, she may save yours."

"You don't know what you're talking about; there is no room to maneuver in there. How are we to operate?"

"The room is tight, I do not disagree, and it will get very hot. But if you are half the surgeon I read about in your dossier, the room will not restrain you from doing your work. I recommend you choose one assistant and perhaps another to help the anesthetist. I will gather your instruments." Lynn placed a hand lightly on Philip's shoulder, "What size gloves do you wear?"

Before Philip knew it, he had answered her, not only with his glove size but a short list of supplies he needed to complete the procedure. He had never met a nurse like Lynn. She had the hypnotic ability to make him want to do what she asked.

Philip sent Connor and Sam to unload supplies. Aryanna was eager to assist. And Pauley wanted to watch. So, they changed into scrubs and cleaned up using the only sink available to prepare for surgery.

The patient was carried into the room on a stretcher by several Haitian workers. She was lightly sedated but awake. Her matted black hair, uncombed and unbraided, still held flecks of concrete. Her skin was a pale brown, beaded with sweat. She was wearing a faded dress, tattered at the hem which reached to her knees. Her left leg and ankle were wrapped in thick gauze stained with brown pus. The pungent odor of death filled the room.

The girl saw the strangers standing around her in masks and blue gowns and began to cry. She looked at each of them in succession, a very ill child searching for a familiar face in a crowd of foreigners. When she saw the instruments on the tray beside her, she began flailing her arms and screaming. She fought each person who approached her, swinging her fists in erratic spurts. Aryanna tried to hold down her shoulders while Pauley attempted to console her, but she bit Aryanna's arm and pushed Pauley away as she shouted a single phrase over and over, "Ou pa fe sa—ou pa fe sa."

Philip turned to Lynn, "What is she yelling?"

"She is afraid. She is saying 'do not do it.'"

Philip watched the disheveled thrashing girl yelling at everyone who came near. Then he pointed at a Haitian man standing at the head of the table, "You. Can't you give her something?"

The young Haitian man nodded. He leaned over the table and injected something into the girl's hip. The girl felt the sting of the needle and became as violent as an injured cat. Then within a few moments, she relaxed, sinking into a trance-like state while staring blankly at the ceiling and still whispering her phrase, "Ou pa fe sa."

Once the patient was sedated, the Haitian assistant started an intravenous line, and Aryanna prepared her leg for the procedure.

Philip turned to Lynn, "What can you tell us about our patient?"

She pulled an assortment of papers written in French from an envelope along with a small x-ray film, "This dear girl is Rose-Marie Sanguine of Port-au-Prince. She sustained a crush injury to her left ankle and distal tibia on January the twelfth. It was initially set and splinted, and she has had one debriding procedure. She developed a fever five days ago with proximal swelling and erythema of the leg. Her sheet recommends a transtibial amputation."

Philip took the paperwork, but he could not decipher the writing, "So, who gave consent? Did anyone speak with her parents?"

Lynn leaned in close and whispered, "The form says her parents and brother died in the building from which she was pulled. Her extended family has not been identified. There is no one to give consent. You must do what you feel is in her best interest."

Philip looked at Rose-Marie lying on the operating table. What a sad case. He had never faced this situation. The girl had no family. No one was outside in a waiting room anxiously waiting for a report. No one was poised to ask endless questions about the surgery, the technique, the recovery time, the second opinion, the cost, the prognosis.

Her father and mother were gone. She had been flown halfway across her country by helicopter to have a surgery performed by strangers who would leave a permanent scar as a lifelong reminder of the day she lost everything. Philip wished for a moment he could change her world. For some reason, her tragic misfortune struck him personally. She reminded him of his own daughter, Alexa.

Cases like this give a father pause. Philip thought, *if my Alexa was the one lying there with a crushed leg would I do something different?* The image of Alexa being under his care was vivid. He was not hallucinating, but the fear of seeing Alexa lying in pain with a limb-threatening injury caused his heart to race. *What would I do for my own daughter?* As a surgeon, Philip had often mentioned his own family members to convince patients that they are making a right decision. More than one patient had asked, "What would you recommend if I were your own father, mother, brother or sister?" Seeing Alexa lying there, if only in his mind, caused Philip to ponder what he would do for his own daughter.

Philip reached for the film and held it up to the overhead light. The x-ray was of questionable quality, and the light was too dim to get a good read, "Do you have a working view box? Where can I see this better?"

Lynn pointed to the door, "Most of us just step outside."

Philip walked out the back door with Aryanna and Pauley and held up the x-ray against the bright sky, "Well, their assessment is good. See here? Her ankle is a worthless comminuted mess. But I disagree with the choice of a transtib procedure. Too much risk of the infection already involving the entire bone. And look here. Is that air in the fascial plane? The quality of this film is too poor to say for sure. But I think this girl could have a serious infection. An above-the-knee procedure is the better option. What do you think?"

Aryanna studied the x-ray, "Is there any chance we can save her leg? Perhaps antibiotics and a bone graft to preserve her ability to walk?"

Philip shook his head, "I don't think so. This girl will never walk again without a prosthetic. Her infection may already be life-threatening. She can either have her leg or her life, but not both. Her walking is not our concern right now. All we can do is give her a chance. What she does with that chance will be up to her."

Pauley wrung her hands, unsettled by the girl's fate, "Do they have rehabilitation?"

Her question was not unreasonable, but it revealed a weakness Philip often pointed out in young doctors. Medical students, in particular, were universally idealistic. They believed every ill in the world had a cure. Philip admitted this could be a valuable trait in those who set out to take care of others, but he believed it came with a tendency to bear the weight of responsibility for matters well beyond the doctor's control. Left unchecked the propensity to ease a patient's load could lead to overtreatment or worse, codependent doctor-patient relationships from which the physician perhaps had no escape.

Philip felt it was important for Pauley to know the truth, "Learn this rule early in your training: The patient *pays* you to fix the broken part; whether or not they use it well, or use it at all, is not your concern."

Pauley cocked her head and pointed toward the operating room, "What if they can't pay us?"

Philip bent down to whisper, "You are a medical student. I imagine at this point patients all look the same. But one day it'll be clear to you that some patients pay and some don't. For those who can't, we make a trade. Free care is given for one reason; patients who don't pay are practice; they are your teachers."

Pauley looked up at Philip, her mouth open and her nose crumpled at the distasteful thought. How could anyone think of practicing on people?

Aryanna saw Pauley's reaction and shot Philip a disapproving scowl. She put a hand on Pauley's shoulder, "Doctor Scott is only half right, your patients are *not* here for practice, but they will teach you more than a thousand professors."

10

Rose-Marie's Amputation

A clock mounted on the wall did not work; its hands hung limp. The operative note said only that it was early afternoon when Philip raised his gloved palm and commanded in ceremonious expression, "Knife."

Lynn slapped a scalpel in his hand.

Rose-Marie had fallen into a medically induced sleep, unaware of the impending, grotesque assault on her body.

Pauley stood at the head of the table with her hand on a bag-mask held over Rose-Marie's nose and mouth. In the absence of a breathing machine, Pauley's hands functioned as a human ventilator. Rose Marie's life was in her grasp, each breath regulated in time with her own. At various moments during the procedure, the Haitian assistant placed his hands over Pauley's hands coaching her to assist Rose Marie's breathing with smooth, unhurried compressions of the bag.

Philip studied the surgical field before him. He tasted salty sweat dripping down his forehead along the edges of his nose and under his mask. The lack of air movement compounded the sensation of suffocating heat, and the sleeves of his surgical gown stuck to his arms. Philip looked through the condensation on his goggles, took a deep breath and applied the scalpel to the skin making a smooth incision across the front of Rose-Marie's leg. Blood trailed the blade and filled the gap of exposed subcutaneous tissue.

Aryanna saw the blood. She reacted with gauze, lightly dabbed to reveal the tiny bleeding vessels each of which she clamped with hemostats and tied off.

Lynn stood next to Philip, and Aryanna stood across the table. It took a few minutes for them to get the feel of working together with a limited, scarcely adequate set of instruments. Without the conveniences of modern technology, they were forced to use older techniques, dividing living tissue and controlling bleeding using small clamps and ties. They had no cautery. A small hand pump was their only source of suction. Philip and Aryanna wore headlamps like the ones found in an outdoors supply store. A still fan slumped in the corner. It had been turned off to prevent contamination of the surgical field.

Gradually the three picked up speed, learning each other's moves and anticipating each other's needs. Lynn demonstrated her value as an operating room nurse, supplying both Aryanna and Philip with what each needed while simultaneously performing her own surgical tasks. Before Philip even called for an item, she had it at the ready.

"Scissors."

Scissors were smacked into his palm.

"Pickups."

A set of oversized tweezers appeared in his hand.

"Sponge."

Gauze, perfectly rolled onto the end of a clamp, was ready for use.

"Silk."

The thread used to tie off a bleeding vessel was immediately placed between Philip's fingers.

"Retractor."

Lynn used a flat piece of metal with a bent end to pull back the edge of the surgical wound.

Once the structures above Rose Marie's knee had been dissected, Philip proceeded to the less interesting task of separating the muscles and tendons that connected the upper and lower leg. His conversation, however, turned to more stimulating subjects, "So, Nurse Lynn, tell us what brought you to this Caribbean paradise?"

Nearly every surgeon Lynn had assisted over the course of her career engaged in this sort of playful banter. She had come to realize that conversation lightened the mood and made even the lengthiest and most tedious procedures more enjoyable. While a patient was asleep, surgeons would talk about all manner of things unrelated to the procedure itself. For the most part, she considered the chatting constructive. Surgeries are repetitive. Doing the same thing over and over could get monotonous, raising the risk for errors. So, Lynn accepted the question, knowing Philip would likely become more garrulous, gossiping on topics peripheral to the procedure itself.

Lynn continued to hand over instruments and supplies, "Have you heard of the Order of Malta?"

"No, but it sounds intriguing."

"It's an old society of knights, formed a thousand years ago by the Knights Hospitaller. They provide medical care and support for vulnerable populations all over the world."

Aryanna looked over her mask, "So, you're a knight?"

Laughing, Lynn answered, "No, technically I would be a dame, but I'm not in the order. I just work for them."

Aryanna handed Lynn a used instrument, "So, the order of Malta sent you here?"

"Sort of. This hospital was founded by a modern-day Knight of Malta who happened to be a surgeon. The order has a strong presence in my country. I had some time after completing my degree. So, when I heard the story of this place, I volunteered to come."

Aryanna asked, "Where is your home?"

"Southern France, I grew up in a Ville called Lourdes, a small town in the foothills. Have you heard of it?"

Aryanna shook her head, "No, but it sounds lovely."

Philip held up a thread of suture to be cut. As Lynn leaned over to make the cut he whispered through his mask, "And is there a knight waiting for you back in France?"

Aryanna shot a look at Philip, "Doctor Scott? I'm sure that's a private matter."

Philip pointed across the table at Aryanna, "The esteemed doctor Vito here has already found her knight."

Lynn's mask stretched as she smiled, "Is that so?"

Philip answered, "You saw him earlier. Doctor Wayman. One of the sharpest men I've ever met. If jousting involved the regurgitation of medical minutia, he'd be a world champion. This young dame can't keep her eyes off him. It's going to make you sick to see them together."

Lynn, "Is that so?"

Aryanna shrugged, "He's a great guy."

Lynn looked at Aryanna, "I think this is a wonderful thing you are doing together."

Philip continued to banter with Lynn, "So, are you a nun or something?"

Lynn breathed an irritated sigh, "No, I'm a lay nurse."

"Then you are Catholic?"

"I am a Christian, Catholic by religion."

Philip reached for a retractor, "I see, so you obey the Pope and all the church rules?"

"I follow teachings the Pope is authorized to give."

"All of them?"

"Well, I'm not on track to be a saint, if that's what you are implying."

"No, I'm just curious, just trying to find out if there is someone guarding your honor?"

Lynn looked again at Aryanna, "He really doesn't give up, does he?"

Philip stood erect and swayed his head like a man strutting as he spoke, "I'd like to think I'm worthy to inquire as to the status of a woman of such noble stature as the lovely lady Sable."

Lynn thumped an instrument down on the metal tray causing a sudden rattle, "Well, there is one thing about American surgeons: you are reliably aggressive. But I'm afraid you will find no time for fraternizing here."

Philip looked at Lynn. Her eyes, framed by the mask and surgical cap were made all the more beautiful in the glow of his headlamp. Perhaps she did not appreciate the attempts at flirtatious humor, but for his part, Philip sensed that she alone could make his trip more tolerable. She stimulated an urge in him to take up the chase, "So, am I to take that as a rejection?"

Lynn pointed back at the open leg wound. An artery had been nicked causing pulsating threads of blood to squirt onto Philip's gown, "You are to take it as a reminder that we are here for more important work. You will do well to keep your eyes on your task."

She handed Philip a hemostat, and he clamped off the vessel. His demeanor fell as he said, "Well, now I'm embarrassed. Here come the complaint letters. I can already hear the ombudsman."

Lynn grinned, "I think you will find your professional conduct is judged here by higher standards than supervisory oversight."

Philip again stood tall, "I don't know about that. We're proud of our standards. You know, people come to our hospital from all over the world."

Lynn did not immediately answer. She looked down at Rose-Marie. The young girl's eyes were closed, and she was peacefully unaware of the gruesome step-wise confiscation of her leg. Then Lynn spoke in a tender, soft voice, "Look at her. She would never make it to your hospital. The best is out of her reach. Any doctor can wait for patients to come to him. But I think your standards are higher because you came to her. Isn't that the rule we are taught: to love your neighbor as yourself? Of all the doctors in the world, who was a neighbor to this young angel? Isn't it the one who has shown her mercy? At this facility, we like to think the one who shows mercy has practiced to the highest of standards."

Aryanna was holding the surgical wound open with a retractor in each hand. She took a broken breath and then gently cleared her throat. A tear hung on the corner of her eye. Then the lone drop ran down her cheek and disappeared beneath her mask. Something about Lynn's comment had touched her. She sniffed and tried to hide her emotion by asking a matter-of-fact question, "So, Nurse Lynn, what types of injuries, are you seeing mostly?

Lynn answered in a kind voice, "We see many wounds. We do surgeries every day for infected injuries. Most of the people who make it to us have severe trauma to the arms and legs. Some have complex hand injuries. Not many chest or abdominal injuries make it to us. I think they are treated in Port-au-Prince or the military hospital ship. Or more likely, people with crush injuries simply don't make it. Those with internal injuries died at the scene or soon after. We reduce and fix many broken bones, but unfortunately, for many people by the time they get to us, the only option left is to sever the dying limb."

Lynn handed Philip a wire-like saw, and within a few minutes, they completed the amputation. Aryanna began closure of the skin over the end of the femur. Only a stump remained.

Philip lifted the few precious pounds of lifeless grey tissue that once formed Rose Marie's leg and placed it on a side table. Philip felt strange looking at a human leg, removed, yet still within reach of its owner. It was on this leg that Rose Marie took her first steps. It was on this leg that she kicked a ball, walked to school, ran to her mother, jumped rope, and likely tried to outrun the falling debris as the earth shook around her. That part of Rose-Marie was dead. For a moment, Philip felt like a guest at a funeral, but it was only a partial funeral. The body part that threatened Rose-Marie's life was being laid to rest; for this, he quietly mourned. But the injured part was successfully removed so that Rose-Marie could live, and for this he was proud. Technically, the surgery, in that paltry nook of an operating room, was a success. But Philip did not feel good about the outcome. He had no way of comprehending the nightmare this little girl faced when she awoke, but he knew enough to wish better for her, and though it seemed morbid, at the time he could not help thinking that it would have been better for her if she would just be allowed to die. Philip saw nothing good in her future.

As Philip looked at the amputated leg, a fly landed on the dusky, motionless skin. He watched it crawl a few inches, return to flight and then land again on the leg. For a moment he did not know what to do. What a bizarre sight. He had never had a fly in his operating room. What was the etiquette? Should he wave it away? Should he kill it? It was an odd sight. Suddenly a fly swatter swung past his face bringing the life of the fly to an abrupt end.

Without saying a word, the Haitian anesthetist who killed the fly looked at Philip, his mask widened from an underlying smile, and then he stepped back to the head of the operating table.

Having completed the operation, Philip rinsed Rose-Marie's surgical wounds with an antiseptic solution and Lynn wrapped the remaining stump with layers of gauze.

Suddenly a beam of orange light shone through the doorway of the small operating room, and an older surgeon with a grey stubble beard leaned into the room, his mask pulled down over his chest. He smiled and said,

"Good evening everyone. Would you join us for the brief-ing when you are done here?"

Philip and the others removed their surgical gowns. They followed Lynn across the campus to a humid, packed room in a building near the front of the hospital. A crowd of people wearing sweat-stained scrubs and dingy white coats, some with surgical caps, sat crammed into pews with about fifty others standing around the perimeter of the room. The din of a hundred conversations reverberat-ed off the walls muffled only by the clank of off-balance overhead fans.

A man called for attention, his voice booming off the concrete walls. He was Haitian with a thin frame and a black mustache that separated in the middle when he smiled. He introduced himself as the hospital's chief exec-utive officer and welcomed new volunteers. Then he broke into a speech with the cadence of a diplomat, "We know that in your countries, when a hospital closes its doors, the people can go to another hospital or another town. But here in Milot, if the hospital closes, people die. We could not do this without you. We are thankful for your coming. But we ask that you remember that this hospital is run by the Haitian people. They will be here long after you go. Please respect the hospital policies and keep accurate records for those who will follow you in your work."

The CEO introduced another administrator who made assignments for the following day and answered questions.

Philip rubbed his heavy eyelids. After a day of travel fol-lowed by draining work, Philip struggled to stay awake, not out of boredom but out of pure fatigue. Once the meeting ended, Philip pushed his way to the door and walked out into the courtyard.

He found a spot where cell service was accessible and texted the following message to Amanda:

Made it to Haiti. Safe. First patient was girl from earthquake. She was scared but did ok. Crazy conditions. Hug my huskies.

He never received a reply.

11

The Guest House

Victor drove toward Cap-Haitien, weaving along a shadowy two-lane highway made all the darker by the absence
of street lights. Philip felt the warm night breeze wash over
his face in the open air of the truck. He shouted to Connor
who was bobbling on the seat across from him with
Aryanna leaned against his shoulder, "It'll be nice to get
something to eat, huh?"

Connor yelled back, "I'm starving for a good night's
sleep."

On the outskirts of the city, Victor turned the white
truck onto a pothole-ridden dirt road, and after about a
mile, he pulled into a walled compound. On the gate,
Philip saw a painted scene of what looked like people in
robes leaving a prison. Under the mural, in large letters
was written a scripture reference, ACTS 16:16-34, along
with the phrase, EVELYN PHILOMEN MAISON de la
DÉLIVRANCE. Through the gate, the headlights illuminated a dark tropical garden lush with mango, coconut,
and plantain trees, behind which stood a white two-story
dormitory built in the French Colonial style. Light spilled
from open windows along a large room on the ground
floor.

As the truck came to a stop, Philip heard laughter coming from the guest house, and he caught the aroma of
food. He felt a pang of hunger and leapt from the back of
the truck, not waiting for Luckson to place the ladder.

Victor led the team from Seattle through the double-
door entrance into the large receiving room. It was a din-

ing area arranged with long tables around which people sat sharing food and lively conversation.

Victor walked up to a man sitting at one of the tables.

The man felt Victor touch his shoulder. He stood, embraced Victor and then welcomed Philip and the others, introducing himself as Joseph Pierre, the owner of the guest house.

Joseph Pierre was thin, casually dressed in slacks and a short sleeve shirt buttoned to the neck. Distinctive patches of grey hair frosted his temples. He welcomed the group in well-articulated English with a smile that wrinkled the skin at the edges of his eyes. He invited them to sit at an empty table, and then he pulled up a chair to sit with them. "So, where do you come from?" he asked.

Sam leaned back, his hands comfortably behind his head, "Seattle."

"You are surgeons?" asked Joseph Pierre.

Connor nodded, "We're orthopedists."

"Ah, bone doctors?" replied Joseph Pierre. "That's what Haiti needs. We have many problems you know, but you are the ones we need now. Did you begin your work?"

Aryanna laughed, "Did we ever! We started out in a full sprint. They called us into a case before finishing our tour of the hospital."

Joseph Pierre called out to the kitchen in Creole. Soon a woman wearing a faded dress and tattered apron appeared bearing a number of bowls which she placed on the table. One bowl had rice and beans; a second contained rust-colored sauce with slices of onion; another contained pieces of chicken; and another had golden disks of fried plantain. The woman placed a plate before each person and into the bowl of steaming sauce she laid a ladle. Then she held out her hands and smiled, "Bon appétit."

Philip smelled the savory steam rising from the bowls. His mouth became moist, and he reached for the rice and beans. "Let's eat," he said, "I'm starving."

Joseph Pierre saw Philip reach for the food. He grabbed Philip by the wrist. Then he looked around at each of his new guests and asked, "May I ask a blessing on the food and say a prayer for you?"

Philip looked across the table. Aryanna and Polly were giggling. Philip felt his face become warm, and he saw Sam roll his eyes upward. Philip withdrew his hand from the bowl and merely nodded.

The host closed his eyes and said a few words of thanks for the food and appreciation for the safe arrival of his guests. As he spoke, the noise of discordant discussions around the room fell quiet. Then at the final word, amen, the room again burst into merry conversation.

Joseph Pierre handed a spoon to Philip, "Now, refresh yourself."

With a more cautious hand, Philip scooped portions of food onto his plate. Then he took a bite. The savory tang of warm rice seasoned with sauce penetrated his sinuses. Philip felt his limbs relax as sensations of warm flavor filled not only his mouth but his entire body. He grinned, winked at Sam, and in a mocking tone said, "Mmmm, I agree. Thank you, God."

Philip turned to the host. With a mouth half-full, he mumbled, "So, do we call you Joseph or Pierre?"

"You may call me whatever you prefer. My name is Joseph Pierre Philomen. Most people call me Pierre."

Philip nodded, "So, Pierre, how long have you had this place?"

Joseph Pierre cut his eyes upward, "Let me think—about thirty years now. The guest house was built on an old French plantation. We started in a two-story villa serving the tourists who came to see the Citadel. We provided work for about twenty people. Then our home was burned down by Baby Doc. We built this facility a few years later, after he was ousted."

"Who's Baby Doc?" asked Connor.

"Jean-Claude Duvalier. He inherited the presidency from his father in the seventies and ruled unopposed until eighty-six when nationwide riots destabilized his control. He flew to France where he remains in exile. His father, François Duvalier was a physician. So, we nicknamed him Papa Doc. Duvalier, the father, was a harsh man, exploiting the fears of an illiterate nation in order to line his own pockets. The son was no more virtuous, and we called him Baby Doc. The son was as ruthless as his father. But he was immature, living in luxury while his country starved. He even used a network of secret assassins to kill people he suspected of threatening his power. Those were dark times."

Sam probed, "So, you got on this guy's bad side?"

Joseph Pierre's eyebrows lowered, "I had no conflict with the president. But I think anyone with money was a threat to him. One night his henchmen broke through our gate and killed my sweet wife. Then they took me prisoner. I spent three weeks in a dark cell in Cap-Haitien with other prisoners. There was no toilet. No beds. We had only a stone floor. We shared the little food family would bring us."

Pauley's eyes widened, "That's just awful."

"Oh, we managed," answered Joseph Pierre in a perfectly calm tone.

Aryanna laid down her utensil, engrossed in the story, "You were lucky to survive?"

Joseph Pierre broke into a wide smile and closed his eyes, "Ah, lucky is not a word I use. We didn't know if we would survive, that is true. So, we sang. With what little energy we had, we sang; sacred hymns sung a thousand times in our youth without much thought became full of meaning. And you'll remember what happened to Paul and Silas when they sang?"

The group shook their heads and looked at each other. Sam shrugged, "Dude, you'll have to tell me who they are."

Joseph Pierre nodded, "Well, you may have heard of Saint Paul. He was a well-educated Jewish man who arrested and killed Christians. Then he met Jesus, and it changed him. Once converted, he became an advocate for Christianity and traveled the Mediterranean with a man named Silas. In one city they were beaten and thrown in jail. Overnight, while bruised and bleeding, chained as they were in the prison, they sang hymns. Suddenly, an earthquake shook the prison. Doors flew open, and their shackles fell to the ground, unlocked by unseen forces. But instead of running, the prisoners remained; no one fled or escaped. The jailer was so moved by their faith that he took Paul and Silas to his home. Personally, he provided care for their wounds. The next morning the city officials set the men free."

Pauley leaned forward, "So what happened to you?"

Joseph Pierre pursed his lips and took a long contemplative breath, "You may or may not think it miraculous, but we felt like those saints. We did not know if we would live or die. We did not know if we would be executed. We put ourselves in God's hands. And we sang. The songs gave us courage. One night we were singing, our voices echoing throughout the unlit cells, and unexpectedly, in the middle of the night, without a word the jailer came, unlocked our cell, walked us silently to the street and set us free."

"No trial?" Connor asked.

"True justice was a rare thing in those days," answered Joseph Pierre.

Aryanna listened to the story with the intensity of someone showing not only interest but empathy. She felt

an expanding weight upon her diaphragm. It was not fear
or sadness. It was indignation. She had seen more suffering in less than twelve hours than in her whole life up to
that day; the crowded conditions, the abject poverty, the
images of starving people, a patient who lost her leg, and
now the story of wrongful imprisonment. Aryanna felt the
weight of a realization that she was in a place where
Joseph Pierre's story was probably not uncommon. "Could
you at least report the unjust treatment?" she asked.

"When walking out of a jail, one does not ask questions.
I have no idea why they let us go."

"So, you rebuilt this place?" asked Sam.

"Not immediately, I stayed hidden until Baby Doc was
out of power. Then we built this house and landscaped the
grounds."

Pauley complimented her host, "It's beautiful."

"Thank you. We wanted to honor my sweet wife, Evelyn,
and raise a memorial for our miraculous release from
prison. That's how the house got its name. We call it the
Evelyn Philomen House of Deliverance. The scripture on
the gate is a tribute to the story of Paul and Silas."

After a few minutes, the host excused himself and
walked to the center of the room. He tapped a glass with a
spoon waiting for conversations to fade. Then he spoke, all
the while with a smile causing rooster tail wrinkles to
form at the corner of his eyes, "Welcome to our home. I
hope you passed a good day and that your work was rewarding to you. We have new guests from Seattle in the
United States. I'd like to make the introductions. Doctor
Scott, Doctor Wayman, Doctor Vito, Doctor Verity, and—
I'm so sorry, miss, I forgot your name."

Pauley giggled, "It's Paulita Sanders, sir."

The host nodded, "Ah, yes. Thank you. This is the lovely
Doctor Sanders."

Pauley interrupted, "Uhm, I'm not a doctor; just a student."

"Just as well. You are welcome, my dear. Yes, you are all welcome. Thank you for coming to serve our people."

Once the team completed their meal, Joseph Pierre showed them to their rooms.

He opened a room for Aryanna and Pauley; then he led the men to another room.

Philip walked into the small apartment. He saw three single beds and one small desk. There were no other furnishings. He tossed his bag onto a bed and sat upon it.

Joseph Pierre tossed the key to Philip, "Please treat this as your home. Let me know if you have any needs." Then he departed.

Philip felt heat radiating from the concrete walls and tile floor. He looked at the window. It was not glass but merely a decorative opening in the wall, covered with rusted screens. The screens were dotted with mosquitos. He sighed, "Ah, the little ax that cuts down the big tree."

Sam was unpacking his gear on the next bed and turned with an upturned eyebrow, "What?"

Philip laughed, "Nothing. I just remembered an old Caribbean proverb. Don't forget your bug spray."

Philip excused himself. He stepped into a small tiled bathroom and turned on the shower. The spray set a mass of mosquitos flittering from behind the curtain. He undressed and stepped into the shower. The water was cold but refreshing. Philip stood under the stream and felt the water rinse humid, dirty air off his body. After a long day's journey, he finally relaxed.

Having showered, the three men, Philip, Sam, and Connor, retired to their beds. For a time, each of them laid quiet, flat on their backs, the night air still too warm for them to cover with even a sheet. Then from somewhere in the darkness, a distant rhythmic sound pulsed across the compound. Sam was the first to hear it. He sat up, "Hey, dudes, you hear that?"

Philip groaned, "Hear what?"

"Something's going on. I hear it coming from way off. Like drums or something."

Connor listened then said, "Yeah, I hear it. It does sound like drums."

They were drums. Large wooden ones beat with a cadence that quickened and grew louder as if carried by an approaching army. The rhythm was hypnotic, each series of beats vacillating from soft to hard and back to soft, like a swaying sound. The beats eventually grew to a crescendo holding at maximum intensity for several minutes until abruptly it all stopped. The sound vanished. It was as if a mob carrying drums simply disappeared into a silent night. Then, after several minutes the cycle repeated. Slowly, quietly, someone beat a drum far away. Then joined by others the beats became louder, the rhythm moving faster, the sound feeling closer, until again having reached maximum intensity the drums fell silent.

Sam whispered, "Is that what I think it is?"

Connor answered, "Must be."

Sam whispered again, this time with a trembling tone, "Voodoo?"

That was the last thing Philip remembered. The drums, far from alarming him, lulled his exhausted body into a deep sleep.

12

An Interesting Man

Philip awoke to the sounds of crowing in the distance. Though still dark, roosters announced the approaching dawn. Philip checked his watch, woke the others, and then made his way downstairs.

On a table in the dining area, a breakfast of tropical fruit and toast was set under basket covers. Flies bounced over the baskets in search of an entrance to the trays. Philip took a slice of toast and uncovered the fruit. He took a banana, a few slices of papaya, and some pineapple; then he poured a cup of coffee and savored the last few moments of quiet. Within a short time, Victor arrived, and the team loaded onto the truck for an early morning commute to the hospital.

By the time sunlight spilled over the mountain, Philip was standing, gowned and gloved, beside an operating table with Lynn at his side and Sam across the table. Before them lay a man in an anesthetic-induced sleep. His left leg, exposed and cleaned with antiseptic, was bent in a grotesque angle midway between the hip and knee.

Pauley sat on a raised stool at the head of the table squeezing a bag to breathe for the man as she listened to a doctor, an anesthesiologist from Florida, describe the mix of medications used to keep the patient sedated and free of pain.

They were working in one of the main operating rooms. It was larger than the room in which they worked the day before but sparsely equipped just the same. An instrument tray stood beside the table, and a simple monitor stood near the patient's head. The operating table sat on white tiles that reflected the glow of the incandescent lights suspended overhead. The smell of disinfectant rose from the floor around them.

Philip, Sam, and Lynn began their work, and within minutes they were moving in concert like a single organism reducing, repairing, suturing, splinting, plating, and bandaging.

Throughout the procedure, people walked through the operating room, stopping at times to rummage through tubs of unorganized supplies placed in careless stacks along the wall. Many wore sweat-saturated scrubs. Names written on cloth tape affixed across the chest served as badges. Letters written behind the name such as RN, LPN, NP, MD, or DO served as an indication of training. Most of the volunteers came and departed rapidly. Some loitered, pausing to peer over Philip's shoulder.

At one point a nurse passed behind Philip. The timing could not have been worse. Just as he inserted a pair of scissors into the muscle to dissect healthy tissue away from shards of fractured bone, the nurse lifted a tub and bumped into him.

Philip felt the nurse smash against his back. Without looking up, Philip filled the air with obscenities and yelled, "Are you trying to kill this man? If you are not part of this operation, get out of here. I cannot work with these distractions."

The nurse, equally startled, looked at Philip with wide eyes and muttered something in a foreign language. Then she hurried out the door; her nervous, trembling arms bearing a collection of supplies.

Lynn leaned over, "Be professional, Doctor. The materials are needed throughout the facility. She did not intend to disturb you."

Philip slammed the scissors onto the metal tray, "Well, would someone please move this stuff to a storage room."

Lynn held up another instrument, "I wish it were that easy. Every room of the hospital has been converted to a workspace or a treatment room. We get so many donated supplies. We are limited on where to put it all."

Sam placed a retractor in the open surgical wound, "Seems to me you could just build a temporary shed out in the courtyard. Put some of these people to work. Know what I mean?"

Lynn winked at Sam over her mask, "Coordination of care is confounded by the mix of diverse languages, cultures, discrepant medical standards, and lack of clear lines of organization. We have hundreds of volunteers. Some are American, some military, some U.N., many Haitians, a few from Germany and other countries. We are fortunate to get any medical work done in the chaos. There's little time for constructing buildings."

Philip grumbled, "Well, it's not sustainable."

Lynn asked, "What do you mean?"

Philip said, "You can't function in this surgical scrapyard without lowering your standards. I cannot imagine any self-respecting surgeon practicing in this environment for any amount of time."

Lynn sighed, "I disagree."

"Really? You think any of these people would be here if it weren't for the earthquake."

"Well, in my opinion, the earthquake may have brought them to Milot, but something else will bring them back."

"Don't tell me; let me guess. The luxury accommodations?"

Lynn slipped a quiet chuckle, "This work brings out something in everyone. I've seen grown men and women, trained professionals, laughing, crying, and teaching each other in the middle of procedures as if they were standing around a table with close friends. There is no need for competition here. Yesterday I saw an American surgeon on his knees in this very room scrubbing the floor with a Haitian nurse. They could barely speak each other's language, but they laughed and worked together like kids in a playroom."

Philip listened but did not respond. He used a mallet to tap a metal rod down the center of the fractured leg bone. Once the rod was in place, he said, "Listen; your altruistic sales pitch is great. But it is not your heart that will make this man walk again." Then Philip pointed the mallet at Pauley as she watched from the head of the table, "Remember that, the most valuable instrument in this operatory is your brain, not your heart. Use it, and people will live."

Pauley raised an inquisitive eyebrow, but she did not speak.

Sam smirked, "I don't know, doc. Seems you'd have to have a heart in this place."

Philip answered, "Well, forgive my skepticism, but you know what they call a surgeon with a heart?"

Sam shrugged, "No, what?"

"Poor."

Sam, who made himself at home in any venue, smiled behind his mask, "Poor or rich, I think I could get used to the tropics."

"Do you have experience in the developing world?" asked Lynn.

Sam nodded, "Not as a surgeon."

Philip answered, "Sam's a surfer. He's a beach bum in scrubs. It's a wonder we've been able to keep him in Seattle. The boy lives for a day in the sun."

Lynn raised her eyes, "Is Seattle a place of beaches?"

Philip laughed, "Absolutely not. That's my point. Seattle is a rainy parking lot with rocky shores. Sam belongs in Southern California or Hawaii."

Sam shook his head, "I've got one word for you, Doc. Wind. I'm telling you whoever figured out how to mount a sail on a surfboard was a crazy genius. On a windy day, there's plenty of waves to catch anywhere around Seattle."

Lynn asked, "So, where have you traveled?"

"Oh, I've caught waves all over. Madagascar; Spain; Costa Rica. Nothing like this though. I went surfing with a friend in the Dominican Republic a couple years ago. Same island as this I guess, but it looked a lot different." Then he asked Lynn, "How long have you been here?"

"I arrived five years ago. The place grabbed my heart, and I now cannot stay away."

Pauley, still squeezing the bag valve mask asked, "How do you get used to seeing so many desperate people?"

Lynn looked toward the head of the table, "Yes. Well, it gets to you. I would think something was wrong if it didn't. At least once every week or so I go for a walk and have a good cry. But when I walk down the street, I see our friends, the Haitian people I mean. They help each other. Did you see the men filling holes in the road? They just decided to do that so that patients in the ambulance would not have to suffer the bumps of potholes. You will see a lot of this. People in Milot, even the poorest, have opened their homes to families coming up from the south. They bring meals to patients who have no family and change bandages for them. You will find a pure hospitality here, generosity defined not by the magnitude of one's wealth, but by the size of one's heart. Seeing such kindness clears my own heart to carry a little more."

Sam began to irrigate the wound with saline, "Ok, so I get the sentimental thing, I really do, but don't you think there's a point at which you say enough is enough."

Pauley asked, "What are you saying?"

"I'm just saying, you do what you can, but don't kill yourself trying to do the impossible. Obviously, the work will never end. The town here will have to start turning people away. At some point, you draw the line and say, that's it for me. You know? When life's theater ceases to provide the room, just make your exit and move on."

Philip interjected, "Speaking of moving on, get this wound closed and dressed. We've got more cases waiting."

Pauley asked, "Do you ever think maybe there's a reason for all this?"

Philip answered, "Of course there's a reason. You can't control natural phenomena. An earthquake was caused by two tectonic plates slipping, one underneath the other. There's your reason. People died because they crowded into a city made of concrete buildings built on a fault line. You can't put a million people in a city of concrete without codes or building standards and expect anything good."

Lynn looked at Philip, "I think Pauley is asking if you think there is a greater good that will rise out of the tragedy?"

Philip answered, "In my experience, no. I've seen too many tragic lives extended well beyond reason because of some false hope of future happiness. As far as I'm concerned, once life tips toward suffering, a person cannot hope for anything but grief."

Lynn shook her head, "That's an interesting opinion."

"You disagree?"

"I cannot agree or disagree. My experience is just different."

Philip rolled his eyes, "Ok, what's your experience?"

Lynn looked around the room. People swarmed about them, moving in and out of the room, each person on a small mission in search of supplies or instruments. To her the entire world was like that room, people doing small things as part of a larger purpose. She stood tall, "This may not make sense for you, but I believe every one of us is here for a reason. Suffering is a reminder we live in a fallen world. But God placed us here for something greater."

Philip took an extended breath, then he answered, "Well, I have no idea what that is supposed to mean. Look at this man. I'm sure there are many reasons he is suffering. I don't know if it's the government, or corporations, or lack of population control, or as you say, God Almighty, but this gentleman is going to suffer his whole life for being in the wrong place at the wrong time."

Lynn handed Philip a strip of gauze, "You speak like a man in the wrong place too, no?"

Philip answered, "You tell me. God only knows why they sent me here."

Lynn placed tape over the gauze, "You are angry at God for bringing you here?"

Philip held up his hands, "Now don't go there. It's just an expression. I am not a religious man. God may exist, or maybe not. I don't think any greater power put me here or caused an earthquake or set my destiny. Frankly, seeing these conditions, if there is an invisible all-powerful spirit, I have to admit, yes, I'm angry at him for allowing it to happen. So, God or no god, I'm not just a little irritated that I've been pulled into this."

Lynn bit the corner of her mouth and rolled her eyes slowly as if scanning the overhead lights, "You are an interesting man, Doctor Scott. An interesting man."

Philip looked at Lynn. Whether her comment was intended to provoke him or censor him, he could not tell. But he took it as an invitation to join her sarcastic banter, "Hey Sam, did you hear that? Nurse Lynn says I'm interesting."

Sam laughed in a way that made his mask billow outward, "I'm not going to confirm or deny anything."

Philip continued to look at Lynn. Bouncing his eyebrows in a playful cynical seduction, "So, Nurse Lynn, is it true? Do I arouse your curiosity?"

Having placed the final bandage, Lynn backed from the operating table and removed her gloves tossing them into a bin, "Let's just say, you're a man I must keep an eye on."

The others around the table broke into spontaneous laughter. Sam lowered his mask, "Whoa, Doc. I think you and she are going to get along just fine."

Lynn walked toward the door. Before departing she turned and looked at Philip, "If it pleases the Doctor, may we round on patients while the room is turned?"

13
Rounding on Rose-Marie

Connor and Aryanna joined the group and exited the hospital gate with Philip, Sam, and Pauley, each of them following Lynn. Together they walked a short distance along the crowded main street. They passed a row of market stands where the scent of fresh citrus fruit dampened the stench of diesel exhaust coming from the road where trucks, tap-taps, and overloaded motorcycles competed for space, blaring horns at pedestrians precariously walking on the shoulder.

The local people had a peculiar way of greeting foreigners. They looked at strangers with a penetrating and persistent gaze. Aryanna was the first to notice that this was not a sign of animosity. Far from it, she saw it was a sign that her presence was a serious matter. There were no artificial expressions of warmth. No counterfeit gestures of what some would call being polite. Just the serious look of absolute attention, as if to say, I take your being here seriously; how do you take me? Aryanna made it a practice to smile and speak a quick word in Creole, "Good morning." This elicited an almost universally agreeable response. The Haitian people would break into wide, genuine smiles and return Aryanna's greeting.

They came to a series of long, large, walled military tents, tan in color with flaps for the doorway. These tents had been set up as temporary recovery wards, a military-style hospital unit.

They entered one of the tents. Moaning came from every corner. The patients, many without limbs, were lying or sitting up in beds organized with the head of each bed placed toward the outer wall and the foot of each bed facing a central walking aisle. The smell of warm urine and body odor filled the air. Patients were either lying flat or sitting up in the beds. Some patients had metal devices holding salvageable limbs in place. Philip noticed the occasional smell of rotting flesh as he followed Lynn down the center aisle.

Toward the back of the tent, a middle-aged Haitian woman, large in stature, stood beside a bed, her expression stern. The woman wore a simple dress and headscarf. She was broad in the shoulders with a round belly, not obese but stout, with a prominent jaw softened by gentle black eyes giving her the appearance of a protective mother.

In the bed next to the woman, a young girl was sitting looking toward the team, her jaw clenched and her eyes fixed in a solid glare.

Aryanna saw the girl sitting in the bed. She grabbed Connor by the arm, pulling him past the row of beds, "Look! It's Rose-Marie."

As Aryanna called out a greeting, Rose-Marie's face transitioned from a stoic stare into a wide white smile. She began speaking in rapid Creole.

The others gathered around the bed and Lynn translated, "She says she is happy to see you all."

Philip did not engage Rose-Marie. Instead, he grabbed the folder off the end of the bed and ceremoniously flipped through the pages, not because he hoped to find anything meaningful; it was a distraction to avoid eye contact. He was not prepared to answer questions. He could see the bandage on the stump of her left leg was dry and intact. The gauze was white and clean and appeared to have been changed recently. That is all Philip needed to know. No infection. No bleeding. No problems. He preferred to move on.

But Philip could not escape. Rose-Marie pointed to him and spoke to the woman next to her bed, "Eske li se doktè mwen?"

The woman nodded, smiled at Philip and asked Lynn a question in Creole.

Lynn translated as she answered, "Yes, Doctor Scott is one of Rose-Marie's doctors."

Philip cleared his throat. He did not wish to engage in a long conversation and sought for a way to expedite the consultation. *Perhaps this woman will assume responsibility for the patient*, he thought. He pointed to the woman, "Are you a family member?"

The woman answered him using heavily accented English phrases, poised and confident, "I am not, sir. My name is Tabitha. Mademoiselle Sanguine has no family."

Rose-Marie held her wrapped leg. She asked in a whisper, "Poukisa ou te koupe pye mwen?"

Lynn translated, "She asks why you took away her leg?"

Philip's eyes flashed, "Take her leg? We didn't take her leg. It had to be amputated. She would either lose the leg or lose her life."

Lynn motioned for Philip to slow down, "I think she just needs to hear something reassuring from you."

Philip shut the chart, "Fine. Tell her it was a necessary procedure."

Lynn shook her head and said something to Rose-Marie.

Rose-Marie looked up at Philip and murmured, "Eske ou pral repare pye mwen?"

Lynn turned to Philip, "She asked if you are going to fix it?"

Rose-Marie's eyes grew wide, expectant for good news. Her hair was clean and pulled back into countless braided rows. She was pretty. Her face was thin with high cheekbones, and she was blushing slightly. She cocked her head as she waited for Philip to answer. She saw only confusion in his expression.

"Yes, I fixed it. I performed surgery on your leg. It was badly broken and infected, and we had to take it off."

Lynn translated Philip's answer into something a child could understand.

Rose-Marie looked at Philip, speaking at a rapid, anxious pace, "Eske ou pral retache pye mwen an?"

Lynn placed her hand over her chest and looked at Philip. She spoke slowly, trying now to translate Rose-Marie's question into something a surgeon could understand, "She asked if you will put it back on."

The question caught Philip off guard. He shook his head and peered at Lynn, "We don't put amputated legs back on people. What is she asking?" Lynn motioned with her eyes to indicate Philip should answer his patient directly. So, Philip looked at Rose-Marie and stumbled over an answer, "I'm sorry, child, your leg could not be fixed; we had to— throw it away."

Rose-Marie looked at Lynn. Then, hearing the translation and understanding its meaning, she began to cry. Lynn sat down beside her and held her. After a moment Rose-Marie looked up at Philip, her eyes dripping with sorrow, "Konbyen tan li pral pran pou pye mwen an repouse ankò?"

Lynn embraced Rose-Marie pulling her head into her own chest. She spoke to Rose-Marie softly. Philip could not understand their words, but it was clear Rose-Marie was upset. She sobbed; big tears flowed down each of her dark cheeks.

Philip saw her lying there, confused, incapable of grasping the gravity of her situation. He was powerless to help. He could not speak her language. He had nothing more to offer her. He did not feel remorse; he had given her his best. He felt no empathy; she was only one of thousands who needed an operation. What he could feel was his heart pounding under anxious pressure to escape the situation. Philip dropped the chart onto the bed and turned to walk away.

Rose-Marie saw Philip turn. She looked up and cried out, "Eske li pral repouse ankò?"

Her scream was sharp and loud, demanding the attention of every ear in the tent. The tent fell silent. All heads turned to look at Philip.

Philip felt the scream. It not only reached his ears, it penetrated his psyche. Rose-Marie had verbally reached across the tent and struck him from behind. Philip stopped and turned again to face the child.

He called out, "What did she say?"

Lynn gave him the translation, "She asks you if it will grow back again."

Philip threw his arms upward, "No! Legs do not grow back. How can I say this any more clearly? Your leg is gone. Forever." He glared at Rose-Marie to confirm she got the message.

Rose-Marie listened to the translation and then sat up straight, pointed at Philip and yelled another phrase over and over.

Lynn stood up and walked up to Philip. She leaned close and whispered in his ear, "She is asking why you can't make her leg grow back?"

Philip looked around at the patients. They were gazing at him, their eyes eager for an answer. In a sense, Rose-Marie had asked what they all wanted to know. *Will I make it?* Philip looked up at his team. Aryanna covered her mouth, her eyes moist. Connor placed an arm around her. Sam shrugged and looked away. Pauley squatted next to the bed and stroked one of Rose Marie's hands. A lump formed in Philip's throat and his lower lip began to quiver. Never in his career had a patient asked him these kinds of questions. He backed away whispering, "I'm sorry. This is too much."

14

La Pietà

Philip returned to the hospital alone taking long, somber steps, his eyes fixed downward, embarrassed by his unanticipated show of emotion in the tent. Rose-Marie's questions echoed in his mind. Something about the honest hope of a child ripped back the curtain of Philip's professional confidence revealing an imposter playing the part of an insecure wizard, a showman using smoke and mirrors to convince the masses he has powers to save life. But Rose-Marie, that little girl, alone, looking desperately for someone who could mend the pieces of her broken world, without pretense or secondary gain, pointed out the obvious: Doctor Scott was not a miracle worker. He had only the ability to cut and discard; he did not have the power to heal.

Philip's vision blurred with tears. He longed for the safety of his Seattle cocoon where personal questions from children did not penetrate the strata that protected surgeons from the emotional weight of patients' fears. Orphaned children undergoing surgery in a major medical center were supported by waves of medical professionals. Social workers, child psychologists, physical therapists, and child protection advocates swarmed the children's wards. In Seattle, Rose-Marie would have been surrounded by stuffed animals and balloons. Her surgeons, if they were nearby at all, would have been unknown to her; they would have remained invisible behind layers of caregivers who would attend to the child's physical, emotional, and psychological needs. But in Haiti, Philip was not invisible; he was easily spotted, and this exposure left him vulnerable. Philip vowed he would not return to the tents; the emotive burden was too heavy. He was a surgeon accustomed to addressing his patients' problems from a distance, usually while they slept. He was not prepared to address their problems when they awoke.

As he walked across the courtyard, Philip was diverted by the sound of vomiting. He looked up to see a young mother cradling a limp boy over her lap. His head hung over his mother's arm. With a soiled rag, she wiped vomit from his chin. With her other hand, she lifted his limp torso. Straining, she seemed to be trying to hold him away from the reach of a grave.

Philip halted. He could not help staring at the living Pietà. The mother's despondent gaze, attentive only to the suffering child in her arms, caught Philip off guard. He looked around the courtyard; not wishing to involve himself, he scanned the area for someone who could help. But no one else seemed to recognize the severity of the boy's condition. Philip had no way of knowing whether the child needed surgery or medication, maybe both, but he was sure the boy needed help. Whatever the problem, the boy needed to be in an emergency room, not a courtyard. *Who's looking after this child?* Philip thought. *This boy is in trouble.*

Philip knelt and greeted the mother with a nod. Then he lifted the boy and carried him across the courtyard. The boy bounced limply over his arms, unresponsive. The boy's mother trailed behind.

Philip entered the ICU and shouted orders as he laid the boy on a bed. His terse commands sparked immediate action. "Someone get me an I.V. We need oxygen. This boy is going to die if someone does not do something, now!"

The young mother stood quietly, wiping her son's forehead. She looked up at Philip with eyes that could only watch, not understand.

What was she thinking? Philip looked back at her, patted his chest and spoke slowly, "My name is Doctor Scott. We will take care of your boy."

The woman watched Philip's gestures, but she did not seem to understand his words.

Philip could only imagine what she was thinking. Did she know her son could die? Did she wonder why her son was not moving? Was her heart breaking, crushed by the thought of losing a child? She seemed scared; her hands were trembling, and Philip had no words to learn why.

A nurse bent down, placed a needle in the boy's arm and began giving fluid. She saw Philip standing perplexed, and she asked, "Doctor, what would you like to give him?"

Philip looked at the boy, then at his mother, her face frozen in exhausted grief, then back at the boy, his body motionless. Beads of sweat covered the boy's ashen face and arms. Philip did not know what to do. The child was very sick. Anywhere else Philip would have called a pediatrician or an infectious disease specialist. But at that moment, he did not know whom to call. He felt alone. With a shaking voice, he asked the nurse, "So, uh—what do you think we've got here?"

The nurse shrugged, "Could be cholera. Could be malaria. Could be typhoid."

Philip glared at her, "You're not helping me."

The nurse sighed, "You want me to call someone?"

Philip's shoulders fell, "I wish I could help, but this really isn't my area. I have no idea what the kid needs."

Just then an older surgeon walked in, still dressed in a blue gown, his surgical mask pulled down over his neck. He walked to the bedside and placed a hand on the boy's forehead. Bending over he placed his ear on the boy's chest. Then he looked to the nurse and called for a list of medications.

Having recited the verbal orders back, the nurse ran out to find the requested supplies and medication.

Philip looked across the table. He admired his colleague's quick, confident decision making. He asked, "So, what are you treating him for?"

The older surgeon did not answer Philip. Instead, he spoke to the mother, calm and reassuring, using Creole to explain what was happening.

The mother nodded and bent over, kissing her son's cold, damp brow. Then she started crying.

Philip asked, "What did you tell her?"

The older surgeon said, "Not here; let's step outside."

Once in the open air of the courtyard, the older surgeon introduced himself, "My name is Ed Abbott. I don't believe we've met."

"Phil Scott. I'm an orthopedist from Seattle."

"Nice to have you here, Phil." Then Doctor Abbott took a deep breath, "The child is in tough shape. You may have caught him just in time."

Philip asked, "So, what do you think he has?"

Doctor Abbott grinned, "Have no idea. Could be anything."

"Then, what are you treating him for?"

"Well, I'm treating for anything I can think of—malaria, typhoid, cholera, sepsis, dengue—we'll run whatever tests we can and know in a few hours if the cocktail is sufficient."

Philip threw up his hands. How could anyone work under these conditions? Without resources. Without knowing what was being treated. To Philip this was madness. Like drunk men holding loaded rifles, they were shooting into the darkness at random. This was not medical care. It was wishful thinking. Exasperated, he grumbled under his breath, "I think we can do better than this."

That night Philip pulled out his textbook on infectious diseases, the one given to him by his friend, Heidi Kapoor. He placed the volume on a wobbling wooden desk illuminated by the brownish glow of a rusty desk lamp. There, while others slept, Philip started reading the book.

Tucked under the front cover was a note from Heidi. Philip unfolded the note and read the message, a handwritten, plucky statement, the meaning of which was lost on Philip. It simply said:

May your heart be broken by that which breaks the heart of God.

Yours, Kapoor.

Philip grinned. The religious tone of the note was just what he expected from Heidi, sentimental and cryptic. He admired his colleague and found her idealism attractive, but her motivations were not his. And the gift he appreciated at that moment was not her well-wishes, but the reference book on diseases about which he knew so little. So, the folded note became a bookmark which Philip tucked somewhere in the middle of the book.

Then Philip started reading, beginning from page one. While this would be appropriate for most any other book, it was an unusual way to approach a textbook. In medical school, Philip developed a curious compulsive habit of reading any text like that, treating it as a story, starting from the beginning and following the structural lines of acquired information as if the textbook had a plot, not just a theme. It was a strange way to approach a reference book. Infectious disease texts are written for quick reference, like a dictionary or a phone book. But Philip did not think it strange at all to begin on page one. "You don't save lives by skimming books," he was known to tell his students.

A boy was dying at the hospital. Somewhere in those pages was the answer to what should be done. So, starting from the first page, Philip sat up for hours learning about tropical diseases. Rather than enlightening, the exercise for him became an intellectual roller coaster. After reading about malaria, Philip thought, "Yes, that's the boy's problem." Then after reading about dengue fever, he changed his mind. Then he read about typhoid fever, and again, he changed his mind. The symptoms all seemed to be the same. Each culprit had the means, motive, and opportunity to strike the child; but without a microscope, a lab, and a trained technician, there was no way to identify a unique fingerprint of the offending organism. After a few hours, Philip leaned back, barely able to lift his eyelids. He laughed; softly at first, then louder. Rubbing the sides of his head, he whispered, "They're so right. It could be anything."

15

Ambitious Men

On Sunday, Philip and Sam walked from the hospital toward Milot's town center. The streets were less congested compared to weekdays. People passed by wearing the clothing of churchgoers, women in pressed dresses and men in suits, their polished shoes reflecting the afternoon sun.

In contrast, Philip and Sam wore hiking shorts and tennis shoes, Philip looking like an eager tourist and Sam like a blond surfer who had wandered off the beach. They proceeded through the town to a place where the road was paved with cobblestones. There they asked a man sitting by the road where they might find the palace, the place called Sans-Souci. The man pointed up the road.

Philip and Sam continued in the direction indicated until they came upon a large, domed church. Behind the church stood four towering guard houses beyond which rose the ruins of Sans-Souci Palace.

Philip stood at the entrance. His eyes widened. Despite looking like a bombed out European mansion, the palace retained all the details of French opulence. Philip stood transfixed, anxious to hear the story behind the palace. He felt like an archeologist who had stumbled upon an ancient treasure. How could such a breathtaking historical site lay hidden from the world? The individual floors had disappeared, and a roof was no longer in place, but what remained of the four-story palace served to ignite Philip's imagination. His eyes roamed across the palace grounds as his mind filled in the missing portions of the palace and its surroundings. To Philip, the view was a snapshot of

French luxury on a scale he had never seen outside of Europe.

Philip loved history, and there was something about historical sites he found particularly fascinating. Books only record what happened in the past. Historical sites record what people in the past actually saw. Even in ruins, a building allows a modern man to see history through his predecessor's eyes.

Looking up at the palace, Philip could envision royalty looking down through the tall windows. Philip's eyes darted back and forth and up and down in an attempt to grasp the magnitude of the palace and mentally restore the scene to its original state. What did the first visitors see? Were they struck with the same wonder he felt at having rounded the final cobblestone bend to catch a glimpse of the palace with its wide marble steps leading up either side of a grand fountain? What was it like to see the yellow stucco walls and red tiles on the roof blending like a painting into the green of mango and mahogany trees of the surrounding mountains?

"Unbelievable," muttered Philip.

"It's cool alright. But there's no one here. What time are we going in?" asked Sam.

Philip stood like a grinning statue, his hands in his pockets, "You know religious people. They're always late."

Aryanna, Connor, and Pauley had attended a church service with Victor. He had invited everyone, but Philip and Sam respectfully declined, agreeing instead to meet the group at the palace. Lynn said she would join them after she attended Mass.

After an hour, Victor drove up in the white truck. Luckson jumped out of the cab and held the ladder for the others to climb out. Soon, Lynn came walking up the road.

Victor entered the tourist official's office and obtained permission to take everyone on a tour of the grounds.

He led the group up the grand staircase to the back of the palace with its view of a terraced lawn stretching out behind the mansion. Victor described an opulent garden, now only grass-covered, that once graced the estate, blooming at one time with trees and plants from across the Caribbean.

From this vantage point, Victor told the story of Sans-Souci, "Haiti is the only country in the world who has won its independence in a slave revolt. In 1789, the Haitian people rose up against plantation owners in northern Haiti. After many battles, in 1803, the Haitian leader Dessalines won the final battle of the revolution at a location near Cap-Haitien. The next year, 1804, we were declared free. The city of Cap-Haitien was first called Cap-François, but it came to be known as Cap-Haitien because the Haitian people won their independence from the French. After the war, Haiti was divided into a north and a south, like your own country in the time of your civil war. Here in the north, they made a Haitian general named Henri Christophe the ruler. He was a ruthless leader who slit the throats of prisoners and burned cities. To many people, he was a harsh man. But you must remember his subjects had been slaves. They remembered how the plantation owners hanged slaves upside down, or cut them with a lash, or burned them in boiling pots of sugar cane, or tied them to stakes to be bitten by mosquitos or fire ants. So, Christophe, he pressed the people hard, forcing the people to work long hours in the fields. But it was to prevent them from ever returning again to slavery."

"Now Christophe, he knew that Napoleon wanted to take Haiti back for France and return the Haitian people to slavery. Napoleon even sent his brother-in-law to retake Cap-Haitien. So, Christophe built fortresses along the Northern coast. The largest fortress, called the Citadel, is on the mountain behind us. The forts were to protect Haiti from an attack by the French. But Christophe also knew that for Haiti to be accepted as an equal, he would have to show France and Britain and Spain that Haiti could match their wealth and independence. So, he built palaces made to host the new Haitian royalty and foreign dignitaries.

Victor looked around at the ruined mansion, "Christophe also had another motivation. He was ambitious, but he was also a smart man. He knew his contentment depended on keeping his wife happy." Victor pointed to Connor and Aryanna, "Am I right? You must keep this woman happy. If she's not happy, you will not be happy."

The group laughed, and Connor blushed.

"And Christophe, he was a smart man too. He built many palaces across northern Haiti, but this one, the largest in the Western world, he built it for Marie-Louise, his wife, his queen, and he called the palace Sans-Souci, which means in French, 'no worries.'"

"In 1811, Christophe declared himself king of the North and was crowned by the Archbishop in Milot. But he did not have a good relationship with the church. One day he had a disagreement with a priest in the church building. The priest said to King Christophe, 'You may be king outside of here, but in here I am king.' This made Christophe very angry, and he had the priest put in prison and executed. Later King Christophe attended a Mass in a town nearby. Before communion was served, legend says that the dead priest appeared and struck Christophe with a stroke. When the people saw that the King was weak, there were many plots to kill him. But before they could attack him, Henri Christophe took his own life in an upstairs room of this palace using a pistol with a silver bullet. To prevent mutilation of his body, his servants took his body up the mountain to the Citadel and buried him in the lime used to make mortar."

Philip walked to the edge of an opening in the wall looking out over the road leading up to the palace. He pondered what he had just heard. *History,* he thought, *is like science. It has a way of teaching lessons by way of experiment. This Henri Christophe was an ambitious man, rising to power, standing up to Napoleon, building fortresses and palaces that would ensure his name would become legend. A man after my own heart, really. Yet on his final day, Christophe stood in this very spot, peering out a large window as his enemies approached. What went through his mind? Escape? Retaliation? Was he still in a state of mind to strategize? Whatever his thoughts, he elected to retire to an upstairs room and complete the morbid task for which his adversaries had come.*

Philip contemplated the irony. Christophe's end was not unique. If history is the laboratory of human lives, Christophe's experiment had been run many times, and the outcome had always been the same. Pharaoh, Cyrus, Atilla, Alexander, Augustus, Genghis, Napoleon. Philip whispered, "So, this is how ambition ends, not with a parade but in a coup." *Strange,* Philip thought, *you never see things clearly until you are peering out another man's window.*

Philip called out to Victor, "Did they ransack the palace? Why is it only a shell?"

Victor laughed, "An earthquake. Twenty-two years after Christophe's death, in 1842, a big earthquake hit northern Haiti. The shaking destroyed buildings in Cap-Haitien and the surrounding towns. Then a tsunami killed many people. The quake left Sans-Souci Palace in ruins as you see today."

Sam scanned the walls, "Still, this place is impressive."

Victor smiled, "If you think this is impressive, wait until you see the Citadel. It will—how do you say—take away your breath."

Victor then drove the team up a bumpy, one-lane stone road winding behind Sans-Souci Palace and up the steep tropical ravine. The town of Milot and the palace fell out of view as they ascended into the refreshingly cool mountain air.

The road ended about two-thirds of the way up the mountain. Victor pulled into a parking spot near a trailhead, "From here, we walk. It is a steep climb. Please take your time. For you who are in good shape, the Citadel will take away your breath, but for you who are not in shape, well—the difficult climb will take away your breath." Victor laughed at himself, "Now, follow me."

The others darted after him, except Lynn. She turned to Philip and said, "There was a day when I too could run up this mountain. But I so enjoy the leisurely pace. Will you walk with me?"

Philip swallowed hard, stumbling over a response, "You come up here much?"

"When there is opportunity. I find it is a good place to get away from our work and pray for our work without being too far from our work. When you see the view from on top, I think you will understand. It's truly magnificent."

Lynn held out her hand, reaching out like a young girl inviting a friend to join her.

Philip saw her hand, petite and smooth, extended toward his. He felt a flutter in his chest. He smiled at Lynn and reached out to accept her invitation. Suddenly, Luckson came between them, his big brown eyes open wide, "Hello, D-D-Doctor Scott. I will walk with you. I-I-I am your friend."

"Yes, Luckson. You are my friend."

"You don't worry, D-D-Doctor Scott, I will be with you today."

Luckson grabbed Philip's hand and pulled him toward the path of paving stones. Philip felt the firm, eager tug.

He resisted the urge to shake his hand free. Though he preferred to hold the first hand he was offered, he chose not to refuse Luckson's gesture of friendship. Philip looked back at Lynn and shrugged, "Maybe next time."

Lynn returned his childlike grin and gave an approving smile.

The three of them walked up a steep path of paving stones through a grove of plantain trees and past several mud huts. Then the path broke into open, rocky terrain above the tree line. Philip felt his heart pounding, his lungs hungry for oxygen.

Then he saw it: the Citadel. An enormous stone battleship cresting a mountainous surge, its pointed bow turned upward with clouds drifting above, the Citadel created the illusion of a solid fortress in motion. The Citadel commanded Philip's instant respect. He could see why this bastion was a deterrent to any would-be attacker.

Luckson leapt upon a boulder beside the path, "You need rest, Miss Lynn? You too, Doctor Scott? I can tell you everything about the Citadel. I am *your* guide today."

Philip took a deep breath and wiped sweat from his forehead, "I'm good, Luckson. Let's keep going."

Lynn reached for Luckson's hand, "Come and teach us about this place."

Luckson took her hand and set off at an excited pace, his laceless shoes flopping on the stones. Lynn could not have given him a more well-chosen gift: a chance to be needed; acknowledgement that he was important, coupled with a request for help that allowed him to practice his English. He stood tall, sticking out his chest and motioning with grand sweeps like a professional guide, "The Citadel, it was built by King Henri Christophe starting in eighteen o-five. They s-s-still work on it when he died in eighteen twenty. It is put together with stone and brick built onto the mountain top. It has no foundation, only the mountain.

And it has no concrete. Its stones stick together with lime, molasses, and cow's blood. It was built to protect Haitian people from the N-N-Napoleon army who try to take back Haiti. It has three hundred and sixty-five cannons. Some cannons they take from the French. You will see them in the Citadel. They were moved here by people only, no horses used to move the cannons."

Philip's opinion of Luckson began to transform into a sort of admiration. He was a bright kid, eager to help. And he knew his history. Philip wondered how articulate his own children could be about their national monuments. "I'm curious, Luckson. Is this the fortress you pointed out to us that first day, the one we could see from the airport?"

"Y-Y-Yes, sir. The Citadel was built in a good place to see Cap-Haitien and the coast. Nobody can sneak up on it. And no one can hide from it. It can always see you."

Lynn broke in with the voice of a school teacher, asking questions to which she knew the answer, "Tell me, was the Citadel ever attacked?"

Luckson shook his head widely, "No, the Citadel, it was never used, its cannons never get fired."

Philip, Lynn, and Luckson eventually caught up with the rest of the team waiting at the base of the fortress.

Victor took over the tour and repeated much of the trivia Luckson had recited on the way up. When Victor mentioned something Philip had learned, Philip would give Luckson a knowing wink. Built to repel Napoleon, wink. Quicklime, molasses, and cow's blood—wink, wink. Three hundred and sixty-five cannons—point, wink, smile.

Luckson grinned and nodded at the affirmations.

Victor walked the team through the entire structure showing the long stacks of unused cannon balls and rows of cannons, many with French emblems, still strategically aimed out thin openings in the otherwise thick stone walls. They shuffled through a dungeon, stood under a domed chapel, and walked past large stone ovens. Victor led them to the top of the Citadel and pointed out a rain-water capturing system, an engineering marvel designed to provide water for the fortress and the fountains of Sans-Souci Palace in the valley below. He explained that even before completion, the fortress could sustain five thousand troops with enough food and water to defend the fortress for up to a year.

The team sat down on a wall near the top of the Citadel looking out over a lush northern plain extending to the shores of the Atlantic Ocean. Even at this altitude, thousands of feet above the plain and miles from the coast, they could see distant waves marked by white foam beyond the patchwork of cane fields punctuated by villages, identified by rising ribbons of smoke. The smell of salt in the ocean air blew against their faces. To the northwest, the airport and the city of Cap-Haitien were visible. It was obvious the engineers of the Citadel knew something about the strategic advantage of an elevated position.

Victor continued to tell stories about Henri Christophe, "While the Citadel was under construction, an admiral in the British navy came to visit. Christophe shows him everything, and the admiral was impressed. He looked out at the soldiers working, and he asked Christophe, 'How do you maintain such discipline in your soldiers?' Christophe shouted an order. The soldiers took up arms and started marching along this wall single file to the edge and then one by one they marched off the edge, each man falling to his death. After ten men marched over the side, Christophe yelled, 'Halt!' Then he turned to the admiral and says, 'That is how I discipline my troops.'"

Sam, who sat swinging his legs off that same precipice, looked back at Victor, "So, really? Is that a true story?"

Victor smiled, "It is a legend. It may be true, maybe not. But even if not true, it tells you a truth about the man who built this place. Twenty thousand people died building the Citadel."

Pauley raised her hand, "But how many lives did it save? I mean maybe the Citadel prevented more deaths."

Victor shrugged, "Only God knows. The Citadel was never used. Its cannons were never fired. The great battle between Henri Christophe and Napoleon Bonaparte never took place. Each man lost, but not to each other. Christophe, as you know, had a stroke and committed suicide at Sans-Souci Palace. Not seven months later, Napoleon died of stomach cancer in exile on an island in the South Atlantic."

Lynn sat with her knees pulled up under her dress. Her face was raised to the warm sun, her eyes closed. Philip nudged her, "Hey, Lynn. How does it feel to be a woman from France sitting in a fortress built to keep you away?"

Lynn opened her eyes. She breathed deeply and smiled, "I take no offense."

Aryanna looked at each of the men, "No man can build a fortress strong enough to keep out a powerful woman. Am I right?"

Lynn grinned, "As a French woman, I take no offense at the construction of the fortress, but I do consider it personally. These stones were laid by men from Africa, men who believed freedom was worth defending. Their fathers were brought to this island against their will, forced into slavery, subjected to all manner of torment. But those atrocities were not unique to France; other imperialists, Great Britain, Spain, the United States, they each profited off the trade of human beings. These cannons point not at any one of us; I believe they point toward all of us."

Suddenly, they heard the rhythmic hum of an aircraft approaching up a ravine somewhere behind the Citadel, its engine growing louder. Philip stood up and looked around. A Navy helicopter appeared from behind a cloud, hovered briefly just below them and then descended toward Milot.

Lynn stood up, "They're bringing us more patients; we should be back to the hospital."

16

Warnings and Work

The sun had set. Philip stood again in the operating room with Connor. Mosquitos bounced around the lights overhead. Connor held the arm of a woman lying in somnolent sedation as Philip wrapped gauze around a pink healing wound that involved most of the woman's shoulder and upper arm. She was the last case of the day.

Lynn tugged at the back of Philip's surgical gown, "Philip, there's been an incident. Everyone's meeting in the hall. Please come."

When Lynn walked out, Connor looked over the top of his mask, "She's calling you Philip, huh? I don't think I've ever heard a nurse call you by your first name."

Philip did not look up. He continued to wrap gauze calmly in circles around the patient's arm, "You know we worked hard to earn our titles. We paid with sacrifice and sweat. 'Doctor'-- that's what they call us. There was a point in my training when that term, 'Doctor,' sounded sweeter to my ears than hearing my own name." Then Philip winked and whispered, "But hearing my name spoken by that angel is sweeter than any title known to man. I suspect you know what I mean. I've seen the spell Aryanna holds over you."

Connor did not answer with words. He simply nodded. His attention falling back on the work he was doing.

Once they completed the case, Philip and Connor walked across the campus toward the assembly hall. But they arrived too late. People were leaving the hall in small groups, eyes darting around, most of them walking toward the road in somber groups. The gathering had concluded. The staff left in slow steps as if departing a funeral.

People greeted Philip, if at all, only with their eyes. Philip entered the hall and scanned the remaining crowd for Lynn. She was standing near the far wall with Sam, Aryanna, and Pauley.

Pauley had bloodshot eyes. She was being held by Aryanna. Sam stood with his arms crossed; he saw Philip and Connor approaching, and he spoke in a dry tone, "Hey guys, you missed the drama."

Philip asked, "What's going on?"

Lynn looked up toward the ceiling, "Some days are just harder than others."

Philip asked again, "Yeah, so what's going on?"

Connor put a hand on Aryanna's shoulder, "Sounds serious. Why's everyone shook up?"

Lynn answered, "We received two pieces of bad news. A little boy died today. He deteriorated rapidly while we were on the mountain and he passed despite the medical team's working hard to save his life. They say he was recovering from cerebral malaria. He started seizing and could not pull out. The doctors and nurses did everything within their power, but they lost him. People are tired and emotional; something about that boy's losing the struggle hit everyone hard. Sometimes a common loss just feels like a pure failure. One of his doctors was overcome with heartache for not recognizing the boy had abnormal labs. The medical team second-guessed their reporting procedures. In the end, everyone shared the grief. Even for those of us who were not directly involved, it was a reminder of the heavy burden we've come to bear."

Philip asked, "Did the boy have a woman with him, a mother?"

Lynn nodded, "I believe so. They said he was her only child."

Philip felt his chest constrict. It was as though his breath had just been sucked out of him. He sat down and put his head in his hands.

Lynn asked, "Are you alright?"

Philip did not look up, "I think that was my patient. I mean, I treated him for sepsis, but I didn't follow his case. I don't think I'll ever get his mother's eyes out of my head."

Lynn placed a hand on Philip's shoulder, "I'm sure you did what you could."

Philip wiped his eyes and tried to divert attention away from his grief, "You said there were two issues?"

Lynn took a deep breath, "Yes, a UN official came and reported that a woman was shot dead in her car today—somewhere near Port-au-Prince. She was American; they think she was targeted. She oversaw an orphanage and was driving back to the home with a car full of children. Apparently, four men in masks approached her car. When she refused to open the door, they shot her. The orphans who rode in the car with her opened the doors and scattered. One of them could not get away. He was kidnapped. They are holding him for ransom."

Sam shook his head, "Of all the lowlifes. Who takes advantage of people trying to help when so many are suffering?"

Lynn continued, "They think the perpetrators are escaped prisoners. The prison crumbled in the earthquake. Some of Haiti's most dangerous criminals escaped."

"The officials say there are reports that some of them have been seen in Cap-Haitien. We were told to use precautions. The UN will park a vehicle and maintain a presence in Milot. But we are to avoid walking the streets alone, especially at night."

Aryanna whispered, "Should we be worried?"

Lynn shook her head, "Just cautious. Milot is a safe town. The people have been protective of visitors. They know you have come to do good. They even watch out for things you may take for granted. So, Milot is a safe place. But we have people coming from Port-au-Prince and other places. So many new faces. It's hard to feel secure."

Philip stood up, "May we drive you to your place?"

Lynn nodded, "I would appreciate that."

The team escorted Lynn back to her housing complex. While others waited in the truck, Philip walked her to her porch and stood with her under a single dim light. Shifting from foot to foot, he stood with his hands in his pockets like an awkward teenager dropping off his date while the family watched from the car. He could not think of words to say. For a moment the only sound came from bugs tapping at the bulb overhead.

Eventually, Lynn looked up at Philip, her eyes glistening in the incandescent light. She touched his shoulder and said, "I appreciate what you did for Luckson today."

Philip bit his lip and tasted the mix of oil and sweat. The day had been full of history and trauma, artifacts and emotions. For the first time in several days, Philip felt a sense of satisfaction, if not outright enjoyment in the experience of being in Haiti. Lynn's statement was puzzling to him. He cocked his head, "What do you think I did for Luckson?"

"I watched how you listened to him. On our walk, you gave him the gift of your attention. You may never know how much it means to him to have a dignified, wealthy man come from America and listen to his stories. You made him feel important."

"Well, he's a great kid. The little guy knows his history. I enjoyed learning from him. It's not every day you get a tour of a national treasure with a local."

"Do you know his story?"

"Whose story?"

"Luckson's."

"No, he never said anything about himself."

"Luckson's parents died when he was an infant. He grew up as a scavenger sleeping in different homes and eating scraps. A few years ago, a friend talked him into trying to get to your United States on a boat. Somewhere in the Caribbean, they were caught in a storm. The smugglers went through the boat picking out the weak ones. Luckson watched as they threw his friend overboard. The next day the Coast Guard captured the boat and took Luckson along with the other survivors to Guantanamo Bay. He was there for two months. Then they returned him to Haiti. That's when he met Victor, waiting for him at the dock. Victor's story is similar; he grew up on his own. Now he runs a program for boys like Luckson, teaching them job skills, giving them a chance."

"I had no idea."

"I saw how Luckson looked up to you today. He thinks you are a hero. And you asked him such good questions. You made him think he was someone important in this world. He was so proud to give you the history of his homeland, and you were so kind to listen."

"Lynn, I think you give me too much credit. I really just enjoyed hearing his stories."

Lynn placed her palm on Philip's chest, "I saw you listen here, not just with your ears, but with your heart."

The mood was suddenly broken by beams of light shining from headlamps coming from the back of the truck parked along the street. Aryanna, Connor, Sam, and Pauley had all looked over at the same time.

Philip had no idea what they were thinking, much less what they were discussing, but something caused all four of his companions to look his way. Philip grinned, "I suppose I should be going."

Lynn held a hand over her eyes, squinting against the lights, waving with the other, "Good night, friends."

17

A Time to Dance

The following days blurred together in Philip's mind. Day after day, he felt suspended in a sort of perpetual motion, rising with the sun and closing out cases long after the sun had set. Volunteer teams of surgeons and anesthesiologists came and went, sometimes completing over thirty procedures in a day, taking only brief breaks between cases. Philip worked harder than he had worked since residency, yet each day the work became more interesting. Residency was the last time he remembered feeling what he could only describe as joy in his work. That feeling returned in small waves.

Like residency, every day in Milot brought new challenges. The sound of the arriving helicopter became exhilarating. Each case presented a unique challenge. Philip was learning new techniques and sharing expertise with colleagues from around the world. Unlike residency, however, there was little sense of competition. The teams pushed ahead in solidarity, working hand in hand, sharing what they had and what they knew.

Despite the spirit of cooperation, Philip noticed the operating rooms were not free from conflict. Doctors and nurses were physically exhausted and emotionally strained. Pride worked its way into the hearts of even the most principled among them.

One afternoon an argument erupted between Sam and an anesthesiologist over how much blood to give an anemic baby who needed a transfusion. Sam, cocky and sure, spouted off formulae for calculating an appropriate volume, while the anesthesiologist pointed out the blood was whole blood, not packed red cells, and that the formulae, if followed, would kill the child, or at best throw the little one into heart failure. Their voices rose in sequential crescendos, fingers pointing as insult-laden accusations were thrown. At one point, Philip worried they would break into a physical fight.

Then Doctor Abbott, wrinkled and stubborn, raised his hands in the air, "Enough! I will not allow you to contaminate this theater with animosity. Your problem is not academic. The life of this precious soul rests on your judgment. If you cannot stand together as brothers, your patient will die. Now take your dispute to the chapel. Argue your case before God. Ask for a decision, and then, and only then, bring us your answer."

They never made it to the chapel. Or if they did, it was a short visit. Within a matter of minutes, the two returned to the operating room, apologized for the outburst, and proceeded to give the child a transfusion. The child lived. But cases like that continued to test the patience of the volunteers.

The constant work kept Philip away from the recovery areas. Some surgeons would leave to check on patients, but Philip avoided rounds, especially through the tents. Rose-Marie was ever present in his mind, haunting him with her questions, distracting him with the memory of her contorted face, screaming; the thought of her occasionally woke him from sleep.

Philip could only imagine how Rose-Marie thought of him, the stranger who took her leg despite her protests. She naively believed he was the one who could fix it and put it back on or make it grow back. Philip could not get her eyes, dilated with false hope, out of his mind.

Then one night, as he was walking Lynn back to her house, they heard singing coming from the recovery tents. Each of the tents was humming in unison as if they were connected by some common sound system broadcasting human voices. Curious, they approached the row of tents. Even from the outside, the walls pulsed with reverberations of men, women, and children blending in a unified chanting melody.

Philip entered one of the tents. His eyes adjusted to the dim lighting, and he froze. The sound and scene were unreal, like something out of a dream where reality and the bizarre mix inseparably. Rows of cots still lined the walls of the long tent. Dim light bulbs still flickered from overhead. The air still reeked of urine and human body odor. But the patients had been transformed. They still bore the scars and blood-tinged bandages of traumatic surgeries. But their behavior did not match their grave condition. They were dancing. Many were missing limbs. Most had only minimal pain medication. But at that moment they were alive in the fullest sense, singing at full volume, swaying on casted limbs or legs pinned with hardware. Those who could not stand were lifted into the air by others. A little boy who had only one arm, his legs gone, waved to the cadence of the song. Philip had never observed such a transformation in patients.

Philip could not tell how long the song lasted. It seemed endless. And he could not understand the words. He was sure it was something religious, perhaps a Haitian hymn. They all seemed to know it well. It fostered a pure joy in the people, a bliss Philip had not felt for a long time.

Philip could only compare the feeling to a similar sense of elation the moment his son was born. When he was a resident, dazed in a post-call stupor, he remembered the moment he was overcome with a sense of joy when Max was placed in his hands. It was as if for one moment all the world was right. Philip remembered that tiny, naked body raised into the air as the doctor called out, "You have a boy." Just the thought of that moment brought back the happiness, the joy he felt as he held Max in his arms and danced around the delivery room. And that is what Philip saw in that tent of dancing patients. Something in that song connected with them in a way that brought back a feeling of unadulterated delight.

But the scene was also surreal, unsettling even, like an annoying prankster jumping on the planks of a swinging bridge, these patients, dancing on mangled limbs to the songs of their religion, rattled the very foundations of all Philip knew to be possible. Until that moment he bought into the dogma, common enough among men and women of science, that religion is the cause of most, if not all, of the world's problems. Religion causes men to blow up buildings, aircraft, and sometimes themselves all in the name of competing ancient teachings. Religious people molest children and tearfully expect forgiveness. Religion stands in the way of science. Religion stands in the way of equality. Religion numbs the intellect to the true causes of suffering in the world. Yet, standing there in suffocating humidity among dancing invalids, Philip witnessed something different about religion, something he could not explain or weigh in the balance or repeat in the laboratory.

Lynn stood next to Philip. She reached over and grabbed his hand. Then as if keeping time, their hands began to pulse to the melody. The singing was so loud Lynn had to yell to be heard, "Have you ever seen anything like this?"

Philip shook his head, "I've walked through countless recovery rooms, written orders for the strongest of pain killers, but I have never in my life seen a drug do what that song is doing for these people."

Lynn wiped a tear from her cheek, "It's beautiful."

Philip shouted, "Maybe Marx was right. Maybe religion really is the opium of the people."

Lynn shook her head, "This is so much more than opium, Philip. Opium only takes away pain, it cannot give life. What these people have is giving them life."

"What are they singing?"

Lynn did not answer immediately, not because she did not know what they were singing. She did know. But its meaning at that moment was so rich and deeply moving for her, she just could not speak. Finally, in a sentence broken with emotion, she translated the chorus, "Jezi—mesi—pou—renmen—mwen. Jesus—thank you—for loving me."

After a few minutes, Lynn regained her composure and pointed across the tent, "It appears Pauley has found our friend."

Pauley was near the far side of the tent. She was standing with Rose-Marie, both of them smiling, arms over each other's shoulders bouncing to the rhythm of the song. Pauley waved, and Lynn, still holding Philip's hand, pulled him through the swarm of dancing patients to the back of the tent. Sam, Connor, and Aryanna were also there.

No one knows who organized what happened next, but somehow the team from Seattle ended up in a tight circle around Rose Marie, each of them with arms over the shoulder of the others, dancing and singing, swaying to the tune and mumbling words they did not comprehend, for the chorus, sung over and over became easy to mimic, even if the lyrics were not understood.

The song eventually came to an end. Exhausted, Rose-Marie fell back into her cot. Pauley bent over her touching her face, pushing back her hair. Rose-Marie was sweating.

Rose-Marie saw Philip standing nearby. She motioned to Lynn to translate, "I am happy to see you."

Philip blinked several times and lowered his gaze, "I—well—I am happy to see you, Rose-Marie. You are—um—recovering well."

Rose-Marie smiled and held onto her stump of a leg, "When you fix my leg, will you dance with me again?"

Philip's eyes glistened, "Dear girl, I could barely keep up with you on one leg. How could I keep up with you on two?"

The group laughed. Even Rose-Marie giggled. Then she reached out for Philip's hand to assist her in sitting up. Lynn translated Rose-Marie's answer, "I will go slow for you, Dokte Scott."

18

Darkness and Light

Something changed that night. Singing and dancing with Rose-Marie caused a sudden shift in the tectonic paradigms of Philip's worldview, particularly his view of patients. Most obvious, the fault line between Rose-Marie and Philip was no longer distinct. He began visiting Rose-Marie in the mornings. Though awkward, these morning visits became a pleasure for Philip, something he anticipated upon waking. It was not so much that he was rounding as he was visiting. Non-surgical medical staff took care of the day to day medical care of patients. Philip's visits to the recovery tents were social.

Contact with Rose-Marie naturally led to visits with other patients who greeted Philip each morning as he walked the center aisle of the recovery tent. He learned a few phrases in Creole, practicing them each morning as he walked from bed to bed. *Hello. How are you? I am happy to see you. Do you have pain?* No profound discussions, just pleasantries.

Conversations rarely rose to the level of anything meaningful, at least not in words, but Philip noticed how each patient assigned a higher form of meaning to these brief encounters. When he reached out to take a hand and make some paltry attempt at speaking, the person responded with a smile and nod as if to say, *I know you have done all you can; it does not bother me that you have nothing more to give, but it means the world to me that you took the time to show up.*

Rose-Marie's bed was on the far end of the tent. When Philip entered each morning, she pushed herself into a seated position and watched him approach, her eyes wide, fidgeting with braids in her hair, then looking away with a nervous smile as he finally reached her bedside.

One morning Rose-Marie taught Philip a new phrase, "Ou-se-zanmi-mwen."

Philip stood at her side, struggling to get his mouth to make each syllable, like a toddler learning to speak.

Rose-Marie was a strict teacher. She would not tolerate the slightest error in Philip's pronunciation.

Philip said, "Oo."

Rose-Marie furrowed her eyebrows, "No, ou."

Philip nodded, "Yes, that's what I said, 'ew'"

"No," Rose-Marie shook her head and placed her palms over Philip's cheeks, pressing inward to force his mouth into an oval shape, "Ou."

Philip finally said it correctly, "Ou." Suddenly the tent fell quiet, and Philip cut his eyes to the side, Rose-Marie's hands still holding his face forward. In his peripheral vision, he could see they had an audience. Patients throughout the tent were watching.

Rose-Marie spoke again with emphatic precision, "Ou-se-zanmi-mwen."

Philip spoke slowly raising and lowering his hands with each word as if beating out a tune, "Ou-se-zanmann-mwen."

Rose-Marie giggled, and the other people laughed.

Philip shrugged, "What did I say? I thought that's what you said."

A Haitian nurse called out from across the tent, "You say, 'you are my almond.'"

Rose-Marie, still giggling, turned Philip's face toward her own, "Ou-se-*zanmi*-mwen."

Philip took a deep breath. He looked at the crowd of patients and then back at his young teacher. With a nervous smile, he said the words, this time correctly, "Ou-se-zan-mi-mwen."

The tent erupted in spontaneous applause and high-pitched cheers.

Philip leaned forward and asked Rose-Marie, "What did I just say?"

Rose-Marie's cheeks swelled into a broad smile. With broken English, she sounded out the words, "You-are-my-friend. Ou-se-zanmi-mwen."

Several days passed, then one morning Philip noticed Rose-Marie appeared tired. She did not sit up. When he walked up to her bed, she lifted her eyelids but did not smile. She was wearing a beaded bracelet, and someone had removed the dressing over her stump. A thick, smelly salve had been applied to her sutured wounds. It had the appearance of what Philip could only describe as a pale herbal paste, but it smelled like feces. This alone concerned him. But what he saw under the emulsion frightened him all the more. Streaks of red skin extended up Rose-Marie's inner thigh.

Philip wiped away the salve to find the surgical wound coming apart, pus oozing from an opening on her inner thigh. When he asked her who gave her the cream, Rose-Marie looked away. His insistence made her even more reluctant to answer.

An American nurse was rounding in the tent. Philip pulled her over to Rose-Marie and pointed out the infection, "Did you know about this?"

She looked at the wound and then at Philip, her brow crumpled. She stumbled over her answer, "I—well—I saw that someone had given her this treatment yesterday; but the redness is new. And now—I agree, this looks bad."

"It's very bad. I want her on antibiotics now, right now."

"Yes, sir. I agree. I'll see what's available. Do you recommend something intravenous?"

"Yes, yes, yes! Use Ancef, vanco, levo, whatever we have; get her on something, now."

The nurse appeared shaken by Philip's abrupt orders. But she reacted in appropriate haste and exited the tent to find supplies and medication.

Philip ran to the hospital to find Lynn. She was laying out instruments in the operating room, meticulously arranging items on a metal tray. Her mask hid a smile revealed only by the creases at the edges of her eyes when she saw Philip enter the room.

Philip did not return a smile, "What can you tell me about the sham treatments being given to our patients?"

"What do you mean? Did you see something suspicious?"

"Rose-Marie has a serious infection starting in her leg. Somebody covered her wound with an awful smelling cream."

"Is she all right?"

"I need this room prepared. I'm going to wash out the wound."

A short while later, Rose-Marie lay again on the operating table, this time unafraid, staring at Philip as she drifted into a deep, anesthetized sleep.

Philip worked quickly. He exposed the wound, red and oozing. His face reddened and his chest filled with fire as he handed an instrument back to Lynn, "Who covered her in this filth?"

Lynn looked down at Rose-Marie's wrist, "Who gave her that bracelet?"

Philip growled, "I have no idea."

Lynn took a deep breath, "Well, I suspect whoever gave her the bracelet also gave her this ointment."

"What are you saying?"

Lynn handed him a roll of gauze, "There's a voodoo practitioner around here, a Bokor. We see his handiwork occasionally. The bracelet came from him, or someone who went to him for help. I'm guessing the treatment is his, no?"

Philip scowled, "A witch doctor?"

"Of a sort. This Bokor is a fringe practitioner, feared by many. They say he practices with both hands, using his power for good and for evil."

"Well, this quack needs a taste of his own medicine. His treatments are dangerous. This is crazy."

"Philip, you should be careful."

"Yeah, of what? He nearly killed Rose-Marie."

Lynn pointed a pair of scissors at Philip, "Not every battle is worth fighting. The Bokor does not share your point of view, and you cannot reason with a man like him."

"I don't plan to reason—I plan to end to his practice."

"You don't know what you're saying. Voodoo permeates every aspect of life here. If you go too far, you will find you are fighting against all of Haiti. Do not make this your Waterloo."

"So, you know this man?"

"I know of him."

"What's his name?"

"He calls himself Theo."

"Do you know where to find him?"

"Up the road a distance."

Philip and Lynn completed the procedure and wrapped the wound. As they wheeled Rose-Marie out of the room, Philip turned to walk out, "I'll be back later."

Lynn knew where he was going, "It's not a good idea, Philip."

Philip did not listen. He was already out of the room. He called back, "If you want to make sure I'm saying the right thing, you'd better come translate."

Philip walked down the road at full stride with Lynn straining to keep up as she shouted directions. It took over half an hour to reach the Bokor's compound. It was a large yard surrounded by a well-trimmed cactus hedge with several cracked mud houses covered by rusting corrugated tin roofs. A tall wooden pole stood in the middle of the compound from the top of which waved a red flag, faded and tattered, flapping in the wind.

Just inside the gate, a woman sat on a short wooden chair. Staring blankly at the ground she made circular motions with a sponge, scrubbing a large aluminum basin as if working under a trance. She remained oblivious to Philip and Lynn.

Philip thought it strange that the woman did not look up even as he approached her, "Excuse me. I would like to speak to the man named Theo."

Philip felt Lynn's hand on his shoulder, "She will not answer you."

"Why not?"

Lynn raised her brow, "Because—she's damaged."

"You mean mentally ill?"

"I mean she's a zombie."

Philip shot back a dismissive glare, "Don't go there. I'm not in the mood."

Lynn could not have been more serious. Her demeanor remained still, "I'm serious, Philip."

"There's no such thing as the undead."

"Believe what you will."

"I believe what's real."

"Her brain is damaged. They say she was poisoned by an enemy and thought dead. They say she was buried in a shallow grave and dug up before suffocating in her coffin. No one knows if it was Theo who did this."

Suddenly a thin man appeared from behind one of the mud houses. He was short in stature with tight elevated cheekbones shaded by a ball cap pulled low over his forehead. His oil-stained jeans were torn at the knees. He rubbed his hands on a soiled rag as he stood in front of Philip, but he did not speak.

Philip looked at Lynn, "Tell this man, I'm here to speak with Theo."

Lynn translated.

The man looked up at Philip. He squinted. Then he laughed and spoke in a thick accent, "Tell this Blanc I speak English."

Philip grimaced, "Very well, where is the man called Theo?"

"Why do you wish to speak with Theo?"

"It's a medical matter."

"Do you seek his service?"

"Absolutely not. I wish to tell him to abstain from practicing—may we speak with him or not?"

"Follow me."

The man led them across the packed dirt compound past a series of open concrete graves marked with black crosses. On the far side of the yard, a group of children were gathered around a water pump, splashing each other, a few wringing out clothing over wash basins.

The man motioned for Philip and Lynn to wait as he entered a small concrete structure.

Philip studied the small building. Compared to the mud huts around the yard, this small building was uncharacteristically clean, walls freshly painted in colors that matched the surrounding tropical flowers.

Philip saw the door was slightly ajar. His pulse quickened, and he stepped up to the doorstep. Through the opening, Philip could see tall drums and rows of shelved jars on the far wall. He pulled a camera from his pocket, hoping to catch a photograph of some dark secret. But as he raised his camera, the Haitian man stood suddenly before him, "Your photos will not take here."

"Excuse me?"

"You may try, but your camera will not take pictures in this room."

Philip took his admonition as a challenge and pressed the door open to gain a full view of the room. It contained ominous objects surrounding a bloodstained wooden table. It looked to Philip like a multipurpose area that functioned as a storage room, ritualistic chamber, or an apothecary, maybe all three. He took several photos, but in each instance, the screen on his camera was washed out as if someone were flashing a light into the lens at the very moment he pushed the camera button.

Philip felt the hair stand up on his neck. He turned to take a photo of the yard to see if it was his camera. Every photo of the yard came out fine, but when he turned again into the building, he could not capture a photo of that room.

Suddenly the sky darkened, and a warm wind blew across the yard. Dry leaves swirled around the doorstep. Philip's heart pounded, slowly at first, then faster. He stepped away from the door, wiping his moist palms on his thighs.

The man stepped out the door, buttoning a clean shirt he had obtained from the room. Then he led Philip and Lynn along a path further back on the compound to an open, thatched-roof pavilion surrounded by a short wooden wall.

The woman from the front gate lumbered behind them. She held three hand-hewn wooden chairs. She moved slowly in a stupor as if drugged, never making eye contact. She placed the chairs under the pavilion and walked away.

The man motioned for Philip and Lynn to sit down. He then sat across from Philip with his arms crossed, not speaking, not moving, just staring, as if he were studying his visitor, examining Philip with his eyes.

Lynn sat next to Philip, calm and confident with her eyes closed. She was mouthing something known only to her.

A small girl wearing a tattered dress ran up to the man. She crawled into his lap and whispered something into his ear. He smiled and gave her a kiss on the forehead, like a man kissing his granddaughter, and then he reached into his pocket and pulled out a mango. She smiled, took the fruit and used her teeth to peel it spitting the rind on the ground. At one point she looked up at Philip and smiled, mango juice dripping from the corner of her mouth.

Philip grew impatient, "May we speak to Theo?"

The man sent the girl back to play with the other children. He then looked at Philip, "All right, you may speak."

"Where is he?"

"Who?"

"Theo."

"I am, Theo."

"You are the Bokor?"

"I am."

"Forgive me. I was expecting someone a little more—dramatic."

Theo smiled, "I am not who you were you expecting?"

"I heard you are a practitioner of voodoo, yet you strike me as more of a..."

"Mechanic? You have a big imagination, Blanc. I work on broken motorcycles; that is my job."

"I see, and do you also work on broken people?"

"You are a presumptuous man, I think. Most Blancs see my flag and pass on by. But you come to see me. Why do you come?"

"Your potions harmed a patient. Whatever you're giving is contaminated. People are getting infections."

"They come to me. I only give them what they ask."

"We give them medication at the hospital. Your treatments are not needed."

"Ah, your medicine is strong, Blanc. But people still die. Haitian people will be drinking from a gourd long after the rich man's cup has been used and thrown away. You have your ways. We have ours."

Philip pointed his finger at Theo, "I don't care whose cup you're drinking from; your potions are killing people."

"You wish me to discontinue my work?"

"Absolutely. I insist. You must stop—and stop now."

"And will you help me to do this?"

"What?"

"Perhaps you would consider a donation to buy tools for my shop. It is hard to get along without good tools."

"So, you want me to give you money to stop selling worthless potions to patients?"

"That is correct."

"That's bribery. You can't seriously think I'd pay hush money."

Philip stood up taking a step out of the pavilion, "Come on, Lynn. We don't have to take this."

"You came to me, Blanc, and you ask me to stop doing what I can do to make money. I am only asking you to cover my loss of income."

"Your income comes from selling false hopes to people who have nothing."

"People pay me to give them hope. They find a way."

"And those who cannot?"

Theo opened a wide smile of corroded teeth. He slapped his thigh and said, "What is it you say—they are for practice?"

That phrase stopped Philip cold. His spine tingled. How did he know that expression? And how had he connected it to Philip? It sounded terribly wrong coming from him, evil even. Philip lowered himself back onto the chair, "How can you in good conscience give people remedies that you know do not work?"

"How can you, Blanc? People go to your hospital; some live, some die. People take a Haitian remedy; some live, some die. The treatments are nothing. The Lwa decide what pleases them and what does not. They may choose to heal or kill."

"The Lwa?"

"The spirits. They decide."

"Listen, Theo. I don't believe in your Lwa. Your concoction is making people very sick. Not spirits."

"It does not matter, Blanc. The Lwa do not need your belief nor do they require your consent."

"Really? You want to put that to the test? Why don't you conjure up something for them to do to me? Right here. Right now. Show me what your spirits can do."

Lynn suddenly opened her eyes. She put a hand on Philip's leg and squeezed hard, "You don't know what you are saying, Philip."

Philip pushed her hand away, "This is all a lie. Surely, you don't buy this smut." He held out his arms, "Come on, Theo, bring them on."

Theo leaned forward. He glared at Lynn then returned his gaze to Philip, "You have come to help my people, Blanc. Out of respect, I will not ask the spirits to do you harm."

"It's because you are a fraud. That's not respect. It's an admission that you are nothing but a charlatan, a seller of snake oil."

"Alright, Blanc, but not while she is here."

"She's got nothing to do with it."

"She is the reason I must refrain."

"Fine, she can leave then."

Lynn shook her head, "I will not leave you here."

Philip shot a look at her, "What is your problem? This man is a fraud. I will not let you—."

Theo interrupted, "Because the spirit in her is strong, I will not act. If I send a spirit to do something to you, it will not be able to touch you as long as she is here. She knows this. The spirit will return the harm to me. But you, Blanc, you do not believe in anything. Without such guards, you are alone, blind and vulnerable."

Suddenly, a woman screamed in the distance. It was Aryanna, yelling. Her voice was desperate.

Philip and Lynn stood and ran to the gate where they saw Aryanna and Conner coming up the road. Philip jogged toward them waving and calling back.

As they drew near, Philip could see that Aryanna was distraught, breathing fast while trying to speak through tears, "It's Rose-Marie. She is sick. Something's wrong. She's in trouble."

Overcome with fear and grief, she could not finish. Connor held her to his shoulder and looked at Philip, "Rose-Marie's condition is grave. She woke up and moaned for you."

19

Rose-Marie Receives a Transfusion

Philip ran to the hospital. On the congested road, he darted between slow-moving vehicles, blurting all manner of
obscenities. Like a wild animal, he darted in front of
trucks and shoved people aside. His heart pounded, his
legs became molten, burning with each stride until he arrived at the hospital gate, his lungs stretched to capacity.
No longer able to speak, he pressed through the crowd.
Breaking free, he lumbered across the courtyard into the
ICU.

A group of doctors and nurses stood around one bed.
Amid them, Sam looked grim, his arms crossed, his face
somber in the dim light.

Philip pushed his way to the bedside. Catching his
breath, he demanded, "Sam, talk to me. What's her
status?"

Rose-Marie lay in pale stillness, her eyes closed. The
faint, rapid rise and fall of her abdomen was the only per-
ceptible sign of life. Her black hair fell across the pillow in
tangled braids. A trail of blood flowed from her nose to
the pillow. Blood also filled the gauze over the stump on
her left leg, and she had many coin-sized bruises across
her body. Above her head hung bags of fluid and medication dripping down a combined tube into an intravenous
catheter placed in the bend of her elbow.

Sam remained silent, his lips pursed, shaking his head.

Pauley held Rose-Marie's limp hand. She looked at
Philip with a quivering lip, "She's sick, Doctor Scott."

Philip's heart pounded. He took deep breaths with an open mouth, still famished for air. Everyone was so still, so silent. Why? He felt a need to act, to shout orders, to do something. Philip grabbed Rose-Marie's wrist. Her pulse was weak. Still out of breath, Philip spoke in short phrases, "Can someone—please tell me what is going on?"

The older surgeon, Doctor Abbott, took Philip's arm. Philip felt the grip and reflexively pulled away as if being threatened.

Then Doctor Abbott grabbed both Philip's arms and turned him around, not with excessive force but with a firmness that demanded attention. He returned Philip's glare with a kind nod, his eyes humble, rising to meet Philip's, "May I speak with you outside?"

They stepped out of the room into the courtyard.

The older surgeon took a deep breath, "The girl has a very serious infection. She developed signs of septic shock and then started bleeding. She is becoming gravely anemic. We believe it's D.I.C."

Philip's face dropped. He looked at the ground shaking his head. *This can't be happening. She can't die; not like this. Not like this.*

The older colleague saw Philip's face fall. He placed his hands on either side of Philip's face and spoke in a firm direct manner, as a father speaks to a son, "I'm sorry; I know the girl is special to you. There is nothing more you could have done."

"Is it the infection?"

"Likely, yes. We suspect it started in her leg. She vomited blood upon waking from the surgery and then rapidly deteriorated."

"Is there any chance she'll make it?"

"Only God knows. She stabilized after the fluids. But she's lost a lot of blood. We thought her best hope would be a transfusion. You know, maybe buy her some time, but the lab has been depleted. We have no supply of her blood type. They've put out the word in the community for volunteers, but there's just been no match."

Something inside Philip clicked. He slapped his inner arm, "Use mine."

"I'm not sure I understand."

"O-negative. That's my blood type. I'm a universal donor."

Philip returned to the ICU, shouting orders. In response, the collection of people could not have jumped any faster if Philip had been a military general calling troops to action, "Get me a tourniquet and a blood collection set. Premedicate this patient for a transfusion."

Lynn had arrived with Aryanna and Connor. She stepped in front of him, "What are you doing?"

"I'm giving Rose-Marie blood."

"Blood? Whose blood?"

"Mine. I'm giving her my blood."

"Are you a match?"

"Forgive me Lynn; we do not have time for this. Rose-Marie needs blood. I'm a universal donor."

"I hope you know what you are doing."

Having set the agenda, Philip pulled a wheeled gurney next to Rose-Marie and climbed atop, stretching out his bare arm to receive the needle.

Rose-Marie lay near him in morbid stillness. Her rib cage expanded slowly, then fell again under the weight of her own chest. Her life was fading before Philip's eyes. And Philip could not let her go. Something was happening to him. Throughout his career, he had maintained an emotional distance from patients. He believed this distance should be kept for a reason. Caring too much clouded objectivity. But suddenly Philip was feeling something quite the opposite, a desire that was altogether new to him. Rose-Marie had found a way into his heart, and he cared.

He cared about her life as if she, his patient, had become family. This care brought clarity. At that moment Philip was willing to give every drop of blood in his body if it meant Rose-Marie would have a fighting chance. Overcome with grief, Philip whispered to her, "Keep dancing, dear child. I'm here."

A Haitian nurse drew a small amount of Philip's blood and performed a bedside test, mixing his oxygen-rich burgundy blood with a sample of Rose-Marie's anemic, almost pink plasma. No reactions occurred. They were a match. Then the nurse filled three pint-size bags; Philip's blood flowed by gravity into each one. She added an agent to prevent clotting and then transfused the life-giving mix of cells and plasma into Rose-Marie's arm.

The transfusion produced few immediate changes in Rose-Marie, certainly nothing dramatic. Her pulse slowed, and her skin took on a less dusky hue, but she remained unresponsive. Philip, on the other hand, felt the instant effects of a bloodletting. He tried to sit up, but every time he raised his head the world turned grey, and he felt queasy. With the sudden loss of blood, Philip's body craved a flat, if not inverted position. Lynn placed a pillow under his raised feet, and he lay on the gurney for over an hour, drifting in and out of sleep.

Philip awoke to find the crowd around him had dissipated. Lynn stood at Rose-Marie's side, stroking her face and arranging her braided hair.

Luckson was sitting on the floor next to them. He was looking down, using his finger to draw shapes in the dust.

Until that moment, Philip had failed to notice the room was full of other patients, lying on beds in ordered rows, many with I.V. poles, all of them unconscious or sleeping. A nurse sat attentively at a desk at the far side of the room, her face illuminated by a dim desk lamp.

Luckson saw Philip was awake, and he stood up, "Dokte Scott, do you remember me? I-I-I am your friend."

Philip reached out and ran his hand back and forth over the tight curls of Luckson's black hair. He exhaled a tired sigh, "Hello, my friend."

Lynn took on the countenance of a mother speaking to a sick child, "How are you feeling?"

"I could use food."

"Yes, of course. Let me see what I can find." Lynn walked out to find something for Philip to eat.

Luckson reached into his dirt-stained pant pocket and pulled out a package of peanut butter crackers, most of which were crushed or broken. He dug into the package and extracted a piece holding it out to Philip.

At first, Philip declined, admittedly rejecting the offer not out of politeness, but because the crackers no longer had any semblance of safety for human consumption, not to mention the fact that Luckson's hands were covered with dirt from the floor, and his fingernails carried traces of black muck from countless other dirt floors.

Luckson pressed the piece toward Philip, "You work hard, Dokte Scott. You need to eat."

"You're kind, Luckson; but I insist you should keep it. There are people who need it more than me. Nurse Lynn will bring me something."

Instead of withdrawing, Luckson held the crackers out and placed the whole pack on Philip's chest. His full arc of white teeth shimmered, "I-I-I saved these for you, Dokte Scott. I'm sorry they got broken. A woman gave them to me. I thought I will k-k-keep these for you, because you are my friend, and I see you work hard and do not eat. But when I sat down, they broke apart, and I felt bad because I wanted to give them to you."

Philip lifted the package of crackers. He sensed this was no small gift. In Seattle, the gesture would have been an inexpensive sharing of a vending-machine snack. But from the hand of Luckson, the crumbs represented a sacrifice. Philip was receiving hospitality on a scale he had never before experienced. In the past, he took pride in being invited to dinners hosted by notable faculty or state dignitaries. But compared to that moment with Luckson, had he been invited to dine with royalty, eating at the finest restaurant, no delicacy placed before him could come close in value to the generosity extended to him by that boy who laid on his chest a package of broken crackers. Philip lowered a piece into his mouth and savored the moment.

Then Philip pulled a broken piece from the package and handed it to Luckson, "I insist you eat with me."

Luckson stood looking back, unsure of how to respond.

Philip insisted, "C'mon, where I come from, friends don't eat alone."

Luckson hopped upon the gurney with Philip, smiling wider than before. He twisted the two halves of his piece and licked one side, nibbling at the cracker, "W-W-When I get to school, I will be a doctor like you, Dokte Scott."

Crumbs spewed from Philip's mouth as he attempted an answer, "Become like me? Ha. I think it is I who should become like you; you're the caregiver around here."

With stabilizing help from Luckson, Philip was able to rise to a seated position. They sat together on the gurney, Luckson and Philip eating crackers, while in front of them lay Rose-Marie, peacefully sleeping on the edge of a mortal abyss. At one point she tensed her face and moaned; then just as quickly, she relaxed back into the mattress, her breathing clear and unlabored.

Luckson cocked his head to the side, like a puppy hearing a sound for the first time, "Do you think she will wake up?"

"I don't know. She is very sick."

Luckson, curious, asked questions about Rose-Marie's condition. And like a scholarly student, he asked follow-up questions until his understanding of the world included new wonders about bacteria and the cardiovascular system.

Lynn returned with a covered bowl of rice and beans smothered in a creole sauce. The salty aroma of chicken and spices made Philip's mouth water. In the bowl lay a spoon.

Philip looked into the bowl. He still felt hungry, but something told him this was not his meal to eat. He smiled and handed the bowl to Luckson, "Eat up my friend, you have worked hard today and need to eat some good food."

Lynn crossed her arms. She raised an eyebrow and dropped the corner of her lips indicating disapproval, or at least unapprovingly acknowledging ignorance of why Philip would be giving away his dinner.

Luckson looked up at Lynn and then down at the bowl. He picked up the spoon filling it high with a mound of bean infused rice and lifted it, not to his own mouth, but toward Philip's. Philip held up his hand refusing to accept the bite. So, Luckson turned the spoon and took the bite himself. Then he filled the spoon again and held it out to Philip. When he again refused, Luckson did not withdraw, but forced the spoon closer to Philip's mouth, "Excuse me, Dokte Scott, I-I-I am your friend. Friends don't eat alone."

Philip smiled and took the bite. In his weakened state, that sensation of spice and oil paired with rice and beans felt like drops of pure energy, each bite adding fuel to his body, and more than that, each bite awakening something greater in Philip. Without knowing it, using a simple spoon, little Luckson had become a thief picking the lock of Philip's heart.

The hour was late. Darkness covered Milot and the sounds of night filled the grounds of the hospital.

Lynn touched Philip's shoulder, "You are looking better. I'll have someone drive you to the guest house."

Philip looked over at Rose-Marie, "Lynn, I think I'll stay here tonight. I can't explain why, but I need to be here. I don't think I would be able to sleep without being able to peek over and see her breathing. I'll be fine."

With further convincing and assurances, Lynn withdrew her protest. She checked Rose-Marie's pulse and hung a new bag of antibiotics. Then she walked over to Philip. She leaned close enough for him to smell the fragrant mix of perfume and sweat. Her ruby lips hovered parallel to his ear and she whispered, "You are an amazing man, Philip Scott." Then she kissed him on the cheek.

As she departed, Philip motioned for Luckson to follow her, "Walk her home for me, will you? Make sure she's safe."

Luckson flashed a large white smile. Nodding with enthusiasm, he ran out the door to catch up with Lynn.

Then, for nearly an hour, Philip sat in silent vigil over Rose-Marie. At one point, she took a deep faltering breath followed by another moan. Was she dreaming? Did she feel pain? Was she conscious at some level? Philip reached over to check her pulse, but she pulled her arm away. Was this a good sign? She was responding to stimuli, but could her prognosis be anything but grim?

Philip leaned forward. What would be the fate of this young woman? His chest burned as he watched Rose-Marie struggle for each breath. He was angry. Her world was so unjust. She was born into poverty then left as an orphan, her parents and siblings taken from her in a matter of minutes. She lost her leg and was now fighting for her life. It was not fair. Philip felt an escalating bitterness. But his anger was undirected. He was mad, though at whom he could not say. He felt the need to blame someone. Rose-Marie was suffering; someone should pay. But who? The Haitian government for lax building codes? International corporations for exploiting Haitian workers, forcing them into crowded cities? Theo for giving her sham medicine? Mother Nature for failing to give fair warning of an impending earthquake?

As Philip ruminated on a target for his simmering rage, none seemed to hold the ultimate weight of responsibility. He increasingly found himself bitter at God, the one entity that he, in fact, could not blame, for he did not believe that God existed; at least not in any meaningful form. His life and training had never made room for spiritual matters, but for the first time in his life, he found himself open to the idea of a supreme being, if only because it gave him a target for his anger and maybe a focus for residual hope.

As he watched Rose-Marie lying on that existential fulcrum, her very being on a balance between life and death, Philip caught himself mouthing something best described as a primordial prayer, a poorly worded and near heretical attempt at making a plea for Rose-Marie's life.

Then he lay down and descended into a restless sleep. In the distance, he could hear two competing sounds: songs emanating from the recovery tents; and farther away, voodoo drums.

20

Papa San

A rooster crowed before there was enough light for Philip to see anything but indistinct shapes. He sat up and looked at Rose Marie's silhouette, watching for signs of life as his eyes adjusted to the predawn darkness.

Her torso was moving up and down with regular respirations, and her arms were crossed as if she were cold.

Philip pulled a sheet over her shoulders, and she sighed, deep in a restorative sleep.

Exposure to the moist morning air gave Philip a chill. He felt feverish. His forehead was warm. Then he noticed intermittent soreness, at first focal across his back then spreading to his arms and legs. The pain was not intolerable; just present, like small gravel between his skin and the mattress. He could sleep, but only for short periods. The irritation made it difficult to find a comfortable position.

About the time the sun spilled over the mountain and onto the hospital compound, the older doctor, Doctor Abbott, walked quietly into the ICU, checking on each patient, speaking to those who were conscious. He came to Rose-Marie and sat on the side of her bed. When he shined a light in her eye to check her pupils, she turned her head away. This made him smile. Then he placed a stethoscope onto her chest, listening, his eyes closed as if deciphering secret messages transmitted from her heart.

Opening his eyes, he noticed that Philip was watching, eager to hear his opinion. He flipped the stethoscope around his neck and said, "I believe your girl's going to live. You saved her life, doctor." Then he pointed at Philip's arms, "But you don't look so good. How long have you had that rash?"

Looking down Philip saw the bright red welts, tender to the touch, covering his arms and body. He felt the lesions over the back of his neck and over parts of his face. Was this why he had a fever? He looked at Doctor Abbott for answers, "This is new. What do think it is?"

Doctor Abbott shook his head, "I can't say I know. It's not like any rash we see around here. Are you allergic to something?"

"Not that I know of."

"Have you had a headache or chills?"

"Well, I get a migraine from time to time, but that's nothing new. I started getting chills earlier this morning."

He placed the back of his hand on Philip's forehead, "You're a bit warm. Low grade I'd guess."

"Could it be bug bites?"

"I don't think so. Those are impressive sores. But it's not like cellulitis or a staph infection either. And it doesn't look like meningitis. You're reacting to something, I'm sure of it."

"What do you recommend?"

Doctor Abbott walked to the pharmacy and returned with a small bag of pills, "This should help. You should go shower and get some real rest. I'll watch over your girl."

Lightheaded and a little short of breath, Philip ambled to the front of the hospital. It was early. The waiting porch was empty of people. He stopped at the gate to rest and watch for a ride. A few women walked by bearing large tubs balanced on their heads carrying fruit or merchandise to market. The street was otherwise free of traffic. But across the street Philip saw a man standing with his arms held at his side, his eyes fixed intently on Philip, his tattered cap pulled low over his eyes.

Philip's heart became leaden. Courage rushed out of him like blood from a wound. He felt suddenly faint. His heart beat rapidly, and he felt his throat constrict. Beads of sweat trickled from his forehead. If he had the energy, he would have withdrawn into the hospital. But at the moment Philip could not move. His body was frozen in place, detained by an unseen force.

Across the street standing like a phantom was Theo, the voodoo practitioner, the witch doctor. He stood waiting for Philip. Why? Had he known about Rose-Marie?

Philip glared back, but he was helpless, unable to move.

Theo nodded with a smirk, proud of his work.

Philip saw Theo nod and felt even weaker. Was he the cause of the rash? Had he poisoned Philip in some way?

Suddenly, Philip heard his name. From up the road, Lynn called out. Theo heard her as well. His head cut toward her, then he looked back at Philip, this time his proud visage melted into a look of alarm. But he did not take his eyes off Philip. He only stepped back into the shadows, his eyes still piercing through the darkness.

Lynn drew near bearing the appearance of an angel. She wore a white dress, crisp and bright in the morning light. Her steps were light, bounding as if carried by invisible wings. Her hair bounced off her shoulders highlighted by morning beams of light.

As she approached, her face took on an immediate expression of concern, "Philip, what happened to you?"

"I don't know. Maybe a reaction to something."

"You look terrible. Let me walk you back to the ward."

"Actually, I was headed back to the guest house. I need to lie down in a real bed."

Lynn supported Philip's arm, and they turned to walk down the road. Philip looked back toward Theo, but he had disappeared, slithering somehow out of view.

The few people along the road were alarmed by Philip's appearance. One woman gave him a surprised, curious stare, her brow furrowed. Then she stepped out of the way and moved to the other side of the street.

Lynn borrowed a truck and drove Philip back to the guest house. They arrived just as breakfast was being served. To avoid a scene, Philip took a back staircase up to his room. When he reached a mirror, he saw why people were reacting to his appearance. He was hideous.

He lay down on his cot, and Lynn pulled a sheet over his shoulders. Within moments he was asleep.

Several hours later Philip awoke to whispering voices in his room. He first heard Pauley say, "I think he's awake."

Philip blinked a few times and sat up. Sam was sitting next to him on his cot. Aryanna and Connor stood in the doorway keeping an obvious distance, and Pauley stood beside them.

Sam leaned toward Philip, "Welcome back, Doc! What did you get into? You are looking rough. You got leprosy or something? Looks like you got beat with an ugly stick."

Sam meant no disrespect. Creative joking was his way of expressing concern, and he had a tendency to make fun of things he did not understand.

In most settings, Philip would banter with him, returning slur for slur. They were both good at the verbal art of insults. But in this setting Philip was not amused. His condition was not humorous. Something was invading his body. Something foreign to him. Philip was an orthopedic doctor, an expert in repairing bones. Rashes of the skin were to him an enigma. In his mind, he was on a forsaken island, far from the type of medical counsel he trusted, and his skin was covered with frightening sores from head to toe. Who knew the culprit or when he had been exposed? He needed answers, not jokes.

Philip did not even look up, "If you have something helpful to add, I welcome your comments. Otherwise, keep the observations to yourself."

Pauley's eyebrows angled to a central point. She placed her hand over her mouth, a gesture of concern as well as a reflexive, perhaps subconscious move of self-protection, "Doctor Scott, is it contagious?"

"Maybe; I got it from somewhere. But why am I the only one with the rash?"

Sam rose to the seriousness of the situation, "So, Doc, what do you think you caught? What's really going on?"

"I don't know. To tell you the truth, the real story may be hard to believe."

Philip told them about his encounter with Theo, how the witchdoctor had threated to do something to him, and then how he was standing in the shadows, peering at him from the road that morning.

Sam asked, "So, you think you're under a curse?"

"Of course not. I don't believe in paranormal gibberish. It's just a reaction to something. But I'm telling you that seeing the witchdoctor standing by the road this morning was spooky. For a moment I questioned whether or not there was a dark magic behind all this. I mean Rose-Marie got sick, and then I get this rash for no reason. Listen to me; I'm out of my mind. It's just a skin reaction, right?"

Connor grabbed his chin between his thumb and forefinger, contemplating the causes of Philip's rash, "Any chance we could get a biopsy?"

Philip looked out the window, "Here? I doubt it. What are you thinking?"

Connor pointed to Philip's arm, "May I examine it?"

Philip was curious. Connor knew something. With a reluctant consent, Philip extended his arm, "Are you thinking of switching to dermatology?"

"Call it a hobby." He ran his fingers across the rash and pressed lightly on one of the lesions, "Tell me; is this painful to you?"

The pressure of his fingers caused a deep, sudden pain under Philip's skin. He jerked away, "It hurts a good deal."

Conner pursed his lips and stroked his chin, "Acute febrile neutrophilic dermatosis."

Philip moaned, "You're speaking gibberish again."

Connor smiled, "Sweet's syndrome. I'd put money on it. Though, I'd need lab work and a biopsy to be sure."

Aryanna touched Connor's shoulder, "Is it serious?"

"Not really. It's uncomfortable and a little unsightly, but it usually responds to a steroid." Then Connor looked at Philip, "Have you got any prednisone?"

Philip nodded, "A colleague at the hospital gave me some this morning."

Sam lay back in his cot placing his hands comfortably behind his head, "So for those of us who skipped the dermatology lectures, give us the skinny."

Connor spent several minutes giving a spontaneous bedside lecture on the rare dermatologic condition. Philip thought the description would have been interesting if they were looking at a slide or picture, but they were looking at him. For the moment he did not feel like a person or even their teacher; he was an impersonal subject, an interesting topic being described with words like autoimmune and cancer.

Philip grew anxious, "So, cut to the chase, Connor. What's the most likely cause?"

"Well, eighty percent of the time it's idiopathic."

Pauley looked back and forth at Connor and Philip, "Idiopathic?"

Sam laughed, "We're doctors. We can't say 'I don't know,' at least not in English. We have to say it in Greek. 'Idiopathic.' It means something like we're pathetic idiots and don't know what we're talking about."

Aryanna grimaced, "Come on, Sam."

Sam shrugged, "Well that's a loose translation."

Pauley looked back at Connor, "So, you're saying it just happened for no reason?"

"I'm saying in most cases we never know the cause. It just resolves as quickly as it started without a clear etiology."

Sam grinned, "Well, it sounds like we can add another possibility to the list."

Aryanna asked, "What's that?"

"Voodoo," Sam chuckled.

Aryanna shook her head, "Really, Sam; be serious."

"Oh, I'm serious. What if we've stumbled on the true cause of acute febrile neutrophilic dermatosis? I can already see the article, published in the most prestigious journals." Sam spread out his hands broadly above his head as if displaying an imaginary banner, "Rashes and the Dark Arts: Which Doctor to See." Then he laughed at himself, "Get it? Which doctor or witch doctor to see? Ha ha."

"Sam, this is no joke." Philip looked to Connor, "Are you saying we don't know what causes this condition?"

"Sometimes it is a sign of something else going on in the body, like cancer or something. But most of the time, we just don't know."

Philip raised a finger, "And in your medical opinion, there are no known cases of the condition's being associated with some metaphysical or psychotic cause?"

Connor shrugged, "Are you asking me a serious question?"

"No. Of course not. I'm just sleep deprived. I'm anemic. I've got a fever. And I just need someone with an objective mind to tell me I'm not crazy."

Connor shook his head, "You're not crazy. Even if we cannot identify the cause, your condition has a perfectly rational and natural explanation. Chances are good you'll bounce right back."

Philip took a deep breath, "Okay then; I'm going with that. We'll leave myths to the uninformed."

But Philip was not entirely convinced. He resisted the temptation to fill gaps in scientific knowledge with supernatural explanations, but something bothered him. It was Theo's haunting words about being vulnerable. What did he mean? Did he cause the rash? If so, how? Connor was absolutely correct. Philip's condition and Rose-Marie's illness had perfectly rational explanations. The biochemistry and pathology were well known. They were textbook cases of medical problems. Philip knew this. Their situations were not unique. Yet, he could not erase the nagging feeling that Theo, that dealer in darkness, had something to do with it.

A few hours later, the setting sun cast an orange glow on the mountains surrounding Milot. The stimulating effects of steroid gave Philip a sense of returning strength. He was able to shower, eat a bowl of fruit, then return to the hospital to check on Rose-Marie. Her wellbeing, more than just a passing thought, had become a priority. Philip wanted her to live, to endure the challenges ahead of her and someday find meaning in life as the only survivor of her family.

Rose-Marie was still lying in her bed. Her eyes were open, glassy and sunken, staring blankly at the ceiling.

Philip saw Rose-Marie lying still. His heart jumped. Was she dead? He stood watching for signs of life. Then she blinked and he saw her chest rise. Philip reached down and took her hand.

Rose-Marie blinked away the opaque film of sleep in her eyes and saw Philip standing over her. He looked sick.

Splotches of red covered his neck and face. She felt his warm hand around her fingers, and she gently squeezed. Then she spoke, uttering a question at a volume barely above a whisper.

Philip saw her lips move, but he could not hear her words. He called for the nurse, "Can you translate for me?"

A Haitian woman walked over.

Philip said, "She is trying to say something. Can you ask her what she is trying to say?"

The nurse listened to Rose-Marie and looked up, "She is asking what happened to you?"

"Tell her I just have a rash, maybe an allergy to something."

The nurse translated and then laid her head near Rose-Marie's mouth to listen to the next whispered question. Then she stood up straight and translated, "She asked me if you are the one who gave her the blood?"

"Yes, you were very sick and needed blood. I gave you some of mine because—" Philip smiled and spoke to her using a Creole phrase she had taught him, "because you are my friend."

Rose-Marie giggled softly and whispered again. The nurse translated, "She asked me if you work for God?"

Philip looked at Rose-Marie, her eyes open with expectation. What could he say? How could he give her an honest answer? The answer was no. But how could he answer such a deeply personal question without crushing her childlike trust? Philip reached out to take Rose-Marie's hand, "No, child. I suppose God has many helpers; my job is to help the people who work for him."

The nurse tried her best to translate Philip's words with its cryptic mix of honesty and compassion. She likely did well because Rose-Marie smiled and spoke rapidly with joy. The nurse turned back to Philip, "She says an angel told her you gave her your life."

Philip responded with a boyish smirk, refusing to believe Rose-Marie was having conversations with celestial beings. If anything, she was talking with one of the nurses who to her looked angelic; Lynn perhaps. Philip just shrugged, "I don't know what she means."

"I think she is trying to say that you saved her life."

"I see. Please tell her, a doctor must do what he can for his patient. I did what I could do to help, but many people worked together to save her."

Rose-Marie listened to the translation. At one time the man standing over her was scary, but as she heard him speak, she wanted to hold him. He made her feel safe. So, despite her weakness, she reached up and put her arms around Philip. Her hug lingered while she whispered a phrase repeatedly in Philip's ear.

He looked to the nurse for the meaning.

The nurse, visibly touched, wiped a tear from her eye and said, "She's calling you her Papa San."

"Papa San? What does that mean?"

"She's calling you her Blood Father."

21
A Spider Story

Rose-Marie recovered quickly. In a few days, she returned to the tent where she was cared for by many volunteers. But it was Philip she looked forward to seeing each day. Rose-Marie called Philip by his new name, Papa San. She would see him from a distance and call out in the endearing way a child calls out to her father, emphasizing each syllable by pursing her lips to say 'Pa-pa' followed by a broad smile as she extended her pronunciation of the adjective, 'Sa-a-a-n,' spoken in a way that made her cheeks bulge. She held the final sound as if the name were being sung. And to Philip that is exactly how it sounded; like a melody floating across the tent, her voice was as unique as the call of a morning songbird.

One morning Philip arrived at the tent. He heard his name from the other end. Squinting against the relative darkness, he saw Rose-Marie hobbling toward him using a crude cane fashioned from plastic pipe. When Philip asked who gave her the cane, she smiled and said, "Luckson make for me."

Thus, began a morning ritual. Each day at dawn, Philip entered the tent. Rose-Marie would see him and call out his name, grab her crutches and hobble to his side. She would follow Philip as he walked from bed to bed, Rose-Marie acting the role of a self-appointed personal assistant.

Her assistance ended at the door of the tent where she waved him off each morning like a girl sending her daddy off to work.

Philip then rejoined the mass of volunteers at the hospital where he continued performing surgeries, often assisted by Lynn, debriding wounds, repairing bones, and occasionally amputating limbs. The rate of flights from the south did not slow. By day they worked without breaks so that by evening they were physically spent, exhausted from doing good.

In the late evenings, Lynn joined the Seattle team at the guest house for dinner. Victor and Luckson also stayed many nights enjoying the meal and stories.

But as weeks passed, the evening meal devolved into a quiet affair. Supper time became increasingly somber; some nights the buzz of a dim light and flopping of an off-balance fan were the only sounds in the dining hall.

Then one night a spider came to dinner. Not just a little house spider, a Haitian tarantula; a creature the size of a man's hand. On that fateful evening, the furry arachnid crawled across the ceiling unnoticed. Then in one freak moment, it fell onto the table squarely between two plates.

Pauley heard the thud as the spider hit the table. She saw it struggle on its back, legs sprawled, gyrating in an attempt to flip over, its fangs flaring outward. Pauley threw a fork at the pest and screamed in panic, her cry loud, long, and shrill.

The spider must have heard the piercing noise and seen the approaching silver object. It caught hold of the table cloth and flipped upright. Before the fork landed, the spider jumped to the side under a plate. Then seeing a clear escape, it ran for an opening between two tall cups.

Sam saw the spider scurrying toward him. His heart jumped. Reflexively he pulled his hand back and swiped at the animal catching it just under the legs setting it to flight along with the two cups of water.

The water splashed onto Aryanna's shirt and face. Then she looked up to see the spider, legs outstretched, gliding toward her. It landed with a thump on her skirt. She felt the weight of the spider on her lap and saw the spider facing her. It raised its hairy front legs preparing to leap. Aryanna could not breathe, much less scream. She looked up at Connor with her arms held up waving frantically.

Connor saw the spider threatening the woman he loved. He grabbed a plate, tossing beans and rice to the side. Then he raised the dish to strike yelling, "Hold your legs apart and don't move."

Aryanna saw the plate. Her eyes widened. She instantly spread her legs and flapped her hands forward in a motion that snapped her skirt taut and set the poor tarantula aloft again, this time landing at Connor's feet.

On the floor, the spider could sense the crushing impact of stomping feet smashing around it in every direction. It sought an escape, running one direction then another, searching vainly for the safety of darkness.

Connor looked down. The spider was jumping back and forth as if searching for someone to bite. His heart trembled, and his mouth filled with a strange metallic taste of panic. He let out a high-pitched yelp and ran backward.

The spider ran the opposite direction toward the table.

Luckson saw it dart toward the shadows and just before it could scamper out of sight, he slammed a tall clear plastic cup down over the creature. It scurried frantically under the cup. The tapping sound of its fangs against the plastic echoed through the room. Luckson slipped a plate under the cup and took the unwelcome visitor out the door.

Aryanna, still shaking, yelled, "Why don't you just kill it?"

Luckson called back, "B-b-because it eats the other bugs, and a spider this big may k-k-keep the rats away too."

Victor looked up from his plate. Despite all the excitement, he continued to eat, unfazed by the furry visitor scurrying about. He swallowed hard. Then he pointed to the other end of the table and started laughing, "You are afraid, Doctor?"

The others turned to see Philip, ghost grey, standing on top of the table, a knife in his hand with the blade held high, ready to strike.

Sam saw Philip standing on the table, and he started to laugh. First a chuckle, then another, then in a bubbling cascade of escalating laughter, he lost control, leaning back with his mouth wide open and his eyes forced shut, tears forming at the corner of his eyes. He had never seen such a funny reaction to a spider.

This caused the others to begin laughing too, first in unison, then in waves of hilarity as one person's sniffling set off another person's laughing until they all ached in the belly and could hardly breathe.

Philip was not laughing. He climbed down and sat in his chair, attentively scooping spilled rice and beans back onto his plate.

Lynn noticed Philip was not amused. She regained her composure and after a deep breath leaned over close to Philip's ear, "Surely you see the humor in this?"

Philip did not look back. He shook his head and just said, "I don't do spiders."

This set Lynn to giggling again.

Philip turned and glared at her.

Lynn said, "I'm sorry, Philip, it's just so funny to see you react with such—agility."

Philip looked around the room. As his heart rate settled, he saw what was happening. Connor was laughing with Aryanna as he wiped the water from her face and shirt. Sam was bent over trying to catch his breath. Pauley was chuckling with her hand over her mouth. And Victor had his head in his hands unable to contain his laughter. It was the first time he had seen his team happy. Not just entertained, they were truly caught up in a moment of pleasure. The spider had done them much good.

Lynn saw it as well. She recognized why the moment was in fact welcome. The team needed a break. She looked up and made an announcement, "I want to take you all to the beach. You have worked hard for weeks without a holiday. It's important for you to know that even in a place like Haiti, there are beautiful places to get away and restore yourself. I hope you brought a swimsuit."

22
Caribbean Beaches

The following morning Victor negotiated the crowded streets of Cap-Haitien in the white truck, making his way to the road leading to the beaches. Sam sat up front with Victor. Philip and the others sat on benches in the back holding onto the canopy frame for balance as the truck rocked along the uneven streets. Luckson again played the role of a tour guide, pointing here and there describing the sites of the city, the famous Catholic church, the town square, the old prison.

Victor turned up a thin pothole-ridden road, its coiled path ascending the mountain west of the city where concrete houses curbed the street. Victor was a good driver, but as they drifted close to the eroded edges, Philip became uneasy. He thought Victor's reliance on the shocks and brakes of the creaking old truck was something akin to blind faith.

Coming over the steep tropical mountain, they passed into a new world, through a portal out of the brown city dust into a lush, verdant, coastal paradise. In the distance, Philip could see whitecap waves advancing over submerged rocks and onto white sand beaches tucked into concave recesses of the corrugated northern coast. This was the land discovered by Christopher Columbus, a reminder of the view first beheld by pirates and explorers. For a moment Philip imagined ancient mariners gathered off the coast in wooden ships with sails unfurled, men rowing to shore on small dinghies as the indigenous Arawak watched from the slopes, unaware of the coming injustices.

The group arrived and checked into a small beach-side resort set within one of the hidden coves. They spent the afternoon playing in the sea and relaxing on the sand under the shade of a lime tree. For the most part, they had the place to themselves.

At one point, Lynn called everyone to a spot in the shade of a low palm tree. She handed a camera to a resort employee and asked him to take a photo of the group.

When evening came, they sat to dinner under an open-air pavilion by the beach. Layers of gold and purple crossed the evening sky as the off-shore breezes pulled the day's humid air out to sea. Sam sipped Haitian rum, not to excess, but in quantities sufficient to lower his inhibitions. The rest drank water or soda.

Sam stood up and raised his glass, "I propose a toast. We have worked hard. And the world is a better place because we came. Here's to the health of our patients and our friends who have allowed us to enjoy the rewards of a tropical rest and relaxation."

Philip ran a finger around the rim of his glass, "It's a beautiful place. But I wonder if there is any real hope? For these people, I mean. They suffer so much. We have worked non-stop for three weeks, yet all our work is for what? It's only a drop in that sea. How can anyone relieve such suffering?"

Lynn grabbed Philip's shoulder, "Your work is not in vain. You saved so many lives. Think on all that you have accomplished. There are hundreds of lives affected by each one of you. They may never be able to repay you, but you will receive your reward; I believe that."

Luckson stood up and held up a bubbling orange soda, a straw floating out the top of the bottle, "I make a t-t-toast, too. To Dokte Scott. And Dokte Sam. And Dokte Aryanna. And Dokte Connor. And Dokte Pauley. M-m-my friends."

The team laughed and held their glasses high, "Hear, hear!"

Then Sam became somber, "What if it's all for nothing?"

Lynn leaned forward, curious, placing her chin on her folded hands, "What do you mean?"

"Nobody knows what comes next. Maybe we all just die and decay. Maybe death is the end of all consciousness. Maybe it is the end of all sensation. If so, then maybe death for some is a welcome relief. Isn't life more about the quality, not the quantity? A happy life seems better to me than a life that is just long. I wonder sometimes if I'm just saving a life to prolong the suffering."

Pauley sat up straight, "You're not saying we should let people die?"

"No, I'm not nihilistic. I mean maybe there's an afterlife. You know, golden streets, eternal bliss and all. I haven't personally been given a description of heaven that makes me not want to miss out, but surely the most boring hour in eternity is better than what people suffer here. Either way, eternal bliss or cessation of existence seems like a good deal. I'm just saying it seems like Mother Nature found a way to rid Haiti of more suffering in an instant than we could relieve in a lifetime."

Victor crossed his large arms. His forehead furrowed, "Would you say the same if your home was destroyed?"

"Sure, I would. But we don't have the same level of misery."

The conversation at the table, previously jovial, fell suddenly into an awkward silence.

Victor glared at Sam, his piercing dark brown eyes held the tension in uncomfortable stillness.

Sam felt the weight of Victor's gaze and shifted his eyes downward; then he looked around at the disapproving eyes.

Aryanna offered a soft rebuke, "Sam, you're a little drunk. Don't insult Victor."

Sam looked back at Victor, "You're so right. I did not mean it that way. You are amazing people. Brilliant. I hold you in the highest respect. I just mean you have many troubles. I think it would be tempting just to give up."

Victor chuckled, and his deep, resonant laugh broke the tension, "I disagree with you, my friend. I have seen your country too. You have many temptations. We may have pain in the body, but you—you have trouble in the soul."

Sam continued to engage Victor in after-dinner banter over the nuances of culture and the philosophies of life. But having no interest in the direction of that conversation, Aryanna and Connor excused themselves for a walk together by the shore. Then Luckson convinced Pauley to join him searching for shells.

Lynn leaned toward Philip. She whispered, "Could I interest you in a stroll down the beach?"

Philip felt the warmth of Lynn's breath on his ear. His heart skipped. He stood and motioned toward the water, "I would enjoy nothing more."

Philip and Lynn walked along the foaming water's edge. The waves splashed and reached up to touch the couple's feet before rushing away, erasing footprints as the water receded down the bubbling shore.

Philip felt comfortable in Lynn's presence. Conversation with her came naturally, like breathing at rest. He gave no thought to the tempo of the discourse, and he felt no temptation to interject words into the pauses of silence. At one point their hands touched, first by chance, then with intent, finally swinging together in a lasting embrace of fingers mutually accepted without a word.

Lynn looked toward the setting sun, "Are you ready to return home?"

"I have to tell you this experience has been good for me, Lynn. But in ways I did not expect."

"How did it affect you?"

"To be honest, I came for selfish reasons. I thought it would be good for my—" Philip paused.

"Good for your what?"

"I don't know. Just good for me."

"You mean good for your dossier?"

"I was going to say good for my career."

"Your career is important to you?"

"Yes. It always has been. Then my boss twisted my arm and made an offer I couldn't pass up."

"What's the offer?"

"Promotion. Glory. Maybe a raise. My superiors believe that humanitarian relief adds a unique weight of value to my résumé. The university will publish stories about our work. Maybe we will be given service awards. And if I'm lucky, I'll be promoted to the top spot in our department."

Lynn's fingers fell limp in Philip's hand, "So this is all just a façade?"

"Well, to be perfectly blunt, yes, that's how it started. But it's become so much more. I've seen things here; things that make me think success is not measured in paychecks or promotions. I get choked up thinking about the patients singing in that tent. There was so much joy. I see Rose-Marie's smile each morning, hobbling on that wobbling cane, the one Luckson made for her. And where do I even start with Luckson? That kid could run the world someday."

Lynn noticed something in Philip's thoughts. He was affected more deeply by his experience than she had realized. She asked, "Philip, may I ask you a personal question?"

"Sure."

"Why do you think you are here?"

Philip took a deep breath, "Well, I'd say I'm here by a quirk of timing and chance."

"Nothing more?"

"I don't believe in fate if that's your question. I suppose that sometimes the random swerves in this universe push us into the lives of remarkable people. That's how I feel about being here. These people have given me more than I brought to give them."

"So, you do not believe in divine providence?"

"Not really. I'm a man of reason. The divine doesn't influence my work or life, at least not in a way I've been able to tell. Don't get me wrong, I respect those who find faith a source of support, and I recognize the contribution great men and woman of different faiths have made in the world, but I've never personally needed to invoke a deity to explain things."

Lynn looked out over the waves, "Well, thank you for being honest with me."

"You disagree?"

Lynn took a deep breath, "Look at the sunset. I see clouds billowing over the sea in orange and purple. I hear the peaceful rhythm of water meeting land. And I think to myself, I'm a woman of science, no? Like you, I can give natural explanations for everything we see, but I have no explanation for why I think it's beautiful. Reason gets me only to the how, but it doesn't give me the why. That's how I felt the other night. I saw you do something beautiful. You laid down your life for another human being. I can explain the clinical reasons for your actions, but I can't explain why you did it."

"You mean Rose-Marie?"

"When you gave Rose-Marie your blood, you didn't hesitate. Was that a scientific decision?"

"It was a medical decision. I wanted her to live. I had no choice; without the transfusion, she would have died."

"Well, I know for you it was professional, maybe an act of kindness, but to me it was the passion of Christ, a reen-actment of the greatest rescue in the history of the world. I saw him do it again through you. You gave your life for Rose-Marie. And as you lay there next to her, I saw his love poured out again through you."

"You really read too much into that. Rose-Marie was sick. I had the blood type she needed. Anyone else would have done the same."

"Perhaps. But I saw the way you looked at her. You did not act out of duty. Yours was an act of love, a sacrifice for someone who could never repay you. Of all the awards that will ever hang on the wall of Doctor Philip Scott, the memory of your looking at Rose-Marie will forever be the image that draws my attention. You are an amazing man, Philip, even if you don't know why."

"And you are a remarkable woman. You bring out the best in me."

Suddenly from a distance, Luckson called out. He ran up the shore carrying an object the size of a football shaped like a spiraling cone with sharp edges. He reached Philip and Lynn out of breath, holding the object up he said, "Doctor Scott, I found this for you. It is a special one. I g-g-give it for you to remember me."

The object was a conch shell, beautiful and large with a shining pearl aperture that reflected the evening light. Philip held the shell, heavy in his hands, and bent down to look at Luckson, "Thank you, my friend. I know just where I'll put it."

Luckson's face stretched to a full grin, then he ran off again with Pauley, his voice trailing him, "We will find one for you too, Miss Lynn."

Philip held the shell, admiring its detail and beauty.

Lynn reached over and took Philip's arm, "So, Doctor Scott, do you see yourself coming back?"

"Someday, I suppose. It's a beautiful place with beautiful people. I could see this being a nice break from the hectic pace of work."

Then Philip looked at Lynn, "What about you? Any chance I could talk you into visiting the States?"

Lynn dug a toe into the wet sand, "I don't think so, Philip."

"Why not?"

Lynn looked back toward the sea. She did not think Philip was ready to hear the real reason. He had no way of understanding her need to avoid such enticements. She took in the salty air and responded simply, "I just think Victor is right. You have too many temptations."

23

The Sunrise

At dawn, Philip stood alone on the beach watching the first scintillations of light reflect off the ocean waves as the sun rose. With both hands he cradled a warm cup of coffee; the strong aroma blended with the smell of salt in the quiet morning air.

The serene colors of the sky and gentle waves triggered meditations on the contrast between the order in nature and the chaos of his troubled mind, matters usually avoided by busy professionals in the city, especially those whose work does not allow for personal reflection, much less acknowledgement of anything spiritual.

Philip had no clear way of explaining his thoughts. It involved his senses and to some extent his mind, but the source of his thoughts was something intangible, something just beyond the intellectual horizon, something unknown from any prior experience. Lynn had cracked open a door to the idea of faith's being something concrete, not just an abstract variation on wishful thinking, but a form of trust, a confidence in the truth of something.

Philip closed his eyes. He wrestled with the thought of a cosmos ordered by a guiding hand. But reason gave him no framework upon which to contemplate the idea of faith. It was for him only a scent, the aroma of something real, something nearby though unseen; like walking into a kitchen where the fragrances of fare and spices, herbs and oils induce a mouthwatering anticipation of a coming meal. Philip detected the allure of something larger than himself, a divine fragrance wafting through his mind causing him to linger at the thought of a life beyond this life.

Philip felt like he was surrounded by people for whom belief seemed to come naturally. Even Luckson seemed to have found it, a sense of purpose uncommon in boys his age. He seemed to be an exception in a generation of self-absorbed adolescents whose minds are open to everything but committed to nothing. Unlike Luckson, most teenagers Philip knew had never experienced the pangs of hunger or found pleasure in doing something for no other reason than a recognition that the other person was in need. Luckson lived as if he were being rewarded, but not by mortal hands. He had something Philip wished for his own children: a sense of joy they once had in the first years of life when every object was a focus of wonder and every sound sparking curiosity. Philip remembered when they would laugh at the simplest act of play. Somewhere along the way Max and Alexa had outgrown that happiness. It had been packed away with the stuffed animals, dinosaurs, dolls, and art projects of their childhood.

And if anyone had a reason for melancholy, it was Rose-Marie; yet Philip had watched her look upon the most uncertain days of her life with a strength he had never before seen in his patients. He thought of how some patients, after minor procedures, would whine for weeks about pain and the inconvenience of rehabilitation. Just for a moment, he wondered how they would react to seeing Rose-Marie, in the humid odors of a sweltering tent, rise onto one leg to dance.

Philip's thoughts returned to his children. How would Max and Alexa react to this place, so foreign to their world of technology? He missed them and imagined what it would be like to sit with them on that beach. Would they have eyes to see the beauty? Philip loved his children. He had spent what time he had protecting them from dangerous philosophies, fitting them with the heavy armor of skepticism. He began to wonder, though, in his well-meaning attempts to protect them if he had prevented them from seeing true beauty in the world. Perhaps he had given them the wrong tools. Instead of teaching them to communicate, he had handed them smartphones. Instead of teaching them to contemplate, he had taught them to question. Instead of time, he had given them money. He was a benefactor, a sponsor of modern teenagers, but he wanted to be a father. In Luckson and Rose-Marie he saw the qualities he truly wished for in his own children. He wondered if it were too late to introduce Max and Alexa to the things he was beginning to see, though he did not have the words to explain it to them, much less to their mother.

While Philip could not articulate what was happening in his heart, Rose-Marie and Lukson provided living examples of what he wished he could describe. They were children, gifted with a sense of awe and a form of trust with which everyone begins life, an unrestrained reliance on the goodness of others. Toddlers laugh at every new experience, not because their eyes are closed to things that are real; on the contrary, their eyes are wide open, unguarded by prejudices and dogmas that cloud the eyes and minds of adults to the good, the true, and the beautiful. Grown-ups, out of a fear of being exploited, voluntarily restrain themselves from the unrestricted awe of investigating the world or allowing themselves the freedom to consider the qualities of the one who upholds the universe. Educated people pretend to control the world around them. God to them is dead, at least tacitly. They are like children who once ran free on the beach collecting shells, building castles and splashing in the waves but now are content to sit down in a backyard sandbox surrounded by fences of their own making, playing with familiar toys, content to say they know what it means to play in the sand. Rose-Marie and Luckson were exposed to the harsh realities of the world, yet despite the wind and waves of their turbulent young lives, they retained a source of peace beyond under-standing. They were fortunate to have acquired the one thing that Philip could name but not fully explain: faith. Suddenly, that single thought captured Philip's full atten-tion: it is called child-like faith for a reason; not because it is immature, but because it is in the young that we recog-nize faith in its earliest and purest form.

Philip's thoughts were interrupted by a hand gently placed on his shoulder, "Good morning, Philip. It's a beau-tiful sunrise."

He turned to see Lynn, her eyes reflecting the light of the morning sun, and he held her hand on his shoulder, "Yes. It's beautiful."

"What have you been thinking about?"

Philip looked back over the waves. He did not answer quickly. He took a deep breath, then shook his head, "Nothing. Nothing at all. Just enjoying the morning air."

Lynn smiled, "Well, I wish we could stay, but Victor says we should get on the road early if you are ready. The group is at the truck."

24

Rose Marie is Taken to the Orphanage

Victor drove everyone back to Milot. He took them first through the historic French gate of Cap-Haitien and north past the monument of Haitian independence at Vertières, then traveling along an inland route, he drove them through a series of tropical rural villages. Taking this circuitous route, he avoided the dense traffic of the city. In the countryside, they passed women bearing tubs upon their heads, sugar cane farmers with machetes, children walking the roads in school uniforms, and groups of women gathered around water pumps washing clothing or bathing their children.

Upon returning to Milot, they drove straight to the hospital compound. Philip was eager to get back to work. The beachside break provided much-needed rest, but more than that, for him, it provided clarity. His time was drawing short, in less than a week the team would board a plane and return home; but the work was far from winding down. Just as they pulled up to the hospital gate, a helicopter flew overhead, a reminder that the injured and ill continued to arrive.

Before picking up a new case, Philip wanted to see Rose-Marie. He grabbed Luckson's arm, "My friend, come with me. I need your help to translate."

Unfamiliar groups of people were gathered at the hospital gates and around the tents; new relief workers had arrived, their eyes wide, unwearied by weeks of work. They appeared eager to help but unsure exactly where to get started. Philip and Luckson walked past them to Rose-Marie's tent.

Philip's eyes adjusted to the dim light inside the tent as his nose adjusted to the heavy smells of wounded bodies and soiled linens. He looked to the far end of the tent, but he did not see Rose-Marie. She was not there. An elderly man lay in the bed once occupied by Rose-Marie. Her crutches and belongings, what little she had were nowhere in the tent.

Luckson suggested she had been moved to another area and ran off to find her. Concerned, Philip asked a Haitian woman in nursing attire standing near the front of the tent, "Where is the little girl, Rose-Marie? She was in that bed yesterday."

The woman just shook her head, "I do not know, sir."

Philip felt his heart race. Where did she go? She had no family. No money. Nowhere to go. No means to provide for herself. Philip asked other patients, frantic to find someone with an answer about Rose-Marie. Most shook their heads or stared blankly at Philip, oblivious to what he was saying.

Finally, Philip approached a woman who might know. She was placing clean sheets on a cot. She nodded and struggled to find the English words, "She is gone."

"Gone? Where? What do you mean?"

"She go to House of Jesus."

Philip's heart sank. What could this mean? Did Rose-Marie take a turn for the worse? Did she die? He could not bear the thought of her dying alone.

Then Luckson returned; Lynn was at his side.

Lynn approached the woman standing next to Philip. The woman explained something to Lynn. Then after a short conversation, Lynn turned and translated for Philip, "Tabitha came this morning and took Rose-Marie with her."

"Tabitha?"

Lynn nodded, "Yes, the lady from the orphanage."

Philip raised an eyebrow, "Orphanage?"

Lynn answered, "That's right. She calls it, Lakay Jezu. The House of Jesus."

"I don't like this at all, Lynn. Rose-Marie is still in recovery. She needs rehab, wound care, a prosthetist evaluation. She was just in the ICU for crying out loud."

"She will be cared for, Philip. Tabitha runs a respectable home for children. Rose-Marie is in good hands."

Philip looked at Luckson, "Do you know how to get there?"

Luckson smiled, "Y-y-yes."

"Take me."

Lynn interrupted, "It's too late to go today, Philip. By the time you get there, it will be dark, and the road is too dangerous at night."

Luckson raised his hand like a boy in the classroom, "I take you in the m-m-morning, Doctor Scott. Victor will pick you up."

25

The House of Jesus

Victor pulled up to the guest house at daybreak. Luckson, after wiping dust from the passenger seat, made room for Philip in the cab.

Victor drove north, keeping to a paved road for about an hour. He ascended high into the mountains, his speed quickening on straightaways and slowing to a crawl when encountering curves or mud-filled craters on the busy two-lane highway.

During the drive, Philip asked Victor if he thought Rose-Marie would return with them. Victor grinned and told Philip he should reserve judgment. Rose-Marie, he explained, was in a very good place.

They turned onto a gravel byway and eventually onto a dirt road corrugated with deep ruts. The road ended at the bank of a river, shallow and wide with water rushing over rounded stones, much of it shaded by the overhanging limbs of mahogany trees. A thin foot trail rose up the opposite bank.

A man with a straw hat and tattered clothing stood beside the river holding the reins of three horses, emaciated animals with long, downcast faces bearing saddles made of straw, their tails swinging at swarming flies. Luckson grabbed a long stick and jumped upon one of the horses using his stick to prod the animal into a splashing gallop across the river. Victor mounted a second horse. The man helped Philip mount the remaining animal, a malnourished mare that smelled of stale, wet hair. Philip felt the prominent backbone of the cachectic creature pressing through the thin saddle into his groin. The horse groaned under the sudden weight and ambled unsteadily into the river. The pony, far from being a full-size steed, was so short that Philip could almost touch his toes to the ground while mounted. He rolled up his pant legs to prevent soaking them during the river crossing. With each rocking step, he grew more worried about Rose-Marie. Who carried her across the river? How did she keep her wounds clean? Was she in pain?

Once across, Victor and Philip dismounted to walk the trail while Luckson, ever the adventurous boy dashed off on his horse pointing his stick like a saber, a curl of dust rising behind him giving him the appearance of a cavalryman in full charge. He was soon out of sight.

The trail meandered through a grove of plantain trees and across an eroded slope through a small mountain village to a grass-covered field. Across the field, the path ended at a rough-hewn wooden gate teetering to one side. A trimmed cactus hedge extended from either side of the gate encircling a compound of small mud-walled buildings and mango trees under which children were playing in the shade. The horse upon which Luckson had ridden was tied to the gate post. Luckson was nowhere to be seen.

Philip and Victor stood for a moment outside the gate. To one side of the compound, Philip saw a wide structure with a rusted tin roof, its central doorway marked with a sign of painted letters spelling out LAKAY JEZU.

A young girl sat on the porch under the sign. Both of her arms were missing. Tan bandages covered stumps at the shoulders. Another girl sat behind her braiding her hair.

Toward the back of the yard, under the canopy of large trees, a boy wearing an oversized, mud-streaked t-shirt kicked a flat ball with his bare feet to another child. When the boy saw Philip, he stopped, yelled something in Creole and ran behind a tree trunk. Suddenly, numerous faces appeared in the doorways and windows of the long-house and several children ran from behind the house. They stopped abruptly when they saw Philip.

Victor opened the gate and invited Philip to follow him, "You are a celebrity, my friend. You may be the first American these children have seen up close."

Then the young boy with the muddy shirt appeared from behind the tree, pushed into the open by larger boys. The child cautiously walked toward Philip, trembling. He held his hands in a wad over his mouth as he shuffled forward, waved on by the older boys.

Philip felt sorry for the boy, so young and bullied. Philip lowered to a squatting position and held out a hand.

The boy looked back at his oppressors and then stepped toward Philip. Quivering, he touched Philip's hand and then his arm, curious to learn the feel of a person with different color skin. Then he turned, and smiling, he called out something to the others, giggling as he yelled.

The others came out from their hiding places, some running, a number of them maimed, and at least one pushing a homemade wooden walker. Within seconds, Philip was surrounded by no fewer than fifty children of various ages, many pressing against his legs or fighting for position at his side and scrabbling to touch his skin or hold his hand, all of them laughing or yelling in a cadence that bordered just on the cusp of song.

If Philip was irritated by the chaotic pawing, he did not show it. His instinct was to step back and push the children away. But he took in a deep breath looking over the swarm of relaxed play going on around him. Then he looked up at Victor, who was leaning against the gate, laughing.

Victor held out his hands, "See, Doctor Scott, you are famous."

Philip smiled. The surge of children encircling him opened his heart to an old feeling, a feeling he had long forgotten. There were not so many people who loved him this way anymore. He had forgotten what it felt like to be adored, accepted, and cherished for no other reason than for walking through the front door. It felt like home.

His entire life, Philip sought recognition through his work and achievements. His fuel was professional pride, a craving to be loved for what he could do, a love expressed by payment, or perhaps awards and promotion; but as he stood in the midst of a different form of recognition, accolades lavished on him in no way connected to anything he had done, he felt himself mesmerized by the attention. These children did not know him. They were treating him as a celebrity, not because of his credentials, but solely because he had taken the time to show up. They did not know him at all. His diplomas, awards, and professional honors were meaningless to them. Perhaps they thought he brought gifts. They were orphans; perhaps they sought his favor as if he had traveled over land and sea to choose one lucky child to return home with him. And in a sense that was true. He had arrived to take one of them back; he had come to the orphanage to find Rose-Marie. But he was unprepared for the feeling of being in a crowd of children, each one of them just like Rose-Marie. They celebrated his arrival as if they had all been waiting for his coming, preparing for his appearance. Never had Philip received such a welcome.

Philip looked up and saw a Haitian woman stepping out of a doorway at the far end of the mud-walled dormitory. She was strong in stature, like the women of West African descent whose bones are large and wide. She wore a faded dress and a golden cloth wrapped around her head. Philip noticed it was a woman he had met a few weeks earlier in Rose-Marie's tent.

The children parted respectfully as the woman approached. She nodded toward Victor, greeting him in Creole, and then she walked up to Philip, "Hello, Sir. Welcome to Lakay Jezu. My name is Tabitha. As you can see, you are most welcome."

"Yes, I remember you. Forgive me; I'm afraid I've created a bit of chaos."

"You are the first American who has ever come to our home. Please pardon the children; they are excited to see you."

Philip separated himself from the children and said, "I've come to check on the girl, Rose-Marie Sanguine. Is she here?"

26

Philip Feasts with the Children

Tabitha led Philip to a room on the back side of the dormitory. A sheet was covering the open doorway of a dark room. After Philip had stepped inside, it took a moment for his eyes to adjust. Dust drifted through sunlight coming through a window, the beam falling at an angle on the foot of a small bed.

A voice came from the shadows, "Papa San?"

Rose-Marie stood up from the bed. She hobbled on her one leg toward Philip, holding the arm of Luckson who was at her side. She embraced Philip with both arms, leaning on him for several moments.

Philip pointed to her stump, "Are you in pain?"

"Oui, pita."

"Yes, a little," Luckson translated.

Philip chastised himself for coming all this way unprepared. He brought dressing supplies but forgot to include pain medication. He reached into his pocket and pulled out what he had, a bottle of ibuprofen, the medication he used for migraines. He poured a few capsules into his palm and gave them to Rose-Marie.

The light from the doorway was suddenly eclipsed by layers of young faces pushing to see what was happening in the small room. When Philip turned to look, the children laughed and ran in different directions only to reappear when he turned back to face Rose-Marie.

While Luckson held a small flashlight, Philip removed the dressing from Rose-Marie's stump. The wound was healing. Philip felt relieved. He saw no drainage or signs of infection.

Luckson watched Philip examine the surgical wound. He was curious, uncommonly bright for his age, and instinctively offered to help, reaching in to hold a bandage, lift the stump or support Rose-Marie. At one point he asked why legs do not grow back, looking at Rose-Marie in a way which suggested it was really her question.

Philip pointed to a tree outside. One of its limbs had either broken or been cut away. He explained that bodies are like that tree when large limbs are cut away, they do not grow back, but the other branches continue to grow, and the tree still bears fruit. "Just because a body is missing a limb does not mean the person will not grow and be able to do good things," Philip said.

Rose-Marie smiled. This explanation touched on one of her great worries. Women in her world walked great distances to survive, carrying produce to market, returning with food and charcoal. Without a leg, Rose-Marie had already made the leap to the conclusion that her entire life was broken. Philip gave her hope.

Philip asked about her trip to Tabitha's. Rose-Marie sat up straight and described her journey in a long rapid sentence, translated by Luckson who had no trouble keeping up. Rose-Marie said she rode together with Tabitha in the back of a small tap-tap crowded with other riders until coming to a dirt road, where a man carried the three of them on a motorcycle to the river where two of the larger boys at the orphanage carried her across the river. She used her crutches to walk the remaining mile to Lakay Jezu. Tabitha was giving her two pills each day for her leg.

All of this was translated by Luckson, standing at the bedside with wide eyes and large gestures to dramatize Rose-Marie's story. Even without the theatrical effects, Rose-Marie's journey sounded harrowing.

Philip took Rose-Marie's hands, "My dear Rose-Marie, do you feel safe here?"

Rose-Marie's eyes glistened in the reflection of the flash-light. Then she began to cry. Softly at first, then in sobs, as she was unable to speak.

Philip pulled her into his chest and allowed her to cry, "What's the matter child?"

Luckson translated her words, "She misses her mama and her papa. Tabitha say th-th-they die. But she did not see them. She did not say g-g-goodbye. She wants to go back to her home."

"Her home?"

"Port-au-Prince."

"My dear child, I don't think your home is there any-more."

This made her cry all the more.

Luckson was not only translating, he was listening to his friend as she spoke. He felt her sorrow, his eyes becoming moist while he translated her words. He touched Rose-Marie's shoulder and looked at Philip, saying, "Doctor Scott, Jesus raised people from the dead. Why c-c-can't He give back Rose-Marie her mama and papa?"

Philip was taken by the fact that Luckson was serious, academic in his tone, asking with a formality equal to that of a resident, and with the same eagerness that he had asked about bandages and bacteria just moments before. He really wanted to know.

And Philip wanted to answer with the same honesty, but he did not have the vocabulary. The gift of faith had not come to him. The capacity to believe that people could come back from the dead belonged to the religiously minded, not Philip. And even if he had such convictions, he still had nothing in his experience to which he could point for help. There were no examples like a tree in the yard to which he could point and say look, that is just how things work. Philip was not a philosopher; even if he were, even if he were well read in such matters, these were children; what could they possibly understand about life or death? More than that, how could he explain suffering to them? Bad things just happen. It is tragic. It is painful. But it is a part of existence. Religious people, thought Philip, do children such a disservice by perpetuating stories that give them a false hope in the miraculous. Why not tell them the truth? When people die, they are gone, forever. As far as Philip was concerned, children had the right to know this. But when the moment arrived, when two children sitting under a tin roof looked to him for the truth, he could not find the words, much less the courage to give an honest answer.

Philip looked into the bloodshot eyes of Luckson and Rose-Marie. He thought for a moment and then shook his head, "I cannot answer for God. I am just a man. But I am a father, and I can say that your papa and your mama have reason to be very proud of you—both of you."

"Why do you s-s-say that, Doctor Scott?"

"Because I am also a teacher. I teach doctors how to take care of people who have been hurt badly. And when a person is hurt, you get to see the kind of person they really are. Some people are weak, some are selfish, others are sad and just give up. But you are strong. And one thing I see about both of you is that you do not give up."

Philip spent about an hour visiting with Rose-Marie and Luckson. At one point, he pulled out a simple ruler to determine the dimensions of Rose-Marie's stump, taking care to write each measurement in a small notebook. When Rose-Marie asked him what he was doing, he smiled, "I have a friend who makes legs for people; I'm going to ask him to make a special one for you."

Victor interrupted them, poking his head in the doorway, "You hungry?"

Philip looked up, "Why do you ask?"

"Because they invited you to eat with the children."

"Ok, I suppose I could use a little something."

Victor laughed, "Ha, a little something? I hope you are hungrier than that; they have prepared you a feast."

Philip stepped out of the room into the courtyard. He saw a square table under the shade of a mango tree surrounded by four rough wooden chairs. Philip carried Rose-Marie to the table and sat down with Victor and Luckson. The crowd of other children sat on the bare packed earth encircling them. Two children walked through the crowd up to the table, one holding a washbasin with water and the other holding a towel and a bar of soap. Philip recognized the gesture of hospitality and thanked the young servants.

Tabitha stood at the periphery directing the children. One boy brought out large bowls of food, steaming white rice and beans, lightly fried chicken, an aromatic creole sauce, and a platter of deep red tomatoes and bright orange carrots. Luckson took it upon himself to measure food onto each plate on the table.

The children sitting around them held bowls into which a woman wearing a matted skirt scooped beans and rice followed by a spoonful of creole sauce.

Philip looked down at his plate, portioned modestly with a chicken leg on top of rice and beans and a small serving of tomato and carrots to the side. Luckson and Rose-Marie ate with voracious delight. But Philip could not eat. He looked around at the children sitting in silence eating what little they had without complaint. He said, "Victor, I appreciate the gesture here, but I cannot eat in front of these children."

Victor laid down a chicken bone and leaned forward, his voice muffled by partially chewed food, "They are giving you a meal, and you are giving them your time. In their mind, it is a fair trade."

"May I give them my food?"

207

"Do you have enough for all of them?"

"Of course not."

"Then do not start a riot over a chicken leg. But if you wish, you may choose one of them to sit with you and eat."

Philip turned and looked over the crowd. One boy stood out. It was the young boy with the dirty shirt, the one who was brave enough to greet Philip at his arrival. Philip pointed at the boy and waved him toward the table.

The boy saw Philip pointing at him. His heart jumped, and he looked away. Then, pushed by the others to the front, he shuffled with dragging feet up to the table.

Philip reached down and lifted the boy onto his lap. The boy held Philip's arm and looked up to study the face of this man who held him as a father holds a child. It was the first time he had been held this way. Then together, one bite at a time, they shared the chicken, rice and beans.

At one point, Philip looked up to see Rose-Marie, her eyes moist with a tear running down each cheek, "What is the matter, child?"

Luckson listened to Rose-Marie's whispered answer and summarized for Philip, "She says the way you feed that boy, that's h-h-how her papa fed her."

The remainder of the meal was shared without much said. Philip still had questions. He satisfied himself that Rose-Marie would be safe at Tabitha's; but would she thrive? How would she get to medical care? Would she be educated? Would she return to the city? What if something happened to Tabitha? Rose-Marie would need a benefactor. In fact, the entire orphanage needed a patron. In his mind, Philip began to plan his own return. Someday, he would come back to Lakay Jezu.

When the time came to depart, Philip pulled Tabitha aside. He gave her money along with an address scribbled on a piece of paper, "This is to take care of Rose-Marie, and this is my address. Please write me and let me know how she's doing."

Philip could not bear extended farewells. He hugged Rose-Marie and walked through the gate with Victor. Luckson mounted his gaunt stallion and rode ahead. The crowd of children stood behind the cactus fence waving as they walked away, Rose-Marie among them holding onto another girl's shoulder. She was crying.

Philip looked back. He saw Rose-Marie standing there on her one leg. In Creole she called out, "I love you, Papa San."

27

The Medical Evacuation

Two days later Lynn ran into an operating room with Pauley, both of them out of breath. Pauley was crying. Lynn tugged at Philip's surgical gown, "Philip, can you break away?"

Philip looked over his mask at Sam, "You mind closing up?"

"I got it. Go ahead."

Philip followed Lynn onto the porch, "Tabitha sent for you. Rose-Marie is sick."

"Why didn't they bring her here?"

"I do not know. The man who brought the message says only that Rose-Marie is sick. Very sick. She was vomiting and now is having seizures. They did not think it was safe for her to travel."

Philip grabbed his hair, "This can't be happening. I knew better than to leave her there. Gather anything you can think to take. We have to go get her."

Victor was waiting at the hospital gate. Philip jumped into the cab. Luckson, Lynn, and Pauley climbed in the back. It took more than two hours to get to the orphanage. The hurried, jarring drive took place in near silence. As Victor pulled the truck up to the bank of the river, he said simply, "It will be a long drive back. You should not stay long."

Philip did not wait for the others, he splashed across the river and within a few minutes arrived panting at the gate into Lakay Jezu. A collection of children stood in hushed attention around the doorway of the dormitory. Philip pushed through the children into the dim room. He turned on his headlamp, illuminating the dust-laden air which carried the stale aroma of a crypt. In a bed along the wall lay Rose-Marie in pale silence. When Philip saw her, he froze. Her body drooped motionless to one side with sweat on her forehead glistening in the light of the headlamp.

Then Philip reached to check Rose-Marie's pulse. Suddenly, she stiffened and began to quiver, slowly at first, then violently, her entire body jerking in the uncoordinated convulsions of a seizure. Her eyes rolled back, and a white froth dripped from the corner of her mouth. The seizure lasted thirty seconds. Then Rose-Marie lay still again, unresponsive, her eyes staring blankly into the distance.

Philip looked to Lynn, "What is happening?"

"It could be anything—malaria, meningitis, sepsis. I brought some medicine and fluid. I could start an I.V."

"Yes, do that. Give the antibiotics and get her fluid. We need to get her back to the hospital. Pauley, you and Luckson find a large sheet or blanket we can use to carry her and keep her warm."

Lynn started an intravenous line and gave the antibiotics and medication for seizures. In a soft voice, she prayed the lines of a prayer over and over as she completed each task, "Your kingdom come, your will be done…"

Then Philip leaned over the bed. He wrapped Rose-Marie in a sheet and hoisted her limp frame off the bed. He first noticed the heat of her body; then he felt the moisture of her drenching sweat soaking into his shirt. He hurried out of the compound carrying her over the long, humid trail back to the truck, Rose-Marie's stiff neck held against his shoulder.

About halfway back to the truck, Philip stumbled and dropped to a knee. He was struggling to lift Rose-Marie.

Breathless, his heart pounding, Philip whispered to Rose-Marie, "Hang in there, child. It's going to be okay."

Victor saw Philip stumble. He reached for Rose-Marie and offered to help. But Philip refused. In a bolt of emotion, he stood and again began running.

Philip splashed across the river, and then, ashen with exhaustion, he handed Rose-Marie to Victor. Then bent over, gasping for breath, Philip motioned for the others to board the truck, "We have no time to lose; let's go, go, go."

Victor laid the girl onto the padded bed of the truck. Then he leapt from the back and climbed into the cab.

Lynn moved quickly to secure the bag of saline to a rail in the truck's canopy.

As Victor started the truck, Rose-Marie started convulsing. Lynn saw the seizure and dug through the medicine bag to find injectable sedative. Philip nodded approval and Lynn pushed the medicine through the intravenous line into Rose-Marie's veins. Within seconds her body relaxed.

On the bumpy road, Rose-Marie's head fell to the side, causing a snoring sound. Pauley heard the sound and, recognizing the partially obstructed airway, she placed Rose-Marie's head in her lap, holding it steady between her hands. She sat in this position monitoring Rose-Marie's breathing for the entire ride back to Milot.

It was dark when they arrived at the hospital. Luckson jumped out of the truck and ran into the compound, returning with Sam, Connor, and Aryanna. They were followed by a team of volunteers dressed in scrubs carrying a backboard onto which they strapped Rose-Marie and then conveyed her to the ICU.

Philip watched as they lowered Rose-Marie, comatose, onto the bed. Separated from any conscious awareness of the excitement around her, she appeared serene. Her peace in the midst of the surrounding panic made Philip feel suddenly weak. He placed a hand on Lynn, "I don't know what to do. Why is this happening?"

Aryanna leaned over the top of the bed, taking Rose-Marie's head between her hands. With a stiff lip she was trying to remain calm, "Hang on, sweet girl; you're going to be okay. Stay with us."

A team of doctors and nurses flooded into the room. They swirled around Rose-Marie in the choreographed chaos of a medical emergency. Philip felt dizzy. The suffocating crowd of medical personnel encircling him moved with a semblance of purpose, but at a frantic pace, doing he knew not what.

Doctor Abbott entered the room and began directing staff. With the smooth efficiency of dancers in a well-coordinated response, the nurses examined Rose-Marie and placed a second intravenous line. Then Doctor Abbott placed a hand on Rose-Marie's forehead, "How long has she been like this?"

Philip stepped forward, his eyes red and moist, "She was brought from an orphanage in the mountains. We were told she had a fever and headache early this morning. She threw up and started convulsing several hours ago."

"Lakay Jezu?"

"Yes, you know it."

"We know it well; Tabitha is a saint. This young one has no family here?"

"No, sir. Her family died in the earthquake."

Doctor Abbott turned to a nurse standing next to him, "Draw her blood; I want a blood count and malaria smear. And get the kit for a lumbar puncture."

Philip leaned forward, "What do you think is going on with her?"

"I cannot say at this point. Her amputation seems to be healing well. I do not think it is sepsis. It could be cerebral malaria, or, worse, meningitis."

"That's serious."

"Most serious." Then he turned to Lynn, "Nurse Sable, will you assist me with the lumbar procedure? I would like to look at her spinal fluid under microscopy."

Philip dug through his supply bag. He was looking for the book given to him by his friend, Heidi Kapoor. When he found it, he sat down at Rose-Marie's side. There he started reading, hoping to find what he could to help Rose-Marie. His eyes swelled, moist and dilated. The little girl was slipping out of his reach. He sat anxiously thumbing through the section on malaria. Then a note fell from the pages. Philip picked up the note, handwritten by Doctor Kapoor. He held the note up in the light and read the words aloud:

May your heart be broken by that which breaks the heart of God.
Yours, Kapoor.

This time the meaning was clear. Philip's chest constricted. He could not breathe. His heart was in fact breaking. *How did Heidi know this would happen?* he thought. He stuffed the note into a pocket and looked at Rose-Marie.

Over the next several hours, Philip sat in an off-balance wooden chair at Rose-Marie's side reading, studying each page as if for a final exam, looking up the names of drugs to ensure Rose-Marie was being given the correct medications at the proper dose.

The book became more confusing than reassuring. Like the boy who died a few weeks earlier, Rose-Marie had symptoms of many diseases. None had a good ending.

Rose-Marie's breathing was irregular, often slowing to the point Philip wondered if intubation was an option. It was not; he asked but was told it was considered futile in such cases.

Philip accepted the unwelcome fact that the staff had exhausted every available resource; he was mentally spent. Soft light from a small lamp on the nurses' desk lingered over the far end of the room. In the quiet, Philip laid his head on the mattress, holding Rose-Marie's limp, livid hand. It was after midnight. He drifted to sleep with his head at her side.

About an hour later, Philip felt someone touch his shoulder, "Philip, it's time to say goodbye."

He looked up to see Lynn behind him. He wiped the sleep from his eyes and noticed Rose-Marie's hand, now cold and stiff. Rose-Marie had passed. Philip jumped up and started shouting orders. He bent over the young corpse, pushing on Rose-Marie's chest. Then locking his lips onto hers, he forced breaths through her rigid mouth.

Others entered the room, but no one joined in to help. Lynn stood with a hand over her mouth making no effort to withhold tears dripping from her cheeks. Rose-Marie was gone, but Philip, in a futile nightmare of denial, was trying to summon her back to life.

Doctor Abbott entered the room and gently pulled Philip away from the bedside, "Doctor Scott, we thought you knew. Please stop. Do not bother the girl. She is at peace now. There is nothing more for you to do."

Philip pushed Doctor Abbott away and walked over to Lynn, collapsing into her arms and weeping bitter, hard tears, at times having trouble catching his breath. He had never cried this way before.

In a few minutes, he regained composure. He wiped his eyes and looked back at Rose-Marie. Her body lay in peaceful repose under a clean white sheet. Philip lowered the sheet and bent down to kiss Rose-Marie on the forehead whispering his lament, "I'm sorry, sweet child. We tried—I tried."

Taken again with emotion, Philip walked out of the room into the darkness of night. The others saw his silhouette come to a stop in the courtyard. There he dropped to his knees, threw dust into the air and repeatedly screamed in shrill sorrow, "Why?—Why?"

28
Parting Thoughts

A few days later, Luckson stood behind a chain-link fence at the airport. He saw the DC-3 lift off the runway. He waved a cloth with large sweeping motions hoping the passengers on the departing plane would see him.

Lynn and Victor stood next to him.

As the roar of the plane subsided, Victor asked, "Do you think he will return? Doctor Scott, I mean."

"I doubt it," Lynn answered, "I don't think he has the strength to come again. Rose-Marie's death affected him. He has not spoken for these few days, and I fear his memories of this place will not be good."

Luckson continued to wave, "He will r-r-remember me, Nurse Lynn. He is my friend."

Lynn stroked Luckson's hair, "This is true; he is very fond of you."

Victor crossed his arms and after a thought-filled pause, said, "He is a strange man. He did not seem to care much for people; but he came around, I think."

Lynn squinted as she watched the departing plane reflect a ray of morning sun, "Maybe," she said. But she was torn. Philip sparked something in her; not the romantic twinge of fleeting infatuation, but the lure of a like-minded soul. Philip was confident and secure in his skills. Lynn felt safe at his side. And his struggle with the austerity of Haiti somehow made him all the more attractive. But his departure fostered only bitterness. Philip was just another ambitious man passing into and then out of her life, an actor with a minor role. He had played his scene on the humanitarian stage and then walked away.

Lynn tried to articulate her feelings, "I don't know if a doctor can recover from that kind of blow. I don't think he will even try."

Victor nodded, "Ah, when a cat is burned by hot water, even when he sees cold water, he will be scared. I think Doctor Scott will not be the same. Maybe he will come back, maybe he will not. I do not know. But Rose-Marie will never leave him."

Lynn cut her eyes toward Victor, "Mark my words; this is the last we will see of Philip Scott. Better men have gone never to return. He is no different."

Later Lynn recorded these words in her journal:

There went another over-educated doctor who swept in under the misguided, egotistical notion that letters behind a name and a philanthropic attitude can overcome centuries of ravaging oppression and poverty. Now look at him, drowned in his own selfish sorrow having stood before a tsunami with a bucket, knocked over by the waves; now he scurries back to the comfort of his world where he can watch from a judgmental distance. Rose-Marie's death was not his fault; there is nothing more he could have done for her. But I don't think he realizes that. He failed her. He failed at the one thing his dossier said he could do well.

Philip looked down from his window. He watched concrete neighborhoods fall away, and the landscape of Haiti fade into a steamy distance. The Citadel high on its mountain came into view prompting a month's worth of memories. Countless surgeries, little sleep, roosters crying out in the night, hypnotic drums, Luckson's stories, long walks with Lynn, dancing patients, arguing with a witch doctor,

220

trying to eat while surrounded by hungry orphans, and then Rose-Marie, first her smile, then her tears, then her death, finally her funeral.

The team donated money to purchase a simple casket and a plot for her burial. The service had been simple. A few hospital staff attended. Sam and Connor helped carry the casket with a few hospital workers, trudging at a somber pace down the street of Milot as onlookers stood in silent respect watching the procession pass. Philip's final memory of Rose-Marie was a shovel of soil thrown onto her grave followed by the slamming of the shovel onto the dirt. The ring of that shovel reverberated in his memory, a definitive closure.

Philip felt his throat tighten. Reflections on the funeral magnified his feelings of failure. Rose-Marie found a way into his heart, and her death was a blow to his very being, his mind unable to find calm amidst the din of thoughts about what could have been done. In self-condemnation, Philip dropped his head against the window.

Pauley called from across the aisle, waving toward the ground, "Doctor Scott, can you see him? Luckson is waving."

Philip just shook his head and looked back out the other side of the plane.

Sam leaned over, "You going to be okay, doc?"

"I'm fine. I'll be fine."

"Well, I just wanted to say thanks."

"For what?"

"For leading us. I had a cool experience and learned a lot."

"That's nice, Sam. You did good work."

Sam took note of Philip's effect. "Hey, I know that girl's death really shook you up, but you did right by her. You gave her a chance. There is nothing more we could have done. I remember the first lesson you taught me. Keep your distance. We save some and lose some. But the outcome is not in our hands. We just repair the bones; the patient decides whether or not to recover."

Hearing his own words from Sam's mouth made Philip wince. What always sounded wise in his own mind came across as cold and foolish in the words of someone else, "You know, Sam, I'm starting to question if that's really true."

"That Lynn's a keeper, huh? You gonna come back to see her?"

Philip looked back out the window. He could not see her because he was seated on the opposite side of the plane, away from where Lynn and the others watched from below. In his mind, he could see her face. In a flash, her expression was in the foreground of a hundred memories reaching all the way back to the moment he saw her for the first time, her white dress swinging gently over her confident frame as she walked up to greet him. But now, in his mind, her face was no longer that of a welcoming stranger. Her eyes, once calm and beautiful, were now red and moist, like those of a woman who was being abandoned. That is the way she looked at Philip in the terminal just before he turned to walk to the plane. Placing her hand on his chest, Lynn simply said, "You are a good man, Philip Scott, a good man." Taken with emotion, she could say no more. When Philip tried to kiss her goodbye, she offered only her cheek. So, Philip walked away, leaving her to her tears, taking only one memory of her face, the expression of a jilted friend, contorted with love and sorrow.

Phil turned back to Sam, "I don't think I'll be coming back to this place. Sometimes it's just best to move on. Tomorrow we'll all be home, back to living a different dream."

Sam leaned his head back and pulled his cap over his eyes, "Or a different nightmare; sleep while you can, Doc. The work's been piling up back home."

29

Reverse Culture Shock

Philip followed Aryanna, Connor, Sam, and Pauley through the Seattle-Tacoma airport. He walked slowly behind them without saying a word, occasionally glancing into shops and airport restaurants with a sort of agitated wonder. He was eager to be home, but the familiar sights bothered him. The abundance of food, overpriced gadgets, and mindless entertainment was to Philip nothing but a thousand unwanted solicitations. Having come face to face with the realities of suffering, he found himself troubled by familiar comforts, little diversions he once took for granted now appeared extravagant, wasteful even. Seen from a different perspective, these conspicuous luxuries produced in him a fresh emotion: resentment.

Philip stepped into the crowd of waiting travelers wedged around a baggage conveyor, each of them impatient to claim luggage. An unkempt teenager caught his eye. The kid was complaining to a lady, presumably his mother, about having to carry bags. The boy spoke to the woman in a sharp whine, feigning oppression in a public display of laziness. Exasperated by the passive aggression of her child, the mother hired a porter. Philip shook his head. He remembered how willingly Luckson, smaller in frame, carried bags of considerable weight, throwing them onto a truck with ease and without complaining.

Aryanna was standing near Philip. She heard the boy's outburst and saw Philip glaring at the boy's lack of self-reliance. Aryanna leaned over to Philip and whispered, "Some people just don't know what work looks like, huh?"

Connor pointed across the crowd and waved, "Doctor Hu is by the door."

Anderson Hu and his wife, Monica saw Connor and the group. Using a crutch for balance, Anderson lumbered cautiously through the crowd, one foot in a cast boot. Monica followed closely behind him. Anderson walked up to Philip, shook his hand, and asked, "How did it go?"

Philip's eyes cut downward. His mind raced through a cascade of possible answers.

Anderson fixed his attention on Philip, waiting. He was not being superficial. He was sincerely curious.

How does a person explain such an experience? Philip thought. *It's like shaking hands with an astronaut returning from the moon and asking 'How was your trip?' Some experiences require a lifetime to explain.* Philip shrugged and answered simply, "It was all right; about what we expected."

Anderson waited for more, but Philip changed the subject, "So, how's the ankle?"

Anderson lifted his leg, "Better every day. I expect to be out of this cast boot in a week or so. Expect to be back to full speed by summer. I've been back to work, and other than feeling a little off balance in the boot, I'm getting around pretty well. But don't tell Monica," Anderson feigned a whispered voice, "I've grown to enjoy the concierge benefits."

Monica walked up behind them. She cut her eyes toward Anderson and gave him a look that spoke both love and annoyance, "I heard that."

"You'll remember my wife, Monica; she's driving one of the university vans. We'll get you back to campus or wherever you need to go. You guys need a cart?"

Sam laughed as he extended his back like a weight lifter preparing for a competition and then picked up two bags, "Who needs a cart? We've been carrying stuff for weeks."

Once loaded and on the road, Monica coaxed the over-loaded van into the flowing northbound Seattle traffic. Anderson sat in the passenger seat. Philip and Sam sat with Pauley in the middle row. Aryanna snuggled with Connor behind them. The back of the van was stuffed with luggage.

Pauley looked out the window watching the world drift by. Without potholes or pedestrians, the landscape appeared to move by as if on a screen. The parked planes of Boeing Field glided past as cars passed in the foreground. Pauley giggled, "Are we floating?"

Aryanna yelled from the back, "I thought it was just me. It feels weird to be on a smooth highway."

Anderson interrupted, "I think you'll find your whole world will feel strange. Like when you first take off skates, you know what I mean? After your brain has become accustomed to the jarring of potholes, you have trouble riding on paved roads for a bit, feeling just a little off balance. Don't be surprised if everything you once knew feels a little off like that for a while."

Then Anderson asked, "I'm curious to hear about the trip. How did it go?"

The team glanced at each other. Then Aryanna shouted from the back, "Where do we start? It was unbelievable. It is a beautiful place, but there is so much misery. People were doing so much with what they had. I don't think I've ever felt so happy and so traumatized at the same time."

Connor nodded, "It was the most intellectually engaging work I've ever done. It should be a required rotation. What we did, in, I don't know, like a hundred cases, was incredible. The surgical challenges alone are worth a year of training."

Sam interrupted, "Totally. I mean—who would have thought we could do major surgery with a hand drill and a screwdriver. Unbelievable."

Pauley leaned forward, "Doctor Hu, have you ever seen the Citadel?"

Anderson smiled, "One of the wonders of the modern world. What did you think of the view?"

Pauley answered, "It's breathtaking. One day we sat on top and could see the entire coast.

Connor spoke from the back, "I'm surprised places like that aren't well known. The historical sites reminded me of places we've visited in Europe. Aryanna and I talked about going back, maybe just to visit."

Anderson continued to ask questions. He probed for interesting medical stories, favorite foods, and descriptions of sights, sounds, and smells that would be hard to forget. Then he asked about people. He was happy to hear about his friend, Victor, and enjoyed the stories about Luckson and Lynn. Aryanna told him about Rose-Marie, and for a few minutes, the van fell silent as if in a moment of respect for the part she had played in their experience.

With simple questions, Anderson drew out their stories. He seemed to understand the need for each of them to debrief. In reality, whether he knew it or not, he was preparing them for the fact that most people would not care, much less attempt to understand their experience. For the moment he gave them what they needed, an attentive ear.

At one point, Anderson looked back at Philip, "How about you Phil? What did you think of Haiti?"

Philip looked out the window. He felt as if putting even one thought to words would make the troubling parts of his experience too hard to forget. He said simply, "I don't know, Anderson; I think it will take time to process."

The van slowed in downtown traffic. Monica looked up into the rearview mirror, "Sorry, guys. I thought we'd miss the rush. Looks like we may be stuck for a bit."

"This is not traffic," Sam scoffed, "Where are the people darting between cars? I don't hear horns. We are not breathing diesel exhaust. The motorbikes have no more than one occupant."

Pauley laughed, "And look we are still moving. It's a rush hour speed record. I'm never going to complain of traffic again, ever."

Everyone laughed with her. Except for Philip; he caught the humor, but it did not strike him as funny. He looked out the window. Somewhere a world away, people he could not get out of his mind were stuck in traffic, real traffic. He started thinking about Victor, smiling at the wheel of the white truck, creeping down the street of Milot, honking at people who stepped into and out of his way. Luckson and Lynn were likely in the cab at his side, perhaps carrying a new group of wide-eyed, inexperienced volunteers to the hospital.

Philip was startled from his daydream by a buzz on his phone. It was a text from Amanda, "Welcome home. Call when free. Kids need you."

30
Philip Has a Weak Stomach

Philip did not unpack. He threw his bags onto his living room floor and departed to pick up Max and Alexa.

He parked on the curb of the Duberstein waterfront estate and walked up the wide glowing stone path to a veranda lit by an overhead crystal chandelier. Stanley, Amanda's husband, greeted Philip at the door. Stanley was dressed in faded jeans, sandals, and an untucked, open-collared shirt. He pushed back his wavy, dark hair, giving him the look of someone ready to be photographed in the act of relaxing on a yacht or sipping wine on the terrace. He saw Philip and flashed his bleached smile, "Doctor Scott, welcome back. How was your trip? Amanda tells me you were in Guatemala or something?"

"It was Haiti, actually, and the trip was fine. I'm glad to be back."

"Oh, yes, they had the big earthquake. Good for you for helping out." Stanley stepped back to welcome Philip into the high-ceiling, stone-tiled foyer, "Come in. The children are pulling their things together. They'll be out shortly. Can I get you something to drink?"

Philip looked up the curved staircase wishing his children would hurry. He hated this ritual. Stanley had such a false air of friendliness and hospitality. Philip would just as soon keep a rock in his shoe as prolong a visit. It was all a show, anyway. Philip smirked, "No, thank you. I'm fine."

Amanda walked out from the kitchen and gave Philip a kiss on the cheek, "So good to see you, Philip. Tell us about your trip."

Philip shrugged, "There's not much to say. It was over-whelming really, but we did some good and helped some people."

Amanda crossed her arms, "Well, it was good of you to go. I know I gave you a hard time about taking off, but now that I've seen the news, I see why they needed some-one with your expertise."

"Thank you, Mandy. I wish the images could tell half the story. It's a sad situation."

Amanda sensed that Philip was reluctant to say more, but she knew how to probe for open areas in his thinly shielded psyche, "How's the girl you operated on, the one you texted us about?"

Philip shot a look at Amanda. Why did she remember that? She never answered that text. And why did she care? Philip hated the way Amanda could see through him. His eyes dropped, "She didn't make it. She died from—a bad infection."

"I'm sorry to hear that, Phil. I sensed her case was im-portant to you."

Just then, Max and Alexa came down the curved stair-case, each with a duffel. They raced past Philip, giving him a dutiful greeting before pushing through the front door, competing to win the coveted front seat.

Philip shrugged, "Priorities, huh?"

Alexa won the race and controlled the music during the drive to dinner.

It was Friday; the U-district was packed, and the kids' favorite pizza parlor had college students standing around the door waiting for a table, but Philip had called ahead. The owner had a small round table reserved for them with three empty seats.

Philip sat down with his children.

Max smelled the aroma of warm bread and melted cheese floating in a thin haze over the dining room, he looked up from his menu, "Let's order; I'm starving."

Something about Max's statement and tone struck Philip in a way he did not expect. He felt suddenly angry. Without thinking he became stern and pointed a finger at Max, "Don't use words when you don't know what they mean."

"Whoa, Dad. Cool down. What did I say?"

"I've seen what starving looks like. And you are not starving."

Max looked at Alexa. She rolled her eyes and slunk behind her menu.

Philip realized he had overreacted, "I'm sorry, Max. I'm jet-lagged. Let's just order our usual pies."

As they waited for the pizza, Philip asked about school and friends. Max talked about the Mariners. He asked about taking a trip to Arizona to see them play in spring training. Alexa confided she had been asked to join a band, an amateur group with an outlandish name. Max teased her about playing music more akin to organized noise than actual notes with a melody. She pointed out his lack of taste. Philip listened, but without a deep interest in either baseball or popular music, he felt further than ever from understanding his children.

Max took a sip of soda, "So, Dad, did you see any zombies?"

Philip leaned forward. He looked both ways as if about to share a deep secret. Then he whispered, "I actually saw one; a real live zombie."

Alexa dropped her straw back into her drink, "How did you escape? Did it try to infect you?"

Max derided her, "It's not like the movies, dork. Zombies aren't infectious. It's the witch doctors; they do it. Right, Dad?"

Philip shook his head, "No, it's not what you think. The one I met just sat there washing a large pan. They told me she was just brain damaged from a drug a witch doctor gave her."

Max looked skeptical, "So, she was dead?"

Philip folded his hands on the table and shook his head, "She was not dead, but I can't say she was really living either; she was just existing. Like some people. You know, just existing but not really living."

Max extended his arms and deepened his voice, "Beware, Alexa. Dad's turned into a boring zombie."

Philip held his temper but not his words, "That's not funny, Max. There are a lot of things you don't understand."

The waitress lowered a large deep-dish pizza onto the table. Steam from the pie rose from the center of the table, its fragrant scent wafting across the dining room, drawing the attention of others waiting nearby.

Max and Alexa grabbed at the pizza, each of them stretching the warm cheese from opposite pieces to their respective plates and stuffing large wads in their mouths, chewing in between muffled sounds of epicurean delight.

Philip placed a small piece on his plate. He watched his children eat, selfishly taking for granted that the food placed before them was a luxury not known to most of the world. They seemed oblivious to the fact that very real children not so far away would gratefully wait for just one bite of the crust. To some, even the leftovers would be a feast. But Philip's kids did not care, and this disturbed him deeply.

Philip poked a fork into the slice on his plate, but he could not eat. He looked around the room at people enjoying the various stages of dinner—eating, laughing, waiting, drinking. A little boy at a nearby table looked back at him.

The boy reminded Philip of a little boy at Tabitha's orphanage.

Suddenly Philip slipped into a daydream. Images of children appeared all around him. It was not a hallucination, but a vivid thought, as clear as if it were real; in his mind, the dining room was suddenly filled with children, orphaned boys and girls, each of them holding up empty bowls. Philip imagined one of them walking up to him. Philip felt paralyzed. He wanted to hand his food to the imagined boy, but he could not move.

Suddenly, Philip heard Max whispering forcefully, "Dad, snap out of it. You're embarrassing us. What's wrong?"

Philip blinked. He wiped his moist eyes and looked around. The scent of heavy oil and garlic filled his nose and caused a sudden unease in his abdomen. He leaned over toward his kids, "I'm sorry guys; I don't feel well. You take your time. I need to step out for some fresh air. I'll wait for you in the car."

Philip stood, paid for the dinner and walked out.

31

That Which Breaks the Heart of God

Standing before a surgical sink, Philip held a sponge under the stream of water. In a meticulous ritual, he scrubbed each hand until every finger was fully washed. Then, with clean hands raised, he backed into the operating room.

For several days Philip had worked with little rest. He started each morning before dawn operating and overseeing the work of young surgeons, instinctively keeping occupied in a fearful evasion of memories that remained suppressed while he was busy. It was only in the quiet moments that his mind flooded with images from Haiti: Lynn's tear-filled eyes; the sounds of Haitian traffic; stuttering words of Luckson; the sight of traumatic wounds; the thumping of approaching helicopters; the scent of creole chicken; and the smiles of Rose-Marie. These memories haunted Philip, each recollection returning in a painful flash, ripping through his chest.

Even in work, however, he could not fully avoid these memories. Colleagues asked about his experiences, most inquiring out of polite respect, few caring to hear details. Philip learned to answer in well-mannered clichés; the particulars he kept to himself.

Still, Philip grew frustrated by just about any conversation. When people talked of politics or golf or boats or investments, he would often respond with a curt censure. To him, people seemed enamored by menial matters he had come to consider of minor importance. Philip had seen the real problems of the world: suffering; disease; poverty;

and injustice. Among colleagues, these issues were either too distant to have relevance or just too painful to be discussed in casual conversation. Regardless, Philip learned to keep his new feelings private. Amid the social elites, he felt alone.

Occasionally someone would show genuine interest. One day, Philip saw a patient, a professional baseball player, in the surgery clinic. The patient, a man in his early thirties, sat on the exam table, his shirt removed, exposing a well-healed surgical scar over his right shoulder. He was seeing Philip for a follow-up.

The man grinned when Philip entered the room, "Hey, Doc Scott. Welcome back. I missed seeing you. Shoulder's doing great. The nurses told me you just got back from Haiti."

Philip closed the chart responding simply, "That's right."

"What was that like?" the man asked as he leaned forward on the soft edge of the exam table. He was not merely being polite. He wanted to know.

Philip told a brief story about Luckson. "There was a remarkable boy who made a cane for a little girl I had operated on." Something about the story resonated with the man. He told Philip about his own experience, being brought to the United States as a child where foster parents raised him. Early in high school, he made himself resourceful around ballparks, becoming a bat boy, then a minor league player and eventually making it to the big leagues. At the time, he played for the Seattle Mariners.

The man asked more questions than most, and when Philip drifted into more stories about Luckson, the man's eyes widened, his lips spread in spontaneous smiles followed by eager nods, a way of acknowledging understanding and genuine interest. A few days later a Mariners baseball cap arrived on Philip's desk. It was signed under the bill with a note attached, "If you ever have reason to return, give that young man the hat for me."

On the same morning, he found the hat on his desk, Philip had a case with Sam, their first together after returning from Haiti. Having scrubbed, Philip entered the operating room and slid his arms into a surgical gown held for him by a nurse. Then he looked over the table at Sam.

Sam peered over his surgical mask. The patient before him was asleep, prepped for surgery, "All ready for you, doc."

"Well, good morning, Sam." Seeing Sam had a calming effect, like breaking free of a congested room of strangers into the fresh open air with a friend; in this case, a friend who had shared a life-changing experience.

The procedure that morning was an extended surgical case that took several hours, time that passed quickly as Philip and Sam shared memories of unique surgical cases in Haiti and dinner on the beach and climbing to the Citadel.

During the surgery, Sam pointed to the lady on the table before them and made a most unusual comment, "Is it just me, Doc, or do these cases seem boring?"

"Boring? I'm not sure I follow you."

"These cases used to give me such a rush. Now they seem mundane."

"You don't like the routine?"

"I don't like the lack of a challenge. With these instruments and a good scrub nurse, my kindergarten teacher could do the procedure. A few weeks ago, I was repairing major life-threatening wounds with only a suture set, a hand drill, and few sterile plates. In Haiti, I was a craftsman. We were heroes. Here I'm a hand on the assembly line. Know what I mean?"

Philip laughed under his surgical mask, "Yes, Sam, I'm afraid it makes perfect sense."

After the procedure, Philip left Sam to close the wounds, and he walked through the recovery room, an open area lined with large hospital beds, each separated from the other by thin curtains suspended from tracks in the ceiling. As Philip looked around the room, he felt his heart throb.

He saw patients stirring as they awoke from an anesthetic sleep. The scent of sanitizer, intermittent beeping of monitors and the quiet hum of fluid pumps caused Philip to stop; it all seemed strangely wrong. He watched the nurses, compassion-fatigued, going through comatose routines, out of touch with the reality that the room was full of actual human beings; not just medical cases, but people—husbands, fathers, mothers, daughters, brothers, and sisters from every walk of life. Trauma, that great equalizer, brought them together in one room. Lying there were drug dealers and community servants, wealthy women and homeless men, teachers and felons, teenagers and grandmothers, each of them waking up from an encounter with the surgeon's knife. Tragedy was the one thing they all shared. Their stories were similar but heartrending: car crashes; assaults; falls; gunshot wounds; and career-ending injuries. They would recover, but Philip saw something more, a truth previously unseen in the countless times he walked through the recovery room; their lives would never be the same.

Philip scanned the room. Most patients were treated by algorithms and checklists, waiting for open rooms, then moved upstairs once all boxes were checked. The way in which cataclysmic personal events were treated as mere routine only added to Philip's unease. He saw individuals whose bodies remained broken and whose brains had not fully recalibrated to the conscious world waking in various

240

stages of delirium. Some of them were frightened; some were in pain, and most were disoriented, waking in a room of unknown people asking repetitive questions. From overhead speakers, Philip heard calming music played to soften the patients' bewilderment.

Philip sat on the edge of an open bed and for a moment closed his eyes. In his mind, he could hear the faint sounds of a different recovery area, a tent in Haiti bursting with a rhythmic hymn sung by a hundred dancing patients, people not free from pain but for a moment free from suffering. Having lost their fears in the transcendent hope of a life beyond this life, they sang. Across the tent, Philip could imagine Rose-Marie dancing with Aryanna and Pauley, pounding claps keeping time, their heads thrown back while shouting out a sacred melody.

The memory made Philip smile. Then he felt someone grab his shoulder. The competing beeps of monitors and humming pumps came back. He opened his eyes to see a nurse looking at him, "Doctor, are you alright?"

"Yes, I'm fine. Thank you. We had a long case. I'm just resting my feet."

But Philip was not fine. He needed to talk with someone who would understand the psychological undertow keeping him from fully coming home. He walked over to the nurses' station and after dialing the office of a friend, said, "Hello, this is Doctor Scott. Is Doctor Kapoor available?"

That afternoon Heidi Kapoor welcomed Philip into her office. She sat next to him holding a cup of warm coffee, "Thank you for coming by, Phil. I've been eager to hear about your trip."

"You know, Heidi, I've had a lot of people say that, but no one really means it. When I begin to tell stories about our trip, they rock impatiently and find ways to move on. I have to be honest; it was a new experience, but I've had a hard time explaining it. It's as if the whole world changed, and I returned to find that nobody has noticed."

Heidi smiled, "The world has not changed, Philip; you have changed. The rest of the world has stayed the same."

Philip shrugged, "Maybe. I've seen some disturbing things, and as much as I'd like to talk about it, I'm not sure anyone understands; worse, I imagine I'd just be wasting good people's time."

"Well, you've come to the right place. I do want to hear what you thought. Did anything inspire you?"

"I met some incredible people. Some of them reminded me of you. There's a French nurse, a brilliant woman, beautiful and smart, a leader who could run any hospital in the world but seems content to volunteer. I met a Haitian woman, equally smart and strong who manages an orphanage by herself. There was also this orphan kid, a boy named Luckson who became our personal helper. That boy found joy in every little thing we did, and we had this driver who protected us in ways I don't even know, yet never once did he ask me for a tip or money."

Philip placed his coffee down on a side table and pulled a folded paper out of his pocket, discolored with worn corners from being opened and closed many times. He held it out to show Heidi, "I found this in the book you gave me."

Heidi smiled, "You found my message?"

"I did, and it's bothered me for weeks."

"Bothered you? Why?"

"We lost a patient. A little girl. Her family was killed in the earthquake. She survived but sustained an extremity injury; I had to amputate her leg. Over the weeks we took care of hundreds of people, but somehow that little girl won us over. She would dance on her one leg and sing and teach us Creole phrases. But she acquired a bad infection, malaria or meningitis or something, and she died. It hit us all pretty hard."

Heidi leaned forward, "What was her name?"

Philip shot a look at Heidi, her eyes open in full attention.

Philip felt his throat suddenly constrict. He could not respond. No matter how hard he tried, he could not bring himself to speak her name. Each time he tried his lips would move, but his throat would tighten, and his eyes would tear. Then his nose began to drip.

Heidi handed him a tissue box.

Philip waved it off, "I'm sorry Heidi; this is embarrassing. You don't need this."

Heidi's words became warm, "What is her name, Phil? Tell me."

Philip stiffened his lip, "Her name was Rose-Marie—Rose-Marie Sanguine."

"That's beautiful. She sounds like a special young lady."

"She was, but I can't tell you why she stands out to me. It's just the circumstances, I guess. I wanted her to live, to run again, to dance. I think we just got too close."

"You can never get too close. Rose-Marie lost something; it sounds like you gave her the one thing she needed most."

"What's that?"

"A family; you gave her a father after she lost her own."

Philip heard those words, and it took him instantly back to the night Rose-Marie died. His lungs filled with the sensation of impending doom and he felt his throat constrict. He could not swallow. He could not speak. Then he broke down. Like the night she died, Philip sobbed without the ability to control the sudden flow of emotion.

Heidi pulled Philip into her arms while allowing him to weep. It was a strange sight: one competent doctor consoling an equally competent grieving colleague over the loss of a patient.

Through his tears, Philip asked, "How do you know this?"

"Know what?"

"That's what she called me; she called me her Papa San, her father."

"Oh, Philip. I'm so sorry you had to tell her goodbye."

It took several minutes for Philip to regain his composure. He felt awkward--embarrassed, yet somewhat relieved. As the weight lifted from his shoulders he sat up, wiped his eyes, and patted the note Heidi had written, "I found your note the night she died. And you were right. You were so right. It broke my heart."

"I'm sorry to hurt you, Phil. The note was meant to give you courage, to confirm you were doing the right thing."

"You knew?"

"Knew your heart would break? Yes. But until now, I did not know how."

"How do you know these things?"

Heidi pulled a small picture frame from her desk. She looked at it and then handed it to Philip. In the frame was a yellowed piece of paper with worn edges pressed under glass. On the paper, in beautiful handwritten script, were the words, "May your heart be broken by that which breaks the heart of G-d."

Heidi explained, "Years ago when I came to medical school, our Rabbi gave me that note. It was one of his favorite lines. I remember the way he read from Isaiah. He would raise a finger and say, "There are five things that break the heart of God, six things for which we fast: the chains of injustice; the yoke of oppression; the pangs of hunger; the exposure of the homeless; the shivers of the naked; and the loneliness of a soul without a family." Then he would point at us and say, "May your heart be broken by that which breaks the heart of God." I don't know how he knew, but somehow, he knew that would be my life's work, addressing suffering in its many forms. Now when I pick up this list, I think of names, hundreds of precious people whose suffering has broken my heart."

Philip looked at the framed message. How could so few words articulate so much? The words of a thousand poems could not express the entangled feelings of love and pain any more fully, and the weight of a thousand psychology textbooks could not explain how the loss of one human being could affect a caregiver with any more clarity. Philip felt his body begin to shake. His heart quivered, and the foul constriction returned to his chest. He handed the frame back and tried to fold the note Heidi had written for him, but his anxious fingers could not make the edges align.

Heidi looked down at Philip's trembling hands. She took the paper, folded it for him, and held it firmly into his palm, "You now have a name on your list: the lovely Rose-Marie Sanguine. I pray her name will not be your last."

32

A Little Life and Peace

Having lost Rose-Marie, Philip feared for his own children. He became keenly aware that time was precious and bound by beginnings and endings over which he had no control. Haiti had opened his eyes to the fact that even his children were bound to him only for a moment, nothing more. Any time remaining with them was not guaranteed.

Over the following months, he took time off to spend with Max and Alexa. He took Max to Arizona to see the Seattle Mariners play in spring training. There they spent hours together, two boys kicked back in the sparsely filled baseball stadium eating hot dogs and talking about life. Another weekend Philip drove Alexa to an outdoor music festival in Portland to watch her favorite band. It was a strange experience comprised of standing in a crowd of tone-deaf teenagers jumping to songs he could not understand. At one point, Alexa leaned over, her hair dyed jet black and hanging from underneath a knit cap of pastel colors matching a loose-fitting, sack-like dress glistening under the outdoor lights and yelled, "You're the best, dad!"

For Philip, his growing love for his children came with a fear of loss. He suffered from a festering mental wound spreading from the emotional gash he had sustained during his final week in Haiti. It left him with the fear of some unseen impending harm. He began to wake up in cold sweats, his sleep interrupted by a recurrent dream of patients who drop suddenly unconscious then seize, convulsing for a time before falling limp. One night he dreamed the patient was Alexa. Philip woke up trembling, his pillow moist, the lingering nightmare having ended with

Philip's standing over a table, exhausted, performing re-suscitative measures on Alexa while others stood watching, unwilling to help. That dream gave birth to an anxiety, at times paralyzing, over the thought that something would happen to Alexa, that she would be involved in an accident or cause herself harm.

Soon his nightmares invaded waking hours. Since early in his career Philip had built up a resistance to the sights and sounds of trauma. To him, the distressing echoes of pain were nothing more than background noise, a part of the ambiance that faded into the unnoticed background of everyday work. But when he allowed his mind to drift toward thoughts of how he would respond if it were his own children suffering, he could not hold his composure. One day, without warning he excused himself from a surgery. The patient was a teenage boy, and the sight of that boy reminded him of Max. Philip passed the instruments to his assistant and walked out. The thought of Max's lying on the table was too much.

The feelings of anxiety became a perpetual band-like constriction around Philip's chest. He could not explain what frightened him, at least not by pointing to any objective signs of impending disaster. Yet no amount of self-reassurance or attempts at relaxation could allay the sensation that something in the world was not right. He feared the loss of his children. He feared the loss of his health. He feared the loss of his job which led to a fear over losing his house, his career, his freedom, his ability to live near his children. He feared the loss of prestige. He feared that his trajectory toward success had reached a plateau and he would soon be overshadowed by ambitious young colleagues in their own rises to power.

Philip stopped eating in quantities sufficient to maintain a healthy weight, and he began to look thin in the face.

Colleagues noticed, making comments but without probing.

Philip felt the growing anxiety. He pushed through each day, making rounds and overseeing complex surgical procedures, but heart palpitations and growing mental fatigue did not abate even when he went home at night. He experimented with brandy, a drink or two, to wash away the anxieties of the day, but even liquid spirits provided no lasting respite from the demons that tormented his soul or the night terrors that haunted the cellars of his subconscious mind.

Then Philip met a former patient, an elderly gentleman lying in the intensive care unit with a traumatic hip fracture, his pelvis crushed in a high-speed car accident. Philip thought he recognized the name, but he could not remember why. He had taken care of thousands of patients, but for some reason, this name appeared familiar.

Seeing the patient did not help. His grey hair was tousled and his face swollen and covered in the purple hues of resolving bruises. The man lay in a hospital bed wearing a thin blue gown, the head of his bed elevated. Intravenous lines wove around wires clipped to various spots on his chest, and a monitor hung on the wall behind his bed beeping out a rhythmic rate of breaths and heart beats.

The patient opened one eye and peered from under a swollen lid. When he saw Philip, his cheek lifted in a reflexive grin as he breathed out a mumbled greeting, "Doctor Scott? You've lost weight."

Philip looked puzzled, "Thomas Palmer? Have we met?"

Thomas fumbled with wires crossing his chest and pointed at Philip, "You fixed my back. I broke my spine. You saved me from paralysis."

Philip looked out the window as a series of disconnected memories, first in isolated pieces then in a more complete picture, came back together like a jigsaw puzzle. He remembered the elderly man with a spinal fracture, a doting spouse, a protracted recovery, then the angry face of Aryanna Vito standing in his office doorway. Suddenly it all came back. Philip remembered yelling at this man and cutting off his pain medication. Philip looked at the swollen man in the bed, and through the bruises, he saw traces of a man he had once treated with disdain. It was Thomas Palmer, the old man who would not quit climbing ladders to help people.

Philip felt embarrassed. His last memory of speaking with his patient had been shameful. He reached down and took Thomas' calloused hand, the fingernails still stained with oil, "It's been too long. I owe you an apology, sir. I treated you poorly at our last meeting."

Thomas coughed a whisper, "That's not so. You spoke truth. I was trapped. I had come to rely on you and the drugs. You reminded me who was my surgeon and who was my savior. You did me much good that day."

Philip pulled up a chair, "May I sit with you for a moment? I feel there's more to you that I should know."

Over the next hour, Philip learned plenty. Thomas was retired from the Navy. He was an aircraft mechanic in the 1960s—that turbulent era when world superpowers held nuclear handguns to each other's head. He joined the Navy out of high school, eager to see the world, a young sentry standing watch among thousands of young soldiers trained to keep the fragile peace. After training, he was stationed on Adak Island, a remote military base that was set like a watch on the wrist of the long arm of Alaska's Aleutian Islands. He described that time period as "the years in the wilderness when I learned to trust that benign parent of all mankind who provides manna from heaven for those who first wander far off the path while en route to the Promised Land."

On the remote outpost of Adak, he learned to work with his hands; he was a mechanic tasked with ensuring aircraft could safely punch holes through clouds hanging above the volcanic line of islands between the North Pacific and the Bering Sea. Philip asked him what it was like to work on warplanes in such an isolated place. He shrugged, "It taught me not to fear anything mechanical, a skill that served me well."

On Adak, he learned that happiness could only be tied to virtue. He tried the alternative. He denied himself none of the pleasures on offer to an enlisted man, but with each experiment, he noticed something was lost, not gained. And one day while sitting on a hill overlooking the sea, he wondered why it all seemed meaningless, why his life had no purpose, why he found no pleasure in eating, drinking, or the labor of his days. That night he found his way to the chapel where, after evening prayers, he was invited to dine with the chaplain, a devout man who befriended Thomas and taught him of the meaning of the words, "Remember your Creator while you are young, before the days of hardship come."

Thomas went on to become a Navy chaplain. He was ordained in the Episcopal Church and ministered to young men and women during a long career in Alaska. He married a florist named Carolyn. She was a native Alaskan from Kodiak Island, a woman with blossoming cheeks and a figure that attracted the attention of many young sailors but whose feisty wit kept them all at bay, except one, Thomas, whose simple sermons wooed her like a spiritual troubadour. His prophetic poetry was, to her, the irresistible call of a lover. He was the only man she ever remembered loving, a man she adored from the beginning, and a man she respected more as the years allowed her to see his character revealed by each hardship.

In retirement, Thomas moved with Carolyn to northern Washington where he served as an Anglican priest for a small neighborhood congregation. After leaving the Navy, Thomas parted with the Episcopal Church out of disillusionment with teachings he felt were inconsistent with his understanding of Holy Scripture. In a letter to his bishop he wrote, "For three decades I have pointed my beloved flock toward Him, the shepherd of our souls, who has loved us since the creation of the world. I fear that we have been distracted by a foolish attempt to force Him, the savior of all men to turn and follow us, or worse to wait on us while we tend to our self-centered nets. This is surely a futile endeavor, and with deep sorrow I must leave my nets on this shore and go with my Lord to the other side of the sea, for my first desire is to follow Him who died for me, and not only for me but all the world, and more than that rose again."

Thomas Palmer was not merely religious; he sought to be good, "like him who called me," he would say. He lived in a small house on a fixed income with Carolyn, his wife, partner, and best friend. Together they served a small suburban community as ambassadors of heaven, poor by American standards but happy in their station. Thomas drew a small retirement, and Carolyn supplemented their income by working in a flower shop near their home.

What did not go to pay for rent and meals went to help neighbors. Most days, Thomas could be found under a neighbor's car, having traded his liturgical vestments for a pair of oily jeans. Parishioners were as likely to call on him to repair a furnace or fix a leak as to call on him to pray. He never accepted payment. Instead, he would say, "It seems to me that you bring more value to my life than anything I could do to reimburse you. Please accept this as principal on a debt I can never repay."

One time a young member of his parish, the manager for a local bank, asked Thomas if he could help him make a few good investments. Thomas laughed, "I've never been able to save money." When the young banker pointed out that saving for the future took discipline, Thomas' wife standing nearby overheard the conversation and laughed, "Discipline is not his problem. No, his problem is that he knows too many people who need help."

He loved Jesus. He once told his congregation, "When I was on Adak I fell in love with Jesus and there decided that even if Jesus were in hell, that is where I'd want to be."

Then one day, hell struck Thomas. Carolyn received a summons to appear in court to face criminal charges. The charges were completely false. In reality, her identity had been stolen, and her name and social security number were used by a woman who had been arrested for possession of cocaine. The criminal bailed out and absconded, leaving the elderly Carolyn with a criminal record.

To clear her name, Carolyn had to appear on a certain date at the municipal court in downtown Seattle. Thomas and Carolyn could not afford an attorney, but Thomas knew that if he could just convince the judge to compare Carolyn's photo identification with the photo of the criminal taken at booking, all charges would be dropped. So, they drove to Seattle for the court appearance.

The judge listened to Thomas, the articulate elderly priest guiding him to see the truth. Carolyn stood at his side, her arm in his with a smiling glint in her eye as she looked up at the man speaking wisdom in her defense. After the court dismissed all charges, the couple was given guidance on how to combat identity theft.

The drive home took over an hour. Rain was falling. Then on a road near their home, without warning a car crossed the median and hit Thomas and Carolyn head on at full speed in a collision that peeled back the passenger side of their small sedan. Carolyn died at the scene, and Thomas was airlifted to Harborview Hospital.

A week later, Philip had been consulted to repair Thomas' hip fracture, but on that day as Philip sat at Thomas' bedside, his attention was diverted from the injury to this rich story about life on Adak and the beautiful woman named Carolyn, and the great tragedy this man was suffering.

Thomas' eyes were red, "I have no memory of the accident, and I never had a chance to say goodbye. I wanted to kiss her and tell her thank you, but I could not even attend the funeral. I always imagined we'd meet Him together; Jesus, I mean, kneel together at his feet as unworthy servants who did our best to follow Him all the way."

Philip touched Thomas' shoulder, "I'm sorry for your loss."

Thomas took a stuttering breath as tears dripped from his swollen eyes.

Philip did not move. He remained silent, providing for his patient a form of comfort no drug could offer.

After a long pause, Philip took a tissue and dabbed the corners of Thomas' eyes. Then he asked a question that among strangers would have sounded presumptuous, but in the privacy of a doctor-patient relationship, it seemed to Philip to be appropriate. He asked Thomas if it were stressful being a man of the cloth.

The priest sniffed and raised a swollen eyebrow, cutting his eyes toward Philip, "How do you mean?"

Philip shrugged, "I don't know; it seems like a man in your position would have to deal with so many people with all their problems. But who do you turn to when things like this happen to you? Is there someone I can call?"

The priest closed his eyes. He tugged at the intravenous lines and folded his hands over his lap. Then taking a deep breath, he allowed his body to relax into the bed, "Ah, Lord, sometimes the burden is great. But I've learned the problems of this life are outweighed by our hope in the life to come. I find comfort in that."

Philip looked at his patient. He felt jealous, envious of the faith that had been given to the priest. The manner in which he faced such tragedy reminded Philip of the peace he had witnessed in Lynn during the emergencies they had encountered in Haiti.

Thomas opened his eyes and saw Philip's head drop. He felt compassion for his surgeon. Thomas reached over and touched Philip's forearm, "Doctor, may I ask you a question?"

Philip nodded, "Yes, of course."

"I see you bear a burden of your own. What troubles you?"

Philip felt his face warm with the disquiet of unexpected attention. He sensed the question was more than polite conversation. The inquiry crossed a boundary. Philip treated patients. He did not allow himself to rely on patients for emotional support. But that is what his patient offered: support. Without presumption, the patient extended a gesture of genuine concern. Philip recognized his personal struggles had been exposed.

Philip looked out the window. He paused, then he answered, "Let me just say that today yours is the greater burden. It's an honor to be your doctor. I'm glad they consulted me.

Thomas grinned. He perceived the evasive response but did not press the matter. He simply said, "I see. Well, whatever your burden, however light or however heavy, may the Lord grant you life and peace."

33
Visit to the Church of the Unwelcome

The next day Philip performed surgery on Thomas Palmer. Thomas' injuries were severe, and recovery took several weeks. Every day of the hospitalization, Philip visited Thomas, most days bringing a cup of coffee or a milkshake from the cafeteria as a show of compassion that allowed for extended visits.

In reality Thomas, without knowing it, provided Philip with a refuge, a sanctuary in which Philip felt insulated from the throbbing anxiety of hospital work. More than that, Philip was drawn by Thomas' confidence in the truth of his convictions. Thomas radiated a sense of peace; real peace, not merely the absence of conflict or relief from pain. Thomas displayed confidence in a belief that his life would one day be complete again. He had no delusions of what had been lost. Carolyn was gone. He would never physically be the same again. But he spoke of the future as if he were a child anxious for the next day's adventure. "If it's only for this life that I have hope," Thomas said, "well, you might as well pity me above all." But Philip did not pity Thomas. Quite the opposite, he sought to learn something from him, to understand the source of this man's unflappable response to tragedy upon tragedy.

The secret evaded Philip for some time. Thomas was discharged to a skilled nursing facility in Bellevue. This was good for Thomas. But Philip immediately felt the loss. The worries of work returned, and anxiety over his children compounded in a constricting pressure that daily pressed on his chest. Sitting alone one day in the doctor's lounge, Philip thought of Thomas with his inner source of strength, and this caused him to reminisce about Lynn with her radiant confidence and Luckson with his child-like faith. Philip recognized that these people shared one thing in common. It was something spiritual, something they believed about the unseen world and their place in it.

If asked at that time, Philip would have admitted to becoming open to the idea of God, at best only a theist without a religion, but captivated by the peace he saw in people of faith. Desperate for a personal escape, or at least a diversion from his stress, he began to read about religious practices that seemed to offer people a source of peace. He wanted to know what it was about prayer, or hymns, or meditation, or whatever religious people did that gave them peace. He decided to attend a religious service, albeit only as an observer, reasoning that he might find something helpful to soothe his aching mind. He determined that even if the experience was futile, at the very least he could prove to himself that religion had nothing to offer, and if so, although finding nothing, he would have lost nothing but time.

So, slipping out of the house while his children slept one Sunday morning, Philip walked to a neighborhood church building.

While a man might normally be drawn to the religion of a parent or the denomination of his upbringing, Philip had no formal reason for choosing to walk into a Christian church. His choice of congregation was only a matter of proximity and a process of elimination. He was not Hindu, Buddhist, or Muslim. There were no synagogues nearby. But there was a Christian church near his home, a low-profile brick structure with frosted glass windows and a sign out front that claimed *God Welcomes All*. It was a protestant congregation, though Philip did not know the difference between Catholic, Orthodox, or protestant churches, much less the nuanced differences between denominations. He sought only a sample of the transcendent; a peek through the door to see where people of faith found peace.

Philip entered quietly and took a seat. The auditorium, a dimly lit hall decorated with religious symbols, provided a sanctuary for people sitting in quiet clusters facing forward in a reverent pre-service quiet interrupted only by whispers, sniffles, and the occasional baby's cry. Philip sat to the outside of a padded pew.

A family came in after Philip and asked if he would be willing to move; he had taken their usual seat. Philip moved to the back row.

The service began on time. An older man with round glasses and a face that sagged on either side of his hooked nose rose to the lectern. He wore a vest and contemporary tie, attire which gave him the air of a working professional. He looked out over the congregation until his presence induced a general silence, then he welcomed the people in somber tones, as if thanking them for coming to a wake.

A group of musicians came on stage to lead a number of songs unfamiliar to Philip, tunes full of strange repeated lyrics about chains and mercy and repetitious instructions for God. Philip noticed people around him were mouthing words, but he could not hear them because the sound system was set at a volume that drowned out participation.

Another man came to the lectern and worded a prayer in the baritone cadence of a practiced poet, his supplications loaded with language familiar only to those initiated in the metaphors and idioms of the religion. After the prayer, trays of crackers and wine were distributed in a formal ceremony during which those in attendance were instructed to think about the body and blood of Christ. The meal was clearly designed as a brief mental exercise, a banquet intended to satiate the spirit but not the stomach. In fact, the morsels of bread and the miniscule cup of drink would not have satisfied a mouse, but those around Philip dutifully took the elements with utmost seriousness, sitting solemnly with closed eyes, savoring crumbs. Unfamiliar with the ritual and unclear about how to act, Philip passed the tray without participating and remained seated when those around him stood for a song that followed.

The central focus of the service was a sermon, delivered by a rotund middle-aged gentleman in a dark suit who had an oily face and out-of-date tie that fell over the curve of his belly. He read a biblical passage and after a personal story, he launched into an exegetical scavenger hunt, dropping briefly into verses from various books of the Bible which, though unrelated in context, when viewed in a particular order formed a sort of geometric proof of God's three-dimensional character. The message had little if any relevance to life in Seattle. If it were of any consequence to the meaning of life at all, that meaning was lost on Philip, whose mind wandered back to his personal worries. Even the sanctuary of a church failed to provide a refuge from his fears.

After the sermon, the minister made a general plea for contributions, exhorting his congregants to be generous; it sounded to Philip as though they thought that without the ongoing investment of his human servants the creator of the universe would otherwise have trouble keeping up with the mortgage.

Then the service ended. Thus, the people having been educated and exhorted to avoid temptations or go astray made their way out of the auditorium. Philip was not so moved. He sat for a moment, alone, disappointed, on a back pew wondering why he had come. Had he known church history, he would have recognized a clear divide between what he had expected and what he witnessed, the scandal lost on those leading the service. In fact, during his ministry, Jesus the Christ, whose name was evoked repeatedly in breathy expressions throughout the venerable hour, did not speak approvingly of much of what Philip witnessed during his visit to the church. It had not occurred to any of them that the cross depicted in spotlights on the front wall of the auditorium was in reality the instrument of execution upon which Jesus had been crucified for preaching *against* many of the very practices just displayed. Jesus challenged the privileged to give up seats of honor, to welcome the stranger, to pray in private in clear language, avoiding the blasphemous temptation to babble under the false presumption that the living God is impressed by lofty language. Jesus invited worshipers who did not seek him in temples, or pursue him through empty ritual, but who sought him in spirit and in truth. He did not ask for money but instructed his followers to sell their possessions and give to the poor. And most important to Philip, it was Jesus who said, "Do not be anxious about your life, what you will eat or what you will drink nor about your body, what you will put on...for your Father in heaven knows you need all this...Therefore do not worry about tomorrow, for tomorrow will worry about itself." That is the message Philip needed most, but he did not hear it that day. Not in church.

He stood and walked toward the exit, intending not to speak to anyone. But an elderly woman sitting in the foyer of the church caught Philip's eye. She was staring at him, looking up at Philip from her wheelchair with eyes that suggested familiarity. Philip did not know the woman, but she looked at him as if she knew him, like a grandmother recognizing the face of a grown child.

Philip stepped over to the woman and reached down to take her bent hand in his. He adjusted his grip to accom-

modate her gnarled joints, fingers deviated from rheuma-
tism, "Good morning, ma'am."

The woman held his hand and in a broken voice said,
"Thank you for coming."

"Thank you; you are very kind."

The woman did not let go of Philip's hands, awkwardly
holding him in her grasp, "My name is Gladys Walters.
Most people call me Mimi."

"It is good to meet you, Gladys."

Gladys patted Philip's hands. She noticed they were otherwise empty, "You do not have a Bible?"

"No, ma'am, it is not a book I've had the chance to read."

Gladys reached into her bag and lifted a black bonded
book with a faded imprint. She shook the book to extract
folded papers from under its covers and then handed it to
Philip, "You take this one."

"No, I can't. I appreciate your kindness, but I cannot
take your Bible. I'm sure it is a personal item. I will pick
one up at the book store."

Gladys pushed the Bible firmly into Philip's hand, then
she pulled him close to her with a grip unusually strong
for an elderly woman, "Do not tell lies; you are standing in
a church."

34
A Bible Story

Several days later, Philip sat alone at his kitchen table nibbling rewarmed remnants of takeout food. He was still wearing scrubs, too exhausted after an extended day in the operating room to change his clothes. On his right, under a pile of mail and magazines, he saw the Bible, his gift from Gladys Walters, the elderly woman he had met at church.

Philip grinned at the irony of an ancient religious manuscript sitting on his table under a pile of modern magazines and medical journals. It stimulated a memory. Philip recalled sitting at the dinner table as a boy. He could smell his mother's casserole and picture her sitting silently with her head lowered. He remembered his father sitting somber and mute at the other end of the table. His father would wait, and Philip was expected to wait as well. In childlike honesty, Philip remembered asking his father why his mother closed her eyes for a moment before the meal. His father glanced at his mother, a signal that this was a tense subject, something they argued about between themselves in private. Philip could still feel the tension, and he could hear his father's words again, as clearly in his mind as he had heard them as a child, "People who pray close their eyes to reality."

Philip chuckled to himself. *What would dad say about a Bible on my table? Would he be embarrassed that a son of his sat in a church and accepted the parting favor of an old woman? Would he understand the psychological burden that led him to question whether religion had something to offer? What if dad's concerns were not so much that reli-*

gion was useless? What if he thought it was dangerous, too dangerous for a young boy to dabble?

Old memories competed with these new questions until Philip, curious, pulled the old book toward himself.

For a moment he held the Bible unopened, rubbing his fingers over the stippled leather to make out the worn embossed words on the cover, *Holy Bible*. It had the feel of an old textbook, heavy and well used. The corners were tattered. The once gilded pages had been browned by the oil of fingers flipping through its pages.

Philip looked around the empty kitchen. He was about to do something he once thought forbidden, and though alone, he felt the need to make sure no one was watching.

Then Philip opened the cover to the first page of the first chapter of the first book, appropriately called Genesis, the beginning. What he read surprised him. Philip was expecting lofty language, lists of rules, and fanciful stories about celestial beings floating about as devout men who, ignorant themselves of the laws of nature, offered sacrifices and incantations to appease a deity. To his surprise, what he read sounded more like a statement of a technical fact, something intended to be considered and, if necessary, verified, not just believed. It said, "In the beginning, God created the heavens and the earth."

What followed reminded Philip of an abstract at the beginning of a journal article. The Bible provided a concise description of how life began. He noticed the order of origins fell suspiciously in line with what he understood to be true, yet, rather than time and chance, the author inserted a divine being, and thereby introduced the specter of purpose behind the cosmos.

Philip read late into the night. He felt like an archeologist uncovering treasure with each lifted page.

Most nights for several months, Philip repeated the same routine. He stumbled in late, grabbed a quick bite and sat down to read.

Philip was surprised by a callous realism he found in the Bible. The trajectory of the stories seemed downward, at times descending deep into the worst of human depravity. This was alarming to Philip. The stories were not about good people. The subjects were scandalous, people unfit for inclusion in such a holy book. For the most part, the characters were murderous, sexually oppressive men, sometimes incestuous and ever thirsty for blood. Philip thought, *Is this book really a legitimate foundation for morality?*

As he read, however, he became less offended and more intrigued. The Bible read like a history book, not a book of epic mythological battles or cosmological events. People were not described in platitudes as if the Bible were merely a spiritual eulogy written to gloss over the more unsavory aspects of a person's life. The Bible was different. It described ancient events in actual places with candid honesty, boldly displaying the corrosive character of men and women. Philip was struck by the adult nature of many of the stories. Noah's drunken stupor. Abraham and Jacob's sexual surrogacy. The adulterous affair of David and Bathsheba. The oppression of slavery. The line of tyrannous kings. The clash of world empires leaving entire cultures in ruin. Still, there was a sense that the writers knew that this is not the way things were meant to be.

The reading was not easy. At times Philip struggled with the cultural and historical divide that made events seem foreign or at times strange. But Philip was struck by the fact that though here and there a story was clearly allegorical, the vast majority of events were written as actual historical events, some of them providing the details of cultural conflicts reverberating into modern times. There were battles and coronations, weddings and migrations, feasts and famines, all occurring in geographical locations he could still find on a map.

Philip caught himself reading the poetry aloud. In the recorded verse of ancient writers, he found words that reflected his own feelings. Though the circumstances were far different, he read how powerful men described their own state of mind when in awe or distress, in anger or fear, in hope or disbelief, or in expressing faith, joy, desire, or their longing to know God. Not just know about him; these people sought to know him. And they repeatedly spoke of a day when he, this living God, would come to make the world right again. For some, this was spoken as a warning, for others it appeared to be a message of hope. The writers seemed to think the world was on the verge of an invasion, not of aliens, but of its maker.

It was a good story. And if Philip were not ready to believe its religious precepts, he had at least come to appreciate that the Bible, at the very least, was to be taken seriously as a historical document.

But any appreciation for the Bible as a work of historical literature gave way to skepticism when he began to read the New Testament. At one point he came across a passage that made him throw the Bible down. Not just place it neatly on a shelf. Philip threw the old book against a wall. With a thud, it fell into a corner. What he read was more than unbelievable, it was an offense to any sane person. And for several days the crumpled book lay only in the shadows.

But it was too late; the story had already captured Philip's mind. The passage that bothered him was the healing of a paralyzed man, a paraplegic as far as Philip could discern, who was lying by a pool called Bethesda in Jerusalem. The man had been crippled for thirty-eight years, whether from some spinal cord injury or infection the text did not say. Philip thought of his own patients, some of whom in one tragic moment lost the ability to walk. The gunshot wound victim with a transected cord. The helicopter pilot with a blowout fracture of the thoracic spine. The college girl with transverse myelitis. Then he thought of Rose-Marie, her deep black eyes looking up from her bed, reaching for someone to lift her and help her walk. This Biblical narrative was no random story. This man had a real-life problem. He represented every person who has ever lost the ability to walk or jump or run. This man only wanted to walk again. Philip sat thinking of neurosurgeons he knew who were working on solutions to this very problem: how to restore the mobility of damaged people. They knew it was possible for nerves to grow back; finding how to make this happen remained the mystery.

Philip initially read the story with the anticipation of someone who expected to see the mercy of Jesus. Surely, he would give the man food or money. Or perhaps he would lift the man to a standing position and help him into the pool.

But to Philip, it appeared that Jesus *did* nothing. He only spoke to the man. And what he said was offensive: *Take up your mat and walk.*

Then the man stood up and walked. This was unbelievable. If this had really happened, it must have been a staged healing, or the man had only had some psychosomatic disorder, a mental block broken by the words Jesus spoke. But the writer did not leave room for such speculation. The implication was clear. Jesus had healed the man, not by what he had done, but by what he had said.

Philip shut the cover and threw the Bible against the wall. He was a trauma surgeon. Paralyzed people do not get up and walk. A man with a transected spinal cord does not just stand up and ambulate. In an instant, motor nerves would have to be generated. Muscle cells would have to be restored in both mass and function. Pathways from the frontal cortex to the motor strip and down the spinal cord, unused for nearly four decades would have to be realigned and retrained. It takes a child over a year to learn this. A grown man who has not stood for that long cannot just take up a mat and walk. That cannot happen.

Philip did not pick up the Bible again for several weeks. But he couldn't get the images and words out of his mind. He had spent a career becoming skilled at making it possible for the lame to walk. Then, there in the pages of a Bible, he read of a man who, years ahead of his time, appeared in the operating theater of history and with only a word made a preoperative assessment, performed a complex multi-step procedure and then skipped the entire rehabilitation process. Did anybody seriously believe this was possible?

Philip's curiosity eventually outweighed his skepticism, and he returned to the book, slowly at first, then with increasing momentum each evening, drawn further into the story by other incredible events. Water turned to wine. Bread created on the spot. Blind men given sight. A violent storm calmed. A man walking on water. Skin infections healed. A girl woken from a dead sleep as easily as if she woke from anesthesia, a dead boy brought back to life and given back to his mother, and Lazarus hopping from a tomb after being brought back to life. Then Jesus himself rose from the dead.

Philip found himself struck by a single thought. If any of this were true, a man would have to have control of the entire cosmos—every cell, every element, every possibility within his control, from the first moment of the big bang until the present. This claim was unbelievable; not merely amazing, it was unworthy of belief—too incredible to be true, worthy of myth, perhaps, or allegory, or at least stories with a moral. But the events attributed to this peasant-born preacher defied reality. Yet one nagging thought would not let Philip just walk away: *What if it were true?*

So, one afternoon Philip took off work early and crossed Lake Washington on I-90 to visit a skilled nursing facility in Bellevue. He walked up to the nurse's station and asked, "Excuse me, I'm looking for a Thomas Palmer. Can you point me toward his room?"

The nurse looked over the top of her glasses, "Are you family?"

"No, I'm his surgeon, Doctor Scott from Seattle."

That afternoon, and about once a week for several months, Philip made the drive to visit Thomas under the pretense of checking on his patient's recovery. He was ashamed to admit the real reason for making the trips, but Thomas knew. Ever attuned to a prodigal's return, Thomas opened the way for Philip and provided a safe place to question openly what he was reading.

It was Thomas who introduced Philip to a line in the Gospel of John, "Jesus did more, but these were written that you might believe that Jesus is the Christ, the son of God, and that by believing you may have life in his name."

The distressing question for Philip was simple: *what if it did happen?* What if a man could restore a limb or raise the dead or silence a storm? This would require the power of God himself.

Thomas reminded Philip of the first line he read in the Bible, "In the beginning, God created the heavens and the earth. Did you recognize that John begins his gospel with the same words? You see his point? These miracles were not mere magic tricks, conjured for entertainment. These were the acts of a being who had control of the universe from the moment the first elements exploded into existence, each miracle a replication of the same act of creation. He controlled the waters. With only a word, he created plants and fish. And in a personal creative act, he formed humankind and breathed into the first human being the breath of life. Only God can do that."

Thomas gave Philip much to think about, perhaps too much. Philip's career, indeed his reputation, was at risk of being destroyed.

35

Prospect of Promotion

About a year later, Philip sat in a plush leather chair across the room from a large desk in a spacious office he once desired for his own. A nameplate on the desk still read, Michael Henske, MD Chairman. A walnut coat rack with ivory knobbed brass hooks stood behind the door. Books were placed in tidy rows on hardwood shelves, and framed honors were displayed on the wall, illuminated by small overhead track lights. Light beamed through the plate-glass windows onto the tall, tufted chair behind the desk.

Philip looked at his watch. He had been brought into the room twenty minutes earlier, summoned for a meeting with Doctor Henske, his boss, the chairman of the Department of Orthopedics.

Michael Henske came into the office in a breathless rush, "Forgive my tardy arrival, Philip. I think you'll find your wait is worth it. I have good news."

Philip stood to shake hands with the chairman, "No worries. My time is yours."

Michael gave Philip a firm handshake, clasping the forearm with the other hand in a way that made the reception seem more formal. Then he chuckled and hung his sports coat over a hook on the rack, pulling an envelope from the inner pocket. "You say your *time* is mine? Oh, how the opposite could be true. If all goes well, I hope to soon announce that my *job* is yours."

Philip lowered himself back into the chair keeping his eyes on Doctor Henske as he tried to absorb the meaning of his message, "What exactly are you saying?"

As Doctor Henske sat behind his desk, he laid the envelope down and leaned forward on his clasped hands, "Phil, you are one of the most valuable surgeons in this program. It is no secret that you've ruffled a few feathers along the way; but in spite of your rash manners, you've remained my first choice as a successor. The provost has questioned my judgment. He does not like you. He doesn't think you have what it takes to run this department. He thinks of you as a cocky fighter pilot in an organization that needs the steady hand of a general."

"And what do you think?"

"I know what you're capable of doing. I've watched you mature from the firecracker student who pushed your way past older residents so you could assist in surgeries while your colleagues had to wait their turns. Yes, I remember your drive. And now I see you as a seasoned surgeon, with no less ambition, but perhaps with the experience to lead a program through the challenges of fiscally lean times."

"But the Provost is of another opinion?"

"Well, he was."

"Was?"

"I made a recommendation—a threat, actually."

"What have you done?"

"We were in a meeting with the president and several regents when the Provost grumbled about your lack of— what did he call it? Your 'abysmal dearth of experience in tactful governance,' I think that was his phrase. I asked him to give specifics as to whom he had spoken with to come to this conclusion. He pulled out a stack of complaints saying, 'I have heard from the patients. From their perspective, he is a threat to the reputation of everything for which this university stands.'"

Philip interrupted, "You know Michael, over the years I've come to see that he's probably right. I'm not proud of the doctor my patients know."

The chairman held up his hand, "Stop right there; you speak too soon. I explained how each complaint, every one of them, resulted from decisive action taken by you to save a life. I told them, 'This man is a decisive leader, a man trusted for making life-and-death decisions when seconds count.'"

Philip smiled, "You told him that?"

"That and more. I got carried away, actually. It was a chance to speak my mind at a moment I had nothing to lose. I told the committee that unless they interviewed the people with whom you work, the people you would be leading, then none of them had any right to claim an opinion on the matter."

Philip looked at his boss. He had always admired Doctor Henske for his political deftness, and the thought of his pleading his case before a powerful body made him all the more respectable. Philip shrugged, "I don't know what to say. Thank you for the vote of confidence. Did they kick you out?"

"On the contrary, they followed my advice. They interviewed the staff. Over the last several months they contacted your colleagues: nurses; residents; fellow surgeons; even the heads of other departments."

"All behind my back? I had no idea."

"So, you don't know about the petition?"

"What are talking about?"

Doctor Henske held out the envelope, "Take a look. One of your admirers, the chairwoman from a sister department, was interviewed by a member of the committee, and she took it upon herself to circulate this petition in support of your confirmation."

Philip unfolded the letter. It was a simple typed letter on thick paper worn at the creases from having been opened and closed as it passed through many hands. The one paragraph statement simply read:

We the undersigned, having worked directly with and for Philip Scott, MD, do together with pleasure and without reservation recommend him to you for the position of Chairman of the Orthopedics and Sports Medicine Department of the University. His knowledge of medicine and commitment to this University are surpassed only by his unwavering dedication to the wellbeing of his patients and to the professional development of his colleagues, the trust of whom he has earned from decades of solid service.

Below the passage was a list of names, about a hundred signatures organized in imperfect columns written large and small, in black or blue ink.

The first name on the list signed in sweeping conspicuous letters was that of Heidi Kapoor, MD, the author of the document.

Philip scanned the list of other names, each person bringing to his mind a different memory, a special case, a different reason to be thankful for the people with whom he had been privileged to work.

Philip recognized the signatures of Connor and Aryanna Wayman, now married. The signature of Sam Verity, who, though in solo practice on the East Coast, had signed the letter. He saw the signature of his colleague, Anderson Hu, and Paulita "Pauley" Sanders, who had become one of the program's orthopedic residents. All of these were followed by columns of other names including operating room nurses, anesthesiologists, and even his office staff at his orthopedic clinic.

As his eyes fell to the last name, he stopped and looked up at Doctor Henske, startled by what he saw, "Is this real?"

"Phil, you need to know two things. First, that letter is absolutely authentic. And second, I had nothing to do with it. It was handed to me about thirty minutes ago by the Dean. He had received it from the Provost."

Philip looked back down at the letter. At the bottom of the last column, signed in large rounded letters was the final name, *Lynn Sable, Ph.D., RN.*

Philip shook his head, "I'm, uh—overwhelmed. I don't know what to say. Some of these people live so far away. I haven't seen some of them for years."

Doctor Henske nodded, "I was told the letter has been circulated by certified mail, even to people who knew you overseas. Apparently, you are a world celebrity. Who knew?"

Then Doctor Henske walked over to his coat, still hanging on the rack. He reached into the pocket and removed a photograph, "And, I almost forgot. This photo was sent back with the letter from one of the signers. I recognize you and a few of our former residents in the picture. Do you recognize the place?"

Philip took the picture. He remembered the moment but from a different vantage. In the scene, Philip was standing next to Lynn, Sam, Connor, and Aryanna in front of a palm tree on a beach. In front of them were Luckson and Victor holding Pauley, laughing, in their arms. Everyone in the photo was smiling. The sight elicited a sudden rush of joy in Philip; reflexively he smiled, "That is a picture of the team of students I took to Haiti a few years ago."

The Chairman leaned over and looked closer, "The trip the University sponsored?"

"Yes. You remember these residents who went. The lady next to me is Lynn Sable, the nurse who worked with us at the hospital in Milot."

Philip flipped the photo over. On the back was a date and a phrase, "Quand ils ont trouvé des coquillages beau la plage."

The chairman asked, "What do the words mean?"

Philip shrugged, "I don't know; it looks French."

Henske typed the words into a translation site on his computer. He looked back at Philip, "It means 'When they found beautiful shells by the sea.' Does that mean something to you?"

"It means more than I can explain. It's a good memory."

Then Henske sat on the corner of his desk, resting his arm over his leg. It was his predictable posture, his tell when he was about to pitch an idea, "I have the authority to make you an offer, Phil. My job is yours starting in six months if you accept. I'll stay on for a three-month transition after that, but I doubt you'll need the help. You were made for this. What do you say?"

Phil looked down at the picture. Seeing Lynn's smile resurrected a strange feeling of pride in Philip, not egotistical vanity, but satisfaction with his work. He briefly remembered what it was like to feel successful by a different standard. That small rectangular photo in his hands was worth more to Philip at that moment than a hundred honors hanging on a lit wall. Looking into the eyes of the past, the present offer seemed suddenly small. He had dreamed of Doctor Henske's offer for decades. The announcement of a new chairman. The exciting handshake of acceptance. The party. Move-in day at the new office. The nameplate. High-powered meetings with his medical staff. But instead of feeling elated, he felt numb, as if he were waking from an exhilarating dream to find the dream fading so that what made the dream exciting was not altogether clear. Philip looked at Doctor Henske, "May I have some time to think about it? Your offer's great. I have to tell you that I have worked toward this moment my entire adult life. But, now that the opportunity arrives, I'm just not sure."

"Think about it, Phil. I have not counted them, but there is quite a list of people there who think you are the right man for the job."

36

A Letter from Tabitha

A few days later Philip walked into his house and threw mail onto the coffee table.

He first grabbed a drink and then sat down on his couch, leaning forward to sort the mail. He noticed a small envelope with a hand-written address; it was postmarked from Cap-Haitien, Haiti. Philip dug his finger behind the fold of the envelope ripping it open.

The letter was from Tabitha, written in pencil on lined paper:

Dear Doctor Scott,

I am thanking the Lord day and night for your letter and generous gift. Since you came to visit Lakay Jezu you know we have many challenges. Your letter last month made the children happy because they know you have not forgotten them. We used your money to buy rice and beans, a walker for Francine Antoine, and a brace for Rodney Mompremier. The children know that your gift makes them have hope. Not a hope in money. But hope that they are not forgotten. You give the children yourself, and they will always remember you. We have tears in our eyes to this day because Rose-Marie was with us for only a short time. But she will be in our hearts always as I know she is in yours. There is a boy here named Fred Joel. You

*remember him because he ate with you on your vis-
it to us so many years ago. He say a prayer for you
every night that you will be well and have good
health to take care of many people. When you come
to Haiti, you are always welcome at Lakay Jezu.*

Yours in humble service,
Tabitha

Philip returned the letter to the envelope. The message
gave him an uneasy feeling. He had corresponded with
Tabitha several times over the years, sending donations,
and each time she responded with an accounting of how
the money was spent adding some emotional story about
one child or another. Philip appreciated knowing his money was going to something worthwhile, but he had not become comfortable with her style of writing. Tabitha's blatant religious tone, her play on emotion, and the 'thank
you' which had all the appearances of a veiled request for
more money reminded Philip of manipulative marketing
tactics used by charities of questionable reputation.

Philip was about to toss the letter away when he unfolded it to read the words a second time. And when he read
the letter again, he could not find one word in which
Tabitha had actually asked for anything more. She said
thank you; she gave an accounting; she offered condo-
lences, and she mentioned an admirer. Then the letter
ended, not with a solicitation but with an invitation. Philip
stared at the words, written in meticulously straight lines.
The thought of a woman living in a remote, impoverished
village taking the time to handwrite such a letter made
Philip feel suddenly selfish; this was not an electronic note
or form letter, sent and forgotten in a matter of seconds.
This letter had been written weeks before and traveled
thousands of miles. Philip thought about the distance

Tabitha had to travel just to get the letter to a mail carrier. She lived hours from anyone who could get mail on an airplane to the United States. And she acknowledged that Rose-Marie's death still hurt him deeply. Philip wondered if it was possible that a woman could have no other intent than to provide comfort to a man she barely knew. Then the memory of the little boy sitting in his lap flooded back, dark eyes staring up as they shared food. Philip had never put a name to the memory; now he knew. Philip wondered how Tabitha could have remembered that moment and why she would think to include such a detail.

Philip looked across the room at his mantle. He pondered two items displayed with pride on the otherwise bare shelf. The first item was a conch shell, Luckson's gift with its pearly aperture turned upward, and the second a framed note pressed under glass. The creased paper in the frame was the note from Heidi Kapoor outspread to exhibit her written supplication, "May your heart be broken by that which breaks the heart of God."

Philip stared at the items and allowed his mind to drift back to events in Haiti that had changed the course of his life. He thought about dancing with Rose-Marie, sharing crackers with Luckson, and walking along the beach with Lynn at sunset. He remembered seeing his residents work long hours without complaint.

Philip felt a strange tension between his old dreams and a new desire. He had been offered an incredible job, recognition, and a top spot in his department. But that offer was no longer attractive. It was as if the sun had set on a self-centered dream, and now he waited in a restless nocturnal repose. He was unclear about what would come next. His dreams had changed. All at once he valued something different than the job being offered. He had stumbled on a different prize, a treasure hidden in a field.

There upon the mantle, as if looking at a horizon, he caught the rising glow of a new ambition.

Philip walked to the mantle and took the frame into his hands, thinking about people he now counted as friends, people he had come to care about though they lived a world away. He pressed the glass out of the frame and removed the note, placing it face down on the mantle. On the back of the note he had already written a list of names in a small script:

Rose-Marie Sanguine
Lynn Sable
Luckson St. Marc
Victor Santile
Tabitha Justinian
Thomas Palmer

To these, Philip added a name, *Fred Joel*. Then he placed the note in the frame and displayed it on the mantle.

He sat back on his couch and for several minutes stared at the note. The words of Heidi Kapoor echoed in his mind. She alone seemed to understand the distress he had experienced in Haiti which, rather than subside, had been amplified upon his return to the United States. She had told Philip the feelings would wane but not really go away until he returned to Haiti or a similar location. "You did not go on a vacation," she had said to Philip, "You traveled to another world, and for a time you got to play the role of a man you have always longed to be. You will never rest until you find that man again."

Philip felt like a prehistoric person strangely drawn to the warmth of a fire despite having been burned by its flames. He had been emotionally burned in Haiti. The scars, though hidden from view, remained tense and painful under the sterile dressing of Philip's professional

280

life. He longed for a salve to ease the sting of memories of his own failure. He could still hear the ring of a shovel's final slap upon the dirt of Rose-Marie's grave. Yet he felt the need to go back.

Something of his heart remained under the rubble in Haiti. But the painful memories were mixed with warm memories of a time with people who found satisfaction in a different life, a life of service. Philip had not corresponded with Lynn or Victor over the years, only with Tabitha. The last memory he had of Lynn was her moist, red eyes at his departure from the airport. But something about seeing her signature and the inscribed photo made him long to see her again.

Philip reached for his cell phone and dialed his ex-wife, "Mandy, I'm sorry to be calling so late, but I need your help. I'm thinking of going back to Haiti."

37

Homecoming in Haiti

Two weeks later, Philip looked down from the plane as the pilot descended through billowing clouds over the northern coast of Haiti. He saw the Citadel in the distance and familiar roads coming in view as the aircraft turned toward the runway in Cap-Haitien.

The decision to return to Haiti had been spontaneous, not thought-out or planned. Philip was taking Heidi's advice, returning to the site, but he had not fully considered the ripple effect of his decision.

Chairman Henske, who had been supportive, almost pushy about the first trip to Haiti, threatened administrative discipline when Philip gave short notice of his decision to return. Sparing no coercive lever, he even insinuated he might retract the offer of promotion to the chairmanship. He backed off when Philip promised to resign if pushed.

Colleagues at the hospital were equally annoyed about having to cover extra shifts for Philip, but Philip was quick to remind them of their own brazen requests for leave which had required him to cover for them over the years.

Amanda was angry about the decision, though perhaps less than before. The argument this time was brief: Philip asked if he could take Max and Alexa. Amanda threatened legal action if he did. Philip was not being provocative; he was serious. He tried to convince Amanda that it would be good for their teenage children to see the challenges faced by the developing world, but she would have nothing to do with even the thought of her children leaving the country. So, he let it go.

But Amanda recognized something different about Philip. There was a seriousness in his voice, sadness she had not perceived in a long time. She knew the signs. He was bearing a heavy psychological burden. Amanda did not demand payment for watching the children. Instead, she prodded for specifics about what was on his mind, why he wanted to return. Philip told her about the children at Lakay Jezu and Tabitha with whom he had been corresponding. Amanda listened and then offered to make a donation, "May I send something for the children?"

Anderson Hu was sympathetic to Philip's need to return to Haiti. He dropped Philip off at the Sea-Tac airport and sent an email to a friend in a mission organization who had contact with Victor Santile. But by the time Philip boarded his plane in Florida to fly to Haiti, Anderson had not heard whether his message had made it through.

As the plane taxied up to the terminal in Cap-Haitien, Philip scanned the fence line looking for familiar faces in the crowd or the white truck that would let him know Victor had come. He saw no one he knew.

Philip entered the terminal alone. He took his place in line behind a crowd of other Americans. The group in line in front of him wore garish, brightly colored matching shirts with blatant religious messages. They were yelling to each other about new sights and smells, laughing without any regard to the disparaging way their behavior insulted the citizens of the country of which they were guests.

Philip greeted a stoic Haitian official sitting behind a wooden counter; without a word, she stamped his passport and pointed him toward the crowd waiting for baggage.

Philip felt the room reverberating in the clamor of people searching for luggage. The noise tightened around his head in a band, causing his temples to ache. He reached into his backpack, searching for some medication. He could find none and chastised himself for forgetting to pack it.

The smell of sweat hung in the humid air around Philip. He found his luggage in a pile of bags and boxes being thrown through an open window at one end of the terminal. Philip grabbed his large duffel and an elongated plastic tub; he shuffled these items across the dusty terminal floor.

Philip lifted his items onto the customs table. An overweight man dressed in official uniform with a shirt stretched over the bulge of his fat belly opened the tub and pulled out a walker with larger than normal wheels, "Are you a doctor?"

"Yes, sir."

"You have medical supplies?"

"These are gifts—for friends of mine."

"Come with me."

Philip followed the man into a small customs office. He felt pulsations in his chest and pounding behind his eyes. He was tired. The thought of being extorted for money under the loose guise of taxation made his head throb more.

The official punched numbers onto an old calculator. He turned the calculator around revealing the total as he said, "Two hundred in U.S. for the tax."

Philip leaned forward placing both hands resolutely on the desk; he spoke with a firmness of one taking charge of the encounter, "My items are gifts; they are not for sale. They should not be taxed."

"I'm sorry, Monsieur. It is the law."

Philip smiled. He reached into his pocket and pulled out a fifty-dollar bill and slid it across the table, "Here, I brought a gift for you too. Is it enough?"

The man studied Philip. Then he placed the bill in his front pocket and smiled waving Philip out of the room, "It is enough, my friend. You may go."

When Philip walked out of the office, he saw two thin men wearing the red shirts of hired couriers carrying his things toward the door. He ran up to them and grabbed one by the shoulder, "Excuse me; those are mine."

One man turned, still holding the tub, "You are Dokte' Scott?"

"Yes, I am."

The man motioned with his head toward the doorway, "The lady is waiting for you."

There, just beyond the doorframe stood Lynn, her arms held behind her back. The sun fell on her shoulders as if heaven itself were illuminating the place where she stood. The moment he saw her, she rose onto her toes and gave him a thin, closed-mouth grin.

When Philip saw Lynn, his headache instantly disappeared, and his heart skipped a beat. He felt weak, hesitant to follow his instinct to run to her, uncertain if she were holding back a smile or restraining her temper. He walked up to her slowly.

Philip lowered his backpack to the floor, "Hello, Lynn."

Lynn broke into a full smile and threw her arms around Philip. Then she pulled back and kissed him on both cheeks, "Oh, Philip. You returned. I did not believe them, but it is true. You came back."

Philip touched Lynn's face, "I began to question if I ever left. My mind has been here since the day I departed. How did you know I was coming?"

Lynn turned and pointed to the back of a gravel lot across from the terminal, "Your friends gave you away."

Philip looked. He saw Victor with his arms crossed standing in front of the door of the white truck. Luckson, taller and even lankier, hung off the back helping the porters raise luggage onto the covered bed. The Americans with the bright shirts were climbing into the back of the truck.

Philip asked, "That group is with you?"

Lynn shook her head, "No. They are students from some university. Victor is just giving them a ride to the guest house, I think."

Philip walked to the truck, Lynn at his side.

When Luckson saw them approaching, he leapt to the ground and ran up to them, "Dokte' Scott, d-d-do you re-member m-m-me."

Philip laughed. He knelt down and pulled a gift from his backpack, a Seattle Mariners baseball cap. He placed the cap on Luckson's head, "How could I forget the amazing Luckson? Of course, I remember you. In fact, I told a friend of mine about you, and he sent you a hat. See, he signed it under the bill. He is one of the Mariners."

Luckson took off the hat and looked at the signature, "What's a Mariner?"

Philip felt his face flush. Should he explain that a mariner is a kind of sailor? It had not occurred to him that Luckson would not know about baseball. He looked to Lynn for help, but she shrugged. At a loss as to how to ex-plain the sport, Philip laughed at himself and raised both arms, "Well, Luckson, maybe next time I'll bring the ball and glove. I bet you could make us a fine bat."

Philip climbed into the back of the truck with Lynn.

Pulling away from the airport onto the congested streets of Cap-Haitien, the new group commented on the sights, sounds, and smells of Haiti. They pulled out cameras, shooting photos of everything as if they were riding a tour bus.

Philip watched the young people, laughing, yelling, and making sarcastic statements. His forehead began to pulse, and his neck became hot. But he sat silent. Victor drove the group to a guest house outside of Cap-Haitien, and Philip remained quiet until the truck came to a stop in front of the accommodations.

Then Philip looked at the group, "May I say something?"

One of the young men shouted, "Hey, guys listen up."

Philip looked around the truck at the young people, each of them eager for some adventure, driven by who knows what. Then he said, "Before you get out of this truck, you should think about how you would feel if someone came to your house and made remarks about the way you smell or the way you look. You are about to meet people who have lost everything. Nothing remains but their dignity; do not take that from them. Every time you pull out that camera, think about what *you* look like. Every time you open your mouth, hear your words in the ears of your hosts."

Lynn reached over and squeezed Philip's thigh, a sign to constrain his rising temper.

As Philip felt Lynn holding his leg down firmly, he looked at her and took a deep breath. "Forgive me. None of you know me, and I do not know you. I understand you are excited. Perhaps you are a bit nervous, but please respect the fact that some of us have friends here. Somewhere in those mountains around us once lived a special little girl; her death broke my heart. I predict someone here will break your heart as well. Do not mock them or belittle their home. Instead, treasure every moment you have to get to know the beautiful people you are about to meet. One of them may change your life."

38

Back to Surgery and Lakay Jezu

Philip found Milot to be a different town than he remembered. Three years had passed. The signs of disaster had been dismantled, and Milot had been reshaped and to some extent eroded by the waves of humanitarian aid that brought new technology and higher standards of living. Milot blossomed into a new community with an old façade. The streets remained congested but with the faces of Haitian people, not foreigners. The flow of people and vehicles up and down the main street was no longer the rush of emergency traffic, just the routine ebb and flow of Haitian life. Local people had repurposed relief tents and shipping containers into storage buildings. One of the shipping containers had been converted into a prosthetics lab in which new limbs were constructed and maintained for the many amputees still living in the region. With donations toward a robust building project, the hospital had expanded to accommodate over one hundred and twenty inpatients, down from the over four hundred patients in the weeks following the earthquake, but up from the seventy beds in the pre-earthquake facility.

Thousands of patients still cycled through the hospital clinics. The hospital staff had acquired equipment for testing, monitoring, and treating patients in ways that mirrored the countries from which visiting medical professionals had come. Volunteer surgical teams continued to come for week-long visits, performing procedures and interacting with the Haitian professional community. The Haitian doctors and nurses, those individuals serving their own friends, neighbors, and family members, sought to work with these visiting doctors and nurses to keep up with the standards expected of medical professionals in a modern world.

Philip jumped back into the work. It had been several weeks since an orthopedist had visited the hospital, and the Haitian surgeons were ready to scrub in with Philip, to learn from him, and to gain confidence in making the kind of decisions that save lives and limbs. Philip did not disappoint them. Before the sun set, he had performed three surgeries.

During one of the procedures, Lynn walked into the operating room to find Philip standing beside a Haitian surgeon, both of them leaning over the body of a patient, their blue gowns illuminated by the overhead procedure lamps. Philip had his hands on the hands of his colleague. Though neither could speak each other's language, Philip had breached the language barrier by taking the hands of his colleague. Like a teacher guiding a student through the motions, Philip directed his Haitian friend through the steps required to fix a fractured bone.

As Lynn stood watching from the doorway, she wiped her eyes and covered her mouth to prevent her reaction from becoming audible. The man before her had changed. She remembered the bitter, self-absorbed surgeon who had arrived three years ago, the man who lacked the tough skin of people who work in the rough and remote hospitals of the world, the man who lashed out in the operating room, who was never satisfied with instruments or the skill level of his assistants. She knew his behavior was not a character flaw; it was a protective mechanism, a reflex, the guarded impulse of a person who feared failure. But as Lynn watched Philip's working with his Haitian colleague, it occurred to her that the man before her, the real Philip Scott had broken free of his cocoon.

Lynn cleared her throat. When the two surgeons looked up, she said, "Doctor Scott, Victor says he is taking a load of rice and beans to Tabitha's in the morning. Would you like to go?"

Philip nodded, his voice muffled by the surgical mask, "Absolutely. Can he pick me up at the guest house? I have items for the children. The tub is a bit heavy."

The next day around noon, the white truck bounced along the mountain roads toward Lakay Jezu. Philip sat with Lynn in the cab as Victor navigated the dirt ruts.

Luckson sat in the back, the wind in his satisfied face, his new cap turned around to prevent it from being blown off.

When they arrived at the river, a gaggle of children came splashing through its shallow waters from the opposite shore.

Philip jumped from the cab and walked toward the children, smiling with his arms held out. They laughed and pushed a boy from the center of the group. The boy's square jaw was immediately familiar to Philip; though the face seemed to have been set on a taller body, his eyes could not be mistaken. Philip called out, "Fred Joel, my friend. Come here."

Fred Joel looked back at his fellow orphans and then at Philip. He took a few shy steps and then broke into a running leap into Philip's arms.

Luckson employed several of the other children to unload bags of rice and beans from the truck. Two of the older boys carried the tub.

Then like a line of ants winding along the trail, the children led their visitors toward the orphanage.

Having arrived at Lakay Jezu, the children gathered around Philip in the courtyard. The tub of gifts lay at his feet. The children pushed close to see what treasures lay inside. Philip opened a pocket knife and pried open the lid.

The children giggled as Philip raised the lid. They leaned forward as he reached in and pulled out gifts. First, he pulled out a walker, sturdy with large wheels and a built-in seat designed for ambulation over uneven terrain. And he gave Tabitha several sets of adjustable crutches for use by the children. He pulled out dresses for the older girls and dolls for the younger girls. Shoes for the older boys, a few soccer balls, and everyone got a new watch.

Many of the items had been donated by Amanda, who had surprised Philip with boxes of clothing she had purchased after hearing of plans for his trip.

The children pushed each other and grabbed at the items Philip distributed. Then, once the tub was empty, they scattered to dress up or play with their gifts.

The boys were particularly excited about the gift of a portable radio. To Philip's embarrassment, it did not pick up any stations because Lakay Jezu was too remote. Philip made a mental note that the orphanage needed supplies to erect an antenna.

Once the children dispersed, Philip pulled out a computer for Tabitha, along with a solar charging device. Tabitha stood shocked. She covered her face as if to hide her smile. Then she gave Philip a hug. "You know, Doctor Scott, you have given us access to education. If these children have access to education, they will have hope."

Philip spent the afternoon helping Tabitha assemble and learn to use the computer.

At one point, Luckson interrupted and invited Philip to play soccer, which he accepted, awkwardly trying to keep up with the swarm of kids whose skilled feet kept the ball dancing in the swirling dust around Philip. The kids laughed as he made futile attempts to kick the ball before another child kicked it out from under him. Then, purely by a fortunate swing of his leg, Philip kicked the ball through the goal. This was no act of skill. He had tapped the ball at just the right moment, and it rolled past the other players into the goal. The children cheered and danced around Philip as if he had just made the winning goal for Haiti in the World Cup.

Philip grabbed the ball. He looked down at the swirling group of boys. Their eyes were wide; not just looking at him, but admiring him. Philip felt suddenly proud. It was not a selfish pride, as if comparing himself to a competitor. It was the elation that accompanies a win for one's team. Philip held the ball above his head and yelled, "Yay, us!"

Lynn sat on the porch holding a doll as one of the girls braided the doll's hair. She heard the commotion in the yard and looked over to see Philip surrounded by the boys. He was smiling; his eyes sparkled, and his laughter echoed across the yard. He was happy in a way Lynn had never seen him happy before. This made her smile too.

Tabitha was sitting nearby. She had a computer on her lap and was awkwardly working her callused fingers across a mousepad and clicking keys. She saw Lynn laughing. She leaned over and said, "I see the way you look at him, not only with your eyes but with your heart. He is a good man, that Doctor Scott. I think he would make you a happy woman."

The girls sitting in front of Lynn giggled. Lynn looked at the doll in her hands, "I am sure you are wrong. He's from a very different world. Don't mistake me, he's cute, no? I enjoy his company. But our paths must diverge."

A few hours later, in the courtyard, a group of boys placed a square table in the shade of a mango tree. The table had chairs set for Philip, Lynn, Victor, and Luckson. A crowd of children encircled them on the packed dirt. Each child held a bowl of rice and beans smothered in a creole sauce.

Philip looked down at his plate. The aroma of the sauce rose from the rice and beans. His plate was colored with slices of red tomato, green cabbage, and a piece of lightly browned chicken. Then he looked around at the children sitting all around him. Philip saw their hungry eyes. Then he locked eyes with Fred Joel. He said to the others at the table, "Excuse me, I need to trade places with someone."

Philip stood and walked to Fred Joel.

Fred Joel sat looking up at Philip. He did not know why Philip stood over him. Was he in trouble? Was something wrong?

Philip saw brown eyes looking up at him, and he thought, *You're breaking my heart, kid.* So, he reached down and took Fred Joel's bowl. Then Philip sat down with the other children and started eating rice from Fred Joel's bowl.

Bewildered, Fred Joel cocked his head thinking, *Why is this man eating my food?*

Philip pointed toward the table, "That's your seat, buddy. Take someone with you and enjoy the meal."

Fred Joel did not understand the words, but he caught the meaning. He stood up and cautiously waved to a girl sitting across the yard. The little girl was his sister. She smiled and lifted herself to her new walker and rolled to join Fred Joel at the table.

Fred meticulously divided the items on the plate into two equal portions. Then together with his sister, sharing one spoon, they ate the meal.

After dinner, Victor drove Philip, Lynn, and Luckson back to Milot. They arrived after dark and dropped off Lynn at the staff house. Then they dropped off Philip at the guest house.

As Philip slid out of the cab, he said, "Thank you for the ride. It was a good day, I thought."

Victor did not look at Philip. His eyes remained fixed ahead as he extended an invitation, "Tomorrow you come to my church. I will pick you up at seven."

Philip stood at the side of the truck. He heard the invitation, and he appreciated the gesture, but he had no desire to sit through another religious service. He patted the truck and respectfully gave a string of excuses, "You know, I'm a bit jet-lagged, what with the long flight and all, and I didn't bring a tie to wear. After packing all the gear, I didn't have room for anything dressy. And I still can't understand the language. I wouldn't know what was happening, and besides, there's much work to do, and I shouldn't be selfish with my time."

Victor never looked over. He listened to Philip give a lengthy description of why he should not accept. Then he smiled, nodded, and pushed the truck into gear. As they drove away, Victor and Luckson looked at each other and laughed. Then Luckson said, "Y-y-you have a tie for Doctor Scott?"

39

Worship with Victor

In Haiti, even in rural villages, church services are a grand affair, a community gala.

On a rocky road at the base of the mountains, halfway through a village was a clearing; surrounding the clearing, a cactus fence. At the back of the area was an open-aired pavilion, a church building, a tin-roof structure held up by a series of wooden poles. A low wall of rough wooden planks skirted the base to prevent chickens and dogs from wandering through. Beyond the pavilion, the terrain fell away into a view of tropical valley shouldered by slopes covered in mango trees and terraced plantain fields.

Through the Sunday morning haze, women dressed in brilliant blue and white, their heads covered in broad lace hats, stepped out of mud-walled homes. They walked down the rocky road in heeled shoes trailed by children adorned in little dresses and suits. These mothers and children made their way to the pavilion and took seats on rough wooden benches. The men, most of them dressed in dark suits with thin ties and bleached white shirts, had arrived early to arrange benches to set up for a worship service.

Victor maneuvered the white truck up a rustic road toward the village, careful to avoid large rocks or deep wavy ruts. Beads of sweat formed on his forehead. Despite the humid morning air, he was wearing a tight-fitting wool suit. Luckson sat in the middle wearing his new baseball cap with a button-up shirt. Philip was on the passenger side wearing a wide paisley tie, a loan from Victor. Though it clashed with the color and pattern in his shirt, Philip recognized the gift for what it was, an act of kindness, and he wore it with pride.

The service had already started when Victor, Luckson, and Philip arrived. From the road, they could hear singing coming from the pavilion.

Philip walked behind Victor and Luckson as they pressed their way into the pavilion through worshipers clapping and swaying to a hymn sung at an extreme volume. To Philip, it sounded like screaming in harmony. He could feel his eardrums throbbing.

Victor pushed through the crowd to a pew near the front where a well-dressed family smiled and quickly made room for Philip to squeeze into the row. An elderly man, short and bent at the shoulders with only a few teeth turned and shook Philip's hand.

Victor handed Philip a book of hymns written in Creole and French. There were no notes, only words. Victor opened to a particular page and pointed to the song. Philip noticed none of the people around him held such a book. Most could not read.

But they could sing. Loudly. Over the next two hours, Philip sat through the movements of a Haitian worship service. He did not understand the words or the songs, but one phrase was very clear to him. Throughout the hymns, the prayers, and the extended monologues he heard a familiar phrase repeated many times, "Mesi, Bondye." Though most of the language was unintelligible, Philip knew the meaning of that phrase: Thank you, God.

The phrase puzzled Philip. For what did these people have to be thankful? They lived in abject poverty. The building in which they worshiped had a rusty tin roof. Its beams were half-digested by termites. They were miles from the city, with no running water, no electricity, minimal, if any, land on which to farm. They lived in houses of mud and sticks. The children were malnourished. They existed from one day to the next unaware of the violent historical injustices that left them abandoned to the forgotten penumbra of western culture, doomed to lives shortened by diseases easily prevented. If anyone had reason to doubt the existence of a benevolent deity, it was these people. Yet they felt compelled to gather on the side of the mountain, to raise their voices to the creator of the universe and utter a word of gratitude. Why?

It is a strange thing for a rich man to sit in a congregation of the poor. He feels pity for them, the less fortunate as he calls them, as if one's station in life results from a cosmic game of chance which results in some winners, the fortunate, and many losers, the less fortunate. He cannot help thinking that a blessing, a word he uses as a euphemism for the word fortune, comes in the form of wealth, food, laughter, or notoriety and that the underprivileged who lack such blessings have nothing for which to be thankful. This is, of course, an error. It is like saying that a man from one country is unfortunate because he does not have very much currency in his pocket from another country. Heaven's currency is different from the world's currency. Wealth is not called a blessing in the kingdom of heaven; it is considered a woe, a curse even. In the kingdom of heaven, it is the poor who are blessed, truly happy, not because of affluence, but because of access. As Jesus said, theirs is the kingdom of heaven.

But when Jesus said blessed are the poor, He did not mean the poor are free from the temptation to be immodest. Vanity is universal. The rich do not have a monopoly on pride, and the poor are not immune from greed, envy, or any of the temptations associated with status. Philip subconsciously recognized the pretense of those around him, and he considered himself above their petty displays of power and finery. He disapproved of what appeared to be wasteful spending on gaudy attire; people who are that poor should be thrifty. He noticed the best-dressed women sat near the front in a posture more consistent with pride than penitence. The men rose to speak in order of superiority, the best dressed and most articulate of them, presumably the best educated, commanded the service and took places of honor in the rickety wooden chairs behind the lectern. It was all very sad. How does a person justify extravagant conduct in such austere settings? Was it all a self-seeking spectacle?

Then Philip was struck by a different thought. Every culture dresses up for special occasions. Perhaps the dress and decorum reflected the importance of the gathering as something the community cherished. Philip caught himself in a hypocritical dichotomy. He could not understand how people with virtually nothing could be thankful, yet he also could not understand why these same people would spend what little they did have to dress up as a sign of adoration. Their clothing may have been the most valuable items they possessed. Sure, for some the dresses, the hats, the shoes may have been nothing more than a prideful show of status. But what if it were something more? What if the reverent gathering was of such importance that the people felt compelled to adorn themselves with the best they owned?

It was hearing the voice of a young woman that changed his perspective. The service had entered a period of silence. Loaves of unleavened bread followed by small cups of wine were distributed to the congregation. A young woman then rose to stand before the people. She was thin with high cheekbones, dressed in a blue gown with her hair pulled back into a bun. She swayed momentarily with her eyes closed as if listening to an unseen chorus; then when the time was right, she began to sing.

At the sound of her voice, Philip felt chills flow over his body in waves. The sound was that of vocal perfection.

Her words were cast into the air softly at first, then rising in volume until finally reaching a precise vibrato that echoed down the valley in perfect harmonic tones, not shrill, but inviting as if the sound itself was a spirit sent to wake the souls of all within its reach. Philip looked around him. The people sat in quiet respect, their heads bowed, seemingly unaware that a vocal wonder was in their midst. Had this woman been in Seattle, had she been heard by an agent, she would have been made into a celebrity, singing in the performing arts centers of the world; she would have been sought after by producers. Her shelves would have been unable to bear the weight of awards and golden records. Her voice was soothing and inspiring, the type that heals and then bolsters timid hearts. How was it possible that such talent could remain hidden from the world's view? How could a woman with such a beautiful voice be heard by only God himself and a few destitute but well-dressed worshipers on a remote mountainside? Yet, no one seemed to acknowledge that the woman was singing to them. She was like a bird singing in a fog, one of God's creatures making melody to its creator somewhere in the distance while others went on about their business.

Only Philip watched the woman as she sang. Her voice aroused a sensation to which Philip had not previously been aware. He could hear the beautiful voice and see the angel producing the melody, but the sense of beauty in that rickety pavilion came not from what he could see with his eyes or hear with his ears. Perhaps it was just in his mind, or perhaps it reached deep into his psyche. Something in Philip began to burn as he sat mesmerized by a song he could not understand but could feel deeper than any song he had ever heard. The woman sang as if the living God were her only audience and as if he had reserved the performance that day for himself.

When she finished, Philip, overcome with admiration, stood up to cheer. He yelled out, "Brava," and had clapped about three times before he realized he alone was applauding. A few children looked up at him and giggled, but the congregation otherwise sat silently, unaffected by this foreigner's surge of emotion. Philip sat down slowly, embarrassed by his outburst.

Victor's cheeks grew rosy as he tried to hold back a laugh. He leaned over and said, "Perhaps you thought she was singing for you?"

After this, a young man in a coat and tie stood at the lectern and preached an extended sermon. Philip could not understand the words, and his mind quickly drifted back to the sound of the woman's voice. The charm of the song was like a filament that continued to glow after a light was turned off, even after the woman sat down, the beauty in her voice illuminated Philip's heart.

Near the end of the sermon, the preacher pointed at Philip, and the congregation turned to look at him.

Philip felt awkward with the eyes of the congregation suddenly on him. Then the preacher smiled at Philip and spoke in broken English, "I have just say to the people that you come many miles to be here today. God knows you could worship at any place in the world. But today you worship here. And we are happy you are here today."

Philip acknowledged the man's greeting with a nod. The congregation responded with a stirring, "Amen!"

After the service, the people walked down the hill to a pool, a place where the water had been deepened by a wall placed in the curve of a stream. The group sang a song, and then the preacher walked into the pool with another young man, both of them had rolled up their pant legs in a futile attempt to keep dry while the preacher spoke. They stood side by side as the preacher gave what sounded like a eulogy to those gathered on shore.

Victor translated for Philip. The preacher said, "Evil is not just out there in the world; it is here, in our village, in each of us. We are part of the problem, part of the suffering. Do not point to your neighbor and say he made my life hard; the standard you use will be used to judge you. Who among us is not a thief? But you do not want to steal. Who among us has not committed adultery? But you want to be faithful. Who among us has not hated his neighbor? But you want to be a good neighbor. Who among us has clean hands? None of us. But we wash our hands to feel clean. In this life, we have many troubles, and God knows the evil we have brought into this world. But we are not punished as our sins deserve. Why? Because we are being renewed, we are being washed on the inside. We wash our hands. We wash our clothes. We wash our dishes. Should we not also wash our hearts? Do not be like a woman who washes the outside of the bowl but never the inside. But you say, "I cannot clean the inside." You are right; you can clean the outside; only God can clean the inside. You wish to be good; God can make you perfect. God has come to our village, not so you can have more, but so you can be more. God has proven this by raising Jesus from the dead. And he will raise you from the dead. But if you would join Him in his resurrection, you must first join him in His death. Will you lie down in the tomb beside Him so you can be raised to life with a new body and a new mind?"

Then the young man was baptized, held under water briefly and raised upright in a ritual that symbolized a death, a burial, and a resurrection.

As the young man stepped onto the shore, he looked to the sky and said, "Mesi Bondye"—Thank you, God.

Victor looked at Philp, "Do you understand what you have seen?"

Philip did not answer. As he watched the young man rising from the water, Philip felt a sort of envy. The boy grinned with elation, released from a burden that could not be seen with human eyes. Philip longed for that sort of release. If he could put a word to what he felt he would say he was jealous. That impoverished young man had for the moment found life and peace. It was a treasure Philip coveted. Philip, the rich man, was envious of the poor man; he wanted what that less fortunate man had. Philip never answered the question. He shook his head, turned and walked back to the truck.

40

Confessions with Lynn

Two days later, following a long procedure, Philip walked from the operating room into the hospital courtyard where palm leaves rustled overhead. Night had nearly fallen. The air held traces of salt and floral scents blown from the coast during that evening hour when the sea exhales over the land. Philip sat down on a raised concrete walkway and allowed his body to relax in the satisfying exhaustion that comes with completing a good day's work. He closed his eyes. For several days, a single song had resonated sporadically in the back of his mind. Finally, in the quiet of a hospital courtyard, he could imagine the tune in all its fullness.

Lynn walked out from one of the wards. She saw Philip sitting alone, his head leaned back and his eyes closed as if listening to a distant melody. She approached him and asked, "So, what is Doctor Scott thinking about tonight?"

Philip smiled and patted the space next to him, "Please, join me."

Lynn sat down. She looked up at the stars of twilight flickering through high palm leaves, "You seem to be in deep thought, no?"

Philip said, "Not really. I was thinking of a woman I heard in a church service on Sunday. The sound of her singing is stuck in my head. This woman had an astonishing voice; spellbinding, really. With her voice, she could go anywhere in the world."

Lynn leaned back on her hands, "That sounds marvelous."

Philip nodded, "Absolutely. I just can't see how someone with her gift could be confined to that village."

"Her song touched you?"

"It was incredible; I don't even know what the words meant, but it was beautiful, like an Italian aria performed for a private audience, and I don't know how to explain this, but it's the closest I've come to having a spiritual experience. When she stopped, everything in my being screamed out to hear more. You know how you feel when you wake up from a dream, and you just want to go back?"

"Do you want to go back?"

Philip shrugged, "Victor may be too embarrassed to ever take me again."

"Why would he be ashamed?"

"Don't laugh at me, but I applauded for the woman. I mean I stood up in a church and just started clapping. Is that a pardonable sin? I'm embarrassed even thinking about it."

Lynn started laughing, "I'm sure Victor knows you meant well."

Philip gave Lynn a playful nudge, "I said, don't laugh."

"I'm sorry, Philip. That's just really funny to me."

Philip let her settle down, and then he asked, "So, Lynn, why do you stay here?"

"What do you mean?"

"Why do you stay in Haiti? You're like that young woman, beautiful, smart, with amazing talent. You could go anywhere in the world, and any hospital would be lucky to have you, yet you stay here. Why?"

"I don't think you really want to hear the answer."

"Try me."

Lynn lowered her eyes, "I had a spiritual experience."

"Oh, I see," Philip drew out his words sarcastically as if suggesting understanding without approval.

"No, it's not what you think."

"I'm sorry. Forgive my bad habit. I know your faith is important to you."

"It *is* important to me. But I would be lying if I led you to believe I am a saint."

"You? If you're not a saint, there's no hope for humanity."

"Well, you only say that because you have not opened your eyes."

"Believe me; my eyes have been wide open. I have never seen you be anything but an angel. You treat patients, staff, and egotistical idiots like me the same. I've never seen you say one cross word—not to anyone."

"You speak as if kindness were the cardinal virtue. I can assure you, the noxious fires of hell are not stoked for those who are merely unkind."

"So, what is your vice?"

"Pride. My struggle is pride."

"Now, that does surprise me. You don't strike me as the prideful type. Confident for sure, but not prideful."

"I'm glad to hear you say so. It's not the sort of woman I wish to be. But it's there. Some would say it is a gift, the lesser of two evils or at least an evil justified by good fruit. I began my career with a strong sense of vocation. Somewhere along the way a passion for becoming a nurse became tangled with ambition; first it was just determination to be the best nurse I could be, then it grew into a determination just to be the best. I earned an advanced degree and then a Ph.D. and had all but forgotten why I entered the healing profession. I was a woman driven to outperform and outshine my peers. I even harassed professors and colleagues that stood in my way."

Philip shook his head, "Again, I'd call that self-confidence, not pride."

"Oh, it was pride, I assure you. It was not enough for me to say I was Doctor Sable, Ph.D. In my heart, it made me feel good to know other people around me were not."

"So, are you here on some kind of penance?"

"Well, I've never thought of it that way—maybe it was like that at first. But penance has to do with punishment. I do not think of my work as a sentence; it is a privilege."

"You mean it's rewarding to you?"

"There is one thing that has always meant more to me than my degree or job or status. When I was a little girl, I heard a priest give a homily about a woman at a well. In the story, Jesus asked the woman for some water. It's a beautiful passage. After that, I had this secret wish that Jesus would visit me. I dreamt what it would be like to talk with Him and sit at His feet and listen. In my mind, He would come to me and he would ask me for water. Like the woman in the story, he would say, 'I am thirsty. Would you give me something to drink?' Oh, the honor that would be: to provide a cup of water for the man who died for me. That one fantasy recurred over and over through my years growing up. It was why I chose to become a nurse. And even in the self-centered months of working on my dissertation, that vision seemed to keep me in balance: the thought that if He asked me, I would drop everything without regret. I'm telling you the truth. I came to a point that I would give up every letter behind my name and even my career just for one opportunity to hand Jesus a cup of water."

"So, that brought you here?"

"It was just after I completed my degree. I was accepted for a position in Paris and had a little time before reporting. I heard about the hospital here in Milot and volunteered to come for a few weeks. I found it overwhelming. The people were so poor. And the needs were so great. How could someone like me help in the midst of such suffering? My first day I walked into the ward, and a patient looked up at me and started asking for something. Of course, I did not understand what he said. So, a Haitian nurse came over and translated. The man was saying, 'I'm thirsty. Could you get me a cup of water?' You will think I am lying, but I am telling the truth. I could not believe it. I heard what he said, and I looked at him. Then he winked at me. He smiled and winked at me like he knew who I was."

Philip gave a skeptical grin, "That's either inspiring or just creepy, but in a beautiful way."

Lynn did not stop, "Oh, it gets better. When I brought the man water, I asked him his name. He told me, but it was very hard to understand. He said it a number of times. But it was not clear. So, I checked his record, and when I saw his name, I dropped the chart to the floor. I could not believe it. His name was Emmanuel. That is the same name they gave Jesus, no? At that moment it became clear. It was Jesus in some terrible disguise looking up from that bed and granting my wish. Oh, I know it was not really Him. But at that moment, I felt like it was Him. He tricked me. He put on suffering that day and asked me how serious I was about serving him. I could hear Him saying whatever you do for this man, you have done it for me. That was ten years ago. I'm still here. And I see no end to the days I get to spend with Him."

Philip picked up a stick and started scrawling in the dirt, "So, your faith in a childhood fantasy kept you from going back to France?"

Lynn answered, "I've been back many times, but it never felt like home again. At first, I thought everyone at home had changed, you know, became preoccupied with work and status and politics. Then one day, I realized it was me. I had changed, or more I had been changed."

Philip said, "Hmm? That sounds familiar."

Lynn asked, "So, what made you come back?"

Philip pointed with his stick as if indicating two different points on a map, "My brain was up there where I do my work, good work that's rewarding in every professional way, but my heart was here, drawn to a place where for the first time in my life I wanted to be good, I mean not just be good at doing something, I wanted to be good, to be a good man. But the first person who made me feel that I could actually be that way is dead, and I can't reconcile how a good person would have let that happen."

Lynn took Philip's hand between hers, "Rose-Marie was a special girl."

"Yes, she was."

"She was the first to see you for who you really are."

"I don't even know who that person is anymore."

"I do. You're a remarkable man. That's who you are: a masterpiece hidden under layers of stone. A man made to do good works, stuff only good men can do. I see why she looked at you with such love. She was your Emmanuel."

"I wish that were true. I want to be good. I've spent the last few years driven by the thought that maybe I could become the man Rose-Marie thought I was. I gave it my best. I worked harder, stayed up later, gave up bad habits, and spent time with my kids. I even read a Bible given to me by an old woman."

"And what did you find?"

"Lynn, you need to know something. I'm not a good man."

"Tell me, what do you mean?"

"I carry a sort of grief I guess. My ex-wife would say it's my psyche responding to some fear of lost love, but I have to just call it what it is: guilt."

"About Rose-Marie?"

"Yes. I am ashamed of how I treated her."

"Now, stop right there. You have nothing to be ashamed of. You gave her the best care anyone could give. Her death was not your fault."

"Maybe not. But I wished it on her."

"You did no such thing!"

"It was when we completed her surgery. I was looking at her amputated leg, and I thought what a pitiful thing. Why couldn't she just die and get it over with? It's an awful thing to say, but I'm just being honest. I'd like to think I was being sympathetic. She had nothing to live for, at least that's what I thought. And looking at her pale, lifeless leg, I just wondered why we didn't just allow nature to take its course and let her die."

Lynn sat in shocked silence. She held her hand over her mouth unable to speak.

Philip continued, "I was wrong. I admit that now. She had every reason to live. But I did not see it until later. By the time she got sick, I wanted her to live. God knows I wanted her to live, but it was too late. Then when she died, the faces of a hundred other patients flashed through my mind, people I've written off as hopeless cases, patients in great need who did not get the surgeon they needed, they got me, the surgeon who didn't care one bit if they lived or died. I never killed anyone, but I can't say I saved everyone within my power to save. I remember running a code one night in the ICU, wishing the man would just hurry up and die so I could go back to sleep." Philip bit his lip and looked into the night sky, "Of all the surgeons in Haiti, on that day, Rose-Marie was sent to me, a man who did not care if she lived. Do you remember how she screamed? I have no idea what she thought, but she had every reason to scream. She had fallen into the hands of a monster."

Philip lowered his head into his hands, his heart broken, "I know it all sounds extreme. And God knows I've tried to rationalize it all away. But I cannot. I came here as a king dressed in his finest. Rose-Marie was the little girl showing the world I actually had no clothes. She exposed me for who I really am. If I have to give an account some day of every life placed under my care, God help me. I have no defense. That's why I feel shame. Not just for failing that beautiful little girl, but for being a man who failed a thousand others like her, good people who thought they were getting something more. I used to think sin was just a religious term for forbidden pleasures, but now I wonder if it's something more. Those ancient writers were onto something. Sin is a cancer: it grows unnoticed until it's too late. I'm telling you, if this guilt does not eventually kill me, surely God will. What kind of God would permit such dark indifference, and if God does exist, who will rescue me from the sentence I deserve?"

Lynn placed her arms around Philip, pulling his head into her shoulder, "I can only speak for myself, Philip. I do not know why God allows darkness to grow in us. But I have learned this one thing to be true: we do not follow Christ because He makes us moral. We follow Him because He makes us new."

41

Blood and Water Flowed

The following morning, Philip walked into the operating room. He saw his patient lying on the table. She was prepped for surgery though still awake. Philip greeted her with wide eyes and a broad grin. She did not return his smile.

She was crying, gasping for air in between sobs. Tuberculosis was growing slowly in her lungs, and the space between her lungs and her chest wall was filled with pus, leaving room for her to take only shallow breaths.

Philip saw her distress, and he felt something for her, a feeling that was new for him, not mere pity or sympathy. He felt distress; more to the point, he felt her distress. He sensed the fear she was feeling, but from her perspective. He took her hand and tried to explain he would take care of her. But she cried all the more.

A Haitian nurse stood on the other side of the table and translated for Philip, "She is frightened."

Looking around for help, Philip called out, "Would somebody get me the chaplain?"

In a few minutes, a short man in a black clerical shirt entered the operating room. Philip said to him, "We can't do this alone. Pray for this woman. She is a child of God— and she's afraid." Then he added, "And pray for me; she deserves a good surgeon today."

The chaplain looked at Philip, nodded, and then spoke a prayer in Creole. Even without translation, to Philip, the chaplain's words sounded poetic.

The patient relaxed, and within a few minutes, she was asleep under the influence of anesthesia.

Philip made a small cut through the woman's chest wall and pressed an instrument through the opening he had made. A mix of blood and purulent fluid poured from the wound. Philip remembered something he had read about a soldier who pierced the chest of Jesus on the cross, bringing forth a flow of blood and water. As he set to work, Philip whispered to himself, "I think Lynn was right. You start seeing Him everywhere."

As he was finishing his work, suddenly Lynn burst into the room. She yelled with a shaking voice, "Please, come quickly. A friend has been shot."

Philip completed tying off the final suture. Then he backed from the table. Tearing off his surgical gown, he ran out of the room trailing Lynn as she ran toward the front of the hospital.

Near the hospital gate, a crowd gathered around a pick-up truck. Philip pushed through the people. He looked down into the bed of the truck where he saw a thin man of no more than twenty-five with auburn hair holding the right side of his chest. He was wincing. His skin was an eerie grey. The entire right side of his shirt was saturated with blood. The blood appeared to be concentrated over a hole in the shirt, bubbling with each labored attempt to breathe.

A frantic young woman, equal to him in age, knelt next to the man. Her face was smeared with blood. She held one hand under the man's head, and with the other, she held a wadded cloth over another saturated area on his abdomen. Every muscle in her face quivered as she pleaded, "Oh, Bryan. We're here. It's okay now. The doctors are here. Please, God. Oh, please save him."

In the back of his mind, Philip tried to make sense of the scene. Clearly, these people were Americans, no doubt missionaries.

Philip shifted into trauma mode, seeing the sucking chest wound. He did not hesitate. He grabbed Lynn by the arm and shouted in the firm voice of a trauma surgeon, "Do you have a needle? Any size?"

Lynn pulled a syringe from a pouch and handed it to Philip.

Philip grabbed the syringe and climbed into the bed of the truck. He ripped back the man's blood-soaked shirt and felt for a space between the ribs high on the chest. Then with one swift motion, he plunged the needle into the man's chest.

The man's eyes instantly burst open, and he groaned.

The crowd saw the needle plunged into the man's chest. They gasped. Many covered their mouths. One woman screamed.

The woman next to the man yelled, "What are you doing to him?"

Philip heard the woman. He looked into her eyes and saw that she was terrified. Philip placed a hand on her shoulder, "Ma'am, I'm going to do everything I can to save him. We are going to have to move quickly, and you will not understand what is happening. But I need you to be strong—for him."

The woman nodded.

Philip removed the syringe, leaving the needle in the man's chest. Air whistled through the needle releasing the trapped air from the man's chest cavity. Then Philip placed a latex glove over the needle hub to prevent air from rushing back in. He took the woman's hand and moved it so as to place the cloth over the sucking chest wound.

Having stabilized the wound, Philip turned his attention to the medical staff, "Clear the operating room. Get the surgeons and trauma supplies. Have the table ready for life support. We will not lose this man."

For several hours the operating room hummed with activity as surgeons, nurses, and medical staff worked to save a man's life.

When it was over, Philip walked from the operating room into the hospital courtyard with Lynn at his side. Sweat trickled from under their blue caps dripping onto their blood-stained gowns. Philip looked across the courtyard. He called out to a woman sitting in the shade among a group of people on the far side; the woman's head was bowed.

The woman heard her name. She looked up and squinted against the midday sun. When she recognized Philip and Lynn exiting the operating room, she stood up and brushed the sides of her dress. She was preparing herself for the worst.

Philip walked briskly toward her and spoke quickly, his voice confident and reassuring, "Your husband is going to make it. He has serious injuries and will need to be medically evacuated to the States. But I do not fear for his life."

At hearing those words, tears welled in the woman's eyes. Overcome with relief she began crying, "Thank you. How can I thank you? Thank you, God."

Then she became pale, almost dropping to the ground. Lynn stepped forward and embraced her, "It's going to be alright, dear. Bryan is a strong man. Have faith."

The woman cried for a few moments then wiped her eyes, "May I see him?"

Philip nodded, "Give the staff a few minutes to clean him up. Then you may go in. He is sleeping now."

Lynn motioned to a bench, "May we sit with you for a few minutes?"

Lynn and Philip sat down with the woman. Then Philip asked her, "Can you tell us what happened?"

The woman became pale again. Her lips quivered. She wiped her eyes and explained, "This morning, men broke into our compound. We have a small mission in Lagousette, a farm we run for the community. We saw them coming—four men, I think, and we locked ourselves in the house. They banged on the doors, and we heard them circle the house looking for a way to get inside. They kept saying, 'Is there one called you? Is there one called you?' I don't know what they meant or who they were looking for. I was in the bedroom with our two girls when they broke down the front door. Bryan went out to confront them. They demanded money. There was a lot of yelling. And then came gunfire. It seemed like a hundred blasts just kept going off. When I came out, Bryan was lying on the floor bleeding so much."

Lynn saw the woman shaking. She pulled her into her arms and said, "It's okay now. You are safe now. Are your girls with someone?"

The woman nodded, "Yes, our housekeeper took them to another missionary's home."

Philip grimaced, "What about the men? The ones who attacked you, where are they?"

"I don't know. They were gone." The woman pointed toward the group of people across the courtyard, "Our neighbor says they drove off in our Pajero. They must have found the keys."

Philip listened. But he could not comprehend how this could happen. These were missionaries on a farm. They were not violent people. This was not a shady part of downtown Seattle. They had no political score to keep. Who would attack unarmed humanitarians? His heart trembled in a mix of fear and anger. Then a horrible thought hit him. He grabbed Lynn's arm, "May I speak with you for a moment?"

Lynn answered gently, "Of course. Let me take her to see Bryan. I'll be right out."

A few moments later, Lynn walked back out into the courtyard. She saw Philip there rubbing his chin and pacing the walkway. As she approached, she whispered, "What is on your mind?"

Philip turned to her. His eyes were wide, and he spoke with a trembling voice, "I'm worried about Tabitha. If these thieves, whoever they are, are attacking mission posts, how can Tabitha be safe? Do you think they would go so far—or stoop so low?"

Lynn stood for a moment. She was shocked at the thought. Then she frowned, shaking her head in rationalized disbelief, until having come to the same conclusion, she dropped her head forward into Philip's chest, saying, "I just cannot imagine Tabitha would be in danger. They are so far away. But then—you are right. Her work is well known. I suppose anyone could be a target. I—I will speak with Victor. Perhaps we can check on her tomorrow?" Then Lynn looked up, "Philip, I cannot explain why, but this really scares me."

Philip took Lynn by both shoulders. He could see her brown eyes looking up, glancing back and forth at his eyes as if searching for reassurance. The sight of her trembling caused Philip's muscles to tighten. He answered with courageous firmness, "Tomorrow, then. At the very least we can warn her and find a way to protect the children."

42

Kidnapping at Lakay Jezu

They departed for Lakay Jezu at daybreak. As Victor pulled up to the river, Philip knew something was not right. A dark blue Pajero was parked at the edge of the water.

Philip jumped from the truck and splashed across the river. Lynn, Victor, and Luckson followed closely behind him.

As they approached the orphanage, Philip noticed the gate into Lakay Jezu was open, unhinged at the top and angled downward to one side. There were no children in the yard and no sound from the compound. A walker lay in the dirt outside the dormitory.

Lynn walked in through the gate taking slow, cautious steps. She heard the sound of children crying from one of the rooms. Her pulse quickened. She ran toward the sound of the children.

As Lynn approached the dormitory, a man wearing dark clothing and black boots stepped from the room. He walked straight up to her and pointed a pistol at her head.

Luckson saw the red eyes of children peering out the windows, many of them crying. He bent low and waved for the children to back away from the windows as he ran around to the back of the dormitory.

Lynn looked at the gun pointed at her. Her face became red, not with fear but with intense anger. She slapped the gun out of the way and yelled, "Get that out of my face!" Then she proceeded toward the doorway.

Philip saw the man raise the gun at the back of Lynn's head. Philip had no time to think. He ran at the man yelling at everyone, "Get down! Get down! Get down!"

Victor was also running and reached the man first. He saw the man raising the pistol toward Lynn and swung his fist at the man's jaw from behind, landing a blow with such force that everyone heard the sound of cracking bone. Fragments of teeth mingled with blood flew from the man's mouth.

The man grabbed his jaw, but before Victor could land a second blow, the man raised the gun and fired twice. He had no time to aim. The shots were random, yet one struck Victor in the leg.

Philip saw Victor drop to the ground. His legs were cut out from under him.

The man turned the gun at Philip.

Philip saw the gun, but his focus was on the man's forearm. While Philip was not a fighter, he had the trained eyes of a surgeon. He had repaired many bones from fights and accidents. He knew exactly where the weak points were on the man's forearm and wrist. In one forceful motion, Philip folded the man's wrist with a crushing swing of both hands, causing the gun to fly off.

The gunman looked down. Philip swung his palm upward, full force against the man's jaw. Philip felt the man's jawbone separate, and for a moment the gunman, holding his jaw, stood stunned.

Philip saw the gun on the ground. His eyes widened. He instinctively reached down to grab it.

Then the gunman ran at Philip, tackling him to the ground. Both Philip and the gunman crawled toward the gun, but before either reached it, another blast came from the other end of the dormitory.

At that moment, a short man, bald, with a fearfully scarred face and yellow eyes, pulled Tabitha into the courtyard. He fired his gun into the air a second time.

Two other men, one with a pistol and the other with a rifle, ran from the far room and stood over Philip.

Philip saw he was surrounded and raised his hands. To the side, he could see Luckson and Lynn ushering children quietly out a door through the back side of the dormitory.

Philip knew he must divert the attention of the assailants. He stood up and yelled, "What are you doing? Let the woman go."

The bald man yelled back, "No talking. I will talk. You will listen."

"Look. This man has been shot, and your man is injured. They need to get to a hospital."

"No hospital. We take Tabitha."

"What is she to you?"

"No talking. You give us fifty thousand dollars. U.S. dollars. Or this woman dies."

"No one here has that kind of money."

"You lie, Blanc. Tabitha has many people who send her money. They will pay."

"You want money? Don't take that woman. Take me."

"No, Blanc. You will collect the money."

"You don't understand. I'm offering you more."

"Tabitha and the children will be tortured and die one by one until you bring us the money."

"So, you're stupid."

"What you say, Blanc?"

"I said you are stupid. You take a woman for just pennies. But you are too ignorant to take me. I am a wealthy man. I work for a large university. I have friends who can send you all the money you want. Take me, and you can demand five hundred thousand."

"Fine. We take you both."

"Then you will get nothing. Unless you leave these people, I will not help you."

"Then you will die."

Philip held out his arms, "Take your best shot; you're a worthless thief. If I'm dead, I'm no use to you. You shoot me, you get nothing. But take me, alone, and you get more money than you can imagine."

Victor spoke through the pain in his leg, "You don't know what you are saying. These men will kill you no matter what we do."

The bald man with the scarred face walked up to Philip and studied him, "You are married, Blanc? You have children? Call them now and tell them. No money and they never see you again."

Philip bent down to examine Victor's leg. Blood trickled from one side of his leg, and he could see bone fragments within the exit wound. Philip leaned close, handed Victor a bottle of medicine and whispered, "Sorry my friend, it's all I have. Do not bear weight. When help arrives, splint your leg and get back to the hospital. I will draw them away from the orphanage."

One of the men struck Philip with the butt of a rifle. He yelled, "Make the call, Blanc. Use your phone."

Philip felt the blow. He restrained a sudden urge to lash back. He reached into his pocket and withdrew a cell phone, holding it up to show the bald man, "Look, no service. We are out of range. Take me toward the city, and I'll make the call."

Once again, they tried to take both Tabitha and Philip, but Philip sat down and refused to move unless they allowed Tabitha to stay and tend to Victor.

The kidnappers found that the children had exited the back of the dormitory and scattered into the hills. This frustrated them. The bald man threw up his hands and started cursing. He shoved Tabitha back toward the compound and had two of the other men lift Philip to his feet.

The bald man put handcuffs on Philip and led him out of the gate. The fourth man walked slowly behind them holding his jaw.

As the captors and captive stumbled down the trail and across the river, Philip thought many times about running. It may have worked, but most likely, it would have been futile. Trying to run in broad daylight while cuffed, he would have been tracked and likely killed. Instead, he became intent on drawing the assailants as far away as possible.

The abductors placed a black hood over Philip's head and pushed him into the back seat of the SUV. An armed kidnapper sat on either side of him. Philip heard the vehicle tires spin as they drove off at high speed, bouncing over ruts in the dirt road.

The irregular rocking motion was nauseating. Philip's chest tightened, and his stomach soured. The smothering sensation of his own warm breath under a heavy sack made him sick. He cried out. He needed to vomit and wanted out of the vehicle. But his abductors only laughed at him. Then Philip threw up. His vomit plastered the inside of the sack and then oozed down his chest to form a pool of vomit spreading over the seat. The rancid smell of partially digested slime filled the vehicle. The men lowered the windows allowing air to circulate. It was for the moment refreshing.

His stomach relieved, Philip could feel his heart racing. His mind was also active, darting from thought to thought, not in the random, chaotic desperation of panic, but in the hyper-alert state of being in danger. Using his other senses because his vision was obscured, Philip became keenly aware of his surroundings. The sound of passing traffic became more frequent, the feel of the road switched from dirt to pavement, and with the windows open, the smells of vomit gave way to smells of the countryside which eventually gave way to the fumes of the city.

After an hour or so, Philip could hear the sounds of a crowd outside the vehicle. He reasoned he must be approaching a city, most likely Cap-Haitien. In heavy traffic, he would be surrounded by other vehicles and people, witnesses, someone who might help. Philip threw himself across the seat, yelling as loud as he could while kicking at the door with great force.

The attempt to escape or alert a rescuer was courageous, but it was futile. Philip felt the blow of steel on the back of his head, and abruptly all went dark.

43
Captivity

Philip awoke squinting against the glimmer of a single bulb suspended over his bed. The back of his head was pounding. He reached back with his hands still cuffed. He felt the crust of coagulated blood overlying a sore, swollen knot on his scalp.

Philip saw the bald man with the scarred face sitting in a chair. The man was looking down; the glow of a cell phone screen illuminated his face in an otherwise dark, empty corner of the cinder block room.

Tall French doors with louvered panels opened to an upper story balcony. Through those doors, Philip could hear the sounds of loud music and car horns. The smell of hot oil from fried food wafted from the street below. It was evening, and they were somewhere in the city.

Philip tried to sit up, but the pain in his head became sharp. He rolled to the side and moaned, "Where are we?"

"What is the code, Blanc?"

"Code? Code for what?" Philip moaned.

"The password to your phone. How do I use your phone?"

"I honestly don't remember. Listen, my head is killing me. I need medicine. Can you just take me to the hospital? I can make a call from there."

The bald man snorted, "Do not think I am a fool. If you do not help, then you are a liar. I have no use for you."

"I'm sorry. Really. But I've got a head injury. I can't remember the code."

The bald man threw the phone at Philip and walked out screaming, "Then we go back for the woman and her children. You are no good. No good."

Philip could not tell whether the man was serious or not. It was dark outside. He could not imagine anyone would drive back to Tabitha's at night. But these were not reasonable men.

Philip lay still for several minutes. He heard the man walk down a flight of stairs, slam an outside door and then slide a bolt closed. When he was alone, Philip unlocked his phone and tried to dial the hospital. But he could not remember the number for anyone there. He reached into his pocket, but it was empty. Everything had been removed including his wallet and the small notebook in which he kept important numbers. He glanced around the room for any evidence of the notebook. There was only an empty chair and dark corners.

Philip thought for a few minutes. Who could he call? He scrolled his contact list. He thought about calling Doctor Hu or Doctor Henske in Seattle. Perhaps they could mobilize the right people. He considered calling Amanda. In the entire world, she was the person who for better or worse knew him best. Would she ridicule him despite his predicament, showing contempt for involving her in another one of his irresponsible acts of egotism, as she called them, or would she show compassion? Philip could not maintain his concentration. He suffered the cognitive effects of a concussion; each progression of thoughts was interrupted by sounds from the window or smells from the street, his thoughts of people from home diverted either into memories or worries about what would happen to his children, his job, his house, or his reputation if he were killed. He waffled in his desire to speak to Max and Alexa, to hear their voices and hear their laughter, but he had no wish to drag them into the unknown horror that awaited him. So more out of reflex than thoughtful reflection, he pressed the number for Amanda. The fact that he would need to put in a country code for the call did not occur to him.

The phone rang three times when an automated voice came on the line speaking French in a dry monotone. Philip looked at the phone and cursed. He pushed the number zero and started asking for help, hoping someone on the other end could hear and understand. But the only response was a replay of the automated message in a foreign language.

Suddenly Philip heard a shuffle from a dark corner behind him. Could someone still be in the room with him? He fumbled with the phone, trying to shut it off.

Before he could hold the power key long enough, a man stepped from the shadows and snatched the phone. He yelled something in Creole to others downstairs.

Philip heard footsteps slowly ascending the stairs accompanied by condescending laughter which grew in volume with each step. It was the bald man. He had only feigned leaving, bolting the door for effect while silently waiting at the foot of the stairwell.

He took the phone from Philip and said, "Now we see who you can call for us, Blanc."

He looked at the screen, "Amanda Ward. Is Amanda Ward your wife?"

"No, she's my ex-wife?"

"Ah, but she cares for you I think?"

"No more than you do."

"Ha, I think you must have children with this woman, no?"

"What is that to you?"

The bald man chuckled like a sinister gambler who had been dealt a winning hand; he could not contain the appearance of having won already. He studied the phone number and dialed.

Philip could hear the line ringing, and the sound sparked a feeling, perhaps an instinct, that had lain dormant for years. It was an impulsive desire to protect Amanda. Despite the pain, Philip sat up straight and reached out his cuffed hands, "Give me the phone. She will not talk to you. She will only listen to me."

The bald man looked at the other man, his subordinate, standing by the bedside. He motioned for the man to push Philip down. Philip was their captive, and he seemed anxious, scared even. The phone call was pulling a manipulative lever that elicited a reaction, a sign they were on the right course. The bald man ignored Philip and walked toward the other side of the room.

Philip yelled with such force that the man placed a finger in his ear in order to hear the phone, and when Philip yelled louder, the bald man walked out onto the balcony. Philip saw the man step just out of sight, and so he stopped yelling to listen.

The man said, "Hello. You are the wife of Philip Scott, no?—But you know him, no?—My name is Captain Ranquitte. I am Haiti police. I have your man in my custody. You will not see him alive unless I receive fifty thousand of your dollars, no, five hundred thousand of your dollars." Then the man fell silent.

He walked back into the room and said, "She hung up."

"Of course, she hung up. You don't call Amanda Ward and make demands. She doesn't care about me; we're divorced. You understand that. She hates me. And she certainly is not going to negotiate with someone she doesn't know. I told you to let me talk to her. Now look at where that got you. You got nothing. Nothing."

The bald man did not seem affected by the insults. He calmly dialed again and threw the phone to Philip, "Ok,

Blanc. If the woman hates you why is she the first person you call? I think this woman will help you, no? This time you talk."

As the phone rang, Philip weighed his options. He knew just making the call would drag Amanda and possibly their children into the depths of a nightmare. But if he did not ask for help—Philip felt the chill of a morbid thought. For the first time, Philip considered that he might not survive. Perhaps Victor was telling the truth: they would be killing him either way.

Amanda answered the phone yelling. Philip could tell she was crying, shouting through the phone between sobs of anger.

Hearing her cries sparked a feeling of empathetic anger in Philip, not ire directed at Amanda, but rage toward his abductors. How could someone be so evil? Where does a person develop the audacity to act out of selfish ambition without regard to the well-being of others?

Philip's growing resentment added clarity of thought in the midst of his post-concussion fog. And one thought became fixed. This might be the last chance he ever had to speak to Amanda, "Mandy, cool yourself. It's me now. There is no time. I'm alive and ok, please know that. But I need you to make a phone call to Anderson Hu, my colleague. Tell him that I have been kidnapped in Cap-Haitien and that Victor Santile, his friend, has suffered a gunshot wound to the leg. These men will ask you for money. I will reimburse whatever is paid."

Amanda could be heard shuffling papers in the background. Her voice shook as she spoke at a pace consistent with panic, "Please don't let this be happening. I-I-I need to write this down. Are you in trouble? The man said he was the police."

"That's not true. They are just men who want money."

"Please tell me what to do. Let me call the police, the embassy, somebody who can help."

"Anderson will know what to do. Call him."

Philip could hear the voices of Max and Alexa arguing in the background about something with shrill expressions that brought back memories of times when Philip thought their petty fighting would never stop. Now nothing gave him more comfort than hearing their voices in the distance.

Amanda was quiet. She too was debating whether or not to allow Max and Alexa to speak with their father, "Can you speak to the kids?"

A tear fell from Philip's eye onto the phone, "No, Mandy. Please don't involve them. Just tell them I called to check in."

Amanda bit her lip. She needed to know how this would end and prepared herself to hear the worst, "I understand. Philip, tell me please, is this going to turn out ok?"

Philip looked up at his captors. He did not know the answer. But he felt he would never have another chance to say what he needed to say at that moment. So, he took a deep breath broken by sniffling spasms, and he tried to say what could never be fully expressed in words, "Mandy, I need you to hear me say something, and I'm sorry it has to be in this way. I want nothing more than to say this to you in person. But you need to know—"

Before Philip could finish, the bald man snatched the phone and spoke to Amanda in harsh tones, "You send five-hundred thousand dollars. Or the man dies."

Amanda argued back, "Give the phone back to him. You will get your money. It will take time. You are so far away. Please give us a chance to collect what you want."

"You have three days. I will call you to tell you where to deliver the money."

Then he hung up. Within seconds the phone rang again, but the man laughed and slid the phone into his pocket.

For the next few days, Philip remained chained to a bar bolted into the floor. His captors eventually uncuffed his hands, but his ankle remained secured by a chain just long enough for him to reach a bedside pot used for a toilet. He could only walk in a small circle. Eating only thin potato soup and bread, he felt persistently weak. There was no conversation, no clock, no media; only lonely hours to contemplate his mortality. He could at times hear his captors laughing in a room downstairs. They came and went from the building, each time slamming the door, sliding the bolt, and a leaving their prize to deteriorate in captivity. Philip began to hallucinate about men hiding in the corners or sitting on the stairs listening to him.

On the evening of the second day, Philip gave up hope. He sat on the side of his bed, and there did something common to suffering men: he prayed. Without any confidence in the reality of prayer, but having lost any other hope of survival, he made a simple, desperate request, "I don't know how this happened. I see no way out. You alone have the power to make this go away. Please, if there is any way, let this pass."

Suddenly, Philip had a memory. It was a vague memory; a story he heard on his first day in Haiti. A man named Joseph Pierre, the host of a guest house, had told the story of his release from prison. He had said the prisoners were hungry, thirsty, and barely thought they would survive. So, they sang. They sang hymns like the two men in the Bible story; they sang and then, just when all hope was lost, the jailer set them free.

Philip lay down on his bed. He did not know any hymns. In his mind, he could hear the beautiful tune sung by the woman in the mountain church. The sound of her voice still burned in his mind; this caused his body to relax. But he did not know the words. He attempted to insert his own, mumbling something that sounded childish in his own ears. At that moment, a feeling of dread like a dense, heavy weight pressed on his chest. He could not breathe. It was not air for which he hungered. It was words, lyrics that would allow him to express the burden of standing in the shadow of death. But he had no words. At the moment he most needed the strength that comes from faith, he found himself instead with the expressive aphasia of a man who never learned to sing.

Then one hymn came to mind. The only spiritual song he knew, though he could not explain why he knew it. Its tune and haunting lyrics had been woven into his life at various random points—a funeral, a radio song, a patient who sang it once while drifting off to sleep before surgery. Philip could not explain where he learned the lyrics, but the words along with the tune expanded to fill his every thought. So, he sang:

"A-mazing grace—how sweet the sound—that
saved a wretch like me—I once was lost—but now
I'm found—was blind—but now I see."

After one verse, Philip paused. He stared at the ceiling. He did not know any more of the song. He closed his eyes, took in a deep breath, and in a voice low and strong, he sang that one verse over and over again. For nearly thirty minutes he sang until as if by the touch of an angel, his anxiety fell away.

There was no flash of light. No earthquake. His chains did not fall to the ground. He heard no rescuers or sounds of freedom. But at that moment, something did happen, something miraculous, though not in the typical way one uses the term. As Philip lay his head down, he noticed an absence of fear. His emotions leveled. It was like standing before a barking dog, ferocious, flinging saliva and baring teeth when suddenly having recognized his master's voice, it lowers its ears and begins wagging its tail, eager to play. The threat had lost its power. Philip, though once terrified, relaxed. He did not know if he would live or die. But regardless, he felt peace, and in that state of peace he drifted off to sleep.

44

The Great Escape

Philip awoke on the third morning to the sound and smell of heavy rain, a refreshing sound that softened the blunt reality of waking up in captivity, still trapped, his clothes stinking of stress. He noticed a pool of water had formed just under the balcony doors. Philip lay in stillness, thirsty, listening to the rain and wishing for the puddle of water to extend his direction.

The rain persisted all day. Like a neglected animal, chained and forgotten, he received no food or water. His mouth became dry, and he craved just a drop to soothe his throat. At one point he crawled, stretching his body across the floor. At his greatest reach, he was only able to dip his finger in the pool of rainwater, then bring the water to his tongue one drop at a time.

When evening came, Philip heard the door downstairs unbolt and bang open. The gang of four men, their faces now familiar, led by the scar-faced bald man rushed in; they unlocked his chains, cuffed his hands in front of him and placed a dark sack over his head.

The deadline had come, but Philip could not sense if the movement was favorable or not. Had the ransom been paid? Was he being taken to an exchange? Or was this the end? Philip could not say. But he was not being handled like a man being led to his freedom. He felt his arms grasped, lifted, and pulled. Unable to see, he stumbled across the room and then down the stairwell, held from falling by captors on either side. Only a few steps beyond the outer door, pelted by water falling from the roof, he was pushed into the back seat of a vehicle, flanked by men who smelled of alcohol and sweat, their clothing wet from the rain.

Only the bald man spoke, his voice distinct, serious in tone. He gave short instructions as the vehicle sped up and then slowed repeatedly amidst the sounds of traffic.

Philip heard the muffled speech, but he could not understand the words. He finally asked, "Where are we going? Did you get your money?"

The bald man spoke from the front passenger seat. He was brusque and ill-tempered, "You do not speak, Blanc."

After driving for some time, the vehicle made an abrupt turn. Philip could hear and feel the texture of the pavement transition to a muddy road. This was ominous. The road back to Milot was paved, so a turn onto an unpaved road meant they were taking him somewhere else.

Worse, they remained on the unpaved road for a long time. Philip was increasingly swayed back and forth, to and fro as they drove over ruts and around sinkholes. The general feel of movement was upward as though they were headed into the mountains. There were no sounds of traffic or people on these side roads. Philip could only hear the sound of rain pelting the roof of the vehicle. They were going somewhere remote, in the dark, alone. Philip began to breathe rapidly, his heart pounding at the thought of being driven to his own execution.

At one point they descended and then stopped suddenly. Philip felt the tires skid over wet gravel as the vehicle came to a stop.

The driver shut off the engine, and the men got out.

Philip heard the men standing at a short distance yelling at each other. With cuffed hands, Philip lifted the cloth slightly and leaned his head back to see what was happening. For some reason, the men had left the doors open and the headlights on.

Rain fell through the headlight beams which illuminated a river. They had come to a crossing made impassable by the swollen and rolling surge of the downpour. The bald man was screaming at the men, who were arguing about whether or not to cross.

Philip saw that the men were distracted. He pulled off the cloth hood and slid out onto the muddy ground. He crawled to the back of the vehicle and then stood to run, trying to gauge whether or not his splashing footsteps and muddy footprints would give him away. He darted as fast as he could into the foliage and trees, his cuffed hands preventing him from moving with any degree of speed or agility. He pushed through several meters of bushes and sharp vines. Thorns left deep gashes across his forearms and face. Then he lay down and listened.

It was several minutes before Philip heard shouts from the road, then gunshots. He lie low and waited. At one point, he heard the men beating at the undergrowth not far from him, frantic as they searched for their lost treasure.

Finally, the men departed. Philip heard the engine roar and saw light beams cross over his head as his kidnappers turned the vehicle and sped up the road, empty-handed.

Philip did not move from his hiding spot. The bald man had already tricked him once. It would be consistent to think he left men posted along the road, watching, sending his driver speeding off in a departure contrived to make Philip reveal his location.

So, Philip did not move. He remained still in the rain and darkness, curled up for hours. Too weak to run but too excited to sleep, his heart pounded in anticipation of completing his escape. One day earlier, death was inevitable; now he could sense freedom, but that liberty remained just out of reach. He remained a target, a hunted animal with enough sense to remain out of sight.

Philip drank water dripping from the large leaves hanging over him. The cool drops refreshed him. After several hours had passed, he drifted in and out of a restless sleep, often waking with a shaking chill.

The rain stopped before dawn. At one point, Philip looked up through the trees and parting clouds to see the first hues of blue against the black sky; his surroundings gradually transitioned from blackness, to silhouettes, to distinct shapes colored by the morning light. He had listened intently all night, convinced that the kidnappers were on the verge of finding his hiding place.

Then Philip heard a welcome sound: roosters. Roosters crowed somewhere in the distance. Philip knew that chickens live near people. A village was nearby.

Philip crawled with bound hands toward the road, taking care to move slowly to get a better view without being seen himself. At one point he took a stone and tossed it down a shallow ravine behind him. The rock crashed against wood and vines, the sound descending like someone running downhill. Then Philip listened and watched. There was no movement from the road. No one stood up to look. No one appeared.

Confident that he was alone, Philip walked toward the sound of the crowing, remaining off the road to be safe.

Eventually, Philip came into a rural village. It was a small village with only a few mud houses. Philip stood in front of one of the houses, his hands cuffed in front him, his arms and face lacerated, his bloodstained shirt and his muddy pants hanging wet and limp on his body. A child came out of the house, and upon seeing Philip, ran back inside crying. Then a thin man stepped out. He wore a straw hat and held a machete. The man pointed the machete and spoke rapid phrases, but Philip could not understand him.

Philip held up the cuffs and tried to explain that he was lost and needed help. He had no money. He had no identification. He had no phone. He could only imagine what a horror he must look like. But he needed help and pleaded for assistance.

Something about Philip's demeanor and countenance caused the face and posture of the man to soften. The man looked at Philip. His stern glare melted into a compassionate grin, and he waved Philip into his yard.

The man summoned others. They gave Philip a chair on which to sit while women washed his wounds, applying a salve to his arms and head. A girl brought him a piece of sweet flatbread and a bowl of rice and beans.

Once cleaned and fed, the family lifted Philip onto a small horse. The animal groaned under the unexpected load and lumbered down the mountain, coaxed by a barefoot boy and followed by the man in the straw hat. The unlikely companions followed a trail, leaving the road in deference to a more direct route.

When they came to a paved highway, the man flagged down a tap-tap and haggled with the driver. After settling on an acceptable price, the man handed the driver a few worn bills and then helped Philip onto a bench in the back. Others sat around Philip, wary of his cuffs and rough appearance. As they drove away, Philip saw the man and boy walking with the scrawny horse back up the trail. He never saw them again.

The tap-tap drove for many miles before coming to a stop in front of a police station. The driver stepped around and ushered Philip out, pointing him into the station.

Inside the police station, Philip found an officer who spoke English. The officer removed the cuffs and took a description of the kidnappers. Then the officer told Philip something extraordinary. Four men by that description had been taken into custody near Milot that same morning, their vehicle had been flipped and burned by people of the community, and the men themselves would have been stoned and beaten to death had the police not intervened.

The officer drove Philip back to Milot. As they pulled up to the hospital gate, Philip offered to pay the officer if he could wait a few minutes while he gathered some money, but the Haitian man refused. "You are fortunate to be alive, my friend. I know you have come many miles to help my people, to help us in our home. Seeing you return safely to your home is my payment."

Philip stood before the hospital gates. Inside a crowd was gathered in the shaded waiting area. It was early in the afternoon, four days since he had been abducted from Lakay Jezu. He did not know what had happened to Victor. He did not know if Lynn and Luckson had returned. He felt the need to call home so that Amanda would know that he had survived.

Suddenly a nurse started yelling, ecstatic, with her hands raised. She saw Philip and ran to him throwing her arms around him, calling out his name. The crowd heard the woman's cries and grew silent and watched. Philip could not remember the nurse's name, but she recognized him, and she wept as she held him firmly, as if he were a man come back from the dead.

The commotion drew a number of hospital staff. One of them told Philip they were told he was probably dead, killed by his abductors.

Then Lynn appeared in the doorway of the hospital. Her eyes were bloodshot, sunken and sleepless. She stood with one hand over her mouth and the other over her heart as if she was trying to prevent a scream and a burst heart. She walked slowly toward Philip; then she broke into a run, taking him into her arms.

45

Philip is Reunited with His Friends

Lynn could barely speak. Through tears, she asked, "Are you all right? You look terrible. Did they hurt you?"

"The ordeal is over. I'll explain later. I feel like I need to sit down."

Lynn placed one of Philip's arms over her shoulder and walked with him into the main building. In her excitement, she repeated, "You're alive. I just can't believe you're alive. They told us it was not enough, but you were freed."

"What do you mean 'enough?' I escaped last night during the storm."

Lynn stopped. She looked at Philip and asked, "Last night? That makes no sense. Men came by the hospital this morning demanding a ransom. We took up a collection, but when we could only produce a few thousand dollars, the men took the money and said it was not enough. Everyone thought the worst. People from the community heard what was going on. They were waiting for the men down the road. They destroyed their vehicle and would have killed them if not for the police."

Philip described his escape, "I slipped away when the men argued about crossing a river. It was a cold night, but I did not move until morning. The men never came back. This morning I found my way to a village. A farmer took me to the nearest road and got me to the police. The men must have come by the hospital thinking they could still get something from you."

Philip asked about Victor.

Lynn smiled, "Would you like to see him?"

"Yes, of course."

Lynn again pulled Philip's arm over her shoulder, "Come this way, Doctor."

Victor was in a hospital bed, lying in a row of patients, his leg elevated and wrapped in layers of padding and plaster. Luckson was sitting on the floor at his side, tinkering with a homemade crutch. When Victor saw Philip enter with Lynn, his eyebrows lifted. He struggled to sit up in his bed, but the movement caused a sharp pain in his leg that arrested his movement. The pain did not affect his smile. He looked to the ceiling and shouted, "There is a God who rescues men!"

Philip saw the elevated leg. Despite his weakness, he felt a surge of adrenaline and said, "We need to get you to the operating room. I want to clean out that wound."

Victor looked confused, "The surgery is done."

"Done?"

"Yes. Fixed last night."

Philip cocked his head and ran his fingers through his hair, "Who did the procedure?"

Victor laughed, "The best surgeon I know."

"Who?"

Victor raised himself onto an elbow, "I was told you called him for me. I don't know how you got around the kidnappers to call him. How did you do it?"

"Do what? Who did the procedure?"

"My friend, Doctor Hu. He said you sent for him."

At that moment, Anderson Hu entered wearing scrubs. A mask hung limply across his chest, "What is this I hear? Is it true? My colleague has been returned?"

Philip and Anderson stood face to face for a moment. There were no social norms on how surgeons should greet one another on foreign soil and under such circumstances. The two men nodded and swayed in front of one another, unsure whether to shake hands or hug or dance. Victor, Luckson, and Lynn laughed at them. Finally, Anderson reached over and pulled Philip into his chest, "You are alive, my friend; thank God. You are alive!"

All of them circled around Victor's bed and swapped stories, recounting details from the harrowing days, each of them sharing a different perspective.

Anderson explained, "Amanda called me. She was pretty upset. Understandably so. So, I got on a plane that night and headed this way. I expected the worst."

Victor looked at Philip, "After they dragged you away, Luckson designed a splint for me. Then those children carried me on a stretcher made from a mattress. Oh, that was torture. Lynn drove the truck while Tabitha tended to me during the ride down the mountain. I never want to go through that again."

Lynn added, "That night, one of our Haitian surgeons cleaned out the wound and did what he could to stabilize the leg. We started antibiotics and hoped for the best. Then yesterday morning, Doctor Hu arrived. He just walked through the front entrance and said he had been summoned to treat Victor. So, yesterday afternoon, we took Victor to the operating room and repaired the fracture."

Anderson looked at Philip, "When Victor woke up from anesthesia, he insisted everyone pray—for you. He just kept saying, *We must pray for Doctor Scott*. We assumed he was in a post-operative delirium when waking from the anesthesia. So, we calmed him and he drifted back to sleep, but minutes later he awoke yelling at us to pray for you. So, I pulled the staff into the recovery room. The small area was packed with nurses, doctors, administrators, and even the lab technician. And they prayed. For an entire hour, they prayed—for you."

Lynn continued, "Then it started raining hard, and Victor prayed, 'As you rescued Noah through the waters, rescue my friend.'"

Philip heard those words and his legs became weak. He sat down, faint. He was not ill, at least not in his body. His mind was spinning. Everything he knew to be true was being sifted. He was not sure what to believe. He considered prayer an empty activity, a personal ritual akin to meditation, not something with any power to effect change over a distance. That would be irrational. So, why had he resorted to asking God for help? Why did he do something so irrational? He recalled how it gave him peace. But could it have caused something more? And why would Victor wake up at the very moment he needed help, the thought of Philip his singular concern?

What if the prayers worked? Philip thought he had escaped on his own merits. His friends now presented an alternative view. What had appeared to him as an opportunity for escape had been, at least in their eyes, a rescue. Did God hear their prayers? Had they really argued their case before the Supreme Judge of the world? Did they truly believe he would hear their petition? And even more that he would grant it? Could the one who calmed a storm also stir up a storm at the behest of mortals? How could any man or woman wield that kind of influence? In a swirling atmosphere with weather variations that even the most rational beings on the planet cannot accurately predict, how could anyone be asked to believe that a storm arose over a Caribbean island on a specific day simply because a group of people prayed for help? This was too much to fathom. A power great enough to grant that request would have to have control of not just a local rain cloud; he would have control of the entire system—the entire universe. Such a conclusion would mean not simply that this being answers prayer; it would mean this divine being had provided an answer long before the petition was uttered by human lips. Philip had fallen into the hands of evil men, an act that appeared random. Then he escaped, saved by a deluge. It could have been a coincidental result of time and chance. Or it could be that a storm had been woven into the fabric of history from the beginning of time, at least in part to answer the prayers of a group of people summoned by a man in a post-operative stupor. Either way, Philip felt he had won a great lottery. And even if the Divine Creator had prearranged the entire affair, Philip was not offended; quite to the contrary, he was in awe. Facing death on the precipice of eternity had given him a new perspective. He felt dread at the thought of coming so close to death, but he found peace in the thought that there in the shadow of death, it seemed that God came near.

Lynn saw Philip sit down. The way he bent forward and placed his head in his hands concerned her. She placed a hand on his shoulder and asked, "Philip, are you ill?"

Philip looked at his friends, "No—No, of course not. I'm fine. This is just a lot to take in. I was so cold last night, shivering for hours. And frankly, I was shaking more from the thought of dying than from the cold. Those men were going to kill me. Right there. The darkness felt heavy around me. There were no stars, no moon, and no light. I was as alone as any man can be. Then I thought of you, Victor, wondering who would repair your wound. I worried for Tabitha. Would they attack her? Would they come after you, Lynn? I thought of all of you. For all I knew, those idiots would attack the hospital next. You were suffering too. The thought of your hurting was unbearable, but I could not move. I was scared, and I felt as weak as any man could be. Now I realize I was not alone. None of us were alone."

46

Philip writes Himself a Letter

The following Sunday, Philip returned to the church with Victor. He sat on a splintered wooden bench wedged between others. Despite being the foreigner, he felt at home, and he sang out the few expressions he picked out from the songs. He again experienced the lifting effect of hymns and spiritual songs. Though most of the words remained foreign to him, one phrase he understood immediately, *Mesi Bondye, Thank you, God.* These words mixed with the evocative cadence of hymns triggered pleasant static-like sensations that flowed over Philip's body in waves. Philip closed his eyes; the euphoric feeling grew as his mind swelled with the adoration of a divine being who still seemed far away; but for the first time, at least for Philip, seemed to have come within earshot.

After the service, the congregation descended the hill to the edge of the mountain stream. The Haitian minister stepped into the water, his pant legs rolled up to mid-thigh while from the shore a crowd of well-dressed men in dark suits stood in front of women in bright dresses. Children pushed to the front in order to see. The minister looked up at the crowd and spoke a few words. Then he held out his hand as if to welcome a guest.

From the center of the crowd, Philip stepped out and descended into the water. There he stood, knee deep in the stream with his head bowed. The minister stood next to him. Victor watched from the shore, leaning on a crutch, his injured leg bent at the knee. Next to him stood Anderson Hu, smiling. Sunlight fell on each of them like a hot spotlight angling through the trees.

Philip felt the cool current press against his legs. Then he heard a woman in the crowd begin to sing. When Philip heard the tune, he looked up. It was the very song that had captivated him a week before. The same woman raised her voice, and it seemed to Philip that everything that was beautiful in the world became in that moment a melody that floated from her lips. She looked to the heavens as she sang. Philip followed her gaze upward, and just as he looked up, the leaves parted, and a beam of sunlight flashed in his eyes. The flash was blinding. For a moment his vision was obscured; he blinked and looked downward until the water rushing past his feet again became clear.

After the song, the minister spoke to the crowd about good and evil, life and death, man's fall and God's strategy for making the world right again. Then he asked Philip to make a confession.

Philip looked up to see the eyes of an entire village looking not at the minister, but at him. He smiled in a nervous grin and looked at the people on the shore. He came thinking he was here to help them. In reality, these people had rescued him. As he scanned the crowd his eyes fell upon Victor, Luckson, and Anderson, and he said simply, "I believe it's true. Jesus is the son of God. By him, all things have come into existence, and through him I have life—and I have peace."

At this, the minister lifted a hand, said a prayer and lowered Philip below the water.

When the minister raised Philip, the men and women on the shore leaned forward, watching in anticipation, curious to see what would happen when a foreign man was baptized. There was no visible change. Philip was wet, but there were no signs of a miraculous conversion. There were no doves descending from the sky. There was no voice from the heavens. Philip looked like the same man who had gone into the water.

Then he shook his head, throwing water from his hair in all directions like a wet dog. The children screamed in laughter. When Philip heard them, he glanced up. The scene had a vague familiarity as if he recognized someone in a photograph but had trouble remembering the venue. The faces of twenty or thirty boys and girls were smiling, watching from the shore, white teeth shining from a cloud of dark faces. Philip surveyed the children. He suddenly recognized the smile. It was the same smile he had seen from Rose-Marie, years before in the shadows of a tent; her smile was on the faces of those children on the shore.

Philip raised his hands and said, "Mesi, Bondye. Thank you, God."

Hearing his words, the crowd clapped and cheered. Then an elderly man hobbled forward. He leaned on a worn cane and spoke. Victor gave Philip the translation, "He says, he is eighty years old, and this is the first time he sees an American person baptized. He says he is amazed to see that you are baptized the same way as a Haitian person. This tells him that God's gift cannot be bought with the wealth of a rich man, but it is the same price for all."

That evening Philip went for a walk with Lynn. He told her about his decision and how the smile of the children reminded him of Rose-Marie, "I've been freed from a burden. It was like Rose-Marie was smiling on me today."

Lynn faced Philip holding his hands in hers, "May I make a recommendation?"

"Of course."

"Everyone who gives his life to God is taken through a wilderness. When that happens, you may forget the joy you feel today. I think it will do you much good to write yourself a letter. Seal it and store it away to pull out when the days are not so bright and you doubt the sincerity of your decision."

That night Philip sat down at a small desk in his bedroom. A small lamp illuminated the desk's surface. He pulled out a pen and a sheet of paper, but for a time he wrote nothing, sitting only in silence while contemplating the experiences that had led him to this moment. He thought of his uncertain career, his failed marriage, and his growing children. He thought of Rose-Marie and could hear her voice in his memory. First her screams, then her honest questions, then her name for him, Papa San. He thought of the first time he met Victor and Luckson. He smiled at the thought of Victor's child-like faith and common sense. He remembered Heidi Kapoor's prayer about his heart being broken by what he saw. He now saw the deep wisdom in her words. Then his thoughts turned to Lynn. Like a Good Samaritan, Lynn did not leave Philip to suffer; she was the salve on his broken spirit and was the first to speak of God in a way that made sense.

Finally, Philip lifted his pen and wrote the following:

I made a decision today with limited data. I accepted an invitation to follow Jesus. This does not mean I took a leap of faith. It is not a blind decision or rash act. I chose to become a Christian. The decision was made after much thought. The decision was mine alone; though, I admit conversations with Lynn Sable, Thomas Palmer, and Victor Santile had much to do with it. I did not choose to join a church or a religion. Maybe that will happen someday. When people speak of their religion or their book, I now have a greater respect for their faith. They have found a source of strength I never before understood. But I can't say I was enticed by their faith any more than I would be at-

*tracted to one of their personal friends. Their reli-
gion is important to them, and I respect them
enough to stay out of their relationships. My decision was not based on a mental assent to some
creed or the teachings of a book. Perhaps some
will say I am following a book, the Bible. But for
me, the Bible has been a telescope that brought a
distant image into focus. It spoke of a man; it is
this man I have chosen to follow. As I understand
it, this man did things that only God Himself can
do. Then he said he would forgive me if I would let
him. It's not just that he would dismiss the horrid
things I've said or done; he said he would make the
whole world right again, including the parts I've
messed up so badly. Perhaps I will look back one
day and see I was only curious, but I'm writing this
now as a reminder that what I am actually experiencing today is better described as awe. I think I've
seen how God is changing the world. He is restor-
ing the world by remaking people. Today, I under-
went an amputation. I could either lose my guilt or
lose my life. So, at the hands of an almighty God,
my sin was removed. I left it buried in a mountain
stream. To be clear, this is not an emotional decision or an idle gesture. I have yet to see or hear
from this Almighty One in whose hands I have
placed my soul. But I believe He exists and that He
rewards men who seek Him. And if this is at all
true, it means that part of me is now buried in water and will never grow back. I am told that the Son
of God died for my sin. I suppose that means he*

paid for this operation, and they tell me that is the meaning of his death and that his resurrection is a foreshadowing of my own. For that I am grateful. I do not know how my story will end, but I am convinced that today I only had two options; the other one was killing me.

A black leather Bible lay on the bedside table, the Bible given to him by Gladys Walters. Philip folded the letter and placed it in the fold of the pages.

Then he picked up his flashlight and walked out.

47

The Graveyard

The evening breeze fell still. Stars hung overhead in the black, stippled sky, and the moon, full and bright, illuminated the road in a blueish hue. Alone, Philip walked up the road to a graveyard. He passed through a tilted iron gate and sat down beside the concrete headstone upon which was written the name, Rose-Marie Sanguine.

Philip sat in silence for nearly half an hour.

Then he spoke to Rose-Marie as if she, too, were sitting beside him, "Neither one of us wanted to come here. To this place, I mean. Your journey was longer than mine, and I'm glad you are at rest now. I still can't comprehend the horror you went through. How did you endure the terror of meeting me after you lost so much? You lost your family. You were flown far from your home. Then I took your leg. With no explanation, and no ear to hear your cries, your world was torn from you. You deserved better, you know. So, I came here to say two things. Whether you can hear me or not, it does not matter; certain things must be said. First, I'm sorry. I once thought God was cruel. How could he allow someone as beautiful as you to suffer? Now I see that if anyone is cruel, it is I. He sent me to you. At the moment you most needed help, he put you in my hands. But I was not worthy of his trust, much less yours. I came reluctantly, angry, thinking this place was beneath me. I admit that now. I did not see the princess you are until it was too late. I have never in my life had the honor of being the doctor for a more beautiful, important, and noble person. If I had it to do over, I would fly you home and personally oversee your care. Please forgive me. Now,

I suppose I really came to say thank you. You once asked me if legs grow back. I did not see until now that you only asked because you believed it could happen. Then I read about a man who could make it happen. But you already knew that, didn't you? Did you know that same man made blind people see? It's true, Rose-Marie. He sent me to help you walk. But you—he sent you to help me see."

Philip could say no more. His voice knotted up, and cathartic tears fell to the dark ground beneath him. His body slumped forward as if surrendering to a heavy burden. There he wept.

After several minutes had passed, Philip heard something; a moan followed by the sound of shuffling feet across gravel; then a male voice mumbling, slurring in the cadence of a funeral march.

The voice called out from across the cemetery in phrases that seemed to be a mix of Creole, French, English, mixed in a strange incantation. The words Philip could understand had the ring of an evil spell. "Bwing me da bones. You dead. When I's a child, the Lwa taught me. At my mudder's breast, they bought me. My fadder taught me the Lwa, and they bought me. If not for the Lwa we'd have no deliverance. Yes, if not for the Lwa we all'd perish. Bwing me da bones."

Philip heard the sudden crash of glass. He froze, eager not to be seen.

The voice called out again, "I hear your cries. You's come because you seek Lwa? Bwing me da bones."

Philip rose to his feet, careful to remain silent. His knees shook. He squinted into the darkness scanning the gravestones and monuments for movement. Halfway across the cemetery, a short shadowy figure lumbered toward him, shuffling across the ground as if half dead.

The voice called out, "Why you come, Blanc? The Lwa do not welcome you. The Lwa do not seek your belief or your consent. You leave. You leave."

Philip felt the weight of unseen eyes on him. He turned and ran a few steps, then hearing the voice again, he stopped. He recognized something about the voice. It sounded familiar. He turned to face the bumbling man and called out, "Theo?"

"Why you come here, Blanc?"

Philip turned on his flashlight and held the beam on the man, "Theo? Is that you?"

The man held a hand up to shield his eyes against the light, "Why do you seek Theo?"

"I'm not seeking him. I remember meeting a man named Theo. He lives near here somewhere. Is that you?"

The man stumbled forward and fell to one side catching himself on a large concrete monument. Philip lowered the flashlight, and the moon illuminated the man's features. Philip recognized it was, in fact, Theo, the witch doctor. In one hand Theo held a broken rum bottle. In the other, he held a human skull.

Philip walked toward him, "You are unwell. What is wrong?"

Theo swung the fractured bottle back and forth like a broken sword, still slurring his words, "I'm fine. You—you may not stay here."

As Philip approached Theo, he caught the stench of musty rum and odors of a man who needs a bath. The edges of Philip's face fell in an expression of pity. With cautious movements, he took the bottle and then the skull from Theo, "You are drunk, my friend. Let me help you."

Theo laughed, "The Lwa decide who needs help. I's do not seek your help or your sympathy."

Philip did not argue. He lifted Theo's arm over his own shoulder and took halting encumbered steps toward the road. Together, arm in arm they lumbered up the road. From a distance, anyone seeing the erratic swinging flashlight and broad swaying shadow would say the scene looked like a couple of drunks trying to find their way home.

When they arrived at Theo's courtyard, Philip raised the beam of the flashlight to illuminate the tattered red flag. Philip recognized the place to which he had come years before. Philip helped Theo through the gate and into a small mud-walled house. The one-room structure was illuminated by an oil lamp; the room was otherwise unoccupied. As Philip lowered Theo onto a bed in the corner, the doorway behind him suddenly darkened. He turned to see a puzzled, wrinkled-faced woman.

The woman's callused bare feet and her moist eyes caught Philip's attention. He greeted her though she did not respond. Philip pointed toward the bed and spoke in slow phrases, "Is Theo your husband? He is not ill, he is just drunk. He needs to sleep. Do you understand what I am saying?"

The woman stared at Philip.

Theo mumbled, "You are a crazy man, I think. Blancs never come to me. But you bring me home. Why you do this, Blanc?"

Philip shook his head, "You are drunk. I'm making sure you're safe. It was fortunate I found you. Now, take off your shoes and go to sleep."

At that moment something startled Theo. His eyes opened wide, and he sat up straight. He pointed a finger toward Philip but not exactly at him. Speaking as clear as any sober man he said, "You are not alone."

Philip looked around him. There was no one but the woman. "You are confused, my friend, there is no one here but the lady."

Trembling, Theo repeated, "She is with me. But you are not alone. Not like before."

"What is that supposed to mean?"

Theo never answered. He fell back into the bed with one leg hanging off the side; his breath deepened and his body sunk into the bed with a moaning snore.

As Theo drifted off, Philip stood over him, wondering what to make of the statement. It was likely nothing, just the hallucinations of an intoxicated man. Yet Philip remembered the day they met. On that day Theo threatened Philip saying, "you are alone and blind and vulnerable." Did Theo now see something different? Philip shook his head, not in disbelief but in pity and compassion. As he studied Theo's face, he noticed it was no longer the face of evil. Philip spent three days in the presence of evil; he knew what that looked like. But lying there on the bed was a man whose life was a mess. It was Theo who was vulnerable, living under the impaired belief that through some unseen spirits he could control his world. In a world of trauma, Theo was not the cause; he was just another victim.

Philip lifted Theo's leg back onto the bed. He placed a hand on Theo's forehead and said, "None of us are alone, my friend. May God grant you life and peace."

Philip turned to the woman, still standing in the doorway. He pulled money from his pocket and placed it in her hand, "Buy some strong coffee. He will need it come morning."

The woman looked at the money and then back at Philip. She did not respond. She stood to the side and let Philip make his exit.

Philip walked down the road at a slow, thoughtful pace. He felt the night breeze on his face and allowed his mind to soak in the smells, sensations, and memories of a place that changed him. Before reaching the guest house, he stopped. He turned off his flashlight and looked toward the silhouette of the mountains. Tabitha was up there. He needed to see her before returning home, but it was well past dark. He would need to get up early to leave at daybreak.

48

Philip Visits the Orphanage

A swirl of dust rose around a group of boys, most of them barefoot, pushing for position to see through the upper limbs of a tree at Lakay Jezu. One boy held a radio, his hand on the dial, twisting in slow increments as others bent close, each ear listening for music or a voice from the city. The radio was connected to a long wire. Another boy climbed above them, lifting the wire high enough to capture unseen waves broadcast from radio towers in the valley below.

Groups of giggling girls pretended not to watch as they sat on the long porches. They braided each other's hair or read books. But one of them took personal notice; she leaned on her walker and held a hand over her eyes straining to see the boy climbing in the tree. It was Fred Joel, her brother. His courage made her nervous.

Fred Joel wove his way upward with a wire in his hand, branches serving as rungs on which to climb to a height which he hoped would allow the wire to serve as an effective antenna.

The boys yelled at Fred Joel to climb higher, which he did, a barefoot acrobat on a mission. Then at one point, they started screaming in uncoordinated joy for him to stop. Fred looked down. Through the limbs, he could see the boys dancing around the radio. Then he too heard the rhythmic music billowing upward and outward across the yard.

Fred secured the wire around a limb. Then, instead of climbing down, he sat in the curve of a branch that afforded him a wide view of the land around the orphanage. For a moment he rested, listening to the music, content to remain above the tussle, free to imagine himself sitting in the tower of a citadel, a lookout on his imaginary island fortress.

Less than two weeks had passed since kidnappers forced themselves into the lives of the children in a vicious act that violated the fragile security of the orphanage and left each child nervous, ever wary of another attack. After that horrid day, the children ran for cover anytime one of them heard a peculiar noise in the distance, especially truck engines, and they were suspicious of approaching strangers; often they scattered to their dormitories anytime unexpected visitors arrived.

So, Fred Joel imagined he was the protector, the sentry on watch for the next attack. But that day the scene was peaceful. Across the field, he could see the trail fade into a sea of plantain trees. Beyond the plantains, smoke rose in scattered plumes before the land fell away toward the river. For the moment his world was calm.

Suddenly, the peace was interrupted. There was movement at the far side of the field. Fred rose to his feet, clinging still to an overhead branch. He saw the movement at the far end of the field but could not make out the shapes. Fred blinked and held tightly to the limbs around him, ready to descend at the first sign of danger. He could only imagine the worst: kidnappers returning with guns.

Fred was just about to yell for everyone to run, but he recognized something familiar in the silhouettes. He called to the boys below, but rather than telling everyone to run, he pointed toward the field and just yelled for them to look.

The children gathered at the cactus fence row, peering over the top to see what Fred was pointing out. Curiosity then drew the girls. They too saw shadows coming over the hill. People. First three people, then four, then five making their way up the trail. One was shorter and wearing a baseball cap. One walked with a limp. Two walked arm-in-arm. Their faces were obscured by sunlight reflecting off the ground in a humid midday mirage.

Fred squinted against the light, studying the approaching strangers until he was sure his suspicions were correct. Even before their faces came fully into view, Fred recognized the visitors, and he shouted to the others, yelling in Creole, "Papa San! Papa San!"

The other children came to the same conclusion. They all began yelling out the name.

Philip heard them. Like an echo down a mountain valley, he heard his name reverberate from every direction. It was not his professional name, nor his birth name; it was the name given to him by Rose-Marie Sanguine, Papa-San, Blood Father, yelled in unison by the young chorus. The sound of that name, called in that accent, was to Philip a shot of adrenaline. He broke into a run, extending his legs and arms in a full sprint toward the cheering children.

Fred Joel saw Philip running toward them, and he dropped from the tree, landing just as Philip reached the gate.

Philip pushed through the swarm of laughing children, and he lifted Fred Joel into his arms and swung him in a circle. Then he picked up a little girl, then another. So many children jumped into his arms that Philip fell to the ground and lay in the dust on his back as boys and girls climbed onto his belly.

Philip could not move. He was trapped, not by the weight of fifty children, but by their love. He was not suffocating; on the contrary, he felt he could breathe as never before. In a way, the living God had become incarnate in a human hug of such size that Philip was unable to move in its embrace. His eyes and throat filled with dust, but he loved it. In between breaths, he screamed out in delight.

Victor and Lynn could not tell if Philip was laughing or screaming for help. They ran up and began pulling children back. Lynn yelled, "Stop this; you are hurting him."

Through the mass of children, Philip cried back, "It's okay. They are just tickling me."

Tabitha heard the noise and stepped out of her office. She walked over to the mayhem and shouted one sharp command. The children instantly stood up and parted, allowing her to pass through. She bent over Philip, stern, with piercing eyes and a foreboding stare.

Philip looked up with a boyish grin. He thought she looked humorous because from his perspective she was upside down, and he wiped the dirt from his mouth, "Hello, Tabitha."

Tabitha's cheeks rounded into a warm smile, and she said, "I see God has saved you from evil men only to have you killed by the love of children."

Philip stood up. He brushed the dirt from his shirt and leaned toward Tabitha, kissing her on the cheek, "If a man must die, let him die in these arms."

Tabitha considered the way Philip looked. His countenance had changed. She looked at his stance, his innocent smile, and then his eyes. She said nothing, but her gaze gave away her thoughts.

Philip saw the inquisitive tilt of her head, and he answered her unspoken question, "Tabitha, I'm a new man."

Tabitha blinked and nodded in agreement; then she replied, "I can see that is true."

She never explained what she meant or what she saw in Philip that was different, and Philip never asked.

Instead, Philip introduced Anderson to Tabitha and said, "Doctor Hu and I are flying back to the U.S. tomorrow. I don't know when I'll be able to return. But I wanted to see you and the children before we leave."

Tabitha studied Anderson; then she called out to the children around her. Several scurried off at her command. Then she turned to say, "Then we will celebrate and send you off in a manner worthy of your voyage."

Tabitha turned to Victor and spoke for a moment in Creole. Victor pointed to his leg and seemed to be describing his ordeal. Then Tabitha turned to Anderson and offered to provide him with a tour of the grounds.

Later they sat around a table under the mango tree, eating dinner. Tabitha retold what had happened the day the kidnappers arrived, demanding money, threatening the children. Then Victor and Lynn described coming on the tragic scene. Anderson Hu listened to each of them, intrigued by the nightmare from which they all survived.

Tabitha turned to Philip and said, "You laid your life down for us, Doctor Scott, and we will remember you for all our lives. God will remember what you have done, for He has recorded your deeds, and God's pencil has no eraser. What you have done has saved many lives."

Philip looked around the table. He thought of how much this unlikely group of people had influenced his life: Lynn's beautiful understanding of her place in the world; Victor's tough skin and soft heart; Luckson's energetic mind and endless supply of hope; Anderson's selfless experience; and then Tabitha, who with few words and the simplest hospitality had made him feel welcome in this simple home for lost souls.

Philip turned in his chair to look back at the surrounding crowd of children, their eyes fixed on him. What did they see? A man who brought them gifts? A man who would lay down his life for their safety? Did they know how much they had changed his life? Could they even imagine how much they had to offer the world? How would they escape the poverty?

Fred Joel saw Philip looking at them. He lowered his bowl and stood up. Then he placed a hand on another child for balance. With the other hand, he held his foot behind him, bent at the knee. While standing on one leg, he yelled out in Creole, "I love you, Papa San."

Lynn placed a hand over her heart. Philip looked at her puzzled. What is the boy doing? Then the meaning of Fred Joel's gesture became clear. He was mimicking Rose-Marie, her leg amputated, saying goodbye so many years ago. How did he remember that day?

Philip looked again, and other children began doing the same thing, first one then another, then the entire group, each child standing up, bending the knee and holding onto others for balance, then calling out the same phrase, "I love you, Papa San."

Lynn looked over to see Philip, staring at the children. The entire yard was full of off-balance children, yelling his name. Tears fell from his chin onto the dirt below. Lynn saw Philip mouthing words, but he was too taken with emotion to make a sound.

Philip scanned the dark eyes of the children. It was a strange memorial to a young girl who had changed his life. He tried to push the words out, but could only whisper, "I love you, too. I love you, too."

Turning back to Tabitha, Philip wiped his eyes and said, "You are too good to say I have done anything for you. It is you, my sister, who have saved my life. It is true: this is the House of Jesus."

49

Think About It

Three months later, a long, low horn sounded across the Puget Sound announcing the coming of night upon Seattle. The reverberations stretched out like a yawn across the water, extending up the shore and in between the buildings whose windows reflected orange evening light. Even the Space Needle glowed, giving it the appearance of a lighthouse at dusk.

Behind one of the Space Needle windows, just above the skyline, Philip looked out of a private banquet room, a sparkling drink in one hand. Laughter and conversation behind him blended with a string quartet. Philip noticed in his reflection that his black bowtie appeared tilted. With his free hand, he adjusted the bowtie. Then he stood with a stoic expression, watching as the distant, fading sun descended behind the Olympic Mountains.

Had this been a dream, he would have walked out. In fact, he had dreamed of this day many times, and when he last left for Haiti, he had decided to walk away from this to chase a different dream. He was ready to give up his career, his home, his position. He had planned to decline the offer of promotion and take on the role of a part-time professor. He could make enough money to support trips to the developing world where he could treat people who needed him. There he could support the growth and health and education of children he had come to love. And just as appealing, he could see Lynn.

Yet it was Lynn who convinced him otherwise. Standing in the airport on the day he left Haiti, she listened to his plans and then took his face in her hands, speaking to him like a mother speaks to a child, "Chasing a dream is to chase something selfishly; it is to pursue something for your own pride. But you are no longer chasing a dream. Yours is a calling, no?"

At first, Philip argued with her, "Someone's meant for that job. But it's not me. For me, the job would not be a calling, just a distraction."

Lynn smiled, "The job is not the calling. Your calling is the distant voice of people who love you. Do not close your ears to them. Imagine what a man in your position could do to change the world. There are people all over the world who need a competent surgeon. Who will train these doctors? Who knows, but that you were put here to be their teacher?"

Philip listened to her. When he returned to Seattle, he accepted the offer. Now, a few months later he found himself standing in a tuxedo at his own promotion ceremony. Gazing across the water at the setting sun, he thought about Lynn's words. Suddenly in the window, as if in a vision, he saw her figure. The body of the very angel who taught him not to be afraid was floating toward him, her evening dress reflecting the lights of the city. Then standing next to him, she took his arm and rested her head on his shoulder. She was no apparition; she was the warm living friend whose touch embodied courage.

Philip whispered, "Am I doing the right thing?"

Lynn squeezed, "You are an interesting man, Philip Scott. I did not accept your invitation because I thought you were making the wrong choice."

Across the room, Michael Henske stood behind a lectern tapping on a crystal goblet. The crowd heard the clang followed by a squeal of feedback in the microphone. They fell silent.

Doctor Henske looked over the crowd of guests in formal attire. He took the microphone in his hand and stood beside the lectern. In a casual after-dinner style he boasted of the program he built. Many of the guests had heard the same speech many times, but they listened politely as the retiree took his final opportunity to enumerate his accomplishments as chairman. His comments were uninteresting, but it was clear he was an important man who had done important work. He pointed out distinguished guests from the University, many of them administrators, each in turn receiving complimentary applause. Then the applause thundered along with rising laughter when Henske concluded by saying, "You realize this is the last speech you will ever hear me make."

When the laughter subsided, Henske shot back with a playful threat, "Let me also remind you I have signature authority on your paychecks for another month."

The crowd laughed again.

Then Henske raised his glass in a toast to his successor, "These many years as chairman I have learned one thing: the chairman's office is a lonely place. I do not mean there are few visitors. The phone rings constantly, and there is no stop to the meetings and unscheduled knocks at the door. But not one person in a hundred stops by just to say hello. Everyone has a problem needing a solution. And the problems are never easy; if they were, someone else would have solved them already. The chairman is the goalie at the end of a long field. I have been proud to stand in that goal for this department, this incredible team. And today it is my honor to step aside and allow a fine colleague and surgeon to stand in my place. Please lift a glass with me to toast the new Chairman of the Orthopedics Department, Doctor Philip Scott."

The room swelled with eager applause, "Hear, hear!"

Philip was pushed toward the lectern and handed the microphone. He looked around the room. He saw his ex-wife, Amanda and her husband, Stanley. Anderson Hu and his wife Monica stood together applauding. Aryanna and Connor Wayman waved. Thomas Palmer pointed his cane like a sword in a salute to his surgeon. Heidi Kapoor folded her hands together in a prayer-like pose and winked. Lynn placed her hand over her heart. Philip remembered the first moment he saw her; in a crowd, her face was still the one he could not ignore.

Philip raised the microphone to his lips and spoke, "Thank you for coming. There are many places you could be tonight. It means a lot to me that you chose to come and enjoy the sunset and special occasion. I've learned that success in life is not so much a matter of what you acquire. In fact, some of the most successful people I know are also among the poorest people in the world. Success, I believe, is about people pulling together in a common purpose. It's being resourceful with what you are given. And the greatest thing any one of us is given isn't an object at all. Friends are our greatest gifts. In Haiti, a little girl once taught me how to say in her language, 'You are my friend.' And she taught me what that means: to be a friend. Friendship is not based on status or success. It is the bond between two people who, upon finding themselves in a common struggle, simply say, 'Let's pull together, you and I.' As I look around the room tonight, I recognize I am standing among friends. You all mean more to me than I can say. And in the years to come, we will do incredible work, you and I; not because we were given a sizable budget or state-of-the-art equipment. I will push for these things because I know you need them. But I also know our success will not be defined by the instruments placed in our hands; our success will be defined by our resourcefulness and by the way we pull together. So, when you are in the fray, pulling with everything you've got, every time you look over, I want you to see me, your chairman, right next to you pulling, you and me, pulling together."

After the speech, a reception line of sorts formed. Each guest filed by to shake Philip's hand, providing congratulations or a word of advice before drifting back to the table of hors d'oeuvres and desserts.

When the line faded away, Amanda stepped forward and asked Philip to join her on a walk around the observation deck. They rode the elevator to the upper level and walked out into the evening air.

Amanda stopped and leaned with her back against the railing. Philip looked at her. He was thankful for the moment to be with her alone. There was something on his mind; something he wanted to say.

She appeared lovely. Her eyes reflected the sparkling city, and a gentle sea breeze pushed her hair in a wave over her exposed shoulder. Philip took a deep breath, but he could not find the words to say what he wished to say.

Amanda broke the silence, "She's a lovely woman."

"Who?"

"I'm speaking of Lynn. She is a good woman."

"Yes, she—has meant a lot to me."

"She makes you happy?"

"Well, it's not what you think. We are friends, nothing more. Just colleagues from different worlds. She's helped me through some difficult decisions."

"I see. You know, Philip, I've never seen a woman treat you as she does."

"And how is that?"

"She enjoys being with you, that's clear, but she is confident in her own skin. She doesn't seem to expect anything from you. For what it's worth, which I don't presume to be much, I approve. You're not going to meet another woman like that."

"Is that what you wanted to tell me?"

"No; sorry. I just wanted to tell you congratulations, personally. I know this means a lot to you. And you need to hear me say it means a lot to me, too. They could not have picked a better person for this job. I'm proud of you."

Then Philip said, "May I say something, too?"

"Of course."

"Mandy, this is really awkward for me, but I need to say it. I want to say I'm sorry. When I faced death, I had only one thought: it was of you and the kids. I wanted at that moment to go back and redo the whole thing, our marriage, being there for the kids. I've not been a good father. And God knows I owe you an apology. I can never really make up for not being the husband I promised you on our wedding day that I would be. I can't change the past, but if I could, please know I'd make it right."

Amanda reached for Philip's hand, "Thank you for saying that. You know, I was crushed that day. Stanley was ready to get on a plane with me to come to you. I still love you, Philip, and I want what's best for you. We were so scared. We are just happy to know you're back, safe."

"Mandy, may I make a request? It may seem out of place, but I don't want to act without your permission."

"What's on your mind?"

"I'm worried about our children, and I would like them to hear someone speak. The man downstairs with the cane is Thomas Palmer, a friend of mine. Well, a patient actually. He's a retired minister. He is speaking at a church in Bellevue, and I would like to take the kids."

"To a church? That's a bit much, don't you think? You know how we've always felt about exposing them to—that sort of thing."

"I know, Mandy. It's a big leap, I know. And if it's too much, I'll wait. But I've seen some terrible things. Not just when I was kidnapped. But before, after the earthquake, I saw people young and old, some of them the same age as Max and Alexa, who had nothing but faith. I saw them face the darkest moments of pain with a resilience I wish for our children. Then I faced my own death, and it became clear that everything I'd worked for in my life would be a worthless inheritance if I could not pass on to them some inner source of strength. We tried so hard to protect them from dogma all these years. I just wonder, in our attempt to protect them, if we've hidden something from them that might be helpful when they face their own struggles?"

Amanda turned to look out over the flickering streets below. After a pause, she shook her head, "I don't know, Philip. I'll have to think about it."

Philip took a deep breath preparing to argue. But he knew better. Instead, he exhaled and turned to look over the city, "Yes. Think about it. That's all I ask."

About the Author

Robert T. Lawrence lives, works, and writes in Anchorage, Alaska.

If you enjoyed this book, please consider leaving an online review. The author would appreciate reading your thoughts.

Follow Sulis International Press

Subscribe to the newsletter:
https://sulisinternational.com/subscribe/

https://www.facebook.com/SulisInternational
https://twitter.com/Sulis_Intl
https://www.pinterest.com/Sulis_Intl/
https://www.instagram.com/sulis_international/

39465635R00238

Made in the USA
Lexington, KY
18 May 2019